CAPTURE
MY HEART

ROSANNE
BITTNER

DEDICATED TO A FAITHFUL FAN of many, many years, Barbara Christian, from California. This story came about from one simple Facebook message she sent me one day. It was just a little Native American quote and it mentioned an Indian name. Two Wolves. This is how I write. One little name or event can kick off a whole story for me. For some reason I loved that name and decided it would make a great name for a hero in an Indian/white romance. It's been years since I wrote a Native American story, and for some reason seeing that name lit the fire. This book is the result. Thanks, Barbara.

AUTHOR'S NOTE:

IN THE 1860'S COLORADO TERRITORY was in turmoil, with people fighting over the right and wrong of the War Between the States, and a shortage of soldiers to protect Colorado from Indian attacks on freighters and settlers alike. This shortage was caused by the bulk of the army being needed to fight the war in the South and led to the creation of a territorial militia made up of Colorado's own citizens. One of the leaders of that militia was Colonel John Chivington, a vicious Indian-hater who committed uncalled-for atrocities against peaceful Southern Cheyenne villages, including the killing and mutilating of women and children. To create excuses for such attacks, gangs of white men began committing raids on their own kind, dressed and behaving as Indians, using arrows, burnings and thievery to make Colorado citizens believe the Cheyenne were far more dangerous than they really were and to feed the fires of hatred. That is the historical reality upon which this story is predicated. Also, in this time frame, Denver was known as Denver City, not just Denver, which is why I refer to it as such in this story

CHAPTER ONE

Mid-August, 1864 ...

MAJOR JOHN ANSLEY STARED AT the headlines of a week-old newspaper out of Denver. He scowled with anger at more news about the "victories" of the Colorado Volunteers.

Rabble, he thought. *Nothing but a bunch of murdering rabble.* Their leader, John Chivington, called himself a Colonel . . . worse than that, he called himself a Christian. But he was no more an Army officer *or* a Christian than any skunk that snuck around under porches at night.

Colonel, my ass. That rotten Indian hater will only cause more problems out here for the real Army. If the man kept harassing and murdering innocent natives, there would be more Indian attacks and unrest at a time when the Army had few enough men in Colorado or anywhere else in the West to take care of such problems. Even the half-Indian Bent brothers, successful traders and friends to the Army and whites, were growing restless and resentful.

Through an open window behind his desk he could hear the shouts of soldiers practicing a drill, as well as the shrill clank of the blacksmith's hammer in the distance. Beyond the fort a small settlement was growing, which made being posted out here a little less lonely.

He sighed and stretched his arms, cursing the bum leg that kept him out of the war in the South. An ornery horse had thrown him three years past and left him with jobs that meant sitting behind a desk most of the time. And politics involving Ulysses S. Grant and William T. Sherman, and some arrogant officer named Custer, left him stationed out here at Fort Collins.

His thoughts were interrupted when Private Dean Slater opened the office door. "Two Wolves wants to talk to you, Sir."

Ansley shoved some papers aside. "Send him in." He took a half-smoked cigar from an ash tray and lit it, waiting for the Indian scout. As soon as he came through the door, Two Wolves filled the room with his earthy, warrior presence. Although half white, the man was all Indian in appearance, always fully armed and looking ready to take a scalp.

Today he wore his usual buckskin leggings with knee-high laced-up moccasins and an array of weapons that seemed literally attached to various parts of his body—rifle, bow and arrows, knife, hatchet, and a revolver. And those were only the weapons Ansley could actually see. He had no doubt more weapons were hidden on the Indian's person. His black hair hung long and straight clear to his waist, beaded ornaments and feathers decorating it, and a bone hairpipe necklace graced his neck. The fringes of his vest danced against his dark skin, and beaded arm bands hugged the man's muscled biceps, while silver and turquoise cuff bracelets graced his solid wrists.

Two Wolves faced the major with arms folded in front of him in a way that made those arms look even bigger. A stripe of black paint graced each of his high cheekbones. Ansley thought how few men could appear more intimidating than a fully out-fitted and armed Cheyenne man, and the Cheyenne and Sioux were among the more handsome specimens of Native Americans.

"You look like you're headed into some kind of battle, Two Wolves."

The Indian's dark eyes showed a rare teasing look, and a very faint smile skirted his lips. "With John Chivington on the loose, perhaps I should do just that."

Ansley nodded. "I wouldn't blame you."

"I could start with you," Two Wolves goaded.

Ansley grinned. "Well, it wouldn't be much of a match-up, but if you can keep yourself in check, I'd just as soon keep my scalp today."

Two Wolves lowered his arms. "You do not have enough hair left for me to care."

Ansley couldn't help laughing at the remark. He put the cigar between his teeth, still grinning. "Two Wolves, I wish I could tell when you are pulling my leg and when you're serious. You Indians have such a subtle sense of humor it's hard to tell."

"Pulling your leg?"

"It means I think you're joking with me." The major smiled. "But you keep such a serious look on your face that sometimes I'm not sure. I agree with you, though, that my scalp wouldn't be much to brag about if you took it."

"This is so. But you saved my life when white men wanted to kill me. You spoke up for me, and this I respect, and it is why I call you friend. So Two Wolves will not take your scalp, at least not today." The Indian grinned wider then.

Ansley chuckled. "Well, I am grateful for that!"

He couldn't help liking the young man. There was such honesty about him, a forthright way of speaking that many others did not possess, especially white men. He'd grown to greatly respect that about the Cheyenne. When sitting in counsel, they spoke openly and laid out their thoughts frankly, rather than in the "forked tongue" of the white man. He set his cigar aside. "You've been gone almost a month, Two Wolves. What is it you want to tell me?"

"Much trouble is coming. There have been many attacks by Chivington and his Indian haters. They kill women and children. They attack small parties of Indians with no cause. They even go after them in Kansas, where they have no authority. The Southern Cheyenne and Arapaho trust the commander at Fort Lyon, the one called the Tall Chief, Major Wynkoop. He keeps trying for peace, but Chivington continues to murder my people with no cause, and so they trust no white man."

Ansley leaned back in his wooden desk chair. "And you, my son, are torn between."

Two Wolves nodded. "I tell you these things because you are the only white man I trust. And I tell you because every time you send soldiers out on patrol they should be watchful. The Cheyenne and Arapaho are very angry and very restless. Chivington's men attack innocent Cheyenne camps, and so the Cheyenne fight back–all except Black Kettle. He believes in peace, as do the Bent brothers, but always whatever they agree to, the promise is broken, and the regular Army does little to stop Chivington. Bull Bear is still very angry that his brother, Lean Bear, was killed in his camp, even though he waved an American flag and a white flag. I, too, am angry over this, but I will continue to try for peace and I will tell you true whatever is happening and warn you when you could be attacked."

"I've heard Wynkoop will take Black Kettle and some white captives to Denver to speak with the governor."

"This is so. Black Kettle wishes to show his intent to be peaceful by returning white captives. I have been asked to go along as an interpreter and guide. The prisoners being returned are four white children who are unharmed. One of them wants to stay with the Cheyenne, I am told."

Ansley couldn't help another smile. "Why am I not surprised?"

Two Wolves nodded. "It is a good life, but not now that my people are hunted like rabbits. I do not know how much this meeting will accomplish. Representatives of Cheyenne and Arapaho will meet with Governor Evans, but is rumored that the governor won't make peace because he is afraid of Chivington and his Colorado volunteers, who are hungry to kill Indians. The governor himself has given permission to Colorado citizens to kill any Indian they see trespassing on their land. And Chivington himself will be at this peace conference. I do not see things ending well."

Ansley sobered. "Then you need to be very careful yourself, Two Wolves. I would be very sad if I lost you. I wish you would wear soldier gear instead of looking so Indian when you attend something like this."

"I am proud to show my father's blood."

"And your *mother's* blood?"

A softer look came into the Indian's eyes. "My mother was a good white woman who loved her son."

"That she was," Ansley said with a nod.

Two Wolves sighed. "I think you should send soldiers out to watch for problems with Chivington. Maybe you can stop him from more murders. That is all it is. He does not make war. He commits murder. That keeps the Cheyenne thirsty for war and revenge. It makes things difficult for Black Kettle and those who do want peace."

Ansley closed his eyes and shook his head. "I know that, but I have orders not to weaken this post by sending men *any*where. There are few enough men here to begin with, and we are to protect the settlers and towns in the immediate area, not the Indians. That's orders speaking, Two Wolves, not me."

Their eyes held in mutual understanding. "And you, too, are torn between," Two Wolves suggested.

"Yes, I am." Ansley rubbed at his eyes. "I'll do what I can, Two Wolves, but my hands are pretty well tied."

Two Wolves nodded. "You sent me out to learn what my People have planned. I have told you. I can do nothing more than that. Wynkoop has asked me to go to Denver, so I will again be gone for a while. I should tell you to also be watchful of white traders who bring supplies here and to the white man's towns. There is trouble there, also."

"What kind of trouble?"

"Thieves and killers. White men. It is not the Cheyenne or Arapaho who attack settlers in the south. It is their own kind. This is something I do not understand about your people. You attack and steal from each other at a time when it is the Cheyenne they should be worried about." Two Wolves shifted restlessly, tiny pieces of tin tied into the fringes of his buckskins making faint tinkling sounds.

Ansley looked him over, feeling the man's energy, sensing his uneasiness at being inside. Two Wolves liked the outdoors, liked to be on the back of a horse and always on the move. He refused to sleep inside a room on a bed while at the fort. He preferred sleeping on the ground under the stars. "Have you seen any of these men who are committing these crimes?" he asked Two Wolves.

"I did some scouting across the plains as I rode back here. I have seen the remnants of some attacks. I know the signs and how the Cheyenne make war and what they would leave behind. I find arrows that are poorly made by amateurs who do not know the proper arrow markings of the Cheyenne or how they place the tail feathers. I see signs of shod horses. White men posing as Indians are committing these raids, but no white man would believe such a story from a man such as I. I intend to prove what I know so that what I tell the authorities cannot be disputed."

The major ran a hand through the gray, curly locks that circled the bottom portion of his head, wishing he could transfer some of it to the top of his head, which sported only a few thin curls. When Two Wolves was present, he always became more aware of his own paunchy belly, softening muscles and balding head.

"Two Wolves, I wish I could oblige your warning to watch out for the traders and settlers south of here, but I just told you that with all this other unrest I have to keep my men close. The settlers in the immediate area and between here and Denver need our protection, and with the war going on back East, I'll play hell getting any help in the way of more men."

Two Wolves scowled. "In the meantime, Colorado wants to be rid of all Indians, and so they let the lies be told, and white raiders attack their own kind just so it can be blamed on the Cheyenne."

Ansley watched the Indian's hands move into fists. He was quietly angry, and the major didn't blame him. Life was hard out here for a man who lived in two worlds ... Indian and white. According to Two Wolves, when his Cheyenne father was killed by soldiers in a rescue attempt on his mother, the woman had taken her son with her to Chicago, where the rebellious young ten-year-old fought living the white way but was schooled and raised there until his mother died when he was eighteen. He'd never forgotten his Cheyenne blood or Cheyenne friends and family, and he'd hated city life, longed for the wide-open plains of eastern Colorado, missed the mountains that always "spoke" to him.

And so, he'd come back to live with the Cheyenne, picking up on the culture and habits of which he'd been raised, letting his hair grow long, preferring to reawaken his Cheyenne blood. On her death bed, he'd promised his mother he would not make war against the whites and kill innocent women and children, and so he lived the hell of being torn between two worlds.

Scouting seemed to be the only happy medium for Two Wolves, able to barter agreements between the Cheyenne and the government, able to sometimes live among his People, able to ride free over the Colorado plains and even able to sometimes make war against the Pawnee, a hated enemy.

"Two Wolves, I don't blame you for wanting to prove what lying bastards some of Colorado's riff-raff are. I'd like to prove it, too, but I just can't spare men to go riding around the plains just waiting and watching for one of these attacks. You have my permission to do what you can to prove it yourself. I have no doubt that if one of these attacking parties is made up of only four or five men, you'd be able to handle the whole thing yourself. I know *I* sure wouldn't want to be a man who goes up against the likes of you in battle."

"The only ones who would believe me would be the soldiers I could take with me. No one will believe me on my own. I am Indian. Therefore, they will say I am lying to protect my People."

"Then you need to capture one of these culprits and bring him back to me alive. If you can manage that, I'll make sure they are prosecuted and that the news gets out as to what's going on. That's a promise, and I'm one white man who keeps his promises."

Two Wolves looked around the room as though he distrusted the very walls that surrounded him. Perhaps they would close in on him and crush him. "Then I will scout the plains again and watch for these attacks, unless you have other orders for Two Wolves."

"Well, since you are headed for Denver with Wynkoop and Black Kettle, I have no other orders for now. But you check back here as soon as you're done with that, Two Wolves. You were gone much too long this last time. I was getting worried. You keep that letter I gave you that explains who you are. I don't want my best scout shot down just because he's Indian. Like I said, I wish you would consider dressing and behaving more like a white man, or at least wear a soldier's uniform like some of the other scouts do. Your mother would probably prefer that."

Two Wolves slowly shook his head. "No. My mother loved the Cheyenne. She told me to feel free in my heart to be who I want to be."

"Wasn't she a Cheyenne captive in the beginning?" Ansley picked up his cigar again. When Two Wolves did not answer, he glanced up at him and saw a darkness in his eyes. "Did I say something wrong?"

"You think my father was cruel to my mother - that he did bad things to her and forced her. He did not! He was good to her. She loved my father and his People. They saved her from a Pawnee attack on her family when she was sixteen summers. She *chose* to stay with them. She was not forced. Why do white men have trouble believing that?"

Ansley puffed the cigar a moment before answering. He rose then, rubbing the back of his neck. "I'm sorry, Two Wolves. I didn't mean that the way it sounded. It's just that I know your mother also chose to take you to Chicago and teach you the White way, so maybe that's what she wanted in *her* heart after all–and maybe that's what she wanted for you, too."

"My mother wanted me to know both worlds, so that I could choose. She longed to come back herself and live among my People, but she knew it would never be the same. She found a white husband among missionaries, and they taught me much. But in here . . ." He put a fist to his chest. "In here I am Cheyenne, and to me the one the white man calls Jesus is *Maheo,* and instead of four walls I choose the earth as my floor and the clouds as my ceiling and the forest and mountains as my walls." He shifted the quiver of arrows on his shoulder, the tiny pieces of tin making a tinkling sound again. "I go now."

"Just like that?"

"I have said what I came to say. Is there more you wish to tell me?"

"I guess not. I'm wondering, though, Two Wolves. How many summers are you?"

"I think I am twenty-six summers."

"Don't you want to take a wife?"

"I have no special woman."

"Would you marry a white woman if you had special feelings for one?"

Two Wolves shrugged. "Not many white women would willingly have eyes for a Cheyenne man."

"Your mother did."

Another faint grin graced the Indian's lips. "My father saved her. She was grateful."

"You know, Two Wolves, if you did dress like a white man, cut your hair a little and used your white name, life might be easier for you, and you wouldn't have to worry about being shot down or hanged for being Indian."

Two Wolves frowned. "I can only live the way my heart tells me to live."

"Well, your mother gave you a fine name. Peter James Matthews is very Biblical and a very strong name, so if you ever choose to use it, you should be proud of it. Remember that. Some woman might come along someday who makes you decide to use that name. And surely, somewhere deep inside, you would like to have a wife and children."

"When it is right, I will know." Two Wolves frowned. "Why do you speak of these things?"

Ansley grinned. "I'm not even sure. I am very fond of you. You saved my life once, and I see you as the son I never had, Two Wolves. You just seem like a man who is everywhere yet belongs nowhere. That must be a lonely life. I'd like to see you happy."

Two Wolves raised his chin. "I *am* happy. And at least I am free of the filth and noise of your white man's cities, and free of the sad and useless life of a reservation Indian. If a woman comes along who makes me choose, she will have to be very special, whether she is Indian or white. For now, I am happy only to be Cheyenne." He turned, and without another word, he left.

Ansley stared after him, thinking how there must be any number of Cheyenne women who would jump at the chance to be the wife of such a grand specimen of man as Two Wolves.

I'm guessing there are one or two Cheyenne or Arapaho women out there who gladly take you in at times, Two Wolves," he mused.

He missed his own wife back in Virginia, and he hoped she was doing well. She'd never quite gotten over burying their baby boy ten years before. There had been no more children. A tiny part of him envied the life Two Wolves led … young and strong and free. He walked to a window and watched the scout mount his horse in one swift movement and ride out of the fort. He grinned, thinking how he would thoroughly enjoy learning that some woman had stolen Two Wolves' heart. What happened then would be very interesting.

CHAPTER TWO

CLAIRE CLIMBED ONTO THE WAGON seat to get a better look at the gathering throng of onlookers. A delegation of Indians was to visit Denver City today to talk peace with Governor Evans.

She had her doubts. Peace was such a relative matter. If not Indian attacks, bandits caused just as much havoc as the natives beyond the more civilized cities in Colorado. From what she could tell from news and general talk with others about the Cheyenne, promises of peace would inevitably be broken on both sides. The hatred and misunderstanding would continue, especially with hate-instigators like John Chivington constantly stirring the pot. Chivington called himself a colonel in the Colorado militia, a man who claimed Indians had killed his family and that Colorado's Native Americans were little more than vermin that needed to be eradicated.

Right now she had more important things to think about–like how to stay in business. She took inventory of the well-packed supply wagon that would be part of her next run. She wondered if there might be room for more sacks of flour. The shipment that had arrived from Omaha three days ago included fifty more ten-pound bags of flour than what she'd ordered for her trip to Pueblo and Bent's Fort.

I suppose I can sell them at cost to Huebner's Supply here in town, she considered. Somehow, she had to make decent money on this last run, or she might be finished. Still, she hated the thought of crawling to Vince Huebner for any help at all. He was an arrogant ass who believed women had no place in the business world. He probably wouldn't take the extra flour, in a deliberate effort to rub it in that as a woman she'd failed at business once her father died. She could just hear it. *Your father would not have made this mistake. You know you have to be careful not to store more flour than you might sell because any flour that is stored too long will get worms in it.*

"I didn't over-order," she grumbled to herself. "The warehouse in Omaha made the mistake, not me." As far as she was concerned she'd done a damn good job of taking over since her father's sudden heart attack four months back. It was the debt he'd left her with that made it almost impossible to survive–debts she hadn't known existed until after John Stewart's death. She wanted to hate him for it, but after her mother died when she was only four, her father was all she had. They had always been close. Now she felt terribly alone. And, in a sense, by leaving her in debt, she felt he'd abandoned and betrayed her.

She wanted to hang on to the business out of sheer stubbornness. Most considered freighting a business meant only for men. Women were supposed to be seamstresses or own hat stores, not run a freighting business. She would prove them wrong. So far no one to whom her father owed money would forgive any of the debt. All seemed eager to see her fail, and although she knew Stewart Freighting and Supply from the bottom up and knew all the mechanics of running it, the reality remained that she might have to give it up and find some other way to survive.

And I damn well will *survive!* she swore. She knew how to read and keep books. She knew how to work hard, and she'd grown a thick skin against being ridiculed for being a woman in business. *I'll sell the flour right here in town myself,* she decided. *I can set it out in front of the office and offer it at a price that undercuts Huebner's.*

After the discovery of gold at Cherry Creek six years prior, Denver City, like so many other gold towns, had fast become a bustling town of quickly-built wooden structures and even a few brick buildings. Miners would gladly grab up cheap flour, considering the outrageous prices most supply stores charged. And if this did indeed become her last run, she could surely find some kind of meaningful job in the growing city. After all, hundreds of permanent citizens lived here. Denver City now boasted lawyers and doctors and dry goods stores and schools and hardware stores and pharmacies and grocers and churches, albeit, of course, an untold number of saloons and the prostitution that came with them. Its growth was what had attracted her father to come here to continue his freighting business.

Little did she know when they came here that John Stewart had really left Omaha because of debts owed there, too. Even some of those collectors had come after her when he died. She wanted to cry with disappointment at her father's secret gambling problem and the fact that he'd left her in a bad situation.

"Here they come!" someone shouted.

Claire looked up to see the visiting entourage coming closer, the crowd following it growing even bigger as it approached Claire's location. Several soldiers rode in front, one carrying an American flag. Behind them came the Indians. Real Indians! She could see now that most of them sat in a flatbed wagon pulled by mules. Four young white children were with them.

Another Indian rode behind the wagon, a very grand looking man who held himself a bit different from the others ... straighter ... more decorated. He was bigger in build than the average Indian, wearing an array of weapons including what looked like soldiers' gear—rifle, canteen, an Army saddle and blanket.

Other than some of the gear, there was nothing "white" or "soldier" about the man. He was all Indian, right down to tiny pieces of tin on the fringes of his clothing and on parts of the horse's gear that tinkled with the rhythm of the horse's gate. He carried a white flag and rode beside another soldier, while yet two more soldiers brought up the rear of the procession.

Indians! Right on Main Street! Considering the hatred for Indians here, it could be a big risk. Some tom-fool white man might decide he had the right to shoot them. She was confused about her own feelings. There had been no trouble here close to Denver City, and so far, none of her freighting trips had suffered an Indian attack. Yet here in Denver hatred for the Cheyenne, Arapaho and Sioux just seemed like a natural prejudice, as though it was supposed to be that way. Lately that prejudice had been fed by newspaper headlines declaring Indian atrocities in outlying areas.

Claire sometimes wondered if the stories were even true or just an excuse to rid Colorado of something that might hinder more growth. The fact that Governor Evans had himself given the order that citizens could "shoot on site" any Indian who trespassed on their land made her wonder why he was now calling for peace talks.

What a hypocrite, she surmised.

The procession slowly moved past, the crowd growing noisier now, some of them bumping into Claire's wagon, many shouting obscenities at the natives.

"Quite an odd scene, isn't it?"

Claire looked down to see Vince Huebner standing near the front of the wagon. It irritated her that he'd suddenly appeared in that sneaky way he had of showing up unwanted. "Yes," she answered.

"Those soldiers are escorting some of the more well-known Cheyenne and Arapaho leaders, and those four children are their captives," Huebner told her, as though a man of great knowledge.

"I do read, Vince," she reminded him. "I know what's going on. I've just been too busy with other things to pay much attention." She noted that the youngsters appeared to be fine, but who could tell what they had been through? "I don't see why they need to come here instead of meeting at a fort somewhere," she commented.

"The governor wants them to see our fine city. He probably figures to intimidate them with how advanced we are. I think I'll walk down to where they are meeting and see how it goes. Chivington will be there, too."

"*Chivington?*" Claire shook her head. "His presence won't help much toward peace."

"Either way, the fact remains that something needs to be done about those red bastards. You really shouldn't go with the men on your trips to Bent's Fort, Claire. There have been several attacks on homesteads and wagon trains and freighting businesses in the north, but more are occurring in the south, and you can bet it's the Southern Cheyenne who are killing soldiers and citizens. Just because you run supplies south instead of north doesn't mean you're safe. One of these days you're going to wind up some Indian buck's captive, and it won't be a pleasant experience."

Claire felt anger at the crude remark. She refused to look at the man because she knew there would be a hinting gleam in his eye. He had asked her to marry him more than once, but she considered him an enemy of her father, a ruthless competitor in the freighting business to whom she was in debt. He'd offered to forgive the debt if she'd marry him, but she suspected he'd be just as ruthless a husband as he was a businessman, in spite of his feigned concern for her.

"I'll be just fine, thank you," she answered, keeping her eyes on the procession.

"You heading out soon?"

"What's it to you?"

"Just wondering."

Claire noticed the Indian who held the white flag spoke to the soldier beside him in very plain English.

"Keep your eyes open for troublemakers," he told the soldier.

Indian or not, Claire thought the one with the white flag looked quite grand, the fringes on his buckskin clothing dancing rhythmically—his knee-high laced moccasins decorated with beads—shiny and feathered ornaments in his long, black hair, which was drawn back at the sides.

"You mean besides you?" the solder answered.

Both men laughed. For some reason that surprised Claire—a soldier and an Indian laughing together. The Indian had a nice laugh, very distinct. And when he turned to look her way, still smiling, she noticed how white and straight his teeth were.

Their gazes met, and Claire felt suddenly warm all over. The man was stunningly handsome! She'd not expected that. She'd seen few Indians, mostly the drunk ones who hung around Pueblo and Bent's Fort. Still, there seemed to be a few decent ones, pretty women, lovely, wide-eyed children, some of the men quite good looking.

But this one ... he wasn't like any she'd seen so far. She'd never really seen what she would call a true warrior. This one seemed to be just that–well built, well-armed, very proud. White stripes were painted horizontally across each cheek bone, and the way he held himself ...

He kept looking at her, almost curiously. His eyes moved over her in a way that made her feel ... what? Like a *woman*? She was suddenly self-conscious of her hair, realizing the auburn locks were probably a mass of frizzy curls because the air was humid this morning. And she wore man's pants. He'd probably never seen a white woman in pants before.

The procession passed them, but the Indian man glanced back at her. Why? Who was he?

"Was that one with the white flag Black Kettle?" she asked Vince.

"I don't think so. He's too young to be Black Kettle, and too big. Besides, I don't think Black Kettle is even with these Indians." Vince stepped away a little to watch the procession a moment longer. "I don't like the way that one with the white flag looked at you. I ought to catch up with them and shoot him right off that horse."

Claire noticed symbols painted on the rump of the Indian's bay gelding before the visitors disappeared amid an even bigger crowd. She wondered what the symbols meant. "Really beautiful," Claire answered.

Vince turned to face her, folding his arms. "*What?* The horse, or the *man*?"

Claire turned her attention to Vince, a tall, slender man who was reasonably good looking, but whose personality distracted from his looks. "The *horse*," she sneered.

Vince studied her with icy blue eyes, his gaze making her feel cold. It was far different from the pleasant warmth she'd felt when the Indian had looked her over.

"You should be careful looking admiringly at an Indian, Claire," he warned. "Men could get ideas. I like you too much to have the honor of such a lovely, decent young woman questioned."

Claire wanted to shoot him for the remark. "How dare you say such a filthy thing to me! And what are you doing here?"

He bowed slightly as he grasped the lapels of his obviously expensive suit. "I just came to warn you that there have been Indian attacks on freight wagons lately all over Colorado. I was hoping to convince you to stay here for this shipment and let your drivers take care of things."

"Well, there are rumors that those Indian attacks are really being made by white men who blame it on Indians just to stir up more hatred. And although my drivers are good men, I prefer to handle the money end of my business myself. One never knows for sure who can really be trusted when it comes to money, and Lord knows I need every penny I make on this trip so I can pay *you* off and be rid of you. And what I do is none of your business. Go take care of your own affairs, Vince Huebner."

"Until you pay me off, your affairs *are* mine. If you'd marry me, you wouldn't have to worry about it."

"You know the answer to that." Claire decided to stay in the wagon seat. She didn't like standing close to Huebner, and he had a way of deliberately coming close and towering over her.

Vince braced his hands against the wagon and looked up at her. "Your decision, but you should settle down like a normal woman, Claire—have babies, teach Sunday School. If you married me you'd wear proper dresses instead of those damn men's pants. You'd live in a fine home instead of in the back room of a freight office, and you'd run with well-accepted women friends instead of mixing with a bunch of no-good men. One of these days when you're traveling alone with your drivers, one of them is going to get the wrong idea, Claire. And there you'll be, out on the prairie all alone surrounded by men who might decide to use you for what women are meant for. After all, underneath those pants, plaid shirt and that mess of hair lies a very pretty young woman who's never been with a man. Surely you don't want to learn the hard way what that's like. Marry me, and I'll teach you in a nice way, like a man who loves you would teach you."

Claire glared at him. "*You're* the very man I'd trust the *least*," she seethed. "When a man's mind is constantly in the gutter like yours is, that tells me I couldn't trust you, even as a *husband*! Get your hands off my wagon and go take care of business, Vince Huebner! I wouldn't marry you if you were the last man to walk the face of the earth! You will soon own the biggest freighting business in Denver and I'll likely be out of your way, so go find someone else to marry."

Vince stepped back. The threatening look in his eyes brought a tightness to the pit of Claire's stomach. "Someday you will wish you'd taken me up on my offer," he told her.

"Never!"

Just then Benny Drum, one of Claire's drivers, stepped around from behind another wagon. He walked up to Vince.

"Get on out of here, Vince. Leave Claire alone," he told Huebner. "I heard what you said, and you ought to be shot for it!"

"Is that so?" Vince stepped back a little more. "I'll leave, but Stewart Freighting will soon close, Benny, and you'll be coming to me for work. You'd best remember that when you're talking to me."

Benny's hands moved into fists. He was a middle-aged man who'd been a good friend to Claire's father, and although his belly hung over his belt a bit too far and his hair was graying, he was tough, and Claire knew him to be one of her most dependable and loyal drivers.

"Let it go, Benny," she told the man.

Benny stepped closer to Vince. "I'd rather clean outhouses than work for you," he told Vince. "Now get away from here before I knock you into that horse shit behind you and muss up that fancy suit!"

Vince glared at the man a moment longer, then turned and walked away. Benny looked up at Claire. "You okay, honey?"

Claire climbed down. "I'm fine. I think we can leave out at sunup, Benny." Claire put a hand on his arm, and he helped her down. "Don't be getting yourself into a fight or something, Benny. I can handle Vince Huebner."

"Yeah, well, I'm not so sure. I think he's up to something. He'll keep trying to find ways to make you marry him, and you'd be better off dead."

Claire put her hands on her hips. "No man will ever *make* me marry him, Benny. You know me better than that."

Benny pushed back his hat. "Well, little girl, Vince was right about one thing. You really should think about marrying and living like a normal woman. This ain't no life for somebody as pretty and smart as you. Your pa would have wanted you to settle someday, have kids, make a permanent home for yourself. I'm sure he always figured he'd get out of debt before he died. He didn't figure on leaving you in this situation."

Claire sighed. "What's done is done, Benny. I'll know when the time is right to marry. And I'm sorry for my remark about not trusting my men with money. You know that doesn't include you."

Benny nodded. "I know." He glanced at the extra flour stacked on the boardwalk. "What do you want to do about all that extra flour?"

Claire walked around the wagon and stepped up onto the board walk. "Let's put up a sign that it's for sale at wholesale prices. We ought to get rid of it pretty fast that way, and I'll be undercutting Vince Huebner, something I always enjoy. When we leave out I'll leave Stu here to watch things and take care of sales."

"Whatever you say. I'll go inside and make up a sign," Benny told her. He patted her shoulder and walked inside the freight office.

Claire glanced up the street, where a band began playing the Star Spangled Banner. She thought how hypocritical people could be. The governor was probably there greeting the soldiers and Indians with a friendly smile, pretending to want peace. She couldn't help thinking about the Indian then … the one who'd ridden the beautiful bay horse and carried the white flag … the one who was so stunningly handsome. She would not soon forget the way he'd looked at her, or how it had made her feel.

CHAPTER THREE

TWO WOLVES WAITED WITH BLACK Kettle outside Denver City at Camp Weld. Trader John Smith, a friend of the Cheyenne, joined the small entourage of soldiers and Indians. They all waited for Agent Wynkoop, who'd stayed behind to talk alone with Governor Evans.

Chivington and some of his Colorado volunteers, any of whom would openly kill every Indian in sight if they could get away with it, were stationed nearby, which made Two Wolves uneasy. These talks would probably solve nothing.

Wynkoop finally came into sight, riding toward camp beside a buggy that probably carried the governor. As Two Wolves watched them approach, he gave thought to the woman he'd noticed back in Denver City, the one with curly red hair. He couldn't help being impressed by the way she held herself and looked right back at him, a fierce pride and no fear in her green eyes. He found that interesting for a white woman. Most of them wouldn't look directly at an Indian, as though it was some kind of sin if they did so. And she wore pants ... a man's pants. He'd never seen that on a white woman, either. Something about her reminded him of his mother ... that strong look in her eyes ... the look of a woman who didn't let what others think bother her.

He was well aware of the remarks and looks with which his mother had to contend in her years in Chicago, but never once did she say anything but good things about his father and the Cheyenne. Never once did she allow anyone to believe she'd ever been abused by them. And more than once she'd voiced the fact that she'd loved Moon Dancer in the way any woman loved her husband. He had a feeling the woman in the street was that kind of woman, though he didn't even know her. He'd decided that when this meeting was over, he would try to find out who she was, just out of curiosity.

Evans and Wynkoop reached camp and ordered a meeting of all involved. Wynkoop, a tall man about the same age as Two Wolves, pulled him aside.

"I had to do some fast talking," he told Two Wolves.

Two Wolves frowned. "What do you mean?"

Wynkoop rubbed at his forehead. "Evans is torn between talking peace and satisfying the blood thirst of Colorado citizens, the very people who voted for him. Chivington and his Third Colorado Regiment wear uniforms and fight the Indians only as an excuse to stay out of the real war going on back East, so they don't want peace because they won't have an excuse to stay out of that war."

"Evans himself called these peace talks. Why is he now reluctant to have this meeting?"

"Chivington and the citizens got to him, I'm sure," Wynkoop answered. "But since Black Kettle and the others traveled almost four hundred miles to be here, he'll hold the meeting."

"And lie through his teeth," Two Wolves sneered. "He will make promises that won't be kept, just like all other peace talks."

"Perhaps, but maybe something will happen here today to calm down the Indians, at least for a while."

"The only thing that will calm them down is to find the white men who attack settlements and wagon trains and then blame it on the Southern Cheyenne. I intend to find a way to *prove* it!"

"You'll get yourself killed, Two Wolves."

"If I do, it will be worth it."

Wynkoop shook his head and walked toward the meeting place. Two Wolves followed. He respected the major, was pretty sure he truly wanted to treat the Indians well. At Black Kettle's request, Wynkoop had gone to that chief's Smoky Hill camp not long before to rescue seven white prisoners from nearly two thousand Cheyenne. That took courage. He'd told Black Kettle that if he noted any kind of treachery he would kill Black Kettle, and Black Kettle had replied that the Cheyenne never break their word, which Two Wolves knew to be true. After that meeting Wynkoop had come to respect and admire Black Kettle and his Southern Cheyenne.

Now here they were at another peace talk, turning over four more prisoners as promised. With both Two Wolves and John Smith interpreting for the governor and for a man named Simeon Whitely, who was there to personally record everything that was said, Black Kettle swore he and his people wanted only peace. But Evans accused them of joining with the Sioux, who *were* at war with whites in general.

That got a rise out of Black Kettle, who swore that was not so and that whoever was telling that to the governor was lying. Two Wolves glanced at Chivington, sure he was the one who'd put those ideas in the governor's head.

Evans named specific incidents of attacks and stolen stock that were blamed on the Southern Cheyenne. Black Kettle and another chief, White Antelope, both denied the attacks. Soldiers had come after them, and it had been reported that the Cheyenne fired upon them, which also was not true.

White Antelope spoke up. "The soldiers fired upon us first, without proof we had done anything wrong."

Evans mentioned a massacre at Cottonwood.

"That was the Sioux," Two Wolves answered for Black Kettle. Black Kettle and White Antelope nodded.

"The Sioux intend to keep making war," another chief named Bull Bear told the governor.

"You should tell your Colorado volunteers to go after the Sioux, not the Cheyenne," Two Wolves warned, glaring at Chivington as he spoke. He dearly wanted to sink a knife into the man.

Chivington rose, a tall, thick-necked man with a gleam of hatred in his eyes. The former Methodist minister turned Colonel for the Colorado Volunteers was an imposing figure. Two Wolves thought how good it would feel to be able to fight with him one-on-one.

"All the soldiers in Colorado are under my command," he answered, keeping his eyes on Two Wolves. "I will go after whatever Indians need discipline, and until all of them lay down their arms and decide to live in one place and stay there, I will keep going after them. And since they are so close to Major Wynkoop, let them go to *him* with their complaints, not to the governor. The governor wants what the *people* want, which is to rid Colorado of its Indians."

"That's enough!" Evans spoke up. "I never said any such things. Keep your personal wishes to yourself, Colonel."

Chivington and Two Wolves faced each other boldly. It took all of Two Wolves' strength to keep from striking the man. The council ended with the governor promising not to send soldiers after innocent Indians, as long as Indian attacks ceased. Two Wolves knew it was a weak promise as long as white men continued to commit raids that were blamed on the

Cheyenne. Just as he'd figured, nothing had truly been accomplished, and in spite of their good intentions, the chiefs were left confused, as always.

They all stayed at Camp Weld or the night, then headed out in the morning. Black Kettle, White Antelope and the others decided to head south to Sand Creek. The soldiers headed for Fort Lyon. Two Wolves accompanied them a mile or so past Denver City, then broke away.

"You'd better stay with us, Two Wolves," one of the soldiers told him. "It would be safer for you."

"I need extra supplies. I will be out on the trail scouting for what I believe are white men attacking settlers and supply wagons. I do not have time to go back to the fort first to get them."

"Two Wolves, there are some people back there who are crazy enough to shoot an Indian on sight."

"I will be fine." Two Wolves pulled an Army shirt from his parfleche and draped it over his horse's neck. He began removing his own buckskin shirt. "I can be white enough when I need to be." He gave the soldier a sly grin as he donned the Army shirt. He dismounted for a moment to tuck it in.

"Your choice, Two Wolves. Be careful."

The soldier turned to catch up with the others. Two Wolves remounted, heading toward Denver. He'd only used the excuse of needing supplies to go back to town. What he really wanted was to meet the red-headed young woman who wore men's pants.

CHAPTER FOUR

CLAIRE PULLED ON KNEE-HIGH BOOTS, then checked herself in a mirror. She'd pulled her mound of hair into a bun, as she always did before heading out on another run. She re-tucked her button-front shirt into her cotton pants, then pulled on a leather vest to hide the fullness of her breasts. When going on a run, she preferred to look more like a man. Her father had insisted on it, thinking it would help avoid an attack by Indians looking for a female captive.

For some reason, she'd recently become more aware that avoiding feminine outerwear wasn't just for her safety. Dressing this way helped her ignore deeper longings that had begun to plague her … an unwanted desire to be a wife, even a mother. Such things required marriage, and marriage was the last thing she wanted. The thought of it actually frightened her. She knew little about being a full woman, and she also feared some man might marry her just to take over her business. She was determined to prove that women were good for more than embroidery and producing babies.

More than that, it frightened her to consider what a woman had to put up with to have babies in the first place. She knew how babies were made, and she couldn't imagine letting any man do that to her. She had no mother to talk to about it, and she had few women friends. Women looked at her as though she were something to be shunned, and they stared and gossiped at the way she dressed, sometimes laughing among themselves.

"I'll show them," she muttered, donning a man's wide-brimmed hat, far different from the feathered, flowered and netted fancy hats other women wore. She walked to the outer room to grab her gun belt and strap it on. Just as she buckled it, the figure of a tall, well-built man darkened the front doorway, the sun behind him so bright that she couldn't see him well at first. She moved behind the counter, keeping her hand on the butt of her gun. "Can I help you?" she asked.

The man stepped closer, and Claire's heart raced a little when she realized it was the same Indian who'd carried the white flag in the procession of soldiers the day before. This time he wore a Union army shirt, but he still wore a six-gun on one hip and a hatchet on the other. His long, black hair was pulled back at the sides with beaded ornaments, and he wore tiny earrings. As he stepped closer she heard a tinkling sound. She wasn't sure where it came from because she kept her gaze on his very dark eyes, not sure at first if he was here for good or for harm.

"Do you sell ammunition?"

Claire swallowed. "Can't you get that from the Army?"

"I am not going back to Fort Collins for a few weeks. I need beans, some jerked meat, a few potatoes and ammunition."

Claire kept her hand on her gun. "I can sell ammunition and potatoes, but you'll have to visit a dry goods store for the rest. Most things in here are bulk items for trade. In fact, I'm low on everything because I'm heading out soon with supplies for Bent's Fort and Pueblo. I do have extra flour to sell. It's stacked outside on the board walk."

"I need no flour." He frowned. "*You* are going along to Bent's Fort?"

"I always do. I've helped my father with this business for years. He died not long ago, and now I've taken over. I don't trust people much, so I always go along to make sure I get my money's worth."

He looked her over in a way that made her feel naked. "Such a trip is dangerous for a woman."

Claire frowned and kept her hand on her gun. "Why on earth do you care?"

He paused, looking around the room, then back at Claire. "I care only about white men attacking freight wagons and blaming it on Indians. Has that ever happened to you?"

Claire shook her head. "No, not so far. Traveling south of here is fairly safe."

"That is because the Southern Cheyenne are not raiding. Most of the raiding is in the north, and it is the Sioux doing it. It is white men posing as Indians who raid in the South. Colorado wants to be rid of us, so they do things to make people hate us and shoot us with no excuse. A man named Chivington is stirring up all the hatred and committing terrible crimes against the Cheyenne."

"I know about Chivington. I've seen his lies in the Denver papers."

"So, you believe they are lies?"

"I suspect they are, mainly because I've had no trouble on any of my trips, and I am aware the Southern Cheyenne are trying to talk peace. How did that meeting go yesterday with our governor?"

"Not well. Nothing was accomplished."

It struck Claire that she was standing here alone having an actual conversation with an Indian who was big and strong enough to break her in half and who could probably land a hatchet into her before she could pull out her pistol. "How is it that you speak such good English?" she asked.

"I was raised in Chicago by my white mother."

Claire couldn't hide her surprise. "*White* mother?"

"She was a good woman, and it is a long story. I will buy the ammunition and be on my way."

"What the hell?" Benny Drum came through the front door, carrying a rifle. "You okay, Claire?"

Claire noticed the Indian stiffen defensively. "I'm fine, Benny. This man is only here to buy some supplies."

"Then send him to Vince's or some other dry goods store." Benny stepped closer. "Get on out of here, mister."

"Benny!" Claire scolded. "This man is apparently a scout of some sort for the Army. He's not here to do any harm. In fact, he was warning me about a possible attack on our freight wagons once we head for Bent's Fort."

Benny sucked in his paunchy belly as much as he could, facing the Indian bravely. "Why do you care?" he asked, repeating Claire's own curiosity.

The Indian closed his eyes and sighed, turning his attention back to Claire. "My job is to watch for such attacks and let the Army know about them," he answered. "I only told you about the attacks because you said you were taking supplies to Pueblo. I came in here only to buy supplies. If you do not have any, then I will leave."

He turned.

"Wait!" Claire called, not even sure why she didn't want him to go yet. "I said I could sell you ammunition." She looked at Benny. "Benny, he's okay. Go on out and check the wagons once more before we leave. I don't want to have a wheel come off or a guide chain break once we're out in the middle of nowhere."

"You sure?"

Claire glanced at the Indian again. His gaze stirred feelings deep inside she'd never felt before. Not only did his eyes say he meant her no harm, but they made her feel warm and protected … in a *womanly* way. In fact, the woman inside her that she usually struggled not to recognize was ripping through her in a most unexpected way. "I'm sure," she told Benny.

Benny glowered at the Indian. "You watch yourself, Indian. You bring harm to a white woman, and you won't get two feet out of this town before you're dragged up the street and hanged."

"Benny, that's enough!" Claire told him. "He's done nothing for you to talk like that."

A scowling Benny turned and walked out. Claire kept her eyes on the Indian. "What's your name?"

"Two Wolves. My father was a Cheyenne warrior. And no, he did not kidnap and abuse my mother, as you are probably thinking. And I have a white man's education, thanks to my mother."

"Do you have a white name?"

"Peter James Matthews. I almost never use it, unless it is for something legal. Two Wolves has no legal rights by white man's standards, but Peter James Matthews does, even though we are one and the same."

The words were somewhat sneered. Claire sensed his anger. "Such is the situation nowadays," she told him. "I'm sorry about that, but it's not of my doing, and I can't do much about it." She turned away. "What kind of ammunition do you need?"

"Four magazines of Spencer rim-fire cartridges, fifty-six/fifty-six."

Claire felt his eyes on her as she unlocked a glass cabinet behind her. "I only have three magazines."

"I will take them. I will need a receipt so that the Army can pay me back, or I can give the receipt to the man in charge at Fort Collins. He will see that the government pays you."

Claire took out the three magazines and turned to place them on the counter. "I prefer cash, if you have it. The government isn't exactly timely in paying their bills, especially with a war going on back East." She met Two Wolves' gaze and caught a glint of humor in his eyes.

"Why do you dress like a man?" he asked her with a slight grin.

Claire felt the color coming into her cheeks. Was he laughing at her? "That's my business, but if you really want to know, it's because it's much more comfortable when I'm out on the trail, and I don't have to worry about getting skirts caught in wagon gear. It's also easier for riding. And I prefer to hide –" She hesitated, suddenly embarrassed at what she was about to say. It irked her then to realize Two Wolves was grinning.

"Hides the things that show you are a woman? In your case I think that is probably hard to do."

Claire shoved the magazine cartridges toward him, frowning. "It's safer that way, out on the trail."

He nodded. "I suppose it would be, but no matter what you try to hide, you carry yourself as a woman."

Claire bristled. "I'm not so sure someone like you should be talking to me this way," she told him. "You owe me for these cartridges." She scribbled out a receipt for him. "Pay me–and leave."

Two Wolves reached into a pouch he wore on his belt and pulled out some silver coins, tossing them onto the countertop. He grabbed the cartridges and turned. "Thank you." He started to walk away, then hesitated. "You should be alert between here and Pueblo." He faced her. "I know what to watch for. I could go with you as a guard if you wish."

Claire was flabbergasted at his offer. "*Why?*" she asked.

"I told you. It is my job."

She folded her arms and shook her head. "My men would never accept you coming along. They are experienced, and they know what to watch for. We'll be fine. Just go out there and do whatever the Army wants you to do and don't give us a second thought. Actually, I am confused as to why you walked in here in the first place. We are obviously not a regular supply store. I remember you from yesterday, and now here you are, for no really understandable reason."

Two Wolves backed away, looking her over again. "Yesterday, I saw you on a wagon. And I saw a sign in front saying you sell guns and ammunition. I thought it unusual for a woman to dress like you do, and to be selling guns. I needed ammunition, so I came here to buy it because I was curious about the woman in man's pants." Again, his eyes moved over her. "I think that if you wore a dress and did not hide your hair under a hat, you would look very much like my white mother. She was very beautiful."

He turned and walked out, leaving Claire dumbfounded and confused. *She was very beautiful.* Did he mean he thought *she* was beautiful, too? She didn't think there was one thing about her that was "beautiful," let alone the fact that an Indian had no business looking a woman over the way he'd looked at her and then talking to her about things that were none of his business, like the way she dressed and wore her hair.

Her father had told her once that the few Indians he'd known were not much for "visiting." They were usually men of few words, and when they did speak, they were very straightforward. His opinion of them was that they were totally honest with their words, and they chose those words wisely.

She moved from behind the counter and walked to the front door. Benny was greasing a wagon wheel, and Two Wolves was already mounted and riding away. His visit left her full of questions. He'd pretended the visit was casual and only for supplies, but she couldn't help remembering how he'd looked back at her yesterday when he rode with the soldiers. The whole thing left her uneasy. Maybe she shouldn't have given away the fact that she was leaving soon for a trip to Pueblo. Maybe he had ulterior motives for coming here and questioning her. Uniform or not, he was, after all, Indian.

CHAPTER FIVE

"**D**O YOU REALLY THINK YOU can keep things going?" Benny asked Claire. He rode beside her on a big buckskin gelding.

Claire drove the lead freight wagon, her wide-brimmed hat pulled down to protect her eyes from the morning sun. Leather gloves protected her hands and fingers from blisters. The day had turned chilly, and she wore her woolen jacket buttoned up to the neck. It was really made for a boy, but it fit her perfectly.

"I'm going to try, Benny," she answered. "I'm not one to give up easily. You know that."

"You've always been stubborn as hell, Claire, but I know Bob left you with a lot of debt. I know you don't like Vince Huebner, but he's right about one thing. You're a very pretty young woman, and you've been left with more than is fair for you to have to handle. You ought to think about getting out from under this business—get married and settle."

"Surely you aren't suggesting I marry Vince!"

Benny shook his head. "No, Ma'am. I don't like that man any more than you do. I'm just sayin' you ought to sell while you can get a few bucks out of this business—start wearin' dresses and maybe teach school or somethin'."

Claire frowned and shook her head. "You, too?"

Benny adjusted his hat. "I've watched you grow up, and I had a wife for a lot of years, Claire. So I know women, way down inside, like to wear dresses and fix themselves up pretty and that most want a family. It broke my wife's heart that she couldn't have kids, but if she could have, we'd have ended up with five or six." He spit tobacco juice over the other side of his horse. "I care for you like the kid I never had. You know that. I just want you to be happy, honey. This ain't no life for a young woman, and I ain't seen you smile since your pa died. That's sad, because you have such a pretty smile."

Claire stared at the road ahead, wincing when the wagon hit a rut that gave her a jolt and made the potatoes in the back bounce. She turned to the three wagons behind them. "Watch out for that rut!" she yelled back to them.

"Yes, Ma'am," she heard Pete Brady yell from farther back.

They drove on for a few minutes in silence. Finally, Claire spoke up. "I appreciate your concern, Benny," she told her father's long-time friend. "If I didn't know how sincere you are, I'd tell you to mind your own business. But I know you feel an obligation to look after me." She snapped the reins lightly when one of the four horses pulling the wagon balked. "And I do think about settling. I even think about wearing dresses. Right now I'm just mad that Pa left me in this mess, and I'm also mad at those to whom he owed money and those who keep telling me a woman alone can't run this business. I'm just out to prove I can, because I am very stubborn and proud. It's a flaw, I guess, especially for a woman, but I can't help how I feel. Maybe in time I'll get over it, but right now I am not going to give in and sell."

Benny shook his head. "Well, until you do, I'll stand by you."

"Even if it happens that I can't pay you?"

Benny chuckled. "You'll find a way."

"Yes, well, part of that way is to go on these trips and collect the money myself. I'm here to protect you just as much as you're here to protect me." Claire studied dark clouds over a southwest range of mountains. "I wonder if it's storming up there."

Benny glanced in the same direction. "It's September. This time of year it can snow in the high elevations. We could even get snow in Denver City."

"I am well aware of the weather situation out here, Benny. But we're heading south, so we should be fine. I'm more worried about what could be hiding in the pine trees in those foothills to our right. That Indian scout who visited us yesterday said he suspected we'd have trouble from white men posing as Indians. He claimed it's not the Cheyenne who have been attacking settlers and wagon trains."

Benny spit tobacco juice off to the side again. "For all you know he could be one of them doing the attacking. I don't trust the man. That visit was strange, I thought. There are plenty of supply stores in Denver that are well marked. Why did he stop at a place where the sign clearly stated we were a freighting business?"

"We also have a sign out front that advertises guns and ammunition."

"Maybe so, but I still think the whole thing didn't smell right. He's just one more example of why you need to get out of this business."

"How's that?"

Benny shrugged, then removed his floppy hat and shook his graying, shoulder-length hair behind his shoulders. "You just never know what kind of character will walk into that office when you're there alone, that's all. And you can't trust every man you hire, either. I won't be around forever, you know."

"That Indian offered to ride with us and keep watch."

Benny shook his head. "Probably to help his cronies out there somewhere ready to attack us. What better way to get the best of us than from inside by him shooting me in the back just before the rest of them attack?"

"Oh, Benny, he didn't seem like that kind at all. I found him very interesting. I'd like to know more about him. He was so well spoken, told me he'd grown up with his white mother in Chicago. I could tell he's educated."

"White mother? You know what that means, don't you?"

"He said it wasn't like that."

"I don't care *what* he said. No white woman lays with an Indian of her own free will. The poor woman had to have been an unwilling captive. The soldiers probably rescued her somewhere along the line. I'm surprised she managed in a place like Chicago, though. Most women like that have trouble adjusting to their former life. And it couldn't have been easy for that Indian growing up there. Half breeds aren't well-accepted on either side."

"Benny, you don't know anything about it. You're taking things for granted that might not be true. I haven't made up my mind how I feel about the Indians. They have certainly not given us any trouble, and I find it reprehensible for someone like Colonel Chivington to tell people to just shoot them on sight. As far as being a half breed, that must be really hard, especially for one who is educated like Two Wolves."

"That's what he called himself?"

"Yes. He's an Army scout. He was with the entourage that came through Denver two days ago."

"Well, I don't much care who he is or what he does. I still say it was strange, him comin' into the office yesterday. I think he was sizin' things up, findin' out when you would leave, plannin' somethin'."

Claire glanced toward the foothills. Most of their trips since her father died had been shorter ones. It was a long way to Pueblo, and the chance that Benny could be right made her uneasy. Still, the man called Two Wolves had seemed genuinely sincere in his advice that she should not make this trip. For some reason, thinking that he could be a part of an attack was very disappointing. She wanted to think the best of him, and she had no idea why it mattered.

CHAPTER SIX

FOUR DAYS OF TRAVEL BROUGHT no problems, other than a rainstorm that forced them all to camp underneath the wagons with no fires. Each driver slept under his own wagon. Benny slept with one of them so that Claire slept alone under the lead wagon. Always watching out for her, Benny feared the other men would think less of her if he slept too close. Before this, her father was always along on these trips and she could stay close to him. But now she was on her own, something else Benny kept pointing out was a good reason to get out of the business.

Claire snapped the reins, her shoulders aching today from insisting on doing all the driving. She couldn't help thinking Benny was right that maybe she should sell the business and live like other women. What she hated was the attitude men had that a woman couldn't fend for herself on her own—that she needed a man to take care of her. She was determined to prove that wasn't so.

Her thoughts were interrupted when an unfamiliar cry came from the thick forest to her right. She glanced in that direction, but saw nothing. The mixture of aspen and pine there was growing dark because the sun had already begun to set behind the higher mountains, leaving the foothills dark even though it was still light on the trail. She'd planned to keep going for at least one more hour.

"You hear that?" Pete called from the wagon behind her.

"Yes. Sounded like an owl or something," Claire answered.

Benny rode back to her wagon. "I think we should make camp here for the night," he told her.

"But there is plenty of light left here away from the trees."

"Something doesn't feel right. Circle the wagons, and I want you to come around this side of your wagon where you can't be seen from the trees."

"Benny, what are you talking about?"

Benny grabbed the lead horses and shouted, "Whoa!"

Claire pushed on the brake and wrapped the reins around it. "Benny, we can travel another hour or so."

"Get down off that wagon," Benny ordered. "The rest of you, circle around!" he yelled as he rode back to the others. The drivers obeyed as Claire climbed down from her wagon. Just as Pete drove his rig into position an arrow struck his chest. He cried out, slumping down below the seat.

"Oh, my God!" Claire screamed. She reached for her rifle, but Benny rode up to her and dismounted, grabbing the rifle away.

"Climb inside the wagon and get down underneath the canvas!" he ordered, handing her his six-gun.

"I'll stand and fight like the rest of you!" Claire yelled.

"No, you won't. The potatoes in that wagon will protect you from bullets and arrows."

"Benny!" Claire could hear *yips* and *whoops* coming from the nearby forest.

"If it's Indians and they get to you, use that gun on yourself!" Benny told her. "If it's white men, you'll have a chance. Now get in that wagon! I have a feeling there are more out there than we can handle, so this is your only chance at living." He threw back the canvas and lifted her by the waist, plopping her inside it. "Get down!"

Another arrow whirred past Benny and into the side of another wagon as it came around the circle.

Claire ducked down into the side of the wagon, able to see a little of what was going on through a crack between two boards. *Benny!* He and Jason were up against her wagon now, while Hal fired frantically nearby. The air came alive with the trilling shouts of Indians, gunfire and whirring arrows, along with the sound of galloping horses.

"Jesus Christ, there's too many!" Jason swore.

Now all three drivers were firing their rifles non-stop. The horses and wild war cries came closer. Claire hunkered down even farther, pulling sacks of potatoes on top of herself and a few between herself and the side of the wagon, leaving a hole just big enough to still see through the crack. Her heart pounded wildly as she realized there was no way Benny and the others could defeat what sounded like at least ten men coming at them. She'd been so sure something like this couldn't happen. She felt sick at realizing that her insistence on making this trip and staying in the business would surely cost Benny and the others their lives. Benny had been so good to her, so loyal.

Jason cried out and slumped to the ground. Claire could see the raiders had ridden around the other side of the circle and were shooting at the drivers from the back side. They had no chance. She stifled a scream when Benny went down next. Shortly after that she heard Hal scream. The attackers swarmed inside the circle then, pumping more shots into the drivers.

She wanted to scream, needed to cry, but she forced herself to remain quiet. All gunfire quieted. Men began shouting orders, and in moments Claire realized by the way they talked that they weren't Indian. Still, there had been arrows. Some of the cries had sounded very Indian. Had Benny been right? Was the man called Two Wolves with these men? For some reason that thought brought heavy disappointment.

"Bring the wagons!" someone shouted. "Let's get this stuff loaded into our own wagons and get on down to Pueblo!"

Pueblo. They knew where she was going! But then a lot of people back in Denver had known where they were headed . . . including Two Wolves. He'd warned her he thought white men were attacking supply trains and blaming it on Indians. Was that because he was a part of some of those attacks? Perhaps a guide for them?

"What about the woman?"

Claire's stomach tightened.

"Did she run off?"

"Check under the canvases," someone ordered.

Moments later the canvas over Claire's wagon was ripped away. She lay perfectly still. Whoever ripped off the canvas yelled out. "Nothing here!"

"Here either!" someone else yelled. "And cover those potatoes back up. There's still a lot of sun."

To Claire's relief, the man near her jerked the canvas back over the potatoes. "Vince said she'd be along," he complained.

Vince! Vince Huebner? Of course! It made sense. Vince knew all about this trip, and he wanted to run her out of business! Could he really do something this despicable?

"He said not to harm her."

"You will give the woman to me," someone answered, his words spoken more like an Indian would speak. "Vince promised I could take her to sell in Mexico."

"He never told us that," one of the others answered.

"He told *me*," came the reply. "Anyone who tries to keep me from taking her with me will feel my knife!"

Was that Two Wolves? He'd worn a big knife! *Sell in Mexico?* Claire felt like throwing up. Surely she'd be found very soon!

"She's got to be here somewhere," another man shouted. "If she'd run off we would have seen her."

"Maybe not. We were pretty busy with the attack. One of you go scour the woods. Let's make camp for now. It will be dark soon. We can switch loads in the morning and get the hell out of here."

Claire could hardly believe it. They wouldn't unload until morning. That gave her time to think. She had no doubt of her fate once they found her, and find her they would, either by tearing through the wagons tonight, or most certainly in the morning.

She watched through the crack in the wagon boards. Several men milled about, unloaded horses, built a fire. One of the men was very tall and dark. . . and Indian. From what she could tell it wasn't Two Wolves, but she couldn't be sure. Two Wolves had been tall, but not as tall as the man she could see now. Maybe she was just trying to convince herself that it wasn't him. She didn't want to think it could be. Still, it made sense, the way he'd turned and looked at her when he rode by her in the street that first time she saw him, as though summing her up. Maybe this was why – trying to determine what she would be worth at some Mexican whore house.

She had to find a way to escape. Some of the men were starting to drink. A couple of them dragged off the dead bodies, and Claire struggled not to cry out with remorse and sorrow. Maybe after dark . . . if they all got drunk . . . She clung to Benny's six-gun. It was all she had now with which to defend herself.

CHAPTER SEVEN

THE ONLY ANSWER CLAIRE COULD think of for why she still lay undiscovered under sacks of potatoes was that God Himself must be protecting her. By some miracle, the men camped outside had not torn through all the wagons to find her . . . yet. She'd lain still as a mouse for hours, partly due to such terror that she found it difficult to move even a finger. She'd waited while the men outside ate and drank and talked filth. She'd waited while they dragged off Benny and the others. She prayed they'd at least buried them, but they didn't seem the type to care. She'd waited while the big Indian carried on about being cheated out of getting his hands on "the woman." He'd vowed to hunt for her again, and Claire felt sick at the thought of his intentions. Her only comfort was that she was pretty sure, after being able to watch him for a while, that it wasn't the one called Two Wolves.

Everything was quiet now, but she wasn't sure if someone was awake and standing watch. She wasn't even sure how many there were outside the wagon. If she was going to escape it had to be now, in the dark, while they slept. Maybe by morning they would give up looking for her and steal her supplies and leave. She'd seen and heard enough to know they'd brought along their own wagons. They would load up her supplies and go on to Pueblo to sell them there. She'd heard one of them mention burning her wagons and reporting to authorities that they'd found them, robbed and burned by Indians.

From what she could tell the men were camped inside the circle of her own wagons. Very slowly and carefully she moved from under potatoes, struggling to keep sand that fell through the burlap potato bags from causing her to cough and spit. She blinked from dirt that fell into her eyes as she moved in snail-like fashion, inches at a time, across the top of the potatoes but under the canvas, making her way to the outside wall of the wagon, hoping no one was camped there. Her only hope of escape was to shimmy over that side and head for the nearby woods and foothills. God only knew what she might face there. Indians? Wild animals? A grizzly? Anything was better than these men finding her and doing what she had a pretty good idea they had in mind, let alone ending up in a brothel in Mexico.

Inches. Inches. She reached the other side of the wagon. Very slowly she lifted the edge of the canvas and looked out. She waited for her eyes to adjust to the soft moonlight. She saw nothing.

She had no choice. It was now or never. She had to at least try to get away. It might be a useless attempt, but what choice did she have? As slowly and quietly as possible, she slid from under the canvas, swinging a leg over the side, glad she was wearing boy's pants. This would have been impossible to do quietly if she wore a dress. She moved as lightly as she could, terrified the wagon would squeak and give her away.

She shoved Benny's six-gun into the belt at the back of her pants so it wouldn't catch on anything as she grasped the top edge of the wagon bed with her still-gloved hands and swung her other leg over the side. She felt for the lip of the steel support bar that ran along the bottom edge of the wagon. Catching a boot toe on that, she kept hold of the top edge as she lowered her other leg. It was a big wagon. She would have to let go and jump down once she got her bearings.

She froze there on the side, waiting, listening, making sure no one had noticed anything. She heard nothing but an owl in the distant trees. Farther off in the foothills she heard wolves, something else she would have to worry about once she got out of here . . . *If* she got out of here.

Taking a deep breath, she let go and jumped down, kneeling there for a moment to make sure she remained unnoticed. She sat down and removed her boots, thinking they might make too much noise against the gravelly ground once she started running. After so many hours of lying in wait, along with pure terror in her bones, she had to urinate, but she couldn't take the time for that until she found shelter in the nearby trees.

Grasping her boots to her chest, she took a deep breath and took off running. Her heart pounded wildly, her imagination bringing visions of several men spotting her and chasing behind her. She expected that any moment someone would grab her hair or her clothes and tackle her to the ground.

Tears and dirt stung her eyes as she headed for the pine trees, ignoring the pain of rocks and harsh undergrowth against her stockinged feet. She reached behind her and grasped the six-gun, keeping it in one hand while she hugged her boots with the other hand.

It seemed to take forever to reach the trees. When she did, she headed deeper into them before stopping to catch her breath and get her bearings. She crouched behind scrub brush, waiting, watching, listening. She thought she heard a man's voice out where the wagons were. Had someone woke up? Had someone heard or seen her run off? She strained to see, thought she saw a figure walking near the wagons.

No! She had to go farther—had to find a good place to hide! Afraid to take the time to put her boots back on, she turned and started running again. It was hard to see. She tripped over a log, and her gun went flying out of her hand. She felt around for it, but found only pine needles and fallen twigs. She panicked. She had to have that gun, but she didn't have time to keep looking for it! She thought she heard someone running in the distance.

She got up and began running again, wincing with pain in her feet and from branches that slapped against her face. She ran as fast as she could, fighting an urge to scream, praying that by some miracle she was wrong about someone following her. She fell down a hill, felt herself rolling, grunted when her back hit the trunk of a tree. She got up yet again, realizing that somehow in falling she'd lost her boots. She wished she could see better, hoped she wouldn't wake up a grizzly or some other animal. Maybe it wasn't a man running after her at all. Maybe it was wolves!

She'd always heard how keen the instincts of Indians were. Maybe the big Indian had heard her after all—had seen her shadowy figure head for the woods. She could almost feel his big knife in her back. She struggled not to yell out when pine cones and pine needles poked the bottoms of her feet. She kept running, hoping whoever was after her didn't realize she'd fallen down the hill. Maybe he would go in a different direction.

She found a place where there was softer grass and her feet made less of a rustling noise. She ran faster, not sure when or if she should stop. She would just run until she had no breath left in her, then pray she wouldn't be found.

All her plans ended abruptly when to her horror someone grabbed her. She felt a big hand clamping over her mouth, stifling her screams as a strong arm wrapped around her from behind, pinning her arms to her sides. She struggled wildly as whoever it was wrestled her face-down to the ground and lay on top of her. She closed her eyes against pine needles that poked at her face.

"Lie still," a voice whispered close to her ear. "Do not scream! It is I! Two Wolves! He will hear us if you do not lie still!"

Who would hear them? Was Two Wolves the one who'd been chasing her? She wiggled and tried to scream again.

"*Ho-shuh!*" He gripped her tighter, kept his hand around her mouth. "I cannot help you if you give us away! I will not hurt you!"

Claire was so worn out that all the fight went out of her. She wanted to believe him, that he truly didn't mean her harm. His weight was beginning to crush the breath out of her.

"Do not move!" he whispered. "I am going to let go of you. I have to kill him."

Kill who? What on earth was he talking about? The other Indian? What if he failed? She'd be doomed. Maybe she was doomed either way. She fought tears of terror.

"Promise you will make no noise," Two Wolves told her. "And do not leave this place if I let go of you." He gave her a slight jerk. "*Promise me!*"

Claire relaxed. She felt some of his long hair fall over the side of her face, felt his strength, and strangely, felt a sudden comfort in the way he held her. Slowly he moved his hand from her mouth. He stayed on top of her for a moment, spoke again into her ear.

"I am going to let go of you. Pay no attention to what you hear. Do not move from this place. Do you understand?"

Now Claire could hear someone coming, the sound of heavy footfall somewhere nearby. "Yes," she whispered.

Suddenly, Two Wolves left her. She lay frozen in place, heard someone running. Then she heard a grunting sound, several thuds, a man crying out, and what sounded like a chopping sound. Moments later someone came back to where she lay and jerked her up.

"Come! Quickly!"

It was Two Wolves. Claire wasn't sure if she should be glad or not. What on earth did he want from her? Why was he doing this? He was, after all, an Indian, and he'd apparently just killed a man. He grasped her wrist almost painfully and ran with her, half dragging her because he ran faster than she could keep up. Suddenly he stopped. He leapt onto the back of a horse, then grasped her arm. "Get up behind me!"

Claire blindly obeyed. Two Wolves lifted her as though she weighed nothing. She wrapped her arms him around his waist, and he urged his horse into a hard run. They rode off into the darkness.

How could he see where he was going? There were trees and boulders everywhere. Did Indians really have "night eyes," as some men joked they did? She had no idea how this man had found her or where he intended to take her. She just hung on for dear life, glad at the moment to be fleeing her attackers. She could only pray she wasn't headed for an even worse fate.

CHAPTER EIGHT

CLAIRE LOST ALL TRACK OF time and space. She only hung on, not sure how long they continued riding or where this man was taking her. How he managed to plunge through the heavy pine forest at night without his horse running into something or stumbling, she couldn't imagine. Apparently Two Wolves had plenty of experience in such things, a man who knew the wild country well.

Finally, he slowed his horse. "There is a cave ahead. We are deep in the foothills now. They will not find us, at least not tonight."

"Why would they follow us? They have my cargo. Isn't that all they want?" Claire felt her voice being swallowed by the darkness, a strange quiet surrounding them now. She was glad this man apparently knew where he was, because alone she would be completely lost.

"The one I killed was Comanche. There was another Comanche with them. He will not let this go. And the others—they know now that you must have been there, must have heard them. That means you are a witness. Some will take your supplies on to Pueblo as ordered—others will come after us. The Comanche warrior will be a good tracker."

The one I killed. How could he speak so casually about that? "I've heard terrible things about the Comanche," she said aloud as he guided his horse up a steep embankment. Claire hung on to keep from sliding off.

"What you heard is true," Two Wolves answered. "They are men with no mercy. As warriors, the Cheyenne are just as able, but most do not kill for pleasure or for no reason. That is where we differ from the Comanche."

He halted the horse. "Get down." He grasped one of her arms and held on until her feet touched the ground. Then he dismounted himself. "Follow me." He led his horse into a dark cavern, where its hooves made an echo when they clattered against the stone floor.

"Hold my horse," he told her, handing her the reins.

Claire could barely see. He walked away, and she heard some rustling sounds, then jumped in surprise when he lit a match and set it to some kindling.

"Where did the wood come from?" she asked.

"I have stayed here before when I am out scouting for the Army."

The kindling cracked and spit a few embers. Two Wolves walked away again, then came back with a few more pieces of wood, laying them on top of the kindling. "There is a draft through here that draws the smoke toward an opening at the back of this cave. If you stand away from its path the smoke will not bother you. And there is a soft wind that will blow it away from the direction in which a tracker would come. He will not smell it." He added one more piece of wood to the fire. "We are lucky a bear or wolves did not decide to use this place as their home."

Claire swallowed. "Are there grizzlies and wolves around here?"

"There are always bears and wolves in these hills." Two Wolves went to his horse and unpacked some supplies. He came near the fire and unrolled a blanket. "You can sleep here. Are you hurt?"

Claire met his eyes, dark, unreadable. Was he dangerous? Here she stood completely at his mercy. Then, by the light of the fire, she saw that blood stained the front of his deerskin shirt, which was ripped. Her own feet were cut and bleeding, but she needed this man to get her back to civilization alive.

"No," she lied, "but you are!" She reached out to him. "Let me help you."

He stepped back. "I will take care of it."

"Don't be ridiculous! Take off your shirt and let me see how bad it is."

"It is not bad. I can tell."

"Two Wolves, without you I'll be lost in these woods until I die! You're the only one who can get me out of here! Even if that wound is superficial, it needs taking care of. It could get infected. If it's from that Comanche's knife, heaven knows what he used it on before he cut you with it. It could have been filthy with a dead animal's blood or even human blood."

He stiffened slightly, studying her intently. "I am not used to asking for help."

"Nor am I! I am a very independent woman, but I *did* need your help back there, and you could have been killed going after that Comanche. You helped me. Now let me help *you*."

He seemed to waver a little. Claire wondered just how much blood he'd lost. Finally, he nodded. He went to his horse and unloaded more supplies and his canteen. He sat down near the fire and began removing his weapons—a quiver of arrows, his bow, a belt with a hatchet and knife and a six gun.

"There is a small flask of whiskey in my parfleche," he told her. "It is good medicine for cuts."

Claire rummaged through his parfleche and felt a small bottle. She'd seen drunken Indians a few times, knew the stories about Indians and whiskey. Would the firewater make this man crazy and dangerous?

"I hope you only carry this for medicine." She glanced his way and had to struggle not to react to his physique. He sat there with his shirt off, his dark skin glistening by the firelight, his arms, chest and shoulders nothing but hard muscle. Combined with a handsome face and chiseled jaw . . . and those dark eyes . . . he was a grand specimen of manhood. He smiled at her remark, and the smile only made him more handsome.

"No," he answered. "I like to get crazy drunk with it and kill whites and violate their women."

Her eyes widened at the remark, and Two Wolves actually laughed. "Do you so easily believe such things about my people?"

She found it difficult not to stare, but finally looked down at the bottle. "I'm sorry. I only know what I've seen and heard." She rummaged in the parfleche again, finding some gauzy material. "Can I use this to wash the wound with whiskey?"

Two Wolves nodded. Claire got up, wincing with the pain in her feet as she walked to where he sat. She doused some whiskey on the cloth and reached out to wash his wound, a deep slash across his left shoulder and breast. He caught her wrist. "You lied to me. You said you are not hurt, but you are barefoot."

It was only then that Claire realized even her socks were gone, mostly ripped apart by the rough undergrowth.

"Wash this wound, and then I will take care of your feet," Two Wolves told her. "I will wash them with whiskey and put bear grease on them. I have spare moccasins. They will be big for you, but you can lace them around your ankles so they stay on."

"If you say so." Claire reached out and squeezed the whiskey-laden cloth into his wound. Two Wolves grunted and jerked. "I'm sorry."

"Why? It must be done."

Suddenly everything that had happened caved in on Claire. She couldn't help the tears in her eyes. "You could have been killed." She sniffed and swallowed, cleaning the wound some more. "Did you follow me the whole way? Why did you do that?"

He didn't answer right away. Finally, she met his eyes again, struck by what looked like a hint of adoration there.

"I am not sure," he answered. "There is a spirit about you, a strength. And you remind me of my mother, when she was young and still lived with my father."

More tears came. Never had Claire felt so confused and alone and frightened, realizing what might have happened to her if not for this man she knew nothing about and had met only once before. She hung her head and cried. "I'm sorry. This is all just . . . I don't know what to think of any of this. My father died only four months ago, and I've been . . . trying to hang on to the business . . . and now this." She wiped at tears with the back of her hand. "And here I am alone in a cave with an Indian I don't know . . . and I think you need stitches, but I've never sewn up a wound before. And my feet . . . feel on fire and . . ."

She felt a hand at the side of her face, an unexpectedly gentle touch. "There is a can in my parfleche. It contains bear grease. Put some on the wound and that will help stop the bleeding."

He brushed at her tears with a thumb, then took his hand away and picked up the whiskey-soaked gauze and pressed it against his wound.

Claire sniffed back more tears and obeyed, finding the can. She pried off the lid and made a face at the smell. "Are you sure this stuff will help? It smells awful."

"My people have used it for a hundred years, probably longer."

Claire took a handkerchief from a pocket in her pants and blew her nose and wiped at her eyes. "I don't usually cry so easily. I hate crying."

"And I hated it when my mother cried. She cried when my father was killed, and she cried when the soldiers took her away from my father's people."

Claire had a million questions for him, but right now she was so tired she feared she would pass out, and the sudden mourning of her father and the relief of being safe were overwhelming. She dipped her fingers into the bear grease and reached out to smear some on his wound. "You'll have a scar."

"The mark of a warrior."

She'd been so concerned about the bleeding wound that only then did she realize he had other scars, above each breast. The light was so dim that she hadn't realized they were there. "How did you get these other scars?"

"You would not understand."

She noticed his bleeding had already slowed. It felt strange to be touching a strange man's bare chest. She'd never even seen a man with his shirt off, not even her father. "You were right. It's not bleeding so badly now."

"Wrap it."

She set the can aside and moved closer, holding one end of the gauze at the top of his shoulder and bringing it around under his arm and over his chest, across and around the other side of his neck and back around again. He was so close she could smell the mild scent of sage and leather, manly smells. She refused to meet his eyes, confused over the odd feelings it stirred in her to be so close to a half-naked man. This was unlike anything she'd ever known. Every single thing that had happened to her today was unlike anything she'd ever known. She felt vulnerable, was embarrassed that she'd cried. She thought herself stronger than this, but now she didn't even have Benny.

Benny! He was gone, too. Poor Benny had died trying to protect her. More tears came as she tied off the gauze and gladly backed away from Two Wolves. "That's the best I can do."

"It is fine. You should lie down now. Tomorrow we will have to get out of here."

Claire moved to the blanket. "What about you? Is this your only blanket?"

Two Wolves stood up and walked to his horse. "I have slept sitting up many, many times." He took something else from the horse and came over to her, leaning down to spread a blanket over her. "Here. It will be cold in here tonight once the fire dies down. I will put on another shirt and sleep sitting by the entrance. But first I will tie my horse outside where there is grass and then I will put bear grease on the bottom of your feet. And I will bring you moccasins."

Claire sat on the blanket and let the tears come while Two Wolves tended to his horse. She managed to stop crying by the time he returned. He wore another deerskin shirt with fringed sleeves and fringes around the bottom. It laced at the throat, but he'd not laced it, and the gauze she'd wrapped around his chest showed. She could see blood. "You're still bleeding."

"It will stop." He knelt down near her feet, holding the can of bear grease. He pushed the blanket off her feet.

"Wait. I . . . I have to go . . . you know. I laid in that wagon for hours and then ran. I was afraid to stop for anything . . . and then you told me not to move after you knocked me down . . . and then the ride here . . . I'm about to burst." Claire was glad for the faint light. It hid her red face. To her surprise, Two Wolves knelt down and scooped her up into his arms. "What —"

"Your feet are cut. I will carry you to a place where you can go."

"Two Wolves, this isn't necessary."

He made no reply as he carried her outside. He set her on her feet and walked away. Claire unbuttoned her pants, remembering Two Wolves had commented on the fact that she wore a man's pants. She squatted to relieve herself, thinking how she was totally at the mercy of a complete stranger who was strong enough to throw her for several feet. He'd picked her up as though she weighed nothing. Still, he'd risked his life to save hers. Surely, she could trust him. As it was, she had no choice anyway. It was this or wet her underwear and pants. At least it was dark out.

She finished and reached over to break a twig off a young pine tree nearby, using the thick needled end to clean herself. The needles were soft because the tree was young. She quickly pulled up her pants, mortified that she'd had to do this at all when a complete stranger stood somewhere nearby. Could Indians see in the dark, as she'd wondered earlier? Had he watched her? All kinds of horrors raced through her mind because of her vulnerability. She didn't even have any kind of weapon now.

She started back on her own, wincing with pain, but in moments Two Wolves grabbed her up again. She gave out a startled scream, her nerves still so on edge that any sudden movement reawakened her fears. "I'm not a baby," she objected. "You can put me down."

"I want your feet to heal fast. We have a lot of riding to do. Can you ride on your own?"

"Of course I can. I've been riding horses since I was little."

"Then we will see about getting a horse for you from a rancher tomorrow. There are a few out here I know and can trust. Others shoot at me just because I am Indian."

"That's terrible," she told him.

Two Wolves set her on the blanket. "I am used to it." He dipped his fingers into the can of bear grease. "Lie down and I will put this on your feet. It might hurt a little at first."

Claire lay down on her back. He gently picked up one foot by the ankle and began applying the bear grease. Claire grimaced with pain.

"It will feel better soon."

"I know." Claire thought how incredibly gentle he could be for such a big, rugged man of the wilds. "I took off my boots so I'd make less noise when I ran," she told him, squinting again. "Somehow I lost them, and I lost a gun I was carrying . . . one of those times that I fell."

Two Wolves worked the grease over her entire foot, not just the bottom. He even ran greased fingers over her calf to help her relax. She thought how incredibly ridiculous this was—an Indian—a stranger—someone who could do terrible things to her—and here she lay letting him rub bear grease on her foot and bare leg.

"I would have ended things back there sooner," he told her, "but there is only one of me and there were many of them. So, I was glad to see they did not find you right away. When you ran, I followed, but I had to get the Comanche far enough away that it will take the others a while to track and find his body and figure out what happened. I knew that would buy us some time."

Claire suddenly jerked her foot away and gave out a little yelp.

"I am sorry."

"It's all right. It didn't hurt. It tickled." Claire smiled through her tears.

Two Wolves grinned in return. "If that helped you stop crying, that is good." He picked up her other foot and applied the salve to that one and to her leg. He picked up the gauze she'd tossed after cleaning his wound and wiped off his hands. He turned and covered her feet again with the blanket. "Get some sleep." He walked away for a moment, then came back with his horse blanket. "Put this under your head, unless you do not like the smell of a horse."

He rolled it up and knelt down to put it under her neck.

"The condition I'm in, it doesn't matter if I sleep on a smelly horse blanket. I'm sure my hair is an unholy bush of a mess by now. I need a bath, my clothes are filthy and torn, every crack in my skin is full of potato dirt, and I probably *smell* like potatoes." Claire covered her eyes. "I can't imagine how terrible I look."

When Two Wolves didn't answer right away, she uncovered her eyes to see him just watching her. "You are very much like my mother," he told her yet again. "She was just as beautiful when plain and wearing an Indian tunic as when she had her hair done up in fine curls and wore white woman's clothing with color on her cheeks. She was strong and brave. There is much beauty in that."

The remark surprised Claire. "Do you think I'm strong and brave?"

"I *know* that you are strong and brave. You proved it today." He rose. "Now you must sleep. We will eat something in the morning before we leave. I have jerked meat and some bread. But now you must rest. I will leave my canteen with you." He rose and walked away.

Claire lay there filled with so many emotions and fears and so much curiosity that she wasn't sure she'd be able to sleep at al

CHAPTER NINE

CLAIRE JUMPED AWAKE, SITTING UP and taking a moment to orient herself to her surroundings. There was just a tiny glow left to the fire, and somewhere outside the cave she heard a wolf howl. She ran a hand through her hair and blinked, feeling out of breath from a nightmare in which she was running from a hideous being that was chasing her with a knife.

She remembered then where she was and how she got here. "Two Wolves?"

"I am here." The sound of his voice came from the mouth of the cave. "Try to go back to sleep. You will need your rest."

Had he sit there awake all this time? She wasn't even sure how long she'd slept. "What about you?"

"I can go without sleep. I have done it before. Do not worry."

"Are there wolves out there?"

"There are always wolves. I worry more about men."

"Do you still think they will come after us?"

"The wolves? Or the men?

"Both, I guess."

"The wolves will remain at bay. But, yes, the men will come, or at least one man will come … the Comanche. Those men back there know you saw that they were white and that you can testify to that. The Comanche warrior will no longer come to capture you. He will come to *kill* you. Did those men mention names?"

"Yes. And I know the man they mentioned personally. They said he told them they could sell me in Mexico. His name is Vince Huebner, and he owns several businesses in Denver. I owe him money. He's been trying to get me to marry him, but I hate him."

Two Wolves did not answer immediately. Finally, his voice came out of the darkness. "I do not understand why a man who wishes to marry you would bring you harm."

"Because he's angry with me for refusing his advances."

"Then he is a man with no honor, and you were wise not to marry him. I think he would not be a kind husband."

A kind husband? The words were soothing, as though this Indian named Two Wolves believed a man should be kind to his wife. His words and attitude were not what she would have expected from an Indian. She'd always imagined Indian men just chose a wife and took her into a *tipi* and took her whether she wanted him or not. She had so many questions. His mother was white but had been the wife of a Cheyenne warrior. A captive? Forced? He'd talked as though she'd actually been happy. What had her life been like?

She lay back down, struggling to sleep as he'd ordered, but her mind raced with the day's events and the possible outcome. If she went back to Denver City and told authorities that Vince Huebner had ordered her attack, would anyone believe her? Vince was a well-respected businessman there, with friends in high places. And telling such a story could get Two Wolves in trouble. They would say an Indian had no place in corroborating such accusations. And the men who'd done this would realize the importance of finding her and either taking her away or killing her . . . which meant they would also be after Two Wolves.

She pulled the blanket he'd given her up over her head against a cold draft. For a man who spent most of his time outside scouting, she thought the blanket should smell bad, but it didn't. It smelled of sage and leather. When she was riding with him earlier she remembered his long hair had also smelled good. When she clung to him she realized there wasn't a soft spot on him.

She tried not to think about how he'd looked with his shirt off, but the vision kept returning. Hard muscle was all she remembered . . . but those scars. What were they? His arms looked so strong. The man could hurt her or attack her any time he wanted and she'd never be able to stop him, but there he sat at the cave entrance, quietly guarding her.

She had no experience with men sexually and had been so busy helping her father and then taking over the business that she hadn't even bothered with going to dances or seeing men in any other way. And because she lived a life so different from other women, few young men had bothered showing her any attention. Vince Huebner's advances made her cringe, and she knew instinctively his offers of marriage were simply an attempt to get hold of her business. The thought of him touching her intimately made her ill.

Now here was a man who caused her to wonder what it was like to be held close by a man. The way Two Wolves looked at her, with admiration and such respect, brought out a sudden desire to visit her womanly side. Why in God's name was she having these thoughts? Here she was in the middle of nowhere, likely being hunted by men who wanted to kill her. Benny was dead. All her drivers were dead. Wolves prowled outside. All her wagons would be burned soon after sunrise, and all her supplies stolen. She'd very likely lose her business for sure now. Yet she lay here thinking surprisingly sinful thoughts about a man she barely knew and who would be forbidden to her even if she did have feelings for him.

"I can't sleep," she spoke up.

"Why not? You are safe for now."

Because I am having disturbing thoughts about you. "How can you be so sure they will come after us?" she said aloud.

"As I told you, there was more than one Comanche outlaw with them. It is in their blood to seek revenge, and the men who did this probably had orders to kill anyone who might live to tell who is behind this. The Comanche are good trackers. He will find the one I killed, and he will come after us."

"Where will we go? Will they catch us before we can find help?"

"It is possible. I will protect you."

"You are one man, Two Wolves."

"One man who knows what he is doing and who is determined to protect a loved one can do much."

Claire frowned. "*Loved* one?"

She heard Two Wolves sigh.

"By that I meant true loved ones. That includes someone we feel is worth protecting. You are a woman alone who did not deserve what happened. And you . . . there is something special about you."

"Because I remind you of your mother?"

He took a moment to answer. "It is my job as an Army scout to protect anyone threatened by renegade Indians and outlaws. I will try to get you back to Denver City. After that it is up to you what you wish to do. It is my job to get you to safety, but if this man you hate, this man who you say ordered this attack is in Denver City, you will still be in danger. I think you should come with me to Fort Collins. You will be safer there until this is settled. You will have to file charges against Vince Huebner."

"It will be hard to prove."

"We will find a way."

We? The man was confusing her. "Do you intend to testify in some way?"

"Of course."

"You're Indian. They won't believe you."

"I have friends at Fort Collins who will vouch for my honesty and my knowledge of these things."

"Two Wolves, this will be very difficult. It will divide people in Denver City, set whites against you . . . and I'll suffer, too, because I'm a woman. A woman's word isn't considered worth much, especially one like me, who is considered too independent."

Two Wolves said nothing for several quiet seconds. "I admire your independence," he told her then. "I can tell you are strong. It is right that you testify to these things. My people are being blamed for things they are not doing. It will help people see what is really happening. I would like you to do this for the Southern Cheyenne. There is someone in power who wants to kill all of them, even women and little children."

Claire sat up again. "Chivington?" She could feel Two Wolves's fury from where he was sitting.

"Chivington," he answered, spitting out the word like it was rotten in his mouth.

"I have read his hateful articles in the newspapers," Claire told him. "I felt much of it was lies."

"It is. I would like to kill him."

The statement was straightforward. Why did she care what that could mean for him? "That is a bad idea, Two Wolves. God in His good time will take care of men like Colonel Chivington."

"*My* God tells me to kill him."

"You aren't Christian?"

"I *am* Christian, but I feel a different message than you. My God is *Maheo*, which I believe is simply the Cheyenne name for *Jehova*. They are the same, and He tells me the world should be rid of men like John Chivington. But I know the laws, and I know how it would look for my people if I killed him, so I will wait for the spirit within me to tell me if there is another way. I will fast and pray about it."

Claire lay back down. "You are a confusing man, Two Wolves. I don't know why you risked your life to save me, but I'm glad you did."

Again . . . silence. Finally, he spoke softly. "I did it because you are special," he repeated.

Claire didn't answer. Did he care about her? If so, why? It couldn't just be that she resembled his mother. Was his mother even still alive? She felt she didn't know him well enough to ask for a more detailed explanation. His words moved her in a sweet, emotional way, and she didn't want him to know that. The way he made her feel was embarrassing, especially when she didn't know for sure what he was talking about. Besides that . . . he was a Cheyenne Indian, someone totally forbidden to a white woman in accepted society.

She decided she would leave things alone. If there was something more here, he would tell her. For now, thanks to this beautiful, brave man, she was safe. She would try to sleep and pray they could stay ahead of whoever might be coming for them. Once they reached safety, maybe then she would have time to figure the man out . . . or maybe then he would just ride out of her life, and that would be that.

CHAPTER TEN

CLAIRE HUNG ON, WONDERING WHEN her nightmare would be over. They still had no extra horse. Four months ago she had been working with her father at what she thought was a successful freighting business in a bustling and growing city. Now here she was on the back of a horse with a Cheyenne Indian scout she still barely knew, fleeing one or more Comanche Indians who were likely after her and Two Wolves, both with the intent of killing them. And on her feet she wore Cheyenne moccasins that were laced up her calves so she could keep them on her feet.

This could not be real.

They kept to the foothills for cover and to make tracking them much harder. The pins that once held Claire's hair in a tight bun had long ago come loose so that now her red mane was a mass of curls. She thought what a contrast her hair made against Two Wolves's long, straight hair, which sometimes blew against her face as they rode. She thought how soft it was, how good it smelled. She wished she could see them together in a mirror, had to smile at what a picture that would be, a short, very white-skinned, red-headed woman next to a tall, well-built, dark-skinned man with black hair and eyes.

"Are you sure we have to go all the way to Fort Collins first?" she asked.

"It is best. Denver will be dangerous for you now. My friend Major Ansley will know how to handle this. And there are white women at the fort who will help you with clothes and such. Then we will go to Denver, with soldiers."

After a day of riding, stopping a few times to rest the horse, and eating only pemmican all day, Two Wolves rode up to a small pond of water in a clearing amid thick pines. "It is late. We will rest here for the night.

You can bathe if you wish. I will do the same."

Bathe? With a complete stranger? An *Indian*, no less? Did he actually expect her to trust him? He swung a leg over the horse's neck and jumped down, then reached up for her. Claire couldn't quite get over how easily he lifted her up and down from the horse, and a little part of her took pleasure in his strength and the feel of his hands at her waist. This whole situation was beyond anything she'd ever known—the attack —the danger—the new and intense feelings Two Wolves stirred in forbidden places.

She helped him make camp and hobbled the horse.

"Tomorrow we will see about finding two fresh horses," Two Wolves explained. "This is too hard on one animal. I would have stopped at a friend's ranch today, but I decided we should continue to stay in deep hiding. I did not want to lead whoever is following us to the rancher. They might bring him harm." He began building a fire. "I usually ride with an extra pack animal," he told her. But I was in a hurry and had to travel unseen when I followed you, so I left my pack horse at a small trading post another day's ride from here. I know the men there. We can pick it up tomorrow and perhaps trade for a fresh horse. There you can also probably find clean clothes."

"I'll only need a clean shirt and under . . ." Claire hesitated. "I'll keep wearing these pants until we reach Fort Collins. Pants are much better for traveling than a dress." She felt embarrassed at almost saying underwear. She wished she could wash the underthings she wore now, but she was not about to hang a camisole and under pants over a bush or tree limb in front of Two Wolves.

To Claire's shock then, Two Wolves began undressing. When she realized he intended to strip down to whatever Indian men wore under their leggings, she looked away, fearful he would end up completely naked right in front of her. She was not ignorant of man and woman and what it took to make babies, but she'd never in her life seen a completely naked man and always thought her first time would be when she married.

"Find some wood to build the fire a little more," Two Wolves told her. He was standing closer now and he handed a blanket to her. Claire was forced to look at him in order to take it. She deliberately kept her gaze only on his magnificent arms and chest as she took the blanket, afraid to meet his eyes, and also afraid to look any lower. "Use this to wrap around yourself after you bathe," he told her.

He turned and walked away, and Claire dared to look at him fully, curiosity getting the best of her. Her eyes widened then when she realized that he was indeed completely naked, his bare bottom a little lighter in color than the rest of him! He walked into the pond and lowered himself into it, coming back up to pull his wet hair behind his shoulders. If ever a man resembled the Greek Gods she'd once read about, Two Wolves would be that man. She watched him reach down and take something into his hand. He used it to scrub himself. Sand, most likely.

She turned away, consumed with shame at having watched. She busied herself building the fire while Two Wolves swam around in the pond, then came out of it with a blanket wrapped around his middle. When he came closer he was actually smiling, a teasing grin that told her he knew he was shocking her.

"I like the way you blush," he told her. "It is easy to tell when a white woman is blushing. Her cheeks become very pink."

Claire said nothing. She was not about to satisfy his cocky ego by protesting. She rolled out her blanket as Two Wolves dug through his parfleche. When she cast a sidelong look at him, he'd pulled out a strip of cloth and was tying it around his privates. She quickly looked away again and dug a piece of pemmican out of a leather pouch, then sat down on her blanket to eat it.

"You are not going to bathe?" Two Wolves asked.

"Certainly not."

Two Wolves laid out his blanket and sat down across from her wearing only a loin cloth. "White women like to be clean. My mother always insisted on cleanliness. Why do you not bathe?"

Claire refused to meet his gaze. "If you think I am going to strip myself naked when I'm alone in the middle of nowhere with a strange man, think again. I'll put up with being dirty until we at least reach that trading post. Maybe there I can find private quarters where I can wash." She chewed on the pemmican, feeling angry and now even a bit afraid.

"Claire." He spoke her name in a commanding tone that compelled her to meet his gaze, which was surprisingly gentle. "I will not harm you. I will not look at you. Surely you trust me by now. I am not like white men, who lust after any woman they see and who do not honor women. In my society women are treasured as the bearers of life, and a man does not lie with a woman until she is his wife. Sometimes a Cheyenne woman will allow a man in her bed if she is a widow and needs his protection and needs him to provide for her, but even then, the man only goes to her if he is invited."

And how many widows have invited you into their tipis? Claire wondered, surprised at the odd, piercing jealousy that stirred inside. Never in her life had she felt anything like that.

"I know you wish to bathe," Two Wolves told her. "Go now while it is still light. Soon I will need to watch for wolves and bears. You cannot bathe after dark."

Claire finished the pemmican, longing for some real bread and meat and potatoes. "I can't. I just can't."

"You do not trust me?"

She looked away. "It's been hard enough being alone with a stranger and at his mercy for two days. Bathing around one is an entirely different matter."

"And why would I risk my life to save you if I meant you harm?"

Claire looked away again. "Some men don't think of violating a woman as bringing her harm. They seem to think she . . . she should expect it and put up with it."

"Put up with it? Do you think what men and women do is something to be feared? Something wrong and distasteful?"

"Don't ask me that. I don't really know anything about things like that."

"Do you think I do not sense that?"

"It's not your place to ask."

Claire heard him sigh deeply. "Claire," he stated commandingly again. She met his eyes, her cheeks hot.

"Go and bathe. I will not look at you. I will not harm you. Can you not see I am sincere? I am only aware of our surroundings and the fact that someone is out to kill us. Violating a woman is the last thing I am thinking of," he told her matter-of-factly. "Go and bathe. I order you."

Order me? Why did she feel compelled to obey?

"When there is no soap, you can scrub yourself with sand," Two Wolves told her. "It freshens the skin."

Claire couldn't help being impressed at his desire to be clean. Most white men seemed not to be too concerned about bathing or how they smelled. Some didn't even seem to care about keeping themselves shaved or keeping their hair clean and cut. Her father had been a clean man, but most of the time the men he hired to drive the wagons weren't always the best groomed, and she was well aware they often visited the brothels. She sometimes heard them joking about it, talking about women as though they were just "things" put on this earth to give men pleasure.

Then there was Two Wolves. The sincerity in his look finally caused her to get up and walk to the pond, taking her blanket with her. She glanced back at him. He sat at the fire with his back to her, and for some reason she trusted he would stay just like that while she stripped off her clothes.

She decided that if she was going to do this, she'd best do it quickly. Hurriedly she removed her clothes and stepped into the pond, gasping at how cold it was. She took a deep breath and dove farther in, grasping at sand at the bottom of the pond and scrubbing her arms and legs and underarms and privates as fast as she could. She wished she had soap for her hair, but maybe just getting it wet would help, although she knew that once it was wet her mountain of curls would just get even curlier.

Hurry! Hurry! She told herself. She dipped again and made ready to get out. That was when she saw it . . . a bear at the edge of the pond not far from where she'd left her clothes on a rock.

CHAPTER ELEVEN

"TWO WOLVES!" CLAIRE SCREAMED HIS name as the bear rose up on its hind legs, standing between Claire in the water and where she'd left her clothing on the bank. She barely got the Indian's name out before he was there on the bank, yelling something in the Cheyenne tongue and holding his rifle in the air, waving his arms and charging at the bear.

The bear let out a roar unlike anything Claire had ever heard. "Two Wolves, shoot it! Shoot it!"

Two Wolves stood there in only his loin cloth screaming at the bear. The animal took a swipe at Two Wolves, its incredibly long claws ripping open his upper left arm. Two Wolves ducked away, still refusing to shoot. Claire watched in terror. He'd not even yelled out when the bear clawed him. He roared back at the bear again, then raised his rifle but shot into the air. The bear roared again, its mouth looking big enough to consume Two Wolves' entire head. Two Wolves fired once more, and the bear finally backed away, going down on all fours then and lumbering away. Before she was out of sight two cubs appeared from the underbrush and ran off after her.

Two Wolves turned, blood pouring from his arm. "Out! Get out of the water now!" He staggered but kept hold of the rifle.

Claire just stared at him for a moment. "I'm not dressed!" she finally screamed back.

"Then get out ... and *get* dressed!" He staggered yet again and made his way to a large, flat boulder, where he sat down. "Hurry!" he told her. "I am losing . . . much blood."

His voice grew weaker with the words. Horrified at being naked, Claire knew she had no choice. She had to get out sooner or later, and Two Wolves was bleeding badly. She scurried out of the water, running to her clothes that lay near where he sat. She quickly pulled on her denim pants and tied the rope belt, realizing Two Wolves had seen everything. She started to pull on her shirt, then realized she needed to do something to help stop the Indian's arm from bleeding so profusely. She noticed him watching her, but there was a kind of faded look to his dark eyes.

"Oh, dear God," she whispered. "I can't get out of here without him!" She ran over and pressed the shirt against his arm. "Two Wolves, tell me what to do!"

"Tie it around my arm," he said weakly. "Very tight."

Claire hurriedly opened the shirt more and straightened it so she could begin wrapping it from the end of one sleeve around and around to the end of the other sleeve. She pulled as tightly as she could and tied the two sleeve ends together. "Why didn't you just shoot that bear?"

"It was a she-bear. I knew there could be cubs. My people do not kill a mother bear or the mother of anything else. The cubs . . . would be lost and hungry . . . wolves would have stalked and killed them."

"But that bear could have killed *you!*"

"I speak to bears sometimes. I could not kill it."

Claire felt like crying, unsure what to do next. "Can you make it back to camp?" She carefully took the rifle from his other hand.

"Yes, but we must keep going."

"Two Wolves, you aren't strong enough to keep going." Claire helped him up, and he braced his right arm around her shoulders as they walked back to camp. "We should stay here longer than just tonight. You'll be weak from losing so much blood."

"It is dangerous to stay too long. We are giving them too much time to catch up with us."

"How can you be so sure anyone is even after us anymore?"

Two Wolves sat down onto a blanket with a grunt. "I know such men. It might only be one man who will hunt us down, but he is Comanche, and he will make sure we are both dead if he can." He winced with pain, and Claire realized it was the first time he'd actually shown that he felt anything.

"Put the rifle beside me," he ordered her. "Look . . . in my parfleche. You will find . . . a man's cotton shirt. You can wear that."

His remark reminded Claire he'd seen everything there was to see, and she'd been bare-breasted through the whole time she wrapped his arm and helped him back to camp. She gasped and crossed her arms over her breasts, hurrying over to Two Wolves' supplies and rummaging through them to find the shirt. She quickly pulled it on and buttoned it, hoping the heavy bleeding meant Two Wolves wouldn't remember too much of what he'd seen. She grabbed an extra blanket and walked back to him, carefully draping the blanket around his shoulders.

"I still think you should have shot that bear," she told him. "What if it comes back?"

"She will not come back. And only a white person would think the first thing to do is kill something just because it is wild."

Claire sat down beside him. "I didn't mean it that way. I'm just scared."

"Do not be afraid. I know the animals. She will not come back. It is man who should be feared, much more than wild animals."

"Then I should be afraid of you. *You're* a bit wild yourself, walking up and roaring right back at that bear like a crazy man. I can't believe you did that."

"Sometimes when you stand up to them they back down."

"And if she hadn't, you would be dead . . . and me, too, for that matter. You could *still* die, from infection."

"I knew what I was doing. And if we can keep going we will be at that that trading post tomorrow where we can get help. In three more days we will reach the fort. There is a doctor there, but I heal fast."

"You lost a lot of blood. In fact, it's all over your side and your leg and still bleeding under that shirt I tied around your arm."

"You can go back to the pond and wet one of the cotton rags in my supplies. Bring it back and help me wash off the blood on my leg. We will rest just this night and then leave at first light, no matter how I am feeling. We cannot stay any longer."

Frowning with concern, Claire found one of the cotton rags. She ran to the pond and quickly wet it, then twisted the extra water from it and took it back to where Two Wolves sat looking like he might pass out. "Two Wolves, lie down on the blanket here." She quickly straightened a blanket near the camp fire. To her surprise, Two Wolves obeyed, stretching out on his back.

"Just tonight," he told her, his voice sounding weak. "We must leave at sunrise."

"We'll see." *Don't you die on me*, Claire thought, realizing it wasn't just because she'd be left here alone if he did die. It was because she cared about him, more than she should and in ways she *shouldn't* care. "You've hardly slept since you first helped me the night of the attack," she told him. She began washing the blood from his side. "It's no wonder you feel weak. You need to sleep, Two Wolves, wounded or not."

Two Wolves didn't reply. Claire looked to see his eyes were closed. He was either already asleep or he'd passed out. She could only hope it wasn't the latter. She returned to washing off the blood, and she found herself admiring his magnificent body, the way his muscled stomach caved in a little from lying on his back . . . his broad shoulders and strong arms. She kept washing him, moving down to his thigh and over his calf and back up again.

Was she really washing off a nearly-naked man? All he wore was a loin cloth that covered that most secret part of him. She'd seen a naked little boy once and thought that part that made him male quite funny looking. She was also well aware of the same parts on bulls and stallions. She wondered just how large a man's sexual parts got when they were full grown.

She turned away, ashamed of her thoughts, struggling with curiosity, upset with the feelings this man stirred in her. Everything was turned around and upside down and nothing like it was supposed to be. She felt removed from the real Claire, wondered how she had ended up out here in the middle of nowhere with an Indian who might be dying and chased by men who wanted to kill her. This man she still barely knew had seen her completely naked, and now here she was washing his own nearly-naked body. And horror of horrors, she was actually tempted to lift his loin cloth and peek at what was under it while he was passed out. Maybe she was a little bit crazy from shock after all she'd been through. She reminded herself she couldn't trust her feelings right now.

You should be ashamed of yourself, Claire Stewart! She finished washing the blood off Two Wolves, then found another blanket and covered him. *Please just be sleeping*, she thought. She shivered, suddenly feeling afraid and vulnerable without the sure, strong presence of Two Wolves. What should she do if someone did come?

Things suddenly seemed too quiet. She felt as though the grizzly was watching her. Maybe wolves were watching her. Maybe it was the Comanche who wanted to kill them. A deep fear began moving through her at the thought that Two Wolves might not be able to help her after all. She had no appetite now, and she realized she'd better get some rest herself if he really did wake up and want to leave at sunrise.

She gathered his rifle, hand gun, ammunition and knife and laid them close to him, then unloaded two more blankets. She spread one out near Two Wolves and sat down on it. Two Wolves made an odd groaning sound, and she realized he was shaking.

"God, don't let him die!" she prayed. She touched his cheek. It was cold. He shivered again. Realizing his body temperature must have dropped from loss of blood, she hurriedly built up the fire, then moved her blankets closer to Two Wolves and lay down beside him, covering both of them with the second blanket. She wrapped herself around him and vigorously rubbed his chest and his good arm, trying to avoid the still-wet bandages around his upper chest as well as the new wound on his arm. She concentrated on his hands, his belly and lower chest, hoping her body warmth and the fire would help bring his temperature back up.

"Don't you die on me, Two Wolves," she repeated softly. The sun slipped behind the mountains, and she prayed whoever might still be on their trail wouldn't catch up while Two Wolves was too weak to do anything about it. It struck her full force that her only hope for reaching safety was the man lying beside her. She absolutely must keep him warm and not let him die. She wrapped herself around him as best she could.

CHAPTER TWELVE

TWO WOLVES AWOKE TO A sun struggling to make its way above the eastern horizon. A bird twittered somewhere, and in the deep blue sky that still clung to night he could still see a few stars. He felt something warm beside him, sensed little puffs of air against his cheek. He lay still, thinking a moment, remembering . . . Cold, he'd felt cold . . . the bear . . . Claire.

Frowning, he turned his head slightly to see her . . . so close . . . lying half on top of him, her flaming red hair a tangled mess, her cheeks looking soft and pink, her lips slightly puckered in sleep like a child's. He wanted desperately to kiss those lips, to breathe in the smell of her, to run a hand over the beautiful breasts he'd seen bare the day before, full white mounds with pink nipples he wanted to taste. He'd been in such pain . . . lost blood . . . and in her haste to stop the bleeding she'd wrapped his arm before even dressing.

She was beautiful to behold. He'd been attracted to her when he first set eyes on her in Denver City. It was as though *Maheo* had led him right to her and that she was meant for him. Still … she was white. Forbidden, at least in the white man's world. But his father had loved a white woman, and she'd loved him in return.

Natural manly attraction made it impossible not to take the chance of touching her. He reached over and ran a hand along her side, up and over the shirt she wore with nothing under it. The soft mound of breast under his hand brought out a painful desire to have her, here and now. He would show her how gentle and lovely it could be.

He opened his lips and tasted her beautiful mouth, wanting much more . . . but she suddenly jerked away, gasping in surprise.

"What are you doing?" She threw off the blankets and quickly rose.

Two Wolves rolled to his back and rubbed his eyes. "I was not quite awake, and your lips were there. I wanted to taste them."

Claire stepped back. "I was only lying near you to keep you warm. Last night you were shivering and your skin was cold. I . . . didn't want you to die." She turned away and began picking up camp. "My God, Two Wolves, what made you think you could touch me . . . that way?"

"You are beautiful . . . and I think you are supposed to be mine. I was only adoring you."

"*Adoring* me?" Claire blinked, shaking out her hair. "My God, Two Wolves, that's ridiculous! You hardly know me, and you had no right taking advantage when I was just trying to help you!" Flustered and confused, she grabbed her blanket and walked over to throw it onto the horse's back. Her breast still felt tingly at the thought of Two Wolves touching it. It irked her to realize that for a quick moment, before she came fully awake, she'd liked his hand on her breast, and the thought of how he'd tasted her lips made her curious what it was like to be kissed by a man in desire, to let a man touch her sexually and to respond to those touches.

Her heart pounded with a mixture of awakened womanly desires, and terror that he might decide to take her against her will. Two Wolves was a powerful man . . . and an Indian. An *Indian*! She had to keep that in mind. Indians were wild and untrustworthy and only lusted after white women. They didn't love them in the same way white men loved their wives. Still, the way he talked about his father loving his mother . . .

He'd used the word adore. *Adore!* What an odd word for an Indian to use. And the fact remained he hardly knew her.

She said nothing more as she began busily packing things, then fully doused the nearly-dead fire, all the while feeling embarrassed and self-conscious.

"We had better get going if you feel up to it," she told Two Wolves. "You're the one who said we needed to stay ahead of whoever is following us. When do you think we will make it to Fort Collins?"

"Three days, perhaps." His voice sounded a bit cold. Claire turned to see him dressing. His muscled back and arms were still bare, and the bandages on his injured arm were stained red, a deep red that meant it was only dried blood and not fresh.

"I should put some whiskey and fresh bandages on that arm, Two Wolves."

"Never mind," he answered briskly. "The men at the trading post can clean it up. We might make it there late today or early tomorrow."

"That arm could be infected by then."

"What do *you* care?" he shot back. He pulled on a shirt, glancing side-long at her with a look that stabbed like a knife. "I saved you from a fate worse than death because that is my job as an Army scout. I will take you to the fort, and you can do whatever you need to do to bring to justice the man in Denver who attacked your wagons and stole everything from you and meant to sell you in Mexico. My part in this will be done."

He was angry. Claire suddenly felt like crying. She'd insulted him. It dawned on her he'd truly meant it in a good way when he said he adored her. She reminded herself that this man was blatantly honest. He simply said what he felt and figured there was nothing wrong with that. She'd embarrassed and humiliated him.

"I'm sorry about how I reacted just now," she told him, "but you can't just, just . . . act on your desires like that."

"You are white. I should have known better. We will not speak of it again." He quickly finished dressing and strapped on an array of weapons. Claire couldn't help wondering how he could be so alert and be using his arm as though nothing had happened. She watched him take took some jerked meat from a sack. He walked over to hold it out. "Eat this. It is all we have for now. There is no time to cook. Finish packing and we will go. Whoever is after us has had time to get too close. We will have to keep to the woods for a while longer, which will slow us up."

Claire reached out for the meat. "Are you really strong enough to leave?" She looked up at him, but he refused to meet her gaze. He looked past her, smelling the air for a moment much like a wolf might sniff for food or danger.

"I am strong enough." He turned away and threw his Army saddle onto the horse, then cinched it with deliberate jerks. "By the end of the day we will reach the trading post I told you about and pick up my pack horse. They will have more supplies, food and such, and you can get some decent clothes there and whatever else white women need. Indian women need very little to get by."

Was that supposed to be an insult? Claire could feel the tension in the air, feel his anger. A myriad of emotions moved through her, a desire to hit him. A desire to let him have that kiss. A desire to scream at him. And a desire to gently tell him she thought it was sweet that he said he adored her. A desire to demand that he never touch her again because he was Indian and she was white. And a yearning to tell him their different cultures didn't matter.

But they *did* matter. It was a huge obstacle, and it irritated her that he'd awakened something in her she had no idea how to handle. It was bad enough she didn't know much about loving a man in the way he had in mind, let alone the struggle inside over the fact that he was Indian.

"Please don't be angry, Two Wolves. I hate the thought of traveling with an angry man."

"I am not angry. I am just being practical. I am sorry for what I did. I awoke confused and you were there and I was weak. I will not allow it to happen again." He moved and spoke with a deliberate matter-of-fact attitude. "The sooner I get you to the fort, the sooner I can report to my commander and leave again. I have friends among the Cheyenne I wish to see. I will be out of your life and that will be the end of it. I will make sure of it so that no rumors are told about the two of us. White men look down on a white woman who has eyes for an Indian man. She is considered white trash." He finally met her gaze. "Because Indian men are considered less than worthy of pure and holy white women. Is that how you think?"

Claire was shocked and taken by surprise. "I . . . no, that's not how I think at all."

"I think you *do* think that way. That is why you recoiled from my touch."

"I didn't recoil. I was just . . . just surprised. I've never had relations with a man, not like … like what you were doing. I've never even been wooed by a man or even thought about it. I don't have time for such things, and I never really cared. Because of my job and the way I dress, men don't pay me much attention anyway." She turned away. "I don't even know why we're talking about this. Let's just get started." She rolled up blankets and tied them onto the horse, then pulled on her jacket. She scrunched her floppy leather hat over her hair to hide most of it.

Two Wolves winced as he leapt onto the back of the horse, then reached down for her.

"That's your injured arm," she told him. "Back the horse up to that big rock over there." She ran over to the rock and climbed onto it. Two Wolves guided the horse to where she stood and she climbed on behind him, grabbing hold of Two Wolves' waist. He rode off, and Claire could feel the tension and anger emanating from his body. It struck her that the man might truly have feelings for her other than an Indian man lusting after a white woman, but taking liberties with her was just wrong, and it angered her that it made her feel she couldn't trust him now. She wished she had a woman to talk to because although it should be his touching her that frightened her, she was more afraid of the fact that a little part of her had liked it. Perhaps she could be more practical in her thinking if he'd not said that word.

Adore.

He'd said it as though adoring her was as natural as breathing. Perhaps for Two Wolves, it was.

CHAPTER THIRTEEN

TWO WOLVES SAID NOTHING THE whole morning, and Claire hated the awkwardness that suddenly lay between them. She hadn't meant to hurt the man's feelings, but though he'd saved her life more than once and had been completely respectful until earlier, she argued to herself that she had every right to be upset with him and now distrust him. How was she going to sleep tonight after what she had awakened to this morning?

The most awkward part was that she still had to sit behind him on the horse . . . had to hang on to him as they rode . . . and what she hung on to was solid muscle. After seeing him naked she couldn't help thinking that his body reminded her of Greek gods she'd read about and seen sketches of. He'd awakened thoughts and unwanted desires that seemed totally wrong and sinful. Not only did she know next to nothing about this side of herself, but Two Wolves wasn't an ordinary man. If he were white and had a white man's job and lived in a white man's house, maybe she could more easily deal with the myriad emotions he stirred in her, but he was Cheyenne. Half white or not, he showed only his Indian side and was seen as an Indian by others. Didn't that make every fond thought she had for him deplorably sinful? And he'd *kissed* her! An Indian had *kissed* her!

His intimate touch had startled and angered her. Yet she couldn't help remembering that for one tiny moment, before she'd realized what was happening, she'd liked it. What was it like to truly love a man and lay with him? Would a man like Two Wolves be abusive and demanding? Wasn't that how Indians were? Still, he'd been nothing but helpful and protective. The thought of being with this man in a womanly way wasn't nearly as frightening and appalling as imagining it with a man like Vince Huebner, who always had a way of making such things sound filthy and sinful.

It was late afternoon when they left the shelter of the foothills and rode into an open, grassy area. Claire was amazed that Two Wolves hadn't mentioned being in any pain and he'd not shown any weakness from his wound and loss of blood.

"We have reached help sooner than I thought we would," he told her. It was the first time he'd spoken to her the whole day. "The trading post is just ahead where we will find fresh horses. That is the only reason I have left the shelter of the trees, but we have to hurry. We are still being followed."

Claire's chest tightened with alarm. "How do you know?" Claire asked.

"I just know. I will leave you at the trading post, and I will come back and hunt the man who follows us and get rid of him."

Get rid of him? Just like that? "If you could take him alive, Two Wolves, he could be a witness."

"This I know. I will try, but if he is Comanche, he will not cooperate, and he will be too dangerous to try to take with us to Denver City as a witness. He will try his best to kill me, and so I will likely have to kill him."

Claire's heart pounded even faster. "But you aren't healed enough to fight someone one on one."

"I am healed enough if it means protecting you."

His words touched her heart, but before she could respond, she felt a sudden, deep, horrifying pain in her lower left back. It was so jolting that she only jerked hard and gasped at first, then clung tightly to Two Wolves. She thought she screamed but couldn't be sure, and in her terrified state she also wasn't sure what had just happened to her. She didn't remember hearing a gunshot.

An arrow?

The horse whirled. She felt dizzy and drifting into a world away from the real one. Someone was lifting her down from the horse. "Stay face down!" a man's voice ordered. "Do not move!"

Did she hear a horse riding off?

"Two Wolves!" Everything began floating around her, the tall grass bowing and rising like waves on water. She heard what seemed like a war cry. A horse charged past her. She opened her eyes and raised her head just enough to see them.

Two men. Two *Indians*, both of them looking wild and vicious. They were in a hand-to-hand battle, with hatchets!

"Oh, my God," she groaned. She tried to move but couldn't. An arrow! There must be an arrow in her back! Was one of the Indian men Two Wolves? What if he was killed? He was injured! How could he possibly fight another man? She realized the other Indian must be the one who'd been tracking them. God only knew what he would do to her if Two Wolves lost the fight!

She watched through a haze of black pain, unable to get up and find a gun or anything else she might use to help Two Wolves. The two men landed into each other, both big and dark and wild and vicious. Claire could see fresh blood on the sleeve of Two Wolves's shirt . . . and new blood on his lower right arm from a fresh cut. They fell to the ground, rolled and growled. Two Wolves was on his back, and the other Indian raised his hatchet. Two Wolves held his attacker's arm away, but he had to use his injured arm to do it. Surely he couldn't hold the man off much longer with that arm!

Two Wolves's shirt was ripped and both men's dark skin gleamed in the hot sun, their muscles taut, their eyes on fire. Somehow Two Wolves managed to suddenly kick the other Indian away and get to his feet. Claire realized then that he no longer held a hatchet. He'd lost it! The other Indian came at him again, and Two Wolves whirled and kicked at the same time, slamming a foot into the man's throat. The other Indian stumbled backward, and Two Wolves kicked again, this time at the man's arm. The other Indian dropped the hatchet, and Two Wolves instantly picked it up.

Claire gasped when Two Wolves buried the hatchet into the man's face. She could hear his skull crack.

"God help us," she whimpered. It was the ugliest, most vicious thing she'd ever witnessed.

The other Indian went down with a thud, and Two Wolves just stood over him a moment, panting, looking wild and dangerous. Claire felt her heart tighten when he let out a war cry of victory, a shrill yip that startled and frightened her. In that moment, she saw a wild Indian out to kill. She just stared at him then, unable to move. Two Wolves shook his hair behind his head and walked over to pick up the hatchet. He shoved it into his weapons belt and walked over to kneel beside her. He touched her face with amazing gentleness for a man who'd just killed another in a vicious fight.

"I am so sorry, *Maeveksea.* This should not have happened!"

"It's an arrow, isn't it?" Claire lamented, now starting to cry.

"Ho-shuh, Maeveksea."

What had he just said? He gently pushed her hair away from her face. "*Ai,* it is an arrow. There is only one way to take it out without ripping at the insides, and that is to break it off and push it through."

"No! It hurts too much!"

"This I know."

"Two Wolves, your arm is bleeding again, even worse!"

"Do not worry about that. You are injured much worse. Lie still." He left her for a moment and walked around to her other side. She couldn't turn her head to look at him because it hurt too much to move.

Suddenly she felt it, a pain so deep and unbearable that she screamed for him to stop, but she felt a sickening jerk and heard a snap, after which she cried out from even worse pain. Two Wolves rolled her over.

"It must be done quickly before you have time to think about it and be afraid."

Claire felt him yank at something near her ribs. "No!" she screamed. Two Wolves pulled out what was left of the arrow head and shaft.

"Stop! Stop!" Claire begged.

In the next moment Two Wolves was lifting her. "I will take you to the trading post ahead where we can clean and sew the wound," she heard him telling her.

"Please don't move me! It hurts too much!" Claire wept.

"It must be done, *Maeveksea.* You are bleeding badly."

He'd used the word again. Had he given her a name? He lifted her as though she weighed no more than a bird. He managed to set her on his horse and climbed on behind her, holding her close with one arm as he got the horse into motion.

"You will be fine," he reassured her. "I will make sure of it."

Claire felt the rhythm of the horse, felt Two Wolves arm around her. In her terror and pain she found herself clinging closer. She nestled her face against his chest, surprised at how comforted she felt when he pressed her even tighter against him.

CHAPTER FOURTEEN

CLAIRE AWOKE TO SOMETHING WARM. She stirred slightly . . . opened her eyes. She saw Two Wolves bending over her.

"You are finally awake," he told her.

Claire realized then that he was washing her with a warm rag. She also realized she was naked from the waist up! She tried to move her arms to stop him, but a deep pain enveloped her that prevented her from doing no more than cry out. Two Wolves pulled a light blanket over her and began washing her face.

"I am only cleaning you up, *Maeveksea.* You do not need to be alarmed. You lost much blood. I will pick you up in a moment so others can put clean blankets on this cot." He gently washed her neck and lifted her just enough to run the warm rag over her back.

"Don't move me!" she cried out. "It hurts too much."

"I am trying to be careful, but this must be done. I did not think you wanted others in here."

Someone knocked at the door to the room, and Claire realized she didn't even know where she was. At the moment she didn't care. All she wanted was for the pain to go away. Two Wolves picked her up, wrapping the blanket completely around her when he did so.

"No! Don't move me!" she begged.

"*Ho-shuh,*" he soothed. "It cannot be helped." He carried her to a chair where he sat down with her in his lap. "Come in," he said loudly.

Someone came inside. "She awake?" a man's voice asked.

"*Ai,*" Two Wolves answered. "She is in much pain. Hurry and put the clean blankets on the bed so she can rest.

"Doin' my best, Two Wolves. Will she be here a while?"

"A few days. Send a runner to Fort Collins. I would like Major Ansley to come here. I need to talk to him, and it cannot wait too many days.

And tell him to bring laudanum."

Major Ansley? A few days? Where was she? Who was Major Ansley? How long would be here, and where *was* here? "Two Wolves, it hurts so bad!"

"I know. I have felt it myself. There is laudanum here, but little is left. I will give you some. It will help the pain. They will bring more from the fort."

He pressed her close and put one hand to the side of her face in an amazingly comforting gesture. He sighed then and pressed his lips to the top of her head. She could swear he'd just kissed her, but she was so full of pain she couldn't be sure. Everything was upside-down now, confusing, blurry, frightening . . . yet she realized all the fear and confusion went away when Two Wolves kept her close. What in God's name was happening to her? An *Indian* was holding and comforting her in an almost loving manner. And she didn't mind! She realized that at the moment she'd be terrified if he wasn't here with her.

"Don't' go away, Two Wolves," she whimpered.

"I will stay."

"Promise me. Don't leave me here! I don't even know where I am!"

"You are at a little trading post where we were going to get fresh horses and go on to Fort Collins, but another Comanche scout who was with those who attacked you tracked us down. He put an arrow in you. I made sure he regretted that. He is no longer a threat."

Claire thought hard, struggling to remember the events leading up to her current situation. She had been riding behind Two Wolves on the same horse. Then the awful pain hit. She had a vague memory of watching two men fight. "You killed him?"

"Yes."

"I sent men out to bury the son-of-a-bitch," a man's voice spoke up.

"Are you hurt?" Claire asked Two Wolves.

"A little. He cut me. But I did much worse to him."

Claire breathed in his scent . . . sage . . . grass . . . leather . . . fresh air. She clung closer. He'd saved her life three times now—from the first Comanche who tracked them—from a grizzly—now from another tracker. Why did he keep risking his life for her? Maybe it was just because he needed her to help him prove white men were attacking other whites and making it out to be Indian attacks. He was Cheyenne. He wanted to help his people. That had to be the reason he kept her alive and why he now watched over her so carefully.

"Do not be afraid, *Maeveksea.*"

"What . . . is that?" she asked weakly. "You keep . . . calling me that."

"It means Red Bird Woman. You are tiny, like a bird, and you have red hair. So I have given you this name."

"My name is Claire. It's easier to say."

"For you it is. I prefer to give you a Cheyenne name. It makes it seem more like you are mine."

What? Why was he saying things like this? She remembered then that when she got upset with him for touching her breasts and trying to kiss her that he said he was adoring her. Was that his word for love? How on earth could this man be thinking that way when he hardly knew her, let alone the fact that they were worlds apart in thought and beliefs and culture. She wanted to argue with him, but she was in too much pain and simply too weak to talk. *I'm NOT yours!* She wanted to shout the words at him. Yet here she was, taking comfort in his arms and asking him to please not leave. Why did she feel so safe here? And if he only was protecting her as a witness for his cause, it was silly to think there was any more to it. Still, a little part of her actually *wanted* him to "adore" her.

He lifted her again, then laid her back onto a bed. She groaned with pain from being moved. Two Wolves pulled more blankets over her, and another man came into the room, an older, pot-bellied man with a gray beard.

"Hello, darlin'. I'm Louis Pearlman. Me and a friend run this tradin' post. We know Two Wolves here right good . . . helped him clean out and sew up that wound. That damn Comanche put an arrow right through your left ribs, but you'll be okay. I've got some laudanum here. You ought to take some for the pain now that you're awake enough to feel it."

They helped clean and sew up the wound? How many men had seen her half naked? It was bad enough that Two Wolves had already seen her breasts that day at the pond, but this was too much. She started to cry at the embarrassment and humiliation of it all.

"Go away," she wept. "All of you just go away!"

"She will not feel this way when she is better," she heard Two Wolves tell the other man. "I will give her the laudanum."

"Sure, but not too much. You tell her she ought not be upset. Hell, me and Matt have sewed up more wounds than we can count, delivered a baby once, had to cut off a man's leg once. We've took out bullets and arrows before. Ain't no bad thinkin' goin' on when all you're doin' is tryin' to save a life. I don't like seein' somethin' so young and sweet hurt that way."

"She will understand."

Why did Two Wolves think he could speak for her? Claire heard the door close, and Two Wolves leaned close, putting something to her lips.

"Take a swallow of this. It will taste bad, but you will feel better. Louis also brought a glass of goat's milk. If you drink some afterward it will help take away the taste of the medicine. I poured whiskey on the wound and then put chewed tobacco on it. That will draw out infection."

Chewing tobacco? It sounded hideous.

"Drink," Two Wolves told her.

Desperate for relief, Claire obeyed, choking and coughing once the taste of the awful laudanum hit her fully. Two Wolves raised her up a little and held a glass to her lips.

"Here, drink some of this milk."

Again she obeyed, this time gladly. She realized the milk was fresh, and it did help get the taste of the laudanum from her mouth.

"Now you must rest," Two Wolves told her, laying her back onto a pillow. "By tomorrow you will feel much better. We will stay here until you can travel again. Then we will go to Fort Collins and make our plans what to do next. You should be stronger before we go to Denver City."

Denver City. She remembered then that she would have to face Vince Huebner and try to convince people, and a judge, that the man was a criminal. Facing the man was a daunting thought. No one would believe her.

"Stay with me," she told Two Wolves again, still not sure why.

"I will stay," he again promised. He took her hand gently into his own, stroking the back of her hand with his thumb. Claire felt him lean close then. He kissed her cheek! "I am sorry, *Maeveksea*. I should have known that man was closer than I realized. This is my fault. No one will ever hurt you again. This I promise."

How could he promise such a thing . . . unless he meant to stay with her forever? That wasn't possible. The man talked in riddles. "It's not your fault," she answered as the room began to swirl around her.

"It *is* my fault. It is my job to protect you. Cheyenne men always protect their own with their lives."

Their own? There it was again—his use of words that made it seem as though he thought he owned her. "I am not . . . yours to protect," she answered, not even sure the words came out of her mouth. Maybe she just thought them.

"You *are* mine to protect." His voice seemed more of an echo. Was she just hallucinating all of this? She was in so much pain and felt so dizzy. She sensed someone was close again. She felt warm breath near her mouth, felt a soft, gentle kiss. She was too weak and confused to turn her head away. And to her amazement it felt nice. She fell asleep with someone's hand wrapped gently around her own, and with the sensation of soft strokes to her forehead as someone smoothed back her hair.

CHAPTER FIFTEEN

FOR TWO DAYS CLAIRE KNEW nothing but pain and vomiting from it. When she was sick, Two Wolves cleaned her up. When she shook uncontrollably, Two Wolves held her. When she cried, Two Wolves soothed her and wiped her tears. When she urinated, Two Wolves changed the towels. Pain stripped her of all pride and protest. She needed help, and Two Wolves was the only person she remotely knew and trusted. It began to set in that she had no one now. Her father was gone, and now even all his friends were gone.

And now men wanted to kill her. Her only protector was Two Wolves, but men wanted to kill him, too. The thought made her realize how afraid and alone and devastated she would be if he died. She'd begun to lose her resentment of his treating her as though he owned her, and she'd lost all concern over the fact that he was an Indian. She was beginning to see him as just a man like any other . . . but then he *wasn't* like other men. He was far more handsome than the average man, far braver, far stronger, far more able in combat and survival . . . and he treated her with incredible respect and . . . what word could she give it? *Adoration.* She couldn't get over the time he said he was "adoring" her. She again wondered if he meant love, but that seemed foolish. He'd known her such a short time.

Her biggest problem was realizing she was developing deep feelings for the man. That just didn't seem right or even possible, but how did one control one's heart? Was this how love felt—to feel afraid and alone the minute the man walked out of the room? To actually look forward to his touch? To feel utterly safe and loved in his arms? To *want* those arms around her?

She thought she heard birds singing. *Maeveksea.* Red Bird Woman. Two Wolves had given her that name. Was it an act of love for an Indian man to give a woman a special name? She stirred, realizing things didn't hurt as much. She took a deep breath and didn't smell vomit or urine. She smelled fresh air and clean linen. She opened her eyes. And there he was . . . Two Wolves. He stood at an open window, looking outside, his long, dark hair hanging to his waist. Claire wondered if he longed to leave and go riding off to wherever men like him rode. He probably loved the out-of-doors and hated being stuck inside such a small room.

She waited, wondering if maybe he was praying, wondering what went through the mind of a man like him. She felt under the covers and realized she was naked. It irked her some that Two Wolves had seen her nakedness, and not especially in the most complimentary ways. Somehow, she sensed he hadn't taken advantage. He'd only done what needed doing. She felt bandages wrapped around her ribs. It didn't hurt to move her arms, and her head didn't hurt any more. She didn't feel sick. In fact, she felt hungry. "Two Wolves," she finally spoke up.

He turned. "You are awake. Your eyes look brighter." He smiled and walked to her bed to sit in a chair beside her. "Major Ansley should get here today. He will bring more laudanum. We ran out."

"I don't want more," she said weakly. "I think the laudanum is what made me sick. And now I'm hungry."

Two Wolves reached out and touched her forehead. "It is good that you are hungry. And today I feel no fever. I feared you were full of infection and might die."

She studied his dark eyes. "Tell me true, Two Wolves. Are you afraid I will die because you need me as a witness to help your people? Or do you really care about me as a person?"

He stroked her cheek with the back of his hand. "A Cheyenne warrior does not give a woman not of his clan a special name unless he cares for her as a person."

"I don't know what to make of that, Two Wolves."

"You will, in time. We will not speak of it now. You are still weak and confused. I want you to be strong and think clearly first, *Maeveksea*. Then we will speak of it." He rose. "I will get you some bread. And I told the cook here to keep hot broth ready. I will get you something to eat. If you keep it down, it is a good sign."

He abruptly left. Claire lay there listening to the birds and to the sounds of men's voices outside the door. She looked around the small room—a simple wooden structure with plank floors and nothing more than the bed, a chair and a small table beside it, and a trunk on the floor.

She realized how difficult it must have been for a man like Two Wolves to be stuck in this little room for however long she'd been here. Two days? Three? Four? She had forgotten to ask. She braced her hands and was relieved to realize her pain had eased dramatically as she pushed herself to more of a sitting position.

Just then Two Wolves came back inside. He hurried over to her when he noticed her trying to sit up. He leaned closer and propped pillows behind her, then grasped her under the arms and moved her even straighter. Her blanket fell away, and she quickly grabbed it to cover herself.

"Get me some kind of night gown or a shirt," she told him.

Two Wolves sat down on the edge of the bed. "There are a woman's clothes in the trunk over there," he told her. "They were left here when a couple traveling to California stopped here because the woman was giving birth, but she and the baby died. The man shot himself."

"Oh, how awful! Two Wolves, that's so sad!"

He nodded, his gaze dropping to her bare shoulders.

Claire pulled the blankets up to her neck.

Two Wolves grinned. "You are thinking perhaps I took liberties. I did not. The only reason I did not dress you is because you were so sick, and it would just have meant having to constantly change you and wash your clothes. And dressing and undressing you would have been too painful. You are special. I would never shame you or touch you wrongly."

His gentle words and her own feelings swam through Claire's mind in mass confusion. He sat here dressed in buckskins, looking all Indian, an earring in one ear, a feather and some kind of other trinkets wound into his long hair, a belt about his waist that held a knife. He wore no other weapons this morning. There was no paint on his face, which only accented how handsome he really was—a face so stunning that even a scar down his left cheek did little to detract from his looks. She noticed a fresher scar under his chin. He was the picture of exactly the kind of man to whom a woman like her should never give a second thought.

"How badly did that Comanche man hurt you?" she asked.

"Not so much that I couldn't kill him and then care for you. I will heal."

"I think I remember him cutting your arm, and maybe across your chest."

"He did. But your wound was much worse. My anger at him for hurting you gave me the strength I needed to kill him."

Claire frowned and shook her head. "Why, Two Wolves? You act like

I'm so special to you. You gave me a Cheyenne name, and you treat me like you own me."

"Someday soon I *will* own you. In the white woman's Christian way. The day I saw you in Denver, I knew. When I turned and looked back and you were still watching me . . . I knew. An eagle was circling above you that day. It did not call out, so you did not see it, but I did. It was a sign that we would see each other again, and that something would bring us together. And now something has."

Claire looked away. "You can't possibly know . . ."

"I can. Someday soon you will understand that I am right. That is why I followed you. It is my duty to protect the woman that *Maheo* has brought to me."

"Sometimes you truly confuse me, Two Wolves."

"We will speak of these things another time. You are not completely well. Your head should be clear and your heart open when we speak of these things, but you still have pain, and you still doubt what is happening between us. For now, you must eat. First I will dress you. Major Ansley will be here soon and will want to speak with you."

"He's your friend from Fort Collins?"

Two Wolves nodded and rose, walking over to the trunk. He fished around in it, pulling out a pink flannel gown. "My mother liked this color," he told her, bringing it over. "She was a kind woman, and very strong and brave . . . like you." He came closer and put the gown over her head, then pulled the covers away. "Can you move to the edge of the bed?"

"I'll try."

Two Wolves grasped her arms and half lifted her to help her move her legs over the side. He helped her get her arms into the night gown, then helped her to her feet long enough to let the gown fall down around her. He picked her up and laid her back into the bed then, pulling covers to her waist.

"Thank you, Two Wolves. This feels much better." Claire let out a little gasp when he leaned in and kissed her cheek.

"You *look* much better. Your color is good." He grinned. "And I like to watch you blush. White women blush so easily."

A bearded man walked in then with a tray that held a bowl and a piece of bread. "Here you go, young lady." He handed the tray to Two Wolves. "And I must say, you're lookin' much better."

"Thank you . . . Louis, is it?"

The man looked at Two Wolves. "She remembered! That's a real good sign."

Two Wolves nodded. "It is."

Louis chuckled. "You're a hell of a doctor, Two Wolves. Go ahead and help her eat. I've got chores."

Louis turned and left. Two Wolves set the tray on Claire's lap. "Do you need help?"

"No." Claire just stared at the food a moment. "You've done so much for me." She suddenly wanted to cry. "I feel so alone, Two Wolves."

He touched her shoulder. "Never feel alone. I am here." He turned. "Try to eat all of it. I am going to ride out and see if Major Ansley is coming."

He left again, and Claire realized he seemed to have a habit of just suddenly leaving.

"And you can't wait to get out of this stifling room and get on a horse and ride free," she said softly. She had so many unanswered questions . . . about his mother . . . about why he was out here living part time among the Cheyenne yet scouting for the U. S. Army. He seemed educated, seemed to completely understand the white man's way. He even had a white man's name. She wanted to know more.

She brushed away her tears, realizing she'd actually taken comfort in his words. *Never feel alone. I am here.* What an unusual man he was.

She bit into the bread, then dipped a spoon into the hot chicken broth and ate some of it. It felt good to put something in her stomach. Just as she bit into the bread again she heard it . . . a *yip* . . . a kind of war cry. She saw him through her window then—Two Wolves—riding off on a gray Appaloosa, his long, black hair flying behind him. Was the war cry in celebration over her being better? She imagined it must feel wonderful to him to be out in the open and on a horse again. He'd stayed with her in this little room and constantly cared for her, apparently for several days. How could she not love him for that?

CHAPTER SIXTEEN

TWO WOLVES STRETCHED HIS ARMS to the side as he rode away from the trading post, heading north to see if he could spot Major Ansley coming. He used only his legs to sit the big Appaloosa gelding, keeping the horse at a gentle lope across open plains as he embraced the wind. It felt good to be riding free, breathing fresh air, feeling the sun on his skin. This was his fourth day here, and he'd spent nearly every hour sitting beside Claire, watching her, nursing her, cleaning her up, soothing her, forcing water and food down her throat when she was barely aware of it.

"*Maheo*, make her well," he prayed.

Finally, he grasped the reins and urged the horse into an open gallop for a good half mile before slowing again. He finally reined his mount to a halt and turned him, patting his neck.

"You are a fine steed," he soothed the animal. "I think I will see if Louis will take two Army horses for you. But then I will need one more mount for Claire when I take her to Fort Collins."

How could he leave her now? He knew these feelings he had for Claire Stewart were dangerous and wrong. Knew that once she was completely well she would likely not return those feelings. Yet the thought of each of them going their own way when this was over just didn't seem right— or even possible. He would never forget her bravery and strength. Nor would he forget her beauty. He was tortured by the sight of her slender legs, her full breasts, the red hair that hid that place he wanted to invade and claim for himself.

He could hardly bear the thought of some other man being her first, claiming her lithe body, forcing himself between her legs when perhaps she didn't even want him. She was small and sweet, and a man should be gentle with her. He loved the thought of tasting her full, pouty lips and getting his fingers tangled in her wild, red curls and teaching her how nice it could be to give herself to a man.

He realized now that he shouldn't have touched her the way he did that morning after the bear attacked him, but she'd looked so perfectly beautiful lying there, her lips reminding him of ripe fruit to be tasted. Her reaction had angered him, but now she seemed not to be afraid of the fact that he was Indian. Still, he fully understood all the things that could be wrong about loving her.

Maybe he should just keep riding. Claire was improving. They'd both probably be better off if he left, but incredibly, after only a little over a week with her, he loved her. He could tell she had feelings for him, too, but how far would she allow those feelings to go? He had no problem loving a white woman, but he knew too well that white women had a very *big* problem allowing themselves to love an Indian man.

He finally had his proof about the fake Indian raids, but it could come at a big cost. Not only might Claire believe it was his only reason for being interested in her, but after seeing the kind of men who worked for Vince Huebner, it was obvious Huebner was a cruel and dangerous man. He might look for ways to get rid of Claire . . . or force her to marry him out of fear for her life. And wealthy white men had the means to conveniently silence any man who presented a threat to his fortune and his life.

"And now *I* am that threat, Vince Huebner!" Two Wolves seethed. "Come for me, and you will *die!*"

He'd already killed two of Vince's men, but more would come. Of that he was certain. Huebner would send them as soon as he learned what had happened. And Claire would be in just as much danger. Even if he didn't love her, he'd be obligated to stay with her and protect her until this was over.

The Appaloosa whinnied and shook his mane, prancing sideways a bit. "*Ho-shuh,*" Two Wolves said softly, patting the horse's neck again. He turned the animal, realizing the horse had sensed something. He saw four men coming. He couldn't make them out yet but hoped it was Major Ansley. He sorely needed to talk to the man. He kicked his horse into motion again and rode toward the approaching riders, finally able to see that three of them wore uniforms. He recognized the fourth as Billy Wade from the trading post, the man he'd sent to Fort Collins.

Two Wolves gave out a shrill cry that was a Cheyenne welcome call he knew Ansley would recognize. In minutes, he came within close range.

"*Ha-hey!*" he greeted Ansley.

Ansley nodded, ordering the other three men to ride on into the trading post, so he could talk alone with Two Wolves. The major removed his hat for a moment to wipe sweat from his brow, his face red from a long ride on a hot day. Two Wolves thought how, if the man would get rid of his big belly, he might not get out of breath so easily, but he chose not to insult one of the few good friends he had among whites, let alone among soldiers.

"I thank you for coming," he told Ansley, putting out his hand.

Ansley put his hat back on and grasped Two Wolves' wrist in the way Indians had of shaking hands. Two Wolves gave Ansley's wrist a solid squeeze.

"The woman I rescued is still weak. I could not bring her to the fort yet, nor could I wait too long to tell you what has happened. I have my proof, Major! I know of a man who has planned many of the raids by white men pretending to be Indians."

"Slow down, Two Wolves. Let's get to the post so I can cool off in some shade and get something to drink."

"*Ai.*" Two Wolves turned the Appaloosa and kept the horse at a gentle lope as they both headed for the post. "She is strong and she is smart, and she personally knows this man," Two Wolves told Ansley. "She can help me prove what I have been saying all along. In a day or two she will be well enough to come to Fort Collins, and we will make our plans there."

Ansley frowned, glancing sidelong at Two Wolves. "I hear something in your voice, Two Wolves."

"Hear something?"

"Yes. It's called infatuation. You're well-schooled. You know what that means."

Two Wolves couldn't help a slight grin. "I know, and we have much to talk about."

"Apparently so. All I know at the moment from the man who came to get me is that you rode into the trading post all bloodied up from a fight with some Comanche man, and that you had a young woman with you who'd been badly wounded. You have a lot of explaining to do, both about how you managed to end up at this trading post with a wounded white woman and how you think you'll be able to prove your theory about the raids."

"I will explain. Let's get to the post so you can refresh yourself and we can talk. *Hai!*" Two Wolves kicked the Appaloosa into a harder run and headed for the post.

Well, well, Ansley mused. *Something tells me you're excited about more than proving white men have been raiding as Indians, Two Wolves. God help you if you've fallen for a white woman.*

It didn't surprise him, considering Two Wolves' own mother was white, but she'd raised him mostly away from the hatred and prejudice that existed out here in the West. He liked Two Wolves and didn't want to think about what all this could mean for him. Or for the woman, if she indeed would even consider a relationship with a Cheyenne half-breed.

CHAPTER SEVENTEEN

MAJOR ANSLEY KICKED HIS HORSE into a faster run to catch up with Two Wolves, who was already handing his mount over to Louis Pearlman.

"I wish to buy this fine gelding for myself," he told the major as Ansley halted his horse beside him and dismounted. "It is better than any Army mount I have ridden."

The major tied his horse to a hitching post in front of one of several cabins at the post where people traveling through often stayed, and where Louis Pearlman and his partner Matt Crane lived year-round.

"Then you'd better start wearing at least the Army shirt of a scout and be sure your saddle and all your gear are Army issue, Two Wolves, and that's an order. You keep riding around dressed all Indian and sitting a blanket instead of a saddle half the time, and you're going to get yourself shot right off your horse, Army issue or not."

Two Wolves patted the Appaloosa's neck and rubbed noses with it. The horse rumbled a low whinny and shook its head and mane. Ansley shook his own head, thinking how there were times when it seemed Two Wolves could communicate with horses.

"He is a fine horse." Two Wolves said, smiling. "He looked at me and I looked at him and we knew we must be together."

Ansley had never seen Two Wolves quite so animated. And he very seldom smiled, especially not in the purely happy way he was smiling now. "What in the world has gotten into you, Two Wolves? You are not your usual, rather stoic and serious self."

"I have my answer! I can prove what I have been saying about white men raiding their own people just so my people are blamed for it."

Behind Two Wolves, Louis cast the major a look that hinted at deep doubt in the Indian's statement. "It won't be that easy, Two Wolves," he grumbled as he led the Appaloosa away. "I'll go rub down Peter."

Two Wolves turned, frowning. "*Peter*? That is his name?"

"Yup."

"That is a ridiculous name for such a fine horse. I will call him *Itatane*. It means 'brother.' From now on we will be brothers."

Louis chuckled softly. "Call him whatever you want. Just make sure I get the fifty dollars he's worth."

"I have it. I have little need for what the Army pays me, so I save it up the white man's way."

"Well, if you start livin' the white man's way for that little gal layin' inside, you'll need more white man's money, 'cuz she ain't gonna' live in any *tipi* and skin rabbits for her supper or sleep out on the ground half the time. White women need a real house and real china and a real bed."

Louis glanced at the major again and winked. He walked off with the horse, and Two Wolves turned to Ansley.

"He takes much for granted."

Ansley studied Two Wolves closely. "He just told me what I feared all the way here. You've fallen for this woman you rescued, haven't you?"

"Come! I will take you inside to meet her."

"Wait a minute." Ansley nodded toward a bench beside a stone well nearby. "I don't want to meet her until I find out what's happened that led to all of this. And I want to know the details of how you think you have your proof and what you intend to do with it, Two Wolves. You can't just go riding into the white man's world throwing names around, especially if you're going to keep dressing like a damn Cheyenne warrior, let alone dragging a young white woman into the picture. The man who brought me here told me what he knows, but I want to hear it from you. Come sit down over there by the well with me and tell me everything. Like how in hell you happened to be in just the right place at just the right time to rescue that woman inside. And how you ended up being chased by a Comanche man you killed south of here, and how that woman inside ended up with an arrow in her."

Two Wolves shrugged as they walked to the bench. "I met her in Denver City—and I knew then she would be mine. I call her *Maeveksea*. It means Red Bird Woman."

"Jesus, Two Wolves, slow down. You are way ahead of me here." The two men sat, and Ansley rested his elbows on his knees, watching Louis remove the blanket from the Appaloosa's back. "You start from the beginning, son, and I want every detail. This is damn serious and could get you hanged, and you know it."

"But it is all meant to be."

"It is all a big problem, that's what it is. And you'd better think about that young lady inside that cabin and what you're proposing could mean for her. Now start at the beginning like I told you. You mean a lot to me, and I don't want to see you or that woman inside get yourselves killed over this."

"Nothing will happen to her. I will make sure of it. Indian men protect their women to the death."

"Yes, well, that's what worries me. Start with Denver City and tell me what's happened. Was it when you went there with Black Kettle for the meeting with the governor?"

"Ai." Two Wolves watched Louis begin brushing down the Appaloosa. "She was watching as we rode by, and when I looked at her I saw pride and strength and many things most white women do not have, like bravery and independence. She was wearing white man's pants. It was funny to see, but I could tell she is not one who cares about how she looks. And unlike most white women, she looked right back at me. I saw that she was curious, and I saw that she admired me as a man. She did not look at me with judgment and disdain like most white women, and she did not turn away as though it was a sin to look upon me. She is different . . . brave . . . very strong for being so small."

"And you haven't said one damn word about what actually happened. I'm already seeing a very dangerous situation here, in too many ways to count. Just tell me what happened and leave out the details of your own opinion or feelings. I need some facts right now."

Two Wolves sobered, glancing sideways at the major. "I am glad you came. I thank you for that. I wanted to explain things before I bring her to Fort Collins, and she is still very weak."

Ansley rubbed at his eyes. "Jesus Christ," he muttered. "You're in love with her."

"Yes."

Ansley sighed, removing his hat. "Tell me all of it."

He listened without comment as Two Wolves went on with the details, how and why he followed Claire's wagon train out of Denver City, how he rescued her and killed the Comanche scout as they fled . . . about the grizzly attack . . . what Claire knew about Vince Huebner because of what she'd heard . . . how he'd been nursing her himself for nearly four days now since a second Comanche man attacked them.

"She is a good person, and she is very much alone. She is trying to keep her father's business going. This Vince Huebner is trying to destroy that business. And he wants her to marry him, but she hates him. I fear he will try to take advantage now that she has lost so much and is alone. Her father's friends who watched over her are dead now, too–killed in the raid. I do not trust this Vince Huebner not to attack her. He is a dangerous man, and I will make sure everyone knows what he has done. She will be safer if he is gone."

"Gone? Don't tell me you're thinking of killing him yourself."

Two Wolves did not reply.

"Two Wolves, if you intend to be around to protect this young lady, killing a white man is a sure way to *not* be! You'd be hanged within twenty-four hours."

"I know. Killing him is just a pleasant thought."

"Well, we *all* have those thoughts about various people in our lives. In your case, it's even more dangerous because of how people feel toward the Cheyenne right now."

"But that is my point!" Two Wolves answered, facing Ansley. "They need to know the truth–that many of the attacks they hear about are *not* by the Cheyenne!"

Ansley could see the passion in his dark eyes, realizing how simple and easy it seemed to a young man like Two Wolves. The truth was the truth, but that didn't always matter. He put a hand on Two Wolves' shoulder. "Listen to me. You know how much I like you. I lost a son who would be your age now if he'd lived, and you're so damn honest and brave, and I feel sorry for the fact that you live in two worlds. That has to be hard for you." He rose and paced. "Are you willing to listen to my thoughts on this?"

"That is why I sent for you. You are one of the few white men I trust."

Ansley smiled softly. "Coming from you, I take that as a compliment." He sat back down. "I completely understand what this means to you, but you're looking at it from the Cheyenne point of view, and you're seeing this whole situation in its literal sense. A supply train is attacked, there is a witness to claim it was white men who did it, one who can name names. It should be easy to prove it all and send this Vince Huebner to prison–maybe even get him hanged. Now I'm going to give you the *white man's* viewpoint."

Two Wolves looked away. "I fear I already know it."

"Number one–this Vince Huebner is apparently well known in Denver

City. He probably has a lot of money, and he's likely a respected businessman who is very good at hiding his evil side. Number two–Huebner owns his own freighting business. People will say Claire Stewart is lying and just trying to get rid of her competition in a desperate effort to save her own business. Number three–it's the word of a prominent businessman against a young girl most townspeople probably don't like because her behavior and the way she dresses are totally abhorrent to the prominent people of Denver City. They see her as a little strange and not believable. Number four - people already hate the Cheyenne and want them out of Colorado. They won't be ready to accept anything that supports the Cheyenne. They are too ready to believe the worst. And last but not least–You're an Indian, and therefore you are just trying to find ways to help your people. Even though you're half white, they will see you only as Indian. To make things worse, your feelings for Claire Stewart will show right through–an Indian lusting after a white woman–that's what they'll call it. And if she returns those affections, she'll be called every filthy name in the book. The fact that she's already a bit odd in her behavior will just make it worse for her."

Ansley could feel the Indian's anger.

Two Wolves suddenly got to his feet. "It is *wrong!*"

"Of course it's wrong. But in a sense, you have absolutely no proof other than your word and Claire's against a respected citizen of Denver City. He's going to deny everything and will find it easy to turn everyone against you."

"We can go back and find the wagons and the bodies!"

"They've gotten rid of both by now. They probably put all those supplies into Huebner wagons and delivered them to Bent's Fort by now. And whoever was in on it will just take up their normal lives and say nothing about it. Huebner probably pays them well to keep their mouths shut. There won't be anything left to use as evidence."

Two Wolves whirled. "What about the Comanche man I killed just south of here? Men from this post went out to bury him. They can testify."

"To what? That a renegade Indian attacked you and Claire? People will just claim he was some wild, lustful Indian who meant to kill you and capture Claire for himself."

"Huebner was going to *sell* her into prostitution in Mexico! She heard them talking about it."

"She *heard*. That's not proof, Two Wolves, not against a man like

Huebner. Our only hope here is to find some of the men who were a part of this and figure out a way to make them talk. Did she know any of them?"

Two Wolves shook his head. "No." His hands moved into fists. "What about the men who worked for Claire and were killed?"

"They were either buried by those who did this, or left for crow bait. Either way, people will simply think it was an Indian raid that killed them, which of course is what Huebner wants them to believe. I don't doubt he's a fan of John Chivington, who is also capable of blaming things on the Cheyenne. Our only hope is to catch some of these men in the act, and that's not likely to happen. It's a big country out there, and I don't have enough men to use them to run around half of Colorado hoping to find men involved in a fake Indian attack. The only reason you happened to be there is your infatuation with this Claire Stewart. You were worried for her safety. But I can't send a man out to spy on every supply train in Colorado or to watch every farm and trading post and rancher in this territory. It's an impossible task."

Two Wolves turned away, his hands still in fists. "I will find a way! And we will first at least plant suspicion in the minds of others about Huebner. If Claire goes to Denver City and tells the authorities what she knows, at least they will begin to wonder."

"Possibly." Huebner rose. "Two Wolves, the messenger you sent said you were wounded in that fight with the Comanche warrior. Are you all right?"

Two Wolves turned, pulling up the left sleeve of his buckskin shirt to reveal an ugly, still-healing cut on his left arm. "I am cut here, and I have a cut across my belly. I also have cuts from the bear attack that are still healing. But I will be fine. It is Claire who was hurt the worst. The hardest thing I have ever done is to push that arrow completely through her. It had to be done. I have been caring for her ever since. I washed the wound and changed the bandages twice a day. I bathe her and feed her, and she is so small—like a little girl sometimes—but she is twenty summers. She is old enough to be a wife."

"A *wife*? Does she know your thoughts?"

"She knows."

"And does she feel the same?"

"She has not said so, but I know that she does. She is just afraid because I am Indian."

"You are also *white*. You have a white name, and if you dressed like a white man and *used* that name, it might help you win her over . . . and it might also help you in going up against a man like Huebner. Would you be willing to be the white man that you are for Claire? And to help you in this case?"

Two Wolves closed his eyes. "In my heart I am Cheyenne, and she knows that. If I turn to white man ways, it will be to help bring down Vince Huebner, not to please a woman. A woman should love me for who I really am. Claire is that kind of woman. You will see when you meet her. And then when we get to Fort Collins, we will make our plans." He faced Ansley. "Will you help us?"

Ansley nodded. "I'll do my best. We can at least use Louis and Matt to testify as to what they saw and heard when you first got here with Claire. But like I said, people will say this Comanche man was just a wild Indian panting after a white woman. They might even say that about you."

"It is *not* that way!" Instant rage showed in Two Wolves' dark eyes.

"Of course it isn't. But you have to be ready for ugly words, Two Wolves, and you have to *not* react to them. Getting angry and landing into someone will only prove them right—that you are wild and danger-ous. We at least have a lot of men at the fort who can testify as to the kind of man you really are. You let me look into this before you go run-ning off to Denver City."

Two Wolves grinned. "And I have two weapons they will not expect. I have white blood, and I am *educated.* My mother once told me that I should always remember these things if white men come against me." He stepped back and yanked a hatchet from his side and a pistol from the other side, holding them in the air with powerfully-muscled arms. "I can think and speak well—and I can use *these* just as well. I can fight *both* ways." He shoved the weapons back into the rawhide loops that held them. "I fear no danger that comes my way, Major, but *Claire* is afraid, and now *she* is in danger. I will not let anything happen to her. Together we will prove the truth, but whether we do or not, I will not leave her alone in this. I know in my heart this Vince Huebner is a bad man, and he will either kill her or sell her. And maybe even try to force himself on her." The dark anger returned to Two Wolves' eyes. "I will *never* let that happen!"

Ansley ran a hand through the sparse hair on his head. "Let me look into the right way to go about this. And you let that young lady in there make her own decisions. I don't want to see her just yet. I'm tired from a long ride, and I want to clean up first and get something to eat. And when I talk to her, I want to talk to her *alone*. I want her reactions and answers to be *hers*, not something she says because you're standing there and she thinks she has to say what *you* want her to say. Understand?"

"I understand." A grin sneaked across Two Wolves' lips, his countenance changing from anger to humor. "She is her own woman. She will be truthful with you. It is one of the things I love about her. She is afraid of what might happen, but she does not fear the *truth*. And she is brave enough to *tell* the truth. She does not need me to be there. See her alone if you wish. It does not matter to me." He walked away.

"Where are you going?"

"I do not want you to think I will try to influence Claire Stewart," Two Wolves called back. "I walk far away to think and to pray."

"But I'm not done . . ."

Two Wolves kept walking. Again, as he'd done many times, the Indian had abruptly finished talking and left. Getting the man to follow his orders had always been difficult. He was his own man and had his own way of thinking and that was that. Even if this woman he'd rescued did love him and decided to marry him, living with a man like Two Wolves would indeed be a true test of love. But then maybe she could tame him.

Ansley shook his head in resignation. He turned to the well and pulled up a bucket of water so he could wash. He had much to consider, and he didn't intend to do it on an empty stomach. He'd get something to eat first. And now he was anxious to meet the woman who'd apparently won Two Wolves' heart. He wondered if she had any idea what she was in for, both from the outside world, and from the complicated man who wanted to claim her as his wife.

CHAPTER EIGHTEEN

"YOU WHAT?" VINCE HUEBNER'S HANDS moved into fists as he came around his desk to face Johnny Sanders, a decent-looking young man with steely-blue eyes. Johnny liked to think he was good with the six-gun he wore on his hip, but Vince suspected it was all bluster.

Johnny stepped back a little. "We lost her."

Vince's pale blue eyes told Johnny in a smoldering glare that he'd like to kill someone. "How in God's name can you lose one helpless woman after a raid that killed all of the men who were with her?"

Johnny swallowed nervously, embarrassed that Claire Stewart had somehow slipped right through the hands of six men. "I don't know, boss." He ran a hand through his thick, blond hair, trying to think straight. "At first we thought maybe you were wrong. Maybe she wasn't with them at all."

"She weighs all of a hundred pounds and has red hair that would have made her stand out in any crowd, but she's damn good at hiding those features! Even so, you were in wide-open country! It doesn't make sense that you could have missed her!"

"Somehow during the attack she must have managed to run off without us noticing," Johnny answered. "We searched the wagons, and she just wasn't there. Then one of those wicked-looking Comanche breeds you hired went off into the foothills to look for her, but he never came back. It was dark by then."

"The next morning we sent two more men to go look." The words were spoken by Bill Powers, one of Vince's best freight drivers. Powers scratched at a scraggly beard as though thinking. Stringy brown hair hung from under his floppy leather hat. Vince thought him fat and slovenly, but the man obeyed every order given him and knew how to keep his mouth shut, so he kept him on his payroll.

"And what did you find?" Vince asked.

Bill glanced at Johnny, who closed his eyes and turned away.

"Well?"

"We found Fox Hunter dead. He'd been hacked up some–obviously killed in a fight with someone."

Vince frowned. "*Who?*"

"We don't know, Boss," Johnny answered. "We can't figure it out. Somebody was out in those woods, and whoever it was must have helped the girl escape. And from the looks of the fight that took place and the vicious way Fox Hunter was killed, it was likely another Indian."

"And that means we have a *witness!*" Vince picked up a vase and threw it against the wall of his study, then paced. The other two men stepped farther back, waiting for instructions. "What sonofabitch would have been out there in the hills? And *why*? An *Indian*? I don't get it! All of Claire's men were with her and were killed. It doesn't make sense she could have survived! It doesn't make *sense!*" He paced more, trying to think. "You sure it was probably an Indian?" He stopped and faced Bill.

"All I know, Boss, is that somebody landed a hatchet across Fox Hunter's neck and into the side of his head. He nearly chopped his head clean off." Bill closed his eyes and shook his head at the memory.

"That's the work of another *Indian*, all right," Vince grumbled. "No white man kills that way, let alone being able to fight back against someone as wicked and skilled as Fox Hunter. The man scared *me* to death, but I knew he wanted a white woman, and he had connections in Mexico. It was all set up to work perfectly. I don't understand this!"

"If it was an Indian that killed Fox Hunter, then maybe it was some renegade who'd been watching the wagon train with the intent to attack it himself," Johnny offered. "And maybe if he saw the girl running off, he followed her and captured her himself. Maybe he's raped and killed her by now."

"If we're lucky," Vince seethed. "But what if he *didn't*? And what if by some chance Claire Stewart is still *alive*? Maybe she heard things she shouldn't. Maybe she realized the attackers weren't really Indians. Who knows?" He stepped closer to Bill. "You take some men and you go out there and try tracking whoever killed Fox Hunter!"

A pained look moved into Bill's eyes, and Johnny turned away. "Oh, man," Johnny muttered.

"*Now* what?" Vince demanded.

"We did send someone to keep looking," Bill answered, "the other Comanche you paid to help us . . . Gray Bear. We, uh, we haven't heard from him since."

"We don't know if he was killed, too, or just went back to Texas. We were kind of hoping you'd heard from him, or we'd see him skulking around here when we got back."

"I've not seen one sign of him!"

"He was big and damn wicked," Johnny spoke up. "I can't believe anybody, even another Indian, could get the better of that one."

"Well, we'll probably never know now, will we?" Vince's ire permeated the room. "Jesus Christ, I have to know if that girl is still alive and if she knows anything! And who the hell could have taken her?" He faced Bill. "Did you get rid of the wagons?"

"Yes. We loaded everything into Huebner wagons when the other men got there with them, and they took the supplies on to Bent's Fort. We burned up the Stewart wagons so's it would look like an Indian raid– shot a few arrows into the wagon beds, then shooed off the mules–shot a couple of them to make it look even more like an Indian attack. We left the bodies and all that. Someone has probably found them by now and will report another Indian attack on freight wagons. When people hear about it they'll probably figure Claire Stewart was taken by the Indians and will never be seen again. It should stir up even more hatred, and you'll be a richer man once the men get back with the money they got paid for the Stewart supplies."

"Yeah!" Johnny spoke up. "Heck, Mr. Huebner, Colorado will soon be rid of *all* its Indians. Chivington will make sure of that. When citizens hear of another attack, they'll support anything he wants to do to get rid of them. And the girl is surely dead by now, or wishing she was, and you've run her out of business."

"If it *was* another Indian that took her, then even if she lives through it she'll think it was Indians that attacked the train," Bill suggested. "I don't think you need to worry, Boss, even if she's still alive and somehow survives and makes it back to Denver City. She'll still think it was Indians, and she won't have a business left, so you got what you wanted."

"Have I?" Vince walked to a window to stare down into the street. "I'm not so sure. I don't feel good about this. Not at all. If we find Claire Stewart, or if she shows up in Denver City, I want her *dead*, understand? I want her *dead!*" He watched three soldiers coming up the street and couldn't help wondering if they knew anything. Had the remnants of Claire's wagon train been found, along with the dead bodies of her employees? If so, at least the *Denver Post* could print another story about the depravities of the Southern Cheyenne.

He turned from the window. "You two keep your eyes and ears open. Get a couple other men and spread out. Send them to the various forts and see if they can find out if this has been reported to any of the fort commanders. See what they know. And be casual about it. Tell them you work for me, and that before I send out another train of supplies I need to know the dangers involved. Tell them I want to know if there have been any reports of more Indian attacks. Understand? Don't give anything away."

"Yes, Sir," Johnny answered.

Bill nodded. "I know what to do. I'm damn sorry, Boss. We did our best. It's like she just disappeared before our eyes."

Vince rubbed his forehead. "My worry is that whoever might have taken her was already watching, deliberately following her for some reason. That person might realize it was white men who attacked those wagons. I just don't know if he's good or bad–a government spy, a soldier, just another Indian who only wanted the woman? There's just too much we don't know. I can only hope that Claire Stewart is lying dead out there somewhere in the foothills."

Bill scratched at his beard again. "I expect that's exactly what happened. By whatever means she got away, she ran into some renegade Indian who treated her worse than if she'd been sold to some whorehouse in Mexico. My guess is somebody had a good time with her and then left her dead. I don't think you'll hear from her again."

"I wish I could count on that," Vince complained. "I'd just as soon one of you found her dead body. Take a good scout and go back out there and see what you can find. Tell your guide I'm just concerned because Claire's father was a fellow businessman and a good friend."

"Yes, sir." Johnny headed for the door, obviously eager to get away from an angry Vince Huebner. "We'll find something." He walked out the door and Vince glanced at Bill.

"I don't like this. Something doesn't feel right."

"I think she's dead, but I'll find someone to help us and go back out there. Don't you worry about a thing, Boss. Even if she lived and tried to claim it wasn't Indians that attacked her, that wouldn't have anything to do with you. Hell, Vince, she could name you flat out, and no one would believe her. Everybody in town thinks she's a little crazy, dressin' like she does and actin' like a man and tryin' to run a freighting business. She's no normal woman, and there aren't many people in town who like her, so quit worryin'."

"I can't help it. Go see what you can find."

"Yes, sir." Bill walked out and closed the door.

Vince took several deep breaths, trying to convince himself that everything was fine, and that Claire was probably dead or some Indian's raped squaw by now. It would serve her right for not marrying him. He'd had wet dreams imagining taking her himself and watching her squirm beneath him. That likely wouldn't happen now.

He opened a closet door and looked at himself in a mirror there, studying his slicked-back black hair and straightening his tie. He shrugged into his spiffy tweed suit jacket, thinking how handsome the expensive suit made him look.

To hell with Claire Stewart. There were plenty of single young women in Denver who would be thrilled to marry a handsome, wealthy businessman. And he'd even had a couple of other men's wives in his bed a time or two.

Everything would be fine. Even if Claire survived and tried claiming she'd been attacked by white men and not Indians, there is too much hatred among Denver City citizens to ever believe a story like that. Still, he'd feel much better if he knew Claire Stewart was dead.

CHAPTER NINETEEN

CLAIRE SAT PROPPED UP IN bed when Major Ansley knocked on the cabin door and announced himself. She ran her hands through her hair self-consciously, thinking what a wild mess it must be.

"Come in," she spoke up, wondering how she should dress when she was able to get up—her usual pants, or the way people expected a woman to dress. She hated the bones and stays of a corset, hated the inconvenience of slips and hoops. Apparently Two Wolves saw her as beautiful just the way she was. He was the only man she'd met who'd not told her she should wear dresses.

A burly man with a big belly and thinning white hair walked into the room, his blue uniform looking clean and freshly brushed. He nodded to her.

"Miss Stewart, I'm Major Ansley, and I'm very glad to meet you," he said as he walked closer and put out his hand.

Claire reached out and shook it. "Thank you for coming, Major. I'm sorry I can't be up and dressed and properly greet you with coffee or something."

"Well, from what I hear you're lucky to even be alive." Ansley pulled a wooden chair up beside Claire's bed.

Claire pulled a quilt up to her neck, self-conscious of wearing only a flannel gown under the blankets. "Where is Two Wolves?"

"Hard to tell. I told him I'd rather speak to you alone. He walked off over an hour ago, and no one has seen him."

Claire glanced out the nearby window. "He's probably happy to be out of here. It wasn't easy for him to sit inside four walls for so long, but he did it. For me." She looked down at the quilt and toyed with one of the ties. "He saved my life, more than once, Major Ansley. He's the most unusual man I've ever met. He's brave and skilled and so–I don't know–

so open and honest. He just says things flat out, you know?"

"Oh, I most certainly know, Miss Stewart. He also thinks he owns you and is responsible for your safety. The man is totally taken with you. Do you realize that?"

Claire couldn't bring herself to look straight at the major. She nodded. "Yes."

"And how do you feel about that?"

Claire suddenly wanted to cry. "I don't quite know. He's Indian, but he's the most handsome man I've ever set eyes on," she said quietly. "And right now I can't imagine going on with my life without Two Wolves in it. I feel like he's my only friend in the whole world. If not for him, God only knows the awful things that would have happened to me by now. I'd be sold off down in Mexico, and no one would ever hear from me again. The saddest part is, no one is left who would even care." She couldn't help the tears then. "Two Wolves is all I have." She hastily wiped at the tears.

Ansley sighed and straightened his leg so he could rummage a clean handkerchief from his pants pocket. He handed it to her. "I didn't mean to make you cry, Miss Stewart."

"It's okay. It's just . . . so much has happened so fast."

The Major thought how lovely she was, with that head of wild red curls and big, blue eyes. But at the moment, with tears in her eyes and a few freckles on her cheeks and looking so tiny under all those blankets, she seemed almost childlike.

"I understand," he told her aloud. "I'm sorry about the attack on your supply train and the loss of your men."

Claire blew her nose. "It was Vince Huebner who planned it all!" she said angrily, finally meeting his gaze. "He's a wealthy businessman in Denver City who's been after my business. I heard those men talking. They were hired by Vince. They were supposed to hack up my men and leave arrows in them and ride off with me and sell me in Mexico. They stole all my supplies and by now they've probably burned my wagons. It's a miracle I was able to hide from them down under a pile of potatoes. I snuck out the side of the wagon after dark and I started running . . ." The tears came again. "And running! I didn't even know where I was, but someone grabbed me and held me down and told me not to be afraid. It was Two Wolves."

"He told me how he saw you on the street in Denver City and then purposely looked you up and then followed you. In his mind the Great

Spirit led him to you, and now you belong to him."

Claire wiped at her eyes. "In a way, I guess I do. He fought and killed a Comanche man and rode off with me. And he saved me from a grizzly attack later. Then when I took that arrow, he killed that Indian, too." She shook her head. "I've never known anyone so brave and who could fight like that and who . . ." She blew her nose again. "When he fights, he's so brave, but he can also can be incredibly vicious. But with me he's so respectful and so gentle and so caring. He's had to bathe me and everything. He's the kind of man you know you can trust, and I guess I wouldn't mind so much being his wife like he wants that." She met Ansley's gaze again. "But he's Indian, and you know what that means."

Ansley sighed, shifting in the chair beside the bed. "He's a fine man, Miss Stewart, but I do know how it looks to others to see a white woman with an Indian. And this situation with you blaming Vince Huebner for raids—surely you know how difficult it will be to prove something like that. People will say you just want to run Huebner out of business. The general public is too eager and ready to blame Indians for everything wrong out here, so they won't want to believe your story. When they get wind of something between you and Two Wolves, it will only make things harder for both of you."

"I know. I worry what it could mean for Two Wolves." Claire fought more tears, hating to cry. "This is very dangerous for him. But it's true about Vince Huebner, Major. I saw what I saw and heard what I heard. Vince Huebner is an awful man. He's been trying to force me into marriage to repay a debt my father owed him. He says ugly things to me and has threatened me many times. And now that all my men are dead, one of them my father's best friend who looked after me, I have no one! I don't feel safe now. I have to get Huebner convicted and put behind bars, or I'll never be safe."

"Then don't go back to Denver City," Ansley told her. "Settle somewhere else. And if it's with Two Wolves, that's even more reason not to go back."

"But then Vince Huebner will have won, and I can't let that happen. People need to know what he's done. He's a murderer and a thief and a liar! And Two Wolves has been trying to prove white men have been attacking their own kind and blaming it on the Cheyenne. I owe him the pleasure of proving he's right and helping him bring down Vince Huebner."

Ansley leaned closer, resting his elbows on his knees. "I understand all of that, but ma'am, you're asking for an awful lot of trouble. I've told Two Wolves to let me look into this first. You two can't just go storming into Denver City throwing around accusations. It will be the word of an Indian and an . . . I'm sorry to say this but, you *are* a bit different from most women, Miss Stewart. They'll just say you're–" He hesitated.

"Crazy?"

Ansley smiled sadly. "Something like that."

"I know what you mean. They'll also say I'm a loose woman, but I don't care what they think! I never *have* cared. Women look at me like I'm a freak just because I wear pants and run a freighting business on my own. But I helped my father with that business all my life, and I know it inside and out. It's all I have now." Her lips pouted in disappointment. "I guess I should say *had*. I'll never recover from this, and Vince knows it. By now he probably thinks I've been sold off in Mexico." She met Ansley's gaze with a determined glare. "I *have* to go back, Major, just to see the look on that man's face when he sees I'm alive and well and that I know the *truth*! Allow me that much satisfaction. And I can at least plant the idea in peoples' heads that Vince might not be the upstanding businessman he claims he is. I can plant that doubt, Major. That's a start."

Ansley nodded. "Maybe so, but I don't want you and Two Wolves going there on your own. Two Wolves can be very single-minded, and I fear he'll not listen to me. He'd be in grave danger if he went there, with or without you. You have to help me keep him under control."

Claire wiped at her eyes again, realizing deep inside that she was falling in love with a Cheyenne Indian. "I don't know that *anyone* can control him, Major. Like you said, he's a single-minded and very determined man."

Ansley wondered what she even knew about men. "And you're in love with him."

Claire stared at the tie on the quilt again, a little embarrassed to talk with someone she hardly knew about something so intimate, let alone a man. Still, she hardly knew Two Wolves, either. Right now she wasn't sure she knew her own mind.

"I must be," she answered. "I hate it when he's gone from my sight. He's become my friend and my protector. But there is still so much I don't know about him. He's so . . . different. And he has family among the Cheyenne and lives among them at times. I couldn't do that."

"Don't get feelings of obligation mixed up with love, Miss Stewart. It's easy to do."

She glanced out the window again, worried Two Wolves wouldn't come back.

"I think the same thing happened to his mother that's happening to me," she said absently. "Two Wolves' father rescued her from other Indians, and they fell in love, and Two Wolves is the result."

"I know the story."

Claire met his gaze again. "He wouldn't use me, would he?"

"*Use* you?"

"This thing about proving white men have been raiding—it's very important to him to be able to prove it. He wouldn't protect me and pretend to care for me just to make sure I testify to all this, would he?"

Ansley smiled softly and shook his head. "Miss Stewart, that young man isn't capable of duping or deceiving or lying to anyone. If he says he truly cares for you, then he does. He would never use you for his own advantage."

"It's hard for me to know whom to trust."

The major out and patted the back of her hand. "You can trust me, and you can definitely trust Two Wolves. And most men who know him well also like and trust him. I'm sure you've seen how he gets along with the men here at this trading post."

Claire nodded. "What do you know about him, Major?"

Ansley shrugged. "Not much more than you do. Soldiers came along and rescued his mother from the Cheyenne, or at least that's what they thought they were doing. Two Wolves was pretty young then. His father was killed, and he remembers his mother crying a lot. They were sent to some of her relatives in Chicago. That's where Two Wolves was raised. He's pretty well schooled and he's Christian, although in his mind the Cheyenne God *Maheo* is the same as Jesus. His mother remarried but never had any more children, as far as I know. And she never let him forget his paternal heritage. When she died, he came back out here and decided to learn about that part of his life. He obviously took to it wholeheartedly."

"What was her name?"

"I don't know. Two Wolves isn't exactly a big talker."

Claire smiled softly. "There are times when he talks *too* much. And he's so honest he leaves you a bit speechless at times because you don't quite know how to take what he's telling you. He keeps insisting he will marry me."

Ansley squeezed her hand. "You just get yourself well and have Two Wolves bring you to Fort Collins. There are a few wives at the fort, and they can help you settle in. And if you need a woman to talk to about all of this and your feelings for Two Wolves, I'm sure some of them will be glad to help. How long have you been without a mother?"

Claire pulled the quilt closer around her neck again. "Years. I hardly remember her. It was always just me and Pa. I've lived in a man's world so long I hardly know how to *be* a woman."

"And you've never even been with other young men socially? Gone to dances? Picnics? Things like that?"

"No. I've just gone to school and worked and done Pa's bookwork and gone along on trips with him. I never cared about the rest. Two Wolves is the first man I've thought about . . . that way." She looked away. "You should go, Major Ansley. I've said too much, and now I truly am embarrassed. I shouldn't talk to you about such things."

Ansley rose with a sigh. "Ma'am, I know how you must feel about Two Wolves, but you need to give yourself a chance. You make up your own mind and do what makes you happy. Come to the fort and talk to some of the women there. We'll have a cookout and a dance, and you can meet some of the single young men there. It sounds to me like you need to see to that part of your life and make sure about what you really want. Choosing a man is a big enough decision on its own. Choosing an *Indian* man is quite another thing."

Claire felt like crying again. "But he's so good and so caring, and he saved my life."

"He's just about the finest young man any woman could choose, but you and I both know how people see such a relationship. I don't want to see him hurt, or you either. You need to think this thing out–and Two Wolves needs to see your side of it and consider behaving more like a white man. And as if your feelings for each other aren't enough concern, we have to figure out what to do about Vince Huebner and what happened to your wagon train. None of this is going to be easy."

Claire glanced out the window again to see Two Wolves walking past a corral and toward the cabin. "I know, Major."

She felt only relief at seeing Two Wolves coming back. He walked with such sureness and pride, his long, black hair dancing in the wind, his dark skin glowing in the sun, the sinewy muscles of his arms stirring womanly desires that were quite pleasant. It was impossible not to be attracted to his finely-etched face and those dark eyes that seemed to have a way of looking right into her thoughts, and her heart.

"But when Two Wolves is with me, everything always seems okay, and I'm not afraid." She faced Ansley. "I'm not scared to go after Vince Huebner."

Ansley sighed. "In the meantime, my dear, is there anyone left behind in Denver City who should know what happened to you? Someone who'll be waiting for you to get back?"

"Oh, my." Claire ran a hand through her tangled hair again. "I forgot about that. I left one of my men behind to sell some extra flour I had over-ordered. I wanted to get rid of it fast before it could get wormy, so I discounted it and put up a big sign out front. Stewart Haggarty stayed behind to sell it for me."

"Can you trust him?"

"Why?"

"Well, ma'am, if I go to Denver City, I don't want to give anything away just yet. I'd rather keep this Vince Huebner in the dark. A man who's flustered is easier to catch in a trap. If Huebner finds out you're still alive, it will give him time to think up a story of his own. I'd rather he didn't know just yet, and for all we know this Stewart Haggarty could work for him under the table."

"Oh, I don't think so."

"Well, let's just not tell him anything yet. I'll go there and check out your business for you and see if he is taking care of things properly. Is he a long-time friend of your father's, or a new man?"

Claire closed her eyes and shook her head. "He's fairly new." A lump rose in her throat. "It makes me sick to realize how few people can be trusted."

"It's a fact of life, Miss Stewart, but like I said, you can trust me. And you can definitely trust Two Wolves."

"I know." Claire met his gaze. "I guess that's part of what makes it hard to know my real feelings. It's nice to meet someone I can trust. If nothing else, he's become my good friend."

Ansley grinned. "That's a good start. Believe me, as a married man, it helps to also be good friends. I don't miss my wife just because of her cooking and housekeeping. I miss her friendship, our long talks in the evenings. I'll be retiring in a couple more years. I look forward to living a normal life back in Ohio. That is, if life ever gets back to normal after this war."

"I hardly understand what the war is all about. Here in Colorado it doesn't even seem real, except for arguments that break out in the streets at times."

"We're in a mess, that's sure." Ansley put on his hat. "You take care of yourself, and we'll take care of this little war you have going on with Vince Huebner for now."

"Thank you, Major."

Two Wolves tapped on the door then and came inside, glancing from Ansley to Claire.

"You look better," he told Claire.

"I *feel* better," Claire answered with a smile. "Major Ansley says we should go to Fort Collins first and make some plans, Two Wolves. I think you should let him look into this first. And you were right. He's a good man."

Two Wolves nodded, glancing at Ansley. "Is she not as beautiful and brave as I told you?"

Claire felt the color coming into her cheeks at the remark, and Ansley grinned.

"She is all of that," he answered, "but she's been through a lot, Two Wolves, and she needs to think things through. You bring her to the fort as soon as she's well enough, and we'll decide what to do next. I'll leave in the morning and maybe make a trip to Denver City myself and check out this Vince Huebner. I won't tell him what I know. I'll just see what I can find out."

"Be careful." The look of a warrior came into Two Wolves' dark eyes. "He is a dangerous man. I would take pleasure in killing him."

Ansley closed his eyes and sighed deeply. "I'm sure you would," he said with a bit of sarcasm. "You just calm down and take this slowly and handle it the white man's way. I would be deeply grieved to see you hang, Two Wolves, and that's what you're risking. You're a smart man, so be smart about *this*." He glanced back at Claire. "I'll have the women at the fort make ready for your arrival."

"Thank you, Major."

Ansley glanced at Two Wolves. "Come and see me again over at the supply store."

He nodded. "I will come."

Ansley put his hat on, glancing at Claire once more. "God be with you both," he commented before walking out the door.

Two Wolves walked closer to Claire. "Tell me what you need. Do you wish to get up?"

Now the tears came again. Claire shook her head. "I wish to start taking care of myself now, Two Wolves. I'll be fine."

"You are *not* fine. You can hardly walk yet."

"Then I'll *make* myself walk!" Claire wiped at her tears. "Now that I'm better it's too embarrassing letting you help me. You've already seen all the things you shouldn't see, and I'm not sure I can live with the humiliation of it." She covered her face with her hands.

Two Wolves sat down on the edge of the bed and gently took hold of her wrists. "Listen to me, *Maeveksea.*"

"Don't call me that!" she answered, her hands still over her face. "You say it so lovingly. You get me all mixed up, and I'm scared and alone and hurt. And my only friend is an Indian I hardly know and he's seen me naked and I am so ashamed and confused!"

He gently but forcefully pulled her hands away from her face. "Look at me, Claire Stewart."

"I can't."

"*Look* at me!"

Claire sniffed and met his gaze.

"I helped someone who was badly hurt and might have died. Would you rather I had let those strange white men out there take care of you?"

Claire looked away again.

"When we first left to come here you thought I was angry with you, but I was angry with myself for touching you wrongly and making you afraid," Two Wolves told her. "I was still in pain and confused, and waking up beside you made it all better. I touched you because you looked so beautiful lying there, and because I care for you. I am sorry that I frightened you. But I have never touched you wrongly or even looked upon you in the way you are thinking. I was already your friend, and I felt responsible for your being hurt. I should have sensed that Comanche bastard was near. And when I thought you might die, I knew I would deeply grieve. And I took care of you myself because I knew you would not want those strange men who run this fort to do it. Do you understand?"

Claire slowly nodded. "I guess."

"From now on I will leave you alone, if that is what you wish." Two Wolves rose. "I will knock before I come in, and I will bring you whatever you need. When you feel you are well enough, we will go to Fort Collins and we will decide what to do about this Vince Huebner. As far as my feelings for you, I have told you what they are. And I tell you this,

Claire Stewart. No *white* man will care for you and be as kind to you as I would be."

Claire swallowed against more tears. "Two Wolves, please understand that I don't want to think about *any* man right now. I just want to get well. I want to see Vince Huebner go to prison, and I want to get back to some kind of normal life, whatever that is."

Two Wolves held her gaze. "Tell me you have no feelings for Two Wolves."

Claire looked down at the quilt again.

"Tell me."

Claire wiped at more tears and avoided his gaze. "I *do* care about you, Two Wolves, but it scares me. I don't know if it's real, or if it's just feelings of obligation for saving my life. I think maybe I . . . I could love you in the way that you want me to love you . . . but you're . . ."

"*Indian?*"

"I don't mean it the way you make it sound, Two Wolves. Surely you know that. Surely you understand why I have to consider our differences."

He walked to the door. "My heart tells me you are brave enough to be with any man you want to be with, no matter what others might think. And you are brave enough to stand up to this Vince Huebner. I think that when you are stronger you will be brave enough to face your feelings for me."

Two Wolves abruptly left. Claire wanted to call out to him, hated the thought that she'd hurt his feelings again, or maybe simply lost him. She watched him through the window again . . . walking away.

"Come back!" she whispered. "Hold me!" She wished she was as brave as Two Wolves thought she was. Maybe when she felt better . . . when this pain was gone . . .

CHAPTER TWENTY

Late August . . .

MAJOR ANSLEY STUDIED THE BIG red and white sign over the double-door entrance to one of the few brick buildings in Denver City.

HUEBNER FREIGHTING AND SUPPLY.

He reined his horse to a stop at a hitching post just two doors down from the building and dismounted, amazed at how Denver City seemed to grow even bigger from week to week. He'd not been here for nearly two months, and the change was phenomenal. It was amazing what gold did to men, attracting not just miners but every type of business necessary to feed and supply those miners and their families, until in a matter of days, tent cities sprang up like mushrooms, at first nothing more than whorehouses and taverns with a few supply stores, but soon turning into full-fledged cities with wood and brick buildings and bustling streets that filled the air with dust in summer and mired wagons in mud in winter.

Because of its prime location for traffic moving north and south along the foothills of the Rockies, Denver City was not likely to follow the path of other gold towns and become a ghost town once the gold and silver played out. This city was here to stay. A major fire only a year and a half before, followed by a devastating flood only three months back, had failed to stop the determination of Denver's citizens to build and re-build. In fact, it seemed this thriving city just got bigger and better every time disaster hit. Those citizens included Vince Huebner, who obviously knew a gold mine when he saw one, and not the kind that meant sweating it out below the earth.

Adjusting his hat, the major walked into a saloon, where several men turned their gazes in curiosity. One quick sweep of the room revealed gamblers, drinkers, miners, every-day family men and two men who appeared to be rather wealthy sitting together at a table removed from the others, as though they were too good to mix with them.

Ansley sensed a mixture of warm greetings, distrust and animosity. He walked up to the bar and ordered a whiskey, then waited quietly, wanting to know the rumors in town and having no intention of giving away anything he knew. The bartender set a shot glass in front of him and filled it.

"What's happening out there?" the slender, bearded man asked.

"Out where?" Ansley slugged down the whiskey.

"Hell, you know what I mean." The bartender squinted as he studied Ansley's uniform. "Major, is it?"

"Major Ansley from Fort Collins."

"Oh, *north* of here." The bar tender snickered. "You probably don't know much about what's been going on *south* of here."

"With the Cheyenne, I suppose you mean."

"Drunken filth is what I mean," the bartender answered.

Several men in the saloon snickered.

"Chivington will take care of them," another grumbled.

"The Colorado volunteers ridin' with 'em ain't afraid of no Indians, whether they be Cheyenne or Arapaho," yet another offered. "Them Injuns will pay for all the raidin' down by the Santa Fe Trail. And our volunteers will take care of what your men in uniform don't seem to be able to take care of."

"The war took most of our men back East," Ansley answered defensively. "I have only so much to work with. Besides, south of here isn't my territory. Major Wyncoop down at Fort Lyon is in charge there, although I'm trying to determine if he needs help."

"Wyncoop is too friendly with the Southern Cheyenne."

"Maybe if your militia didn't go around murdering women and children, the Cheyenne would be more willing to talk peace," Ansley suggested, trying to keep his temper under control.

"Peace, my ass!" the bartender broke in. "I hear tell some white family got wiped out south of here, and it ain't pretty what they did to the woman. They're all rapists and killers!"

"Savages!"

"Some of your fine militia do the same to Cheyenne women," Ansley argued. He noticed one of the wealthier men glance his way then.

"Where did you hear such lies?" the man asked.

"I've *seen* it," Ansley answered.

The well-dressed man who'd addressed him just grinned. "Pay back for what those Indians do to our own women," he told Ansley. "I'm sure you know about the meeting a couple of weeks ago between a few Cheyenne and Governor Evans. If it got your hopes up, forget it. That meeting was just for show. Evans wants those worm-ridden bastards out of Colorado as much as any of us does."

Ansley drank a second shot of whiskey, then ordered a beer. He turned to face the man who'd made the remark about the Cheyenne. Animosity and hatred spewed from the man's eyes, and the same could be felt emanating from others inside the saloon.

"Last I knew, most of Colorado was Cheyenne homeland for a few hundred years before all of us got here," Ansley answered. "I suspect you'd fight back, too, if some foreigners came here and tried to chase you off and treated you like vermin to be eradicated."

The room quieted, and the man Ansley faced rose. The major hoped he was exactly who he suspected he was. Vince Huebner. He fit Claire's description. He wore expensive-looking, well-fitted silk pants, and his crisp white shirt was topped with a shiny silk vest and a string tie. He wore no jacket because of the heat. A gold watch chain hung from his vest pocket. Ansley supposed women might consider him handsome, more for the fine way he dressed and for his wealth, but his nose seemed too long and thin, and his steely blue eyes narrowed with hatred in a way that distracted from his looks.

"They *are* vermin that need to be eradicated," the man told him.

The room erupted in a chorus of "You bet!" and "That's right!" and "Damn sure!"

"You tell him, Vince!" another shouted.

So, he was right. Ansley waited as the fancy-dressed Huebner walked a little closer. "Aren't you a bit old and soft to be a leader of soldiers?"

Ansley turned and reached for his mug of beer, taking a drink of it before answering. "Just too old and soft to be riding around in battles back East. There's another kind of war going on there, you know."

"Oh, we know, all right!" a man in the crowd shouted. "Plenty of our own volunteered for the Union. A few took off to fight for the South, but they'll find a real unwelcome greeting when they get home. I expect they won't stay in Denver long, if they live to talk about it."

A few chuckled. Some just grumbled. Huebner stepped up to the bar, facing Ansley. "What are you doing in Denver, Major?"

"I'm here to barter for some fort supplies, for one thing. For another, I'm just trying to get an idea what's been going on farther south, if anyone here knows for sure."

"You said the south was Wyncoop's territory," Huebner reminded him.

"It is, but he's lost men, too. I need to report to Washington just how bad things are in Colorado overall. My scout tells me there have been more raids than usual, and he thinks it's *white* men doing the raiding in order to stir up even more hatred for the Cheyenne."

Huebner diverted his gaze, glancing at the bartender and ordering a whiskey. "Major, I'm guessing that scout is Cheyenne himself."

"Half."

Huebner snickered and shook his head. "Half-breed or not, he's bound to try to convince you it's not his people doing the raiding. I'm surprised you'd take his word on something like that."

"He's as honest as they come, and he just wants to try to keep the peace. A lot of the Cheyenne want the same thing," Ansley spoke up boldly. "They're beaten and starving. And when citizens and militia randomly kill some of them with no cause, it's impossible to negotiate with them. The killing of Lean Bear down by Fort Larned a couple of months ago didn't help. And rumor has it that there are white men out there posing as Indians and attacking farms and supply trains. That just instigates more unrest, and when the Cheyenne retaliate, which they have every right to do, everybody calls it an act of war."

Vince's eyes narrowed at the remark. The irises of his eyes seemed to literally grow smaller, and the major could easily see why Claire Stewart was afraid of the man. A mean streak vividly showed in those eyes.

"What are you *really* after, Major?"

Ansley knew he'd hit a nerve. Claire Stewart was right in her claims about this man, but proving it—especially among angry, hateful citizens like those in the saloon—would be difficult, if not impossible. "As I said, I'm just here to feel things out and to order some supplies."

"You're awfully high in rank to be running around ordering supplies."

"A man gets restless stuck out there in the middle of nowhere. I have the rank to do whatever I want, so I decided to come here myself."

"Why are you asking questions about Indian raids? There are runners who cover news from fort to fort, and we have telegraph lines."

Ansley took another swig of beer. "And your name?"

Vince straightened proudly. "Vince Huebner. And if you are looking for supplies, I'm the man you want to see. I own Huebner Freighting and Supply just a couple of doors down from here."

"Well, then, you must know about Indian attacks on supply trains. I'm just after the truth, Mr. Huebner. After all, I and my men might need to get involved in some of the skirmishes going on out here with the Cheyenne. With all the raiding going on, I try to see some of this from the Cheyenne point of view. If it's true that white men are conducting some of the raids just to stir up more hatred, I need to know that, too, so it can be stopped. Have you heard anything about such raids? Have any of your own supply trains been attacked?"

Vince folded his arms, his eyes glistening as he boldly lied. "Major Ansley, I keep my supply trains well-armed. The Cheyenne know better than to even *try* attacking them. I've heard some farther south have had trouble, but not me." He slugged down a shot of whiskey and frowned. "One of my competitors rode out of here close to two weeks ago, though, headed for Bent's Fort. It only takes ten or twelve days to get there and back, but they still haven't arrived. People are beginning to wonder if *they* were attacked. Maybe you should check it out. The owner went with them, and she's a young woman by the name of Claire Stewart. She's a wild, independent little slip of a woman who's trying to save her father's freighting business, so she took charge of the supply wagons herself. I begged her not to go, but she insisted. If I wasn't so busy with my own several businesses here in Denver, I'd have gone with her. God only knows what's happened to her. Maybe you can find out for me."

"I'm sorry to hear that. I'll look into it."

Vince looked him over again. "You do that, Major. I'm very concerned because I'm actually quite fond of Miss Stewart, in spite of the fact that she wears men's pants instead of dresses, and she doesn't behave at all the way a proper woman should. She fascinates me."

And you're wondering if I know something. "Maybe she left someone behind who's heard from her," Ansley suggested.

"She did leave a man behind, but he hasn't heard a thing. I already checked with him. No runners have come, and there have been no telegraph messages." Vince leaned on the bar. "Finish your beer, Major, and come on over to my place with your list of what's needed. I can send wagons to Fort Collins with the supplies."

"That's not necessary. I'll send men here to pick them up. I wanted to scout around first and make the order myself. Sometimes when I send men with just a list, they come back with the wrong items. And some-times they take a little too long to get back, if you know what I mean."

Vince grinned. "We do have some lovely whores here in Denver."

Ansley smiled in return, wanting to win the man's confidence. "I'm sure you do."

"I can set you up with the best if you're in need."

Ansley finished his beer. "I have a wife back East, and believe me, even at a thousand miles away, she'd know."

Vince laughed heartily, but Ansley saw the nervousness behind his laugh. Worse, he could literally *feel* the man's evil.

"Tell me something, Mr. Huebner. If you're so fond of this woman who runs another freighting business and you're concerned about what happened to her, why haven't you reported it to the Army, or sent your own men out to look for her?"

Huebner seemed to stiffen a little. "I was planning on doing just that later today. You see, Major, a lot of things can happen on a trip like that— wagons breaking down, someone getting hurt. She really isn't *that* late yet. And since your men are stretched so thin, as you were telling me, I didn't want to bother the Army with it unless I was sure."

"With all the Indian raiding going on?" Ansley set his beer mug on the bar and took money from his pocket, plunking it beside the mug. "Mr. Huebner, if it was my wife missing for even one day out there, I'd be out looking for her. If I couldn't get the Army to help I'd get some men on my own, but I'd be looking."

Vince's eyes narrowed more, the jovial look he'd put on having now vanished. "She's *not* my wife. She's just a silly kid who's in too deep, so I feel a responsibility to look after her. And that has led to a more personal interest, that's all." He paid for his own drink. "And you don't understand the freighting business, Major. It's not at all unusual to be a few days late. Claire had plenty of men along, so I'm not that worried. In a couple more days I'll send some men along the same trail she would have taken to make sure she made it to Bent's Fort." He held out his arm toward the saloon entrance. "Come on over to my supply store and give me a list of what you need. I own the biggest store and the busiest freighting business in Denver."

Ansley followed him out.

"Go get them Indians," one of the men shouted to Ansley.

Several of the men laughed.

"Don't worry about it, Major," another joked. "John Chivington and our own militia will take care of things."

Ansley ignored the remark. His main concern was for Two Wolves. If he came here with Claire to accuse Vince Huebner of the heinous crime of white men killing white men and raping white women just to frame the Cheyenne, the result would be disastrous, just as he'd figured. Claire would risk being run out of town, maybe even tarred and feathered first if people realized she had fond feelings for an Indian. And Two Wolves . . . Ansley shook his head. Two Wolves would never make it out of town at all. He'd be hanged, and only God knew what these men would do to him first.

CHAPTER TWENTY-ONE

"I DO NOT THINK YOU ARE ready to go. You are still thin, and your color is not good."

Two Wolves watched Claire gather her thick curls at the back of her neck and then twist her hair up and pin it. She plunked a floppy hat on her head.

"I'm as ready as I'll ever be. I need to get out of here and go someplace where there are other women and people who can help us decide what to do next, Two Wolves. I'm anxious to know if Major Ansley went to Denver City and what he found out."

Two Wolves frowned. "I am afraid for you."

He felt an ache in the wrong places as she rose, again wearing a man's shirt and pants, actually a shirt and pants meant for a boy. He couldn't help wondering how she'd look in a dress, with the undergarments white women wore to boost their breasts and show all their curves. He thought how even Indian woman wore tunics, not pants, except sometimes in winter when they wore fur-lined leggings. But in the night, under a blanket, those leggings came off. He wanted to share his blanket with Claire Stewart. Feel her under him. He wanted to touch her beautiful round bottom and taste her perfect breasts. He wanted to explore the places he'd seen but not touched in the way he'd *like* to touch them.

"You have not allowed me in here to help you for six days," he reminded her. "You have not even spoken to me. Why?"

Claire remained turned away. "Because I have to think, Two Wolves. Most of my time with you was spent confused and in pain. Now that I'm better, maybe I can think more clearly about these . . . these feelings."

"Then they are still there."

"Please let me do this, Two Wolves."

"Do what?"

Claire refused to tell him she was still in pain. It was time to move on. Maybe getting up and around would help her get back to her old self and build more strength.

"Think. Just think. I have to be around my own kind for a while."

"Your own kind? Half of me *is* your own kind. You cannot change what is in your heart, but if this is what you want, then I will let you do it because I promised that I would. But this leaving . . . it is too sudden. Without warning you send for me and tell me you are ready to leave. We need supplies."

"Then get them. And we don't need a wagon. Bring an extra horse besides a pack horse. I'll ride."

"You will *not* ride! You are not ready. And because you are not ready, we can't leave."

Claire put her hands on her hips and faced him. "I *am* ready. And I *can* ride."

Two Wolves stepped closer. "Why are you being this way?"

"What way?"

"You know what way. You treat me as though I work for you, which I do *not*. You speak as though you are in charge of me, and in a way that makes it seem you look down on me. You are *not* in charge of me." He stepped even closer, and Claire stepped back a little. "I think you are being too defensive. This is not you–to speak rudely."

Claire turned away, flustered by how he disturbed her in all the wrong ways. His closeness interfered with her ability to think straight.

"I just want to get this over with, Two Wolves. Going up against Vince Huebner scares me."

"I will be with you."

"Two Wolves, you've been a good friend, and you saved my life. And now I care too much about you to watch you die. I don't think you should go with me to Denver City. I can handle Vince, even when he's angry."

"Can you? If not for me, the men he sent to kill your own men and take you captive would have succeeded. When he finds out you are alive, he will find another way to kill you, except that perhaps he will attack you first to satisfy his own filthy thoughts of you." He stepped even closer, putting a hand on her shoulder from behind. "I think your concern is because you care about me more than you will admit. And I think you are being rude and pretending to be strong because you want to discourage me and make me think you do not care, when actually you care very much."

"Please don't, Two Wolves. You know it could never work."

"Couldn't it? You might be surprised. Did you not miss me the last six days?" When Claire didn't answer, he gently turned her. "This is not you," he told her. "It must have been hard for you to even get up and move, let alone change your bandages. And you look like you have barely eaten. I saw the trays Louis brought back. You hardly touched your food."

"I'm fine. I never eat much anyway."

"When you are healing, it is important that you eat. I do not agree you should ride on your own, but if you insist then that is what we will do."

Claire still refused to meet his gaze. "I just want to get to Fort Collins and decide what to do next."

Two Wolves touched her under the chin and forced her to look up at him. "We will decide together. This means very much to me, too, as you well know. I will *never* allow you to do this alone."

Claire stepped back. "Have someone bring me something to eat, and I promise to eat it while you get some supplies together."

Two Wolves sighed. "Fine. I will gather supplies and prepare the horses. Major Ansley expects me to bring you to Fort Collins. It will take at least three days because I do not intend to allow you to ride hard; and I don't think you are ready, but if you insist, we will go."

He turned and left, and again Claire realized she'd stepped on his pride again. She walked over to her bed and sat down. She'd hoped that not seeing him for several days would help, but as much as she hated to admit it, she'd missed him. What they'd been through couldn't help leaving them with a special closeness that couldn't be denied. But that part of her that warned against such an impossible relationship still fought wildly inside her head to be reasonable and logical. And to ignore her heart. The trouble was, it wasn't working. When he came into a room it seemed filled with "man," and in a very pleasant way. Sometimes in the night she still vividly remembered the beautiful way he'd kissed her that morning they lay together near the campfire . . . the way fire ripped through her when she had realized he was fondling her breasts. He'd given her an Indian name.

"God help me know what to do," she whispered.

CHAPTER TWENTY-TWO

CLAIRE HATED BEING WRONG. SHE forced herself to pretend she was fine. The first day of their journey saw a long, mostly silent ride. Two Wolves in front leading a pack horse, Claire following behind. He seemed to be determined to pay little attention to her, and Claire couldn't blame him. She'd asked him to give her time to think. Her reasonable side told her this was how it should be, but when she considered never seeing the man again, she wanted to cry and beg him to stay. She'd be glad to reach Fort Collins, where she could be around her own type of people and perhaps befriend some of the women there. She kept telling herself that once she was there she'd be able to think more clearly.

"We will make camp soon," Two Wolves called back to her.

Claire's head began to spin, and the image of Two Wolves ahead of her blurred. His voice seemed to come to her in a dream. She'd clung to the pommel of her saddle for the last two hours in an effort not to fall off her horse, but her resolve was dwindling along with her energy and strength. She'd been so sure she could do this, and so determined to get someplace where she wouldn't have to depend only on Two Wolves for help. She'd hoped the pain in her side would subside, or at least be bearable until they arrived at the fort.

It wasn't working. She felt so hot that sweat poured down her face. She knew instinctively it wasn't just the weather. The heat seemed to come from deep inside ... a fever. Two Wolves had been right that she wasn't ready for this, but she'd been so anxious to return to a normal life that she'd convinced herself she was fine. A wave of nausea moved through her then, and she leaned over to vomit. It seemed only a second or two before a strong arm came around her, pulling her off her horse. She felt like a rag doll. Two Wolves pulled her hair away from her face as she finished vomiting . . . helped her wash her mouth out with water . . . fed her a bit of biscuit to soothe her stomach. She was in his comforting embrace again, strong arms keeping her safe. He spoke softly to her.

"I'm sorry," she managed to say, not sure if it was loud enough for him to hear. "I thought I could do this."

"You try to be too brave, *Maeveksea*," he answered, gently touching her brow. "You have a fever! You did not have one when we left this morning. I should have made you wait."

She felt him shift her closer, realizing in a dizzy fog that in the next moment she sat on his horse in front of him.

"I gave in to what you wanted because you seemed so unhappy," he told her, "but I should have listened to the inner voice that told me not to allow you to leave." He touched her brow again, then held her closer. "This is very bad."

They rode a little farther. Claire struggled to keep her thoughts together, but she felt miserably hot on the inside yet cold on the outside, and through it all she felt a blackness trying to close in on her. How could this have happened? She remembered that this morning she'd felt good enough that she was sure they could leave, but she still had no appetite and remembered eating only two bites of a biscuit. Two Wolves had warned her she should eat more. Maybe it was hunger that was doing this to her. She felt angry with herself for not eating more.

Two Wolves. Again, she was taking comfort in his arms, his closeness, his gentle words, his protection. It seemed she couldn't get away from the man no matter how hard she tried, and in moments like this she didn't want to.

She heard a whistle and a shout. Two Wolves yelled something in a strange tongue. She thought she heard someone holler back. A war whoop? That's what it sounded like! Was another renegade attacking them? Maybe it was a whole band of renegades out to kill. What if Two Wolves had to fight someone again? What if he was killed?

"Two Wolves," she muttered.

"*Ho-shuh, Maeveksea. Shi-hen-na* come. I will get help for you."

She had no idea what he'd just said except for the word "help." Had they come upon a ranch? Soldiers? He'd said he could get help for them. *Shi-hen-na.* He'd used that word once when talking about the Cheyenne.

Cheyenne! She heard *yips* and calls, heard men talking in a strange tongue. *Indians?* Through blurred vision she saw a dark-skinned man on a horse close to theirs, his face painted, his long black hair blowing in a gentle breeze. She heard other voices then, realized they were all

Indians.

"Two Wolves," she whimpered weakly, "what's happening?"

"Do not be afraid. They are friends."

"They're Indians!" she cringed closer, grasping Two Wolves' vest in her fists.

"And so am I. I am taking you to their camp. You are too sick to go on."

Claire felt the blackness closing in on her again. "No. We have to go . . . to the fort."

"We cannot go on until you are well. You have a fever, which means you have infection. This is very dangerous."

"But, I'm cold."

Two Wolves shouted something to the others. Claire felt a blanket come around her, then another. Everyone spoke in a strange tongue. Two Wolves kept her close, and she sensed his horse was in motion. Everything went black then.

CHAPTER TWENTY-THREE

CLAIRE HAD NO IDEA HOW long she lay moving in and out of consciousness. She remembered feeling so hot she wanted to throw off her blankets, but someone kept wrapping her back into them. She remembered something cool and wet on her face and hair, someone softly soothing her. When she wasn't too hot, she shivered with cold, felt more blankets come around her, remembered someone holding her close and rubbing at her limbs and saying something about wrapping her in a buffalo robe and heating rocks. And chanting. There had been an eerie chanting.

She opened her eyes and looked around at a haze of smoke in the air, smelled something sweet. As her thoughts cleared, a hand passed over her, and someone began chanting again. A man sat near her, a thousand wrinkles in his face, his hair long and gray, his upper torso bare but heavily painted. He was waving the sweet-smelling smoke over her. She tried to move, but was wrapped tightly in a blanket. She began to panic, at first thinking she'd been deliberately bound, as though a prisoner of the wild-looking man who sat near her chanting. The old man bent over her, waved more smoke over her along with shaking some kind of rattle.

Where was Two Wolves? Had these people killed him and taken her captive? She wiggled inside the blankets to free herself and sat up.

"Two Wolves!" she screamed.

The old man said something to her softly in the Cheyenne tongue and smiled, then got up and left. In the next moment Two Wolves was kneeling beside her.

"Two Wolves!" Claire let the blanket fall and threw her arms around him. "I thought they'd killed you! Where are we? Take me out of here!"

Two Wolves stroked her hair. "Do not be afraid, *Maeveksea*. We are with a small band of Cheyenne. They are my friends and you are safe."

Two Wolves kissed her hair and urged her to lie back down. It was only then Claire realized she was naked. Again. She wrapped her arms over her breasts as Two Wolves checked her bandages. He gently pressed against her wound at her lower left side. "Is there pain here?" he asked.

"No. I feel better than I have felt since I was first wounded."

Two Wolves smiled as he pulled the blankets over her. "That is a very good sign. Your wound became infected. I had to cut and drain it." He touched her face lovingly. "A Shaman prayed over you and I kept you warm. You have been blessed by *Maheo*. I think now you will fully heal."

Claire grasped his hand. "How far are we from Fort Robinson?"

"About two days. We are deep in the foothills where it easier to hide. The Cheyenne have to camp in places where white men do not notice them." Two Wolves reached for something, then put a hand under the back of her neck to support her. He put a canteen to her lips. "Drink some water."

Claire obeyed as he explained more. "You have been very sick. We gave you an herb that put you into a deeper sleep so I could open your wound. I was not sure it would help, but I did not know what else to do. Your cries of pain tore at my heart."

Claire finished with the water and he set the canteen aside. She studied his dark eyes, thinking what a caring man he was. "You keep saving my life."

"Your life is *worth* saving," he answered with a smile, covering her again.

"So that I can testify to the raids?" She saw disappointment in his dark eyes.

"You should know by now it is much more than that. I have told you as much."

Gratefulness and wariness clashed in Claire's mind and in her heart. "How did we get here?"

"We came across a hunting party. There are some women with them. One is the wife of my cousin *O'Kohm*. His name means Coyote. His wife's name is *Tai-in-hkok*. It means Sits-In-The-Night. She speaks English when necessary. She will come in and help you clean up and give you something to eat now that you are better. It is important that you eat."

"Will I have a bad scar?"

Two Wolves studied her lovingly before answering. "Not bad enough to mar your beauty."

Was he referring to how she looked naked? The thought stirred sweet desires that, strangely enough, she no longer wanted to fight. This man had been boldly honest about his feelings, and it struck her how hard life had to be for him, being torn between two worlds. If he truly did love her, it had to hurt deeply to realize she might never return that love just because he was Indian. Right now, she didn't see him that way anymore. He was her good friend, her protector, her only refuge. And he'd been incredibly patient with her.

Two Wolves rose. "I will get Sits-In-The-Night to come and help you bathe and dress."

"No."

Two Wolves looked down at her.

"I want you. I don't want another stranger, not even a woman. I'm scared when you leave. I'm afraid you'll ride away and not come back."

He watched her closely. "I would never do that to you."

"Please don't go."

"You are better now. You need–"

"I need *you*, Two Wolves. I've been mean to you at times. I've judged you wrongly and I, I'm sorry. And I'm not sure of my feelings. I only know I hate it when you aren't near me. I hate it when I think you're mad at me. And I don't say it but sometimes—like now—I just want you to hold me. You rescued me, you've saved my life. You've been a friend and a protector, and I can no longer imagine living without you."

Two Wolves came closer, kneeling beside her. "Your whole world is changed, and you are still not completely well and strong. Perhaps it is only your momentary weakness that makes you speak this way."

Claire's eyes teared. "No. It's more than that. Lie down beside me, Two Wolves."

He just watched her warily for several long seconds. "You are young. And you wear nothing under those blankets. You have no idea what you are asking of me, now that you are better."

"I think I am safer with you than with most white men who would have had to take care of me the way you have. And I think we have hardship and danger ahead of us. Right now, we are safe and we are with people who understand." She couldn't help tears then. "And I really, really need to be held, Two Wolves."

Two Wolves felt torn at her tears, and the way she shivered under the blankets. He frowned. "Sometimes you confuse me, Claire Stewart. I have deep feelings for you, and if I lie with you the way you ask, I will want you more."

Claire smiled through her tears. "That sounds so strange from a man who is so brave and strong and kills his enemy with such ease, but is afraid of one woman whom he could throw all the way across this village if he wanted."

"Injury to the body is one thing. It is an outward pain and it heals. Injury to the *heart* is very different. It is not something you can stitch up and let heal. Sometimes injury to the heart *never* heals."

Their gazes held for several quiet seconds. "Has someone broken your heart before, Two Wolves?"

Two Wolves turned away and called something out in the Cheyenne tongue. He looked back at Claire. "*Tai-in-hkok* will bring water and a cloth to help you wash. I will go through the things you packed and find some clean clothes for you. We have to get on our way to Fort Robinson. Major Ansley will be worried."

Claire realized he was not going to answer her question about a broken heart. Had he loved someone else? Before she could say anything more, Sits-In-The-Night came inside with a pan of water and a piece of cloth draped over her arm. She smiled at Claire.

"You look much better," she told her. "Is the pain gone?"

"Yes." Claire watched her–a lovely woman with a beaded leather band tied around her forehead. Slender of build, her black hair hung long and soft. In many ways, Claire was beginning to see that these people weren't so different from whites in living as family and staying clean and caring about each other. Somehow, she'd imagined they were all dirty and mean and wild, but after getting to know Two Wolves . . .

"It is best I go now," Two Wolves told her. He moved out of the way so that Sits-In-The-Night could sit down beside Claire.

"Two Wolves, please don't leave," Claire asked.

Literal pain moved through his eyes. "You are better now. It is best I no longer be so close to you, as you yourself told me before we left. You can take care of yourself now."

"No! I *want* you close to me. I'm not letting you leave without telling you . . ." Claire sat up straighter, holding the blankets over herself. "Two Wolves, I love you, more than just a friend. I don't want you to be angry with me again. Please come right back."

Two Wolves studied her with quiet intensity. "I want to believe you, but feeling safe with someone does not mean you love them."

"And you are a fool, Two Wolves!" The very unexpected words came from Sits-In-The-Night, who turned to face the man.

Two Wolves frowned. "Why do you call me a fool?" he asked, a note of anger in his voice.

"No one knows better how torn your heart is than I and your cousin *O'Kohm,*" Sits-In-The-Night answered. "And this life we live . . . We know it cannot last. Much as you fight it, your future lies with the part of you that is white, and it is best you love a white woman rather than a Cheyenne woman. I sense that now that this young woman believes she loves you, you are thinking of running from that love. Her words surprised you and put doubt in your heart, but you have told us your feelings for her. Do not run from them now. This is your chance at true happiness." Sits-In-The-Night rose and faced him squarely. "Come back here in a while. I will help her bathe and I will change her bandages. You need to talk more with her."

Two Wolves scowled at her, then sighed. "I will come back soon." He left, and Sits-In-The-Night turned to again sit down beside Claire, smiling. Claire realized that apparently, Two Wolves had been talking to these relatives about his feelings for her.

"You should wash and be clean when Two Wolves comes back," Sits-In-The-Night told her. "And now that you are better, I think by morning you will belong to Two Wolves in every way. I hope it will be so. It is time for him to be happy."

The Indian woman dipped the cloth into the pan of water. Claire touched her arm. "Has he loved before?"

Sits-In-The-Night twisted water from the cloth. "That is for him to tell you. I only know that my husband's cousin has lost his heart to you." She studied Claire's eyes. "Do not break it. That is why he now thinks of running from the love he was hoping you would feel for him." She reached out and began washing Claire's face.

Claire took the cloth from her. "I can do it."

Their eyes held in mutual understanding between women. "Do you have children, Sits-In-The-Night?"

"*O'kohm* and I have four children. We are little different from your own people in these things. We love and we marry and we have families and we want only to be left alone, but now we constantly run and hide. It is a hard life. Two Wolves is torn between helping us and facing the fact that his only future lies with the whites. That does not hurt us. We understand."

Claire washed under her arms, washed her breasts. "I've never known anyone like Two Wolves. He saved my life more than once. He's so, so brave and skilled."

"He is also just a man, *Maeveksea*, which means he can be stubborn and proud and full of silly ideas when it comes to women and love. Sometimes with men you have to take things into your own hands. There are ways to control even a brave warrior like Two Wolves that only a woman can use. You finish washing. I will give you some sweet oil that makes a man unable to resist a woman. I will put a little on your neck and send Two Wolves back in here. By morning he will belong to you, and you to him."

Claire blinked, considering what the woman was telling her, then blushed. "You hardly know me. Why do you care?"

"Because *Two Wolves* cares. That is all I need to know. He is a man of wisdom, and he is lonely on the inside. I wish that he is no longer lonely." Sits-In-The-Night took the cloth from her and re-wet it.

The remark only enhanced Claire's feelings of love for the man. "But I've never been with a man, Sits-In-The-Night. Are you saying –"

"You know what I am saying." The Indian woman handed the cloth back to Claire. "Do not be afraid. It is beautiful. And Two Wolves is a kind man. He loves with as much passion as he has for killing his enemies, and he is a man of honor." She rose. "You finish washing, and I will bring some fry bread and dried meat. You should eat. I will also bring the sweet oil. This *tipi* belongs to the shaman. Tonight, it will belong only to you and Two Wolves."

Sits-In-The-Night turned and left, and Claire finished washing. She felt confused and on fire and afraid and bold, unsure but sure, a thousand emotions swarming through her. Two Wolves might be half white, but he was also half Indian. Cheyenne—the very same Indians most whites thought should be killed or run out of Colorado. Now that she'd met the lovely Sits-In-The-Night—a wife, a mother, someone she could talk to like any woman talks to another, it didn't seem to matter anymore that Two Wolves and these relatives of his were Indian. Hunting these people down and killing them like animals seemed so wrong. So horribly wrong.

She would be far better off not loving Two Wolves, but there was no denying how she felt. It was more than just her feelings of gratefulness that he'd saved her life more than once. It was his utter manliness, his bravery, his kindness in caring for her, his incredibly handsome looks, and he way he made her feel so safe. He was all she had left in the world, and she knew with no hesitation that she could never walk out of his life and would be totally heartbroken if he walked out of hers.

Sits-In-The-Night came back with the sweet oil. "Two Wolves has told me *he* will put the oil on you."

Claire's eyes widened. "*What?*"

"He is bathing. He will return soon." Sits-In-The-Night smiled knowingly and left.

Claire stared at a wooden bowl with the oil in it. She touched her finger to it and raised it to her nose. It truly did smell sweet, a bit like sage, a bit like some kind of flower. Her heart pounded harder at the implications of Two Wolves rubbing the oil on her. She finished washing, then dabbed some of the oil near her throat, breathing deeply of its soothing scent. She curled back into the blankets to wait, her heart pounding with anticipation, fearful of what it might be like to become a woman in the fullest sense, yet on fire with a desire to do just that. She wasn't sure why or when she'd known this had to be and that she was most assuredly in love with Two Wolves. She only knew she'd lost her heart too deeply to ever get it back. Two Wolves had captured it as surely as if he'd captured her physically.

CHAPTER TWENTY-FOUR

CLAIRE RAN HER HANDS THROUGH her hair, shaking out her mass of curls as best she could and wondering how she really looked. She realized this was the first time she'd really cared what a man thought of how she looked. And hadn't Two Wolves already told her she was beautiful—that she reminded him of a little bird? She'd never considered herself pretty.

She looked around the *tipi*. The air inside was more pleasant now that the smoke from the shaman's sacred fire was gone. She was amazed at how clean and neat it was inside, with paintings on the skins stretched on tall poles that met high at the top at the smoke hole. It was dark out, and camp was surprisingly quiet except for voices somewhere in the distance, someone sharing a quiet conversation. Was it Two Wolves talking to his cousin?

A soft breeze rippled across the stretched hides and caused something outside to make a tinkling sound. She'd eaten, and Sits-In-The-Night had helped her outside to a place where she could relieve herself. She'd nervously washed again and now she waited, wondering if Two Wolves would change his mind about coming to her.

Her anxious curiosity was answered when at last Two Wolves came inside, closing the deerskin flap at the *tipi* entrance and just standing there for a moment, studying her. Claire nearly gasped at the sight of him. He looked splendid! He wore no shirt, and his chest and arms spoke of power and strength. His hair was combed long and straight, some of it twisted into skinny braids mixed in with the rest of his hair. A circular hair ornament of leather and beads was tied into one side of it. He wore a long silver earring in one ear, a beaded leather necklace close around his throat. She noticed the unexplained scars on his breasts, a scar on his arm where the bear had run its claws through it, other scars on his chest–put there by the Comanche men he'd killed to protect her. Still, none of the scars marred his magnificent build and looks. He wore white buckskin pants, but his feet were bare. A wide silver cuff bracelet encircled his upper left arm, and another one graced his right wrist.

They said nothing at first. Claire wasn't sure what he would do or what he expected of her. He came over and sat down beside her then, watching her eyes. "Tell me yourself that you want me here," he said softly.

Claire looked him over. Was she crazy to want to give her heart and her body to this man? Is that what would happen tonight? "I do. I meant it when I said I love you, Two Wolves."

"And how do you know for certain?"

"How does *anyone* know? It just–*is*. You have been so kind and so attentive. You've been my only friend ever since you first rescued me. And the times you cared for me, you could have taken advantage of my youth and my ignorance and my weak condition a hundred times over. Yet you never did."

Two Wolves smiled teasingly. "How do you know for sure? You were very sick. Sometimes you were not aware."

"I know because I've come to know *you* all too well." She scooted back a little and pulled her arms from under the blanket so that her bare shoulders showed. "I'm not sure what you want me to do, Two Wolves. All I can tell you is that I still want you to hold me. I want to lie in your arms tonight where I always feel safe. I'm not afraid of you. I'm more afraid when you aren't beside me."

"Perhaps you would regret letting me hold you, because if I share your blanket, I will want more of you. Do you understand?"

Claire swallowed. "You can have whatever you want." Had she really just said that? Was some foreign, wanton being making these words come out of her mouth?

Two Wolves sighed and reached for the sweet oil. "Lie face down and I will put some of this on your back. Massaging the sweet oil into your muscles will help you relax.

Claire nervously did as he said, not truly sure what to expect this time. Two Wolves pulled the blankets down to her hips. In the next moment his strong hands were caressing her back, gliding over her muscles, up and down her spine, over her shoulders, her neck, back down her spine, staying away from her clean bandages.

Claire felt the ends of his hair brushing her skin. He pulled the blankets all the way off her, and her heart pounded at the thought of him seeing and touching her nakedness. This was different from letting him bathe her and treat her wounds when she was sick. She closed her eyes and felt fire begin moving through her as he continued the massage, this time over her bare bottom, the backs of her thighs, down over her calves, her feet, back to her bottom.

"You are beautiful here." He moved his hands to her waist, reaching almost all the way around it with both hands and massaging around her hips. "Tell me you are sure, *Maeveksea*. If I do much more, I will be unable to stop even if you beg me to do so." He massaged her back and shoulders again. "A man can only hold back so much, and then he cannot resist when he loves the woman he is touching. You have truly never been with a man? I want you to be sure."

"I *am* sure, Two Wolves. I want you to touch me like you did that night at the campfire." She rolled to her side, amazed at her own boldness as she let him look upon her nakedness. "I jumped away, but deep inside I liked your mouth on mine, your hand on my breast. You said that you adored me, and you said it so beautifully."

He touched her face, leaning closer. "You test me in a way no enemy could, in a way no one else, man or woman, has ever tested me." He gently urged her to lie on her back, then dipped his hands into the sweet oil and leaned over her to begin massaging her throat, her shoulders, her arms, her belly, and then up over her breasts–gently–ever so gently.

"Everything about you is beautiful," he said softly. "Your splendid hair, your pouty lips, your beautiful, full breasts." He moved his hands down over her hip bones. "Your hips, your slender legs."

The massage continued downward, over her legs again, her feet, back up, his thumbs skirting her most private place, over her stomach, again carefully avoiding her wound. He rose then and wiped his hands on a piece of cloth.

Claire felt mesmerized at the sight of him, unable to look away when he untied his buckskin pants and tossed them aside. He stood there wearing only a loincloth, and she could see a swelling there. She struggled not to show a sudden panic.

"Do not ever be afraid of me, *Maeveksea*," he told her, as though he'd read her thoughts. "When I hold you, you will no longer be afraid."

He knelt down and pushed the blankets farther away. He lay down beside her.

Claire opened her arms and wrapped them around him as he lay partly on top of her. Her naked breasts were pressed against his naked chest, and it felt good. Strong arms embraced her more fully, and she rested her face against his chest. Two Wolves gently ran big hands over her bare back, as he moved a leg over hers.

"I feel safe here," Claire told him. "I'm not afraid. Don't ever leave me, Two Wolves. I can't begin to imagine any other man I would want to touch me. Surely that means that I love you."

She leaned her head back and he found her lips, groaning then as he tasted her mouth in a most surprisingly gentle, delicious kiss. He searched her mouth suggestively with full, soft lips.

Claire couldn't help a whimper from a sudden desire that was much more pleasant than she'd expected. When he moved one hand to fondle her breast she didn't want to jump away like she had that first night. She only responded by kissing him with more passion, her whole body feeling on fire. Suddenly she wanted more than anything to please this man who had done so much for her.

She gasped when he left her mouth to taste her neck, and she didn't object when his mouth found a nipple as he plied her breast. He sucked at it lightly, moving from one breast to the other and savoring them as though he drew nourishment from them. She whimpered his name, her body enshrouded by his hair that fell around her. He moved a hand down over her belly, as he trailed his fingers down between her legs. His kisses deepened as he explored that secret place she once never thought she could let a man touch.

"I want you so," he groaned, licking at her ear. "You are like silk."

Claire closed her eyes and let out a little breathed deeply when he moved a finger deep between her folds and inside of her.

"My God, Two Wolves," she nearly groaned. "I love your touch. Don't stop."

Two Wolves kissed her again, running his tongue deep while he gently explored between her legs, bringing forth a rise of ecstasy that made Claire feel wanton and wicked.

"You must be sure," Two Wolves groaned. "Do not ask me to stop, *Maeveksea*."

Claire leaned up to kiss his chest. "I'm sure," she whispered. She sucked in her breath at a sheer, unbridled desire that made her arch against his fingers. Suddenly she was engulfed in a world beyond where they lay together. A pulsing explosion that created a need deep inside her beyond anything she could have expected caused her to cry out. Two Wolves pressed his fingers against that magical spot for a few moments longer as the wonderful pulsing continued. She felt she couldn't get enough of the wonderful sensation. "Don't stop," she begged, her eyes closed.

Finally, Two Wolves moved his hand away as he kissed her once more, then leaned back to untie and toss aside his loincloth. Claire closed her eyes as he moved on top of her then, gently forcing her legs apart. She felt a hardness against her belly and realized what it was. "Two Wolves," she whispered.

He found her mouth again, gently tasting her lips, her chin, her cheeks, her eyes, her hair. "I want all of you," he told her.

"It's all right," she whimpered. "I trust you."

"I will bring you pain, *Maeveksea.* Do not be afraid."

"I'm not," she whispered.

She never dreamed that letting a man touch her this way would feel so wonderful. She shuddered as he left her mouth and kissed his way over her body.

"You should be fully ready," he told her. "I want you wet and relaxed."

Claire wasn't sure what he meant as he kissed his way farther down, surprising her when he began kissing her in secret places. She felt like a wild, wanton woman. She cried out his name when she realized his tongue was slaking between her legs and over her most private place, exploring, tasting, licking, pulling, savoring her like something delicious. His hair fell over her thighs, and he seemed to be taking over her entire body, claiming it as his own and gently forcing her to give it all over to him.

Again the wonderful sensation of keen desire built inside of her, the same wonderful, erotic need he'd first brought forth with his fingers, only now it was almost agonizing in the craving it created deep in her loins to give herself to a man. She felt as though she was floating, and she wanted desperately to make sure he savored every part of her. His strong hands plied at her bottom as he ran his tongue inside her, bringing forth another glorious explosion that made her cry out his name and grasp his hair, pushing herself against his tongue and lips as he pressed his mouth harder against her. It was as though he knew exactly what she was feeling and that she needed more pressure there for total satisfaction.

He licked his way back over her belly, her breasts, up to her throat, her mouth. She tasted her own sweetness on his lips.

"Do not be afraid," he repeated. "It will get better and then you will want this and enjoy this often."

She cried out then at the sudden pain she felt when his manhood invaded her, pushing deep, while he moved his hands under her bottom to bring her up to him so he could plant himself deeply.

Claire dug her fingers into his shoulders, wincing with the sharp, cutting sensation, yet a bit astonished that it was strangely enjoyable.

"I will not take so long this first time, *Maeveksea*. You are so beautiful, and I want you so badly."

He smothered her mouth in another kiss and groaned deeply as he pushed rhythmically and deep several times. He was all power now, in complete control of not just her body but her soul. She was his captive in every way, and that was what she wanted.

Claire finally felt something pulse inside her and realized it was his seed. He found her mouth again, kissing her wildly, deeply, as though worshipping her.

"You are so beautiful," he again whispered into her ear. "You taste sweet." His kisses lingered as he remained on top of her, making her feel lost beneath his muscular frame and the dark hair that fell around her face. "I have never been so pleased to be inside a woman," he moaned. "I am sorry if I hurt you."

"I can tell it will get better, Two Wolves." She threw her arms around his neck. "I love you! I love you! Tell me you'll stay with me forever! I'd be so afraid without you."

Two Wolves gently pulled himself out of her and held her close. "I will stay with you forever, *Maeveksea*." He reached across her to grasp a clean piece of cloth. He gently pushed it between her legs. "You will bleed," he told her. "Do not be afraid of it. We will lie here together for a while and enjoy touching."

"Will we do that again tonight?"

Two Wolves grinned. "Again and again, if it is what you want, and if the pain is not too much for you."

"It's a nice pain. I want to feel it again."

Their gazes held in mutual love mixed with the wonder of what they'd just done. Two Wolves drew her closer and pulled the blanket over them. "You are mine now. When a Cheyenne man takes a maiden this way, she is his wife."

His wife. It was done. There was no changing any of it, nor would she *want* to change it.

"Do it again, Two Wolves."

Two Wolves grinned. "So soon?"

"Yes. I want to feel you inside me again."

"I do not like bringing you pain."

"It's a good pain, and you told me it gets better. Make it better, Two Wolves."

He grinned and moved on top of her again. "I think my woman might want more than I can give her."

"You are a man who has much to give," she teased.

Two Wolves laughed softly. "And you are a woman who makes me *want* to give all that I have." He pulled the cloth away, and Claire opened herself to him. She winced again when he pushed himself inside her, his penis already large with the want of her yet again.

"*Ne-mehotatse*," he whispered.

"What does that mean?" Claire groaned, arching up to meet his thrusts.

"It means I love you."

"*Ne-mehotatse*," she replied. "Did I say it right?"

"*Aye, Maeveksea*." He met her mouth again, moving inside her as gently as he could. Claire didn't fear it any more, nor did she think of any of this as wrong or even think of this man as an Indian. He was just the wonderful, handsome, brave man she loved. Whatever all of this meant, she wanted nothing more than to be with him forever, no matter what lay ahead.

CHAPTER TWENTY-FIVE

CLAIRE AWOKE TO SOFT TALKING outside the *tipi*. A dog barked and somewhere a baby cried. She realized she hadn't even met most of the people there–only Sits-In-The-Night and the Shaman himself. She lay with her back to Two Wolves, his strong arm wrapped over her. She rubbed his arm.

"Two Wolves," she said softly. "Are you awake?"

He kissed her hair. "I have been awake for a while. I just did not want to disturb you." He turned onto his back "There is a little waterfall not far from here. We will go there and wash and then eat something. It is important we leave for Fort Collins soon. Major Ansley is probably worried."

They lay there staring at the top of the *tipi*. "Two Wolves, I need to know something."

"What is it?"

"Sits-In-The-Night said I should never break your heart. She made it sound like it's been broken before. And when you made love to me you said you were never so pleased to lie with a woman as with me. Have you loved before?"

He lay there quietly for several minutes. "My cousin's wife meant that my heart was broken when my father was killed, and again when they took me and my mother away from the only people I ever knew. Then my mother died and I mourned her greatly. Since then I have searched for where I belong. I came back here, and I cared very much for another warrior's third wife."

"What?" Claire sat up. "*Third* wife? Do you intend to take more wives? I won't allow it!"

Two Wolves chuckled and pulled her back down into his arms. "I have no such plans. I know you cannot live among the Cheyenne or by their culture. You must understand that our women often die in childbirth, or because of their age or for other reasons, they can no longer bear children. When that happens, a man takes a younger wife. It is important to preserve the race, *Maeveksea*. Many are dying from disease and starvation, some are being deliberately murdered by soldiers and the militia. A man needs to produce as many sons and daughters as he can so the Cheyenne will live on into the future, in spite of all the things the white man does to destroy them."

"Well the only way you can take another wife is if I die. And even *that* makes me jealous."

Two Wolves grinned and kissed her neck. "I want no other wife."

She put her hands to his face. "You said you were fond of another man's third wife. You *slept* with her?"

"With his permission. She could no longer bear children. She was still young, but something happened in her second childbirth that left her barren. She craved a man's love and attention, and her husband had other wives to tend to." He lost his smile and pulled away. "I considered asking to make her *my* wife, but I wanted children. And then she was killed in a raid on her camp by Colorado militia. I came back from hunting and found her . . . naked and cut open."

He sat up, and Claire could feel his anger.

"I'm sorry, Two Wolves. I shouldn't have asked."

He shook his long hair behind his shoulders. "You had a right to ask." He turned, smiling softly in spite of what Claire was sure were tears in his eyes. He leaned down, pulling her underneath him. "I know that my only future is with a white woman and in the white world. But you will have to be patient, *Maeveksea*. I have much to think about. My heart lies with the Cheyenne, but now *you* own my heart, and you are white. I see my people's future, and it saddens me." He kissed her softly. "Finding you has helped that sadness, and now I am no longer lonely."

Claire touched his face, tracing a finger over his lips. "Tell me I'm the only white woman you've ever been with."

"You are the only one."

Claire curled closer. "Hold me, Two Wolves."

He pulled her closer again, wrapping strong arms around her. "It is done, *Maeveksea*. You are my wife."

"I'm glad." She ran her fingers over his arms, his chest. "Where did you get these scars at your breasts? Will you tell me?"

"They are from that part of me that is Cheyenne. When I came back here and joined the Cheyenne, I wanted to be fully a warrior, so I took part in the Sun Dance. I am not so sure you should know the details. A white woman might think it is a barbaric ritual, but it means everything to a Cheyenne warrior."

"Your warrior side is one thing I love about you. Tell me."

He studied her eyes. "It is a way of seeking a vision that will guide us through life. First, a man fasts and prays for many days. A sacred pole is erected with long tethers of rawhide tied to it. After fasting and praying, those warriors who wish to make the sacrifice dance around the pole for hours—sometimes a full day or two." He breathed deeply before continuing, fearful she'd be horrified and wonder what kind of man she'd married. "Bone skewers are thrust through the chest muscles, and the rawhide tethers are tied to it so that when the warrior leans away from the pole, the tethers pull at the bone skewers. Sometimes skewers are also put through the calves of their legs with weights tied to them."

Two Wolves watched her eyes widen a little. "The key to bravery and the ability to fight the enemy and ignore pain is to find a vision, and to suffer great pain so that no other pain can compare. I told you once that wounds to the body are only temporary pain and will heal. It is the pain on the inside that hurts much more, and if I should lose you because you feel I am too Indian for you to accept . . . that pain I could not bear."

Claire touched the scars. "I honor that part of you that felt he should make such a sacrifice. I want to understand, Two Wolves, but *you* have to understand that I am Christian."

"I *do* understand that. I have told you I believe *Maheo* is the same as your Jesus. When I lived in Chicago with my mother we went to a Christian church. And I know you would want to be married the Christian way. We will do so when we reach Fort Collins. I promise. But lying with you, adoring you, joining with you—that to me is as much commitment to forever as a Christian marriage. All that matters is what God knows, the Supreme God who created man and woman to come together in love to create children to carry on the human race. What we have done is as right and holy as to be married the Christian way. The only difference is a piece of paper. Do not feel you have done anything wrong."

Claire threw her arms around his neck and drew him to her. "I don't, Two Wolves. You are my husband, and I feel so full and so happy and so protected."

He wrapped her in his arms. "We will go and bathe and get ready to leave. And I want you to meet my cousin and know his children. There are only a few in this camp. The Cheyenne find themselves scattered now. Many have gone north to join with the Sioux and Arapaho. Many things are changing. We were once a strong nation that roamed all of Colorado for buffalo, following the seasons and the yellow grass. Now the white man is killing off the buffalo, and hunts us down. The only way I can help is by scouting for the Army and acting as interpreter to try to keep the peace. There will be many treaties coming–white man's lies–but I will still be there to try to make my people understand that they must abide by the treaties or risk being completely destroyed. Part of me wants to ride with them as a warrior, and the other part of me sees it is hopeless."

"I'm so sorry, Two Wolves. I don't understand why we can't all just live together in peace."

He sat up, then rose to his feet, tying on his loincloth. "It is because the white man is never satisfied with just a little. He wants it all–all the land–all the wealth that lies under the ground–all the water–all the minerals–all the timber. To him the Cheyenne are in the way and they do not count as human beings." He looked down at her. "It is the same with Vince Huebner. He wants all the shipping business for himself."

Claire's heart raced at the mention of Vince's name. She'd almost forgotten they still had to go to Denver City to try to convince people what Vince was up to. She dreaded that more than ever now, fearful for Two Wolves to go into a the city, where the Indians were so hated.

Two Wolves pulled on his buckskin leggings, then reached down and wrapped her in a blanket.

"Do not be afraid of Vince Huebner, *Maeveksea.* God is with us. Let us go and bathe."

He picked her up as though she weighed nothing and carried her out of the *tipi.* Claire covered her face with the blanket as they were immediately surrounded by smiling, doting, laughing women who Claire could tell were making teasing remarks even though they spoke in the Cheyenne tongue. Sits-In-The-Night draped two clean blankets over Two Wolves' shoulders and handed him the leather bag that contained Claire's clothes. Men also began teasing, their barbs obviously aimed at Two Wolves, who shouted something back to them and laughed.

Children chased after them part of the way as Two Wolves carried Claire around boulders and to a small waterfall deeper in the forest. He dropped the blankets and Claire's bag of clothing, then set her on her feet and pulled the blanket from around her. He opened the blanket and spread it out in the grass.

"Let me remove your bandages. The cold water will help heal your wound. I told Sits-In-The-Night to put clean bandages from my gear into your bag of clothing." He removed his leggings and untied his loin-cloth. Claire couldn't help glancing at all that was man about him before quickly looking away.

Two wolves laughed softly. "There is no shame in looking at your husband's nakedness, just as I enjoy drinking in the sight of your own naked beauty."

Claire smiled bashfully. "It's still embarrassing for me."

Two Wolves took a beaded ornament from his hair. "Soon you will not be so embarrassed." He picked her up and dashed to a small pool beneath the waterfall.

Claire screamed as the cold water streaming down from the mountains hit her shoulders and poured over her hair and body. Two Wolves knelt down and grasped some sand in his hands to scrub her with.

"Sand freshens the skin," he told her.

Claire folded her arms over her breasts. "Two Wolves, someone might see us."

"They won't. You can trust them." He pulled her down. "Here. Sit for a moment. The water will clean you and soothe you if you are sore."

Claire couldn't help another little scream when she lowered herself into the cold water. Two Wolves knelt beside her and rubbed more sand under her arms and over her back, then scrubbed his own body.

"We will rinse off under the waterfall."

Claire thought how utterly happy and handsome he looked that morning. He was so different now, no longer a bit angry and defensive around her, no longer holding back in a stoic attempt to pretend it didn't matter to him if she didn't return his affections. She threw her arms around his neck.

"I love you, Two Wolves. I've never been this happy."

He rose, picking her up with him, and carried her to the waterfall. They rinsed off the sand, then just stood there drinking in the sight of each other's naked bodies. Two Wolves grasped her face in his hands and leaned down to kiss her heatedly.

"You are beautiful," he told her.

He kissed his way downward, over her shoulders, her breasts and the pink nipples that were more protruded from the cold water.

Claire closed her eyes and touched his wet hair, amazed at her own boldness as he kissed her scar . . . then kissed the crevice between her legs. She sucked in her breath as he tasted and explored. She continued to be amazed at how brazen this man could make her feel. He rose then, picking her up and carrying her to the blanket in the grass. He laid her on it and knelt over her.

Nothing needed to be said. He began working his magic with hands and lips and tongue, moving over her body lovingly, finding her love nest and leaving her no choice but to open her legs to his touch that left her wanting more. She groaned with ecstasy as he took his pleasure with her, savoring her as something delicious. A thrilling desire made her grasp his head and actually push toward him in a desperate need to bring herself to a heightened climax. She thought how she'd surely go crazy if he would have stopped before the lovely, rippling explosion that made her cry out his name.

Two Wolves kissed his way back to her neck, her lips.

"I love the taste of you," he told her. Before entering her, he lay beside her, taking her hand and moving it to his manhood. "Touch it, *Maeveksea*. Know my body as I know yours."

Claire felt his erection, somewhat amazed that something so big actually fit inside her. She understood now why it had hurt the first time.

"The skin is so soft," she told him.

Two Wolves smiled. "It *has* to be soft to the touch, so I don't hurt you when I am inside you."

Claire dared to look down at his swollen penis and touched his scrotum. He grasped her hand.

"Be very careful there," he teased. "If you ever want to bring a man to his knees, kick him there, and he will be at your mercy."

Claire smiled. "I'll have to remember that."

Two Wolves laughed, moving between her legs. "Right now, it will be much more pleasurable to be inside you." He raised to his knees and entered her, grasping her bottom and pushing deep.

Claire closed her eyes and grasped his powerful forearms, still amazed at how this man could remove all inhibitions, making her actually enjoy lying naked in the sun and letting him mate with her. He had a way of taking over her every emotion and desire and wiping out any bit of bashfulness and reserve she had left in her. She reveled in the sweet rhythm of their mating, glorying in the fact that his promise of less pain was true. At the moment she wanted him to stay inside her forever. For several wonderful minutes he kept up the thrusts before coming down closer to press her against his chest as his life spilled into her.

They lay there in complete, dreamy ecstasy, sharing kisses, touches.

"I will love and protect you forever," Two Wolves told her.

"And I'll be a good wife. I promise."

Two Wolves grinned. "You are already a good wife." He kissed her eyes, smoothed back her hair. "How do you think our children will look—me so dark—and you with green eyes and all this red hair."

Claire grinned. "They will be beautiful because their father is the most handsome man on the face of the Earth."

"It will be because of their mother," Two Wolves answered.

"I hope we find out soon, Two Wolves. I hope your seed is already springing to life inside me."

Two Wolves frowned, lying down beside her and rolling her over on top of him.

"Of course it is already growing inside you. My seed is powerful!" He spoke the words boastfully then broke into laughter, running his hands along her thighs. He reached up and grasped her behind the neck, pulling her down to meet her lips in a heated kiss as he rolled her back over. "I want to stay here and make love to you all day," he told her, "but it is important that we leave for the fort. Major Ansley will be wondering why we are not there yet." He kissed her again. "And I am anxious that we marry the Christian way so that your heart carries no doubt about whether this is right."

"I have no doubts, Two Wolves."

"And you forget that I understand your world better than you think. I know how other whites will look at this if we are not married by a Christian preacher. I will not allow others to look down on you. It will still be hard for you, even if we marry the Christian way. You must understand this."

Claire sobered. "I *do* understand, but I'm not afraid of it. Other women have looked at me scathingly ever since I was old enough to be called a woman. I don't dress like them and I don't behave the way they expect females should behave. I loved my father, and I've helped run his business since I was old enough to add two and two and to help hitch teams and pack wagons. Now it's my livelihood." She touched his face. "But we do have to decide how we are going to live, Two Wolves. If you want me to give up my business and live at the fort while you continue scouting, I'll do it."

He shook his head. "I survive because I need little. What I do does not pay well, but I don't need a roof over my head and store-bought things. I live free, hunt for my food, and live part of the time among the Cheyenne. Most of my supplies come from the Army. But I know all that must change for me because you will need to live another way."

"I just want you to be happy," Claire told him. "I fear you'll long for the freedom you have now and you will grow to resent me."

He sighed, lying down beside her and pulling her into his arms. "That will not happen. There might be times when I need to ride into the hills and be alone. I need you to understand that. But I have declared my love for you and made you my wife, and I lived the white man's way for several years in his city." He gave her more quick kisses, then rose, pulling her up with him. "We must go."

He rose, pulling her up with him. "Which is why we need to leave now and talk to Major Ansley."

"I wish we could stay," Claire said with a deep sigh. "It's so pretty here, so peaceful."

"We have no choice, *Maeveksea*." He kissed her hair. "Let me put on your clean bandages, and we will dress."

He wrapped her wound once more and they quietly dressed, both hating to leave. They faced each other then, and Two Wolves wrapped Claire in his arms. "I will always remember this place," he told her.

"As will I, Two Wolves. We will always be this happy, won't we?"

"*Aye*. We will always be this happy."

The tender moment was interrupted by screams . . . and gunfire . . . all coming from *O'kohm*'s camp.

Two Wolves pushed Claire away and whirled.

"Stay here!" he told her. "And *hide! Hide!* Do what I tell you!" He ran off, still shirtless, carrying no weapons, his feet bare.

"Two Wolves, no!" Claire screamed. She started after him, dodging through pine trees and aspen as she heard more gunfire . . . war whoops . . . screams. Remembering his order to hide, she stopped then. Through the trees, she could see men riding through the camp, killing and destroying. They were white. "My God!" she groaned.

Two Wolves had told her to hide, and she knew instinctively he was right. Running after him would only distract him and possibly cost him his life. She ducked down behind a huge log and waited, covering her ears against the awful screams. She didn't have to look to know the men who'd attacked the Cheyenne camp were likely killing at random. It made her sick to think of it, ashamed of her own race. "God, don't let my husband die!" She'd just found the most glorious happiness she'd ever known, and now her own kind might take it all away from her.

CHAPTER TWENTY-SIX

CLAIRE WAITED IN TERROR. SHE remained hidden behind the log, feeling guilty for not being able to do something to help. There came more gunshots and screams. Then . . . an eerie silence.

Finally, she heard Two Wolves calling for her. Claire jumped up and ran to him, gasping at the sight of a gash on his forehead. Before they reached each other, Two Wolves stumbled forward and fell.

"Two Wolves!" Claire ran to kneel beside him. He rolled to his side and groaned. "Two Wolves, what happened!"

He managed to sit up, putting a hand to his head. "White men. Ranchers. They found the camp and rode their horses through it, destroying everything they could. They . . . the shaman is badly wounded . . . and *O'Kohm!* He is dead!"

"No! Oh, no! What about Sits-In-The-Night and the children?"

Two Wolves struggled to his feet. "My little nephew . . . a horse rode over him. He is four. We have to get help for him." He took Claire's arm and led her toward where he'd left the rest of his clothing.

Claire could feel his anger. The beautiful spell between them was broken.

"I shot one of them." Two Wolves turned from Claire and picked up his shirt.

"Will you be in trouble?"

"I do not know. I am an Army scout, yet I fought on the side of my people; but those men attacked first." He pulled on a buckskin shirt.

"Two Wolves, we still have bandages here. Let me wrap something around your head to stop the bleeding. Come to the pool, and we will wash the blood from your face."

He just stared at Claire for a moment, looking dazed but furious. "These are the reasons I should not have married you in the flesh. Now you are mine, but I will understand if you change your mind, though my heart would fall into pieces."

"Change my mind?"

He turned away and picked up the bandages, walking to the pool. He knelt down, wet some of the bandages and washed his face, then held one to his head. "One of them charged through the camp and swung his rifle at me. After he knocked me down, I ran to my horse and took my rifle . . . and I shot him. His friends picked him up and rode away. They will tell the law." He faced Claire again. "We have to get to Fort Collins and tell Major Ansley what has happened. We will take *Tai-in-hkok* and the children with us. And the shaman. He is still alive. The others . . . they want to run to the south. They were here to hunt, and they have families waiting for them. I will see that *Tai-in-hkok* and the children get safely to the Northern Cheyenne." He wrapped a bandage around his head.

"Let me tie it for you," Claire told him, her heart pounding at his statement that she could change her mind. Why had he said that? She gently tied the gauze. "And I don't want to hear anything more about me backing out of this, Two Wolves. I love you. I've given myself to you in every way, body, heart and soul. I am your wife, and a wife stays beside her husband through the best and the worst. I could never live without you now."

Rising, he pulled her into his arms. "I am sorry, *Maeveksea*. It was so beautiful here. So peaceful." He held her closer. "I fear you will suffer, maybe even physically, for being my wife. I will fight to the death for you if necessary."

Claire rested her head against his shoulder. "You've already proven that." She leaned back her head and met his gaze. "We are husband and wife, and when we reach Fort Collins we will be able to be alone at last in our own cabin. Major Ansley won't let anything happen to you because of this. You had a right to fight back. We will talk to the major and work all this out."

Two Wolves leaned down and kissed her. "We have to pack everything and leave quickly before those men come back. I think we are on their land. Perhaps once we are off it they will not pursue us. We must hurry."

"I'm not sure you should ride."

"I have no choice. Help me pick up our things."

Claire felt everything she did then was like a bad dream, carrying their things back to camp, seeing the devastation in the eyes of Sits-In-

The-Night, listening to her wailing over her husband. Claire struggled against her own tears. Sits-In-The-Night wanted to bury *O'Kohm* on an altar above ground, but there was no time to build one. It was agreed he would be lifted into the trees.

Claire couldn't help thinking how broken she would be if Two Wolves had been killed. Her heart went out to Sits-In-The-Night and her children. The poor woman hardly knew which one to mourn–her husband or her wounded son. The other hunters there quickly wrapped *O'Kohm*'s body in a buffalo robe, being sure to wrap his medicine bag and weapons into the robe with him for his journey to the Great Beyond. They tied leather straps tightly around the robe to secure everything. Two Wolves helped, in spite of his wound. They found a cluster of pines, and two of the men climbed into them, keeping with them long straps tied to *O'Kohm*. The men below lifted the man's body and the others in the trees raised him and positioned him between branches, tying the straps tightly to secure him.

Claire touched Sits-In-The-Night's shoulder, sick at how happy they had all been just a couple of hours earlier. Sits-In-The-Night embraced her–one woman sharing her grief with another–like all women were prone to do. Again, Claire was struck by how normal these people were–loving, laughing, sharing, bearing children and caring for them. These particular women were forced now to be constantly on the run, following their men as they searched desperately for food that was growing more and more scarce because of the systematic slaughter of the buffalo, and the white man's railroad and progress chasing the wild game from the plains and prairies. Claire had never given much thought to their plight until now.

It seemed that they were too quickly on their way, breaking camp and making two *travois* from the *tipi* poles to carry the shaman and Two Wolves' little nephew. Sits-In-The-Night rode beside the *travois* and carried her two-year-old daughter in a cradleboard. Tragedy was written in the new widow's eyes. Two Wolves kept his five-year-old nephew, Little Dreamer, with him, the boy riding behind him with his little arms wrapped around Two Wolves, his head resting against his uncle's back. Claire could tell he wasn't just hanging on to stay on the horse. He was hanging on in pure terror. Another nephew, named He Sings, was seven and able to ride his own horse. He pulled his little wounded brother's *travois*. Claire's horse pulled the *travois* carrying the Shaman.

Claire thought how somber their little group was. Sits-In-The-Night kept looking back, and Claire thought how utterly painful it had to be to leave her husband behind, his dead body tied in the trees. She would never see him again, and she'd had no chance to say good-bye. She wept off and on, and sometimes she softly sang a chant Claire supposed was a song of mourning.

Two Wolves stared straight ahead. Right now, he was more like the man Claire had first met–stoic, angry, and carrying enough weapons to fight ten men. He kept his rifle in one hand, as though he might need to use it so fast that he wouldn't have time to draw it from the straps holding it to his horse's side. He hardly spoke, and Claire knew it was because he wanted all his senses alert to danger. They were riding in the open with Indians who'd already been attacked by white ranchers, men who might come for them a second time. And the Colorado Militia could be anywhere, with orders to kill any Indian in sight. Claire felt sorry for him, wounded, a man alone defending his own relatives and his new wife, torn between two worlds.

They stopped to rest and water the horses. Two Wolves' wounded little second cousin, Dancing Feet, began crying. Claire knelt down beside Two Wolves as he removed a blanket from the boy to check his bruised body. He spoke soothingly to him in Cheyenne, gently stroking his hair. In that moment, Claire knew this man she'd chosen deserved his own children. He'd already mentioned wanting a family, and she felt a glowing satisfaction in realizing what an attentive, protective father he would make.

"I think he has broken ribs, but I do not think anything else is broken," he told Claire as he gently felt the boy's arms and legs. "Look In my supply bag. I have laudanum. I will give him a little."

Claire obeyed, coming back with the sedative. Two Wolves held the brown bottle to Dancing Feet's lips and urged him to drink some. The boy swallowed, then made a face and cried again.

"*Ho-shuh*," Two Wolves soothed. "You will feel better soon." He looked at Claire again. "When he and my cousin reach the Northern Cheyenne a Shaman there can help him." His eyes saddened. "I am so sorry, *Maeveksea*. I did not plan on this. I will not be able to lie with you tonight. I must stay awake and alert for animals and for men who might be following us."

"Has the dizziness gone away?" Claire asked him.

"I am all right."

Claire reached out and touched his head. "Let me change the bandage."

"I will remove it. Let the fresh air heal my wound." He looked her over lovingly. "What about you? Do you have any pain from your wound? We left it unbandaged."

"I have no pain. I think it's finally healing well now."

Two Wolves covered Dancing Feet, then walked over to check the shaman. He helped the old man drink some laudanum, then spoke to him softly in Cheyenne. Sighing deeply, he rose, handing the bottle to Claire, then taking her arm and walking her a few feet away. "He has a bullet in his chest. I do not think he will live more than another day."

"I'm so sorry, Two Wolves! Those men had no business to do what they did."

"In the eyes of Colorado citizens, they had every right. They will say *I* am the one who had no right to shoot back." He pulled her into his arms. "We would normally reach Fort Collins by tomorrow afternoon if it was just you and me, but at this pace, we won't reach the fort until the day after tomorrow. I want you to do something for me if white men should stop us or attack us again."

Claire looked up at him, aching for things to just be sweet and peaceful between them again. "What should I do?"

"You must promise me you will not tell them you are my wife."

Claire pulled away. "I'll do no such thing! I'm *proud* to be your wife."

He grasped her arms. "Then listen to your husband and do what he tells you! If we are attacked and there are more than three or four of them, I will not be able to fight them off. I could even be killed. If you tell them I am your husband, they will treat you badly. They might even abuse you sexually and consider you nothing but a white squaw! I know men like this. You must make them believe you were just wounded in the attack on your wagon train, and that I helped you because I am an Army scout. I was taking you to Fort Collins for help. Nothing more! *Nothing!* Do you understand? Do not even tell them what you know about Vince Huebner. Save that for Major Ansley and let him decide what to do."

Claire couldn't help the tears that filled her eyes. "But I'm not ashamed to be your wife, Two Wolves."

"I know that. But it won't matter to white men how you feel about me or the Cheyenne. If they know you lay with a Cheyenne man they will not respect you. *Promise* me, *Maeveksea!* Do not say anything about being my wife!"

Claire sniffed, tears streaming down her cheeks. She reached out and hugged him around the middle. "I love you, Two Wolves."

He embraced her, kissing her hair. "You know that I love you. I would like nothing more than to share my blanket with you tonight, but I cannot. And my heart will be heavy with worry if you do not promise what I just asked you."

Claire sniffed and wiped at her eyes. "I promise."

"Good. Keep that promise." He leaned down and kissed her cheek. "If I kiss your lips I will not be able to keep from wanting more." He let go of her. "Give me the laudanum. I will put it back, and we will go farther before we stop for the night."

Claire wiped at tears again. "What should I do about Sits-In-The-Night? I feel like I should be able to help her somehow."

"She is in deep mourning. There is nothing you can do. When she reaches relatives in the north she will likely cut off her hair and cut herself to draw blood."

Claire sucked in her breath. "*What?*"

"It is the way of a Cheyenne woman in mourning. Her sacrifice will help make sure *O'Kohm* goes proudly to the land beyond. Someday Sits-In-The-Night will join him there."

Claire turned away. "There is so much I don't know, Two Wolves." She ran a hand into her tumble of red curls. "I only know that I love you and that nothing else matters."

He came closer, touching her shoulder. "When we reach the fort we will have time to talk, *Maeveksea*. And we will marry the Christian way. Somehow we will find a way to always be together in peace. I will do whatever I must do to make that happen."

Claire covered his hand with her own. "So will I. Right now, I just wish we could go back to that pond and stay there forever."

He kissed her hair again. "You are strong and brave, my wife. I am proud of you." He took her arm. "We must go."

Claire walked with him back to the horses. Two Wolves took a moment to speak with Sits-In-The-Night and held her for a moment, speaking to her in his native tongue. For a moment, Claire wondered if he might not be happier to have married a Cheyenne woman. Sits-In-The-Night looked so natural in his arms, and Claire felt a deep jealousy at the thought of Two Wolves lying with anyone else. He helped Sits-In-The-Night onto her horse and handed up her cradleboard. Claire mounted her own horse, and Two Wolves checked the security of the *travois* pulling Dancing Feet. He leapt onto the back of his own horse with ease, then reached down and let Sits-In-The-Night's five-year-old son grasp his arm so he could lift the boy onto his horse behind him again.

They continued their journey, and Claire silently prayed no one was following them. They reached nightfall with no problems, bedding down soon after eating jerked meat and some bread. They all slept in their clothes, Two Wolves keeping constant watch. Sits-In-The-Night slept beside her wounded son once she got her baby daughter to sleep. Claire slept beside the five-year-old, Little Dreamer. Holding the child close only confirmed her desire to give Two Wolves children. Surely they would be dark and beautiful like this little boy beside her. It tore at her heart to think about the future that lay ahead for Little Dreamer, having just lost his father, running from terrible danger and headed into a life of more running. She'd only been with these people five days, and she already understood and sympathized with their plight. It was no wonder Two Wolves lived with so much indecision and torn feelings.

Somewhere deep in the night Claire jerked awake when Two Wolves touched her shoulder. She could make out his muscular build against the soft moonlight, his long hair blowing in a gentle wind. Her first thought was how terrified she'd been of him that first night he'd tackled her to the ground and put a hand over her mouth.

"I just wanted to touch you," he told her softly.

Claire sat up and threw her arms around his neck, and he pulled her to her feet, holding her tightly as he did so.

"I miss you," he whispered. "I am so sorry for all of this."

"And I miss you." Claire kissed his cheek and moved her lips so that he could catch them in his own in a soft, delicious kiss. "Don't be sorry. This helps me understand everything so much more."

He moved a hand over her back, into her hair. "I want you so, but I must be aware," he told her softly.

"I know."

"One more night, and we will be at the fort."

"It will be such a relief."

They kissed once more, and Claire took comfort in his powerful arms. She was always safe when he held her.

"I should not have awakened you," he whispered, "but I wanted to hold you."

"I'm glad you woke me." Claire met his dark eyes, thinking how handsome he was in the moonlight. "Sleeping beside Little Dreamer makes me want to give you babies, Two Wolves."

She could see his smile. "Then we will work on that when we are safe, and I will enjoy making babies with you."

Claire grinned, grasping him tighter again. He held her for several long seconds. "I must let go of you, or I will want to take you into the far grass and be one with you again. I cannot. It is too dangerous."

They kissed once more then he quickly left her. Longing to lie next to her husband and worrying he was not getting any sleep of his own made it difficult for Claire to go back to sleep herself. One more day. One more long day and one more night, and they would reach the safety of the fort.

CHAPTER TWENTY-SEVEN

THEY RODE IN SAD SILENCE, the only sound being a gentle wind and the occasional snorting of one of the horses. Claire was amazed at how alert Two Wolves was, despite his head wound and having gone sleepless all night. He couldn't keep this up. Another long day in the saddle, and he would surely have to sleep. He sometimes urged his horse into a faster lope, scouting ahead, circling around behind, always watching, sometimes literally sniffing the air as though more animal than man.

The sun was high when Two Wolves suddenly halted and whirled, ordering the two women to stop and be very still. Claire heard nothing but a few bird calls and the swish of the wind bending the dry grasses, but after riding several yards away from them and listening again for a moment, Two Wolves rode back to them in a hurry.

"Get into the trees!" he ordered. "Quickly!"

Heart pounding, Claire obeyed, Sits-In-The-Night right behind her. They rode as deeply into the foothills as they could, until the trees were so thick they couldn't drag the *travois.*

"Get off the horses," Two Wolves ordered. "Tie them and get down! Lie across the children!"

He leapt from his own horse, rifle in hand, then pulled the animal farther into the trees and tied it. He ducked behind a half-grown pine tree, crouching on one knee and resting his elbow on the other knee, bringing his rifle up and aiming.

"Two Wolves, is it the same men?" Claire asked quietly.

"I believe so. Remember what I told you about not telling them you are my wife." He didn't look at her. He stayed crouched with his rifle steadily aimed. "We had a good start on them, but *travois* tracks are easy to follow, and pulling them slowed us down."

"But I don't see anything." Claire had no more got the words out than several riders appeared from behind a rise they'd just come over themselves not long before. "Two Wolves! There are too many for you to fight!"

"I can only try. Stay behind the trees."

Claire watched him–a man of sure aim, his weapons belt sporting a hatchet, a knife, six-guns and ammunition. She had no idea how he'd suddenly known they were coming, but from what she could tell there were at least half a dozen men charging toward them. Though a magnificent warrior, Two Wolves was only one man, and against six or seven men with rifles and six-guns, he could only do so much.

"Hurry over to my supplies before they get any closer," he told her. "There is an Army pistol in there. Take it out. You might need it."

"Uncle, let me help," He Sings spoke up. "I can shoot."

"I know you can, He Sings, but we have only one rifle. A pistol would not work now, and I want *Maeveksea* to have it in case these men try to do something bad to her."

The riders came ever closer, stopping to check tracks. One of them pointed toward the trees. Two Wolves took aim, pulling back the hammer of his Army rifle. Claire jumped when he fired. One of the men fell from his horse. Two Wolves quickly aimed and fired again. A second man took a tumble. Claire hoped both men were dead. The other men's horses whinnied in terror and whirled wildly, one of them rearing so high the rider couldn't hang on. He fell off his horse and the other three riders managed to dismount.

"That will hold them for a while," Two Wolves said quietly. "They will be afraid now to come closer. If we can hold out long enough, I might be able to pick them off. I would rather go down there and attack them the Cheyenne way and sink my hatchet into them!"

Claire panicked over the fear he just might try if he ran out of ammunition. She moved to his horse and rose just long enough to grab his Army supply bag. She yanked it off his horse and lay back down to rummage through it, finding the Army pistol.

"Have you ever shot a gun?" Two Wolves asked her.

"Yes–a six-gun and a rifle. My father took me hunting sometimes. He would let me practice with his rifle, and I even shot a deer once. I also practiced with my six-gun. Father thought I should know how to shoot for safety's sake."

Two Wolves watched the men approach. "They are off their horses and in the grass now. I think one of them is crawling to the side. He might try to sneak up here and get behind us."

They waited as the men below shouted to each other. Claire could only catch part of their words . . . "Redskin" . . . "murderin' sonofabitch" . . . "Rout him out of there" . . . "How many are there?" . . . "women and children" . . . "Hang his ass."

"There!" Two Wolves pointed. "One of them got back on his horse and is riding hard to our right."

He took careful aim and fired again. The man cried out and flew from his horse, which stumbled and fell from the jolt of the bullet hitting its rider. It rolled onto its back and on over on top of the rider.

"Fucking sonofabitch!" the man screamed. "My leg's broke!"

"Ain't leavin' 'til they're all dead!" someone yelled.

A volley of shots tore into the trees then, sending wood shrapnel flying all about them.

"Cover your eyes!" Two Wolves told the women. "And stay over the children!"

The shots came so fast and hard that he was unable to shoot back. Now Claire could see their attackers were crawling through the high grass, trying to come up the hill and get closer. Two Wolves fired several shots in return. Then came another volley of shots toward them, ripping and snapping through the trees. Claire's horse whinnied and reared, and she saw a piece of wood sticking into its neck. She shoved her pistol into the belt of her pants and jumped up. She ran to the horse and yanked out the piece of wood, afraid that if she left it in its neck the animal would keep wildly rearing and hurt one of the children or the wounded. The animal ran in another direction. Claire ducked back down when a bullet pinged against a tree so close that wood chips sprayed against her side. She winced with the stinging pain. She hurried back to where everyone was crouched in hiding near Two Wolves.

"Are you hurt?" Two Wolves asked while still watching the men below.

Claire looked down at her arm and brushed chips and dust from her clothing, relieved to realize nothing had penetrated her skin. "No." She laid over Little Dreamer while Sits-In-The-Night remained over Dancing Feet and her baby girl. He Sings crouched nearby, covering his ears and looking ready to cry.

"They will kill us all!" Sits-In-The-Night lamented.

Claire watched the trees above and behind them, afraid one or two of the men had gone unseen and might be coming at them from behind.

"Whoever is doing the shooting, come on out of there!" someone shouted from below. "We can tell by your tracks you have wounded along! If you have women and children, we will let them go!"

"I think you would not!" Two Wolves yelled back, firing several more shots, then letting out shrill war cries that made Claire shiver at the thought of what he was like as a warrior.

More shots came their way before things quieted again.

"You just one man up there?" one of their pursuers yelled.

Two Wolves did not answer. "Let them wonder," he said softly.

"There's a bounty on your scalps now!" another screamed. "Man, woman, kids–doesn't matter! If you're a true warrior, you will give yourself up. We will take only *your* scalp! Women and kids will go free!"

"They will never give up taking as many scalps as they can," Two Wolves told Claire. "Not when it involves money." He glanced at Claire. "Yours is the only one they will not take. Remember what I told you!"

Claire almost felt guilty for being white. "If they kill you, I will not deny you are my husband," she told him, "because I won't care if they kill me for it!"

"No! You *promised* me!"

Another volley of shots rang out and whipped through the trees again. Two Wolves made ready to shoot back, then hesitated. "More are coming from another direction!" he told Claire. She watched alongside him, and suddenly Two Wolves relaxed a little and lowered his rifle. "Soldiers!"

Claire strained to see better, wondering how he could tell. "What if they are the kind who also go after Indians? Maybe they'll join those men down there."

"It is possible." Two Wolves kept watching as men in uniform came closer at a hard gallop. The ranchers below stopped shooting. "At least the soldiers have taken their attention away from us for the moment. Stay here and stay low. I am going to get my Army trousers out of my gear." He left Claire, quietly telling Sits-In-The-Night and the children to stay put. He untied his supplies and took a pair of Army trousers from his gear, unlacing his buckskin leggings and trading them for the Army pants. He came back to Claire and watched what was happening below.

"All my gear and my weapons are Army issue, and I have my papers, but there are soldiers who would shoot before asking questions."

The soldiers reached the men below, and Claire could make out the words of one who demanded to know what was going on. The men below began yelling and pointing to where Two Wolves and the others were hidden in the trees. The leader of the soldiers turned and held his rifle high in a sign he meant no harm, then rode closer.

"Come down from there!" he shouted. "We won't let these men fire on you if you come down peacefully!"

"It's Major Ansley!" Two Wolves told Claire. He still did not stand up and make himself visible as he shouted back. "Major, it is I, Two Wolves! I have only women and children with me. Those men killed my cousin *O'Kohm* who had no weapon. *Okohm's* camp was *tiyospe*. We have a little boy and an old shaman with us who are wounded and need help!"

"Two Wolves!" The major lowered his rifle and turned to the men below. "Is that true? You attacked a peaceful Indian camp?"

"They were on King property!" one of them answered. "I'm Gary King. My pa owns this land, and we have a right to keep Indians off of it!"

"You're idiots!" Ansley looked up into the trees again. "Two Wolves, where in hell have you been? Come on down out of there."

Two Wolves looked at Claire. "Stay here for the moment. I will go first. I do not want those men to see you with us." He rose and started down.

One of the men below raised his rifle. Two Wolves ducked behind a tree. In the same moment, Ansley pointed his own rifle at the ranch hand.

"Fire that thing and you're *dead*! That man up there is one of the best scouts the U. S. Army has. Any of you shoots him will *hang* for it."

"He killed my *brother*!" the ranch hand answered.

"And your brother probably deserved it." Ansley kept his own rifle pointed at the man. "What's your name?"

"Rube. Just Rube."

"Well 'Just Rube,' hand over that rifle!"

"You can't take my gun!"

"The hell I can't! I can even *arrest* you if I want." Ansley turned to one of the other soldiers. "Take his rifle," he ordered.

"Yes, Sir." The soldier rode closer to Rube. "Better do what he says," he told Rube. "You'll get it back when we're through here."

Ansley turned to a third man. "Name?"

"John Hooker. I'm ranch foreman for Henry King, and those people up there illegally squatted on King's land. You know from our own governor's orders that we had every right to chase them off. We could have killed every one of them if we wanted to."

"And I'm sure that's exactly what you were trying to do!" Ansley chided.

The man Two Wolves had shot from his horse still lay in the distance screaming about a broken leg.

"Let me go help him," Rube asked the major.

"Go ahead." Ansley kept his eyes on John Hooker and Gary King. "You two had better also hand over your rifles."

"Bastard!" Gary King sneered as he handed his rifle to Ansley. Another soldier took Hooker's rifle.

"Well, now, aren't you and your cowboys here just the bravest, most honorable men who ever walked?" Ansley said. "It takes guts to attack women and children and old men. You should be very *proud.*"

Hooker glared at the major. "It's the *law*!"

"And you're nothing but cowardly, yellow-bellied murderers. I have a notion to hang every one of you."

"You'd be court martialed."

"It might be *worth* it." Ansley looked up into the trees again. "Come on down, Two Wolves!"

Two Wolves continued on foot down the steep hill and out of the trees, keeping his own rifle in hand. He glared at the attackers when he came closer. "I should kill every one of you," he growled.

"Two Wolves, give me your rifle before bad becomes worse here," Ansley ordered.

Two Wolves turned to Ansley, and in that moment even Ansley felt uncomfortable. He could see Two Wolves was still in a warrior mood. "It's all right, Two Wolves. Are you the only man up there?"

"I am, except for an old, dying shaman. It is as I told you. The rest are women and children, one of them a wounded little boy. There were others with us when these men attacked us the first time, but they headed south. I am taking my cousin's wife and children to the Northern Cheyenne."

"Well, now, Mister King," Ansley spoke up. "Looks like just one man was able to hold off all of yours. I would laugh at that if it weren't for how sad this whole situation is."

"He killed two of my men here today and wounded a third man!"

"In self-defense and in protecting women and children," Ansley reminded him. "Collect your dead men and the one that's hurt and get the hell back to your ranch."

"They killed *O'kohm*, who was unarmed," Two Wolves protested. "They severely wounded the shaman, and rode their horses over a four-year-old boy. They should *hang*!"

"Calm down, Two Wolves. You know Colorado would never stand for us even arresting these men, let alone hanging them."

"But they would easily hang *me* for nothing more than defending women and children. It is *wrong*!"

Ansley had never seen the scout this angry. He suspected the problem was that Claire Stewart was up in those trees with the other women and children.

Two Wolves cast Ansley a dark look of warning and the major realized he was trying to keep Claire out of sight. "I was bringing what is left of my family to the fort for help," he told Ansley.

Ansley nodded. "You know I have to let these men go. I have a right to break up this gun battle, but that's all I can do. I'm just glad I happened along. I was out here looking for you because you should have shown up at Fort Collins at least two days ago. I was getting worried."

"I will explain once these ranchers are out of my sight." Two Wolves looked at King. "I would like to plant a hatchet in your skull!"

"There! You see?" King told Ansley. "Scout or not, he's just a murdering warrior who has probably killed other innocent whites."

"No white man I ever killed was *innocent*!" Two Wolves growled back. He unexpectedly landed into King, grabbing him from his horse and throwing him to the ground. He pulled a hatchet from his weapons belt, but Ansley and two of his men were off their horses to stop it. It took all three to hold Two Wolves back while King rolled to his knees and stood.

"Damn it, Two Wolves, calm down!" Ansley warned. "Drop the goddamn hatchet before you do something I'll have to arrest you for!"

A panting Two Wolves jerked away and shoved the hatchet back into a loop on his weapons belt. "Leave now!" he told King. "And hope that we never run into each other again."

"You dirty savage!" King growled, rubbing at a scraped elbow from the fall.

"*You* are the savage! You are white trash and do not have an ounce of bravery in you. I will enjoy envisioning what the Cheyenne would do to you if they could. You would cry and beg like a *baby*!"

Ansley addressed King. "Get going before I decide to turn this man loose on you. I've seen what he can do, so I would suggest you get the hell out of here–*now*!"

King picked up his wide-brimmed hat that had fallen off when Two

Wolves jerked him from his horse. He glowered at Two Wolves a moment longer before telling his men to go pick up the dead and wounded.

"Give me my rifle," King told Ansley.

Ansley opened the rifle's chamber and began shaking out bullets until it was empty. "When you've gathered everything and are ready to leave you can have this back." He ordered his men to empty the other rifles.

A disgruntled King mounted his horse and the rest of his men began gathering bodies. They slung the dead over their horses, after which King demanded the return of their weapons. Disgruntled and angry, they finally left. Ansley ordered his men to follow them until they were well out of sight. They rode off, and Ansley pulled an angry Two Wolves aside.

"Is Claire up there?" he asked.

"*Aye.*"

"Where in hell have you been?"

"Her wound became infected. I wanted her to wait a few more days to leave the trading post, but she insisted on getting to the fort. We came across the Cheyenne hunting party and Claire was very sick. I had to bed her down and open the wound to drain the infection. The Shaman helped me with herbs and prayers. He is up there, wounded, probably dying. And my little second cousin, Dancing Feet, has broken ribs from one of those bastards riding his horse over him." Two Wolves clenched his fists. "I want to kill them all!"

"And you would *definitely* hang. Just come with us now. We'll go back to Fort Collins and talk about this. And we have to discuss what to do about Vince Huebner. You've got to calm down, Two Wolves. You might be our best scout, but you're also half Cheyenne. There is only so much I can do to protect you. If you go off on a killing spree, you'll be no safer than any other Cheyenne in this territory."

Two Wolves shook his hair behind his shoulders. "And I would be *proud*!" he sneered. He looked up into the trees. "All of you stay up there until the ranchers are out of sight," he called to Claire and the others. He turned back to Ansley. "There is something you should know."

Ansley folded his arms. "Something tells me it will make all this more complicated."

Two Wolves nodded. "I have made Claire Stewart my wife."

"Your *what*?"

"The Cheyenne way. She is my wife now. When we reach the fort, I wish to marry her by a Christian preacher. She would want that. But she is *mine*, Christian marriage or not. I was fighting mostly for *her*! If those men found her with us they would have treated her badly. You know what I am saying."

Ansley sighed, removing his hat and wiping at his sweaty forehead with the sleeve of his jacket. "I know exactly what you mean," he answered with an exasperated tone. He put his hat back on his head. "Two Wolves, sometimes I just don't know what to do with you. Do you understand how hard this will be for that girl? And it will make it harder for us to do something about Vince Huebner."

"We are not afraid. I love her, and she loves me."

Ansley studied the man a moment, having no trouble understanding why and how Claire Stewart had fallen in love with him. "It wasn't long ago that you told me you weren't in any hurry to get married."

Two Wolves finally grinned. "That was before I met Claire Stewart. I call her *Maeveksea*–Red Bird Woman."

"And when I spoke with her back at that trading post, she wasn't sure *what* she wanted. She was just anxious to get to the fort where she could think straight. What happened between then and now?"

Two Wolves glanced up into the trees where Claire still waited. "You would have to ask *her* that."

Ansley noted the proud, warrior stance the Indian seemed to take when making that remark. He shook his head. "Never mind. I think I *know* what happened."

"I do not take this lightly. I will always protect her," Two Wolves answered. "Which is why on our way back I do not want the other men to know what I have told you. They should not know until we marry the Christian way. My people understand and see us as man and wife, but I know how white men think. When your soldiers ride back here, do not say what I have told you until Claire and I can be married by a white preacher."

Ansley nodded.

"I will take good care of her."

"I'm sure you will." Ansley studied him closer. Two Wolves had removed the bandage from around his head. "That's a pretty bad cut. Did those men do that?"

"Aye, in the first attack, but I am fine. And *Maeveksea* is well now. We will both be glad to reach the fort. I will go up there now and bring her and the others down as soon as those ranchers are gone."

"Fine. Go back up there until we're ready to leave."

Two Wolves nodded. He glanced in the direction the attackers had ridden, then back at Ansley. "If you were not here, more of them would be dead. But I was one man alone and might have run out of ammunition before they did. I am glad you came along." He turned and headed back up the hill.

Ansley watched him with a heavy heart. He thought how all of this would have been easier if he didn't care for Two Wolves almost like a son. He couldn't help feeling sorry for the fact that the man had watched his father die at the hands of whites. His world was filled with enough tragedy. He'd only made it all worse by marrying Claire Stewart.

CHAPTER TWENTY-EIGHT

CLAIRE HATED THE FACT THAT none of the men who'd attacked and killed *O'Kohm* could be arrested and prosecuted. When they'd made ready to leave their hiding place in the foothills, they'd discovered the Shaman was dead. Major Ansley had waited while Two Wolves, with the help of some of the soldiers, secured the Shaman's body in a tree, refusing to allow the man to be put into the ground, away from the sun.

Claire easily understood her husband's torn feelings, and now she had to pretend she knew him no better than she knew any other Army scout who'd rescued her and was assigned to getting her to safety. She rode beside Major Ansley. Two Wolves stayed farther back with Sits-In-The-Night and her children.

Claire wondered, if she should die before Two Wolves, if he would bring her to the mountains and put her in the trees. She actually liked the idea of being buried in nature's beauty, facing the sun every day. So far what she knew of the Cheyenne culture, they had an unusually deep spirit connection to nature.

Two Wolves' horse loped up beside her then. Claire faced him, and she saw in his eyes he wanted to hold her as desperately as she wanted to be held. She had to look away so the men behind them wouldn't notice their true feelings.

"How are you feeling?" Two Wolves asked her.

"I'm all right. How is little Dancing Feet?"

"I think there are two ribs broken. He is very lucky the horse did not step on his head or break his legs or arms. He will heal, but he will not forget. It is things like this that turn boys into warriors." He turned his horse and rode back to Sits-In-The-Night, who remained stoically quiet. Claire had a feeling that if the woman were a man, she would have ridden south and joined those who would continue making war. Claire couldn't blame her.

"Are you sure about what you're doing?" Major Ansley asked, interrupting her thoughts.

Claire looked straight ahead. "I have never been more sure about anything."

"Have you considered how you're going to live out your lives?"

"We'll work it out."

"There will be children. You'll need to settle somewhere, which won't be easy for Two Wolves. You'll have to feed those children. There is no future with the Cheyenne now. You can't live all over the land, and Two Wolves can't go out hunting for your food. He will need a steady job. His pay as a scout won't support a family."

"I still have my freighting business."

"*Do* you? A lot of it was destroyed, and Vince Huebner will see to it that what's left is also destroyed once he learns you're still alive."

"Not if I can run *him* out of business."

"I've *seen* his business. I went to Denver City. Whoever you left in charge there has closed the doors and left. A lot of your inventory was stolen in that raid, and your wagons likely destroyed, and now you have no men left to help you. Once people find out about you and Two Wolves, you'll play hell finding more men to work for you."

"Thank you for the bright outlook for my future, Major."

Ansley shook his head. "Miss Stewart . . . or should I call you something else?"

"Apparently, I have to be addressed as Miss Stewart for now."

"I just want you to give things a lot of thought before you're legally married by a preacher. You can still get out of this, maybe move someplace back East and find work there, marry a white man."

Claire looked at him. "I can't believe what you're saying. I would never hurt Two Wolves like that, and you shouldn't want me to. I know you care about him."

"I'm saying it out of true concern because I like you and Two Wolves *both* very much. I don't want to see either one of you hurt, not just emotionally, but even physically, because that could very well happen."

"Major, surely you see what a good man Two Wolves is. He risked his own life to save mine three different times. And if you think he somehow coerced me, you're wrong. I willingly went to him. He's honest and strong and brave and intelligent and schooled and kind and devoted–"

"And he's extremely handsome."

Claire smiled. "There's that."

Ansley reached over and grasped her horse's bridle, pulling her farther from the rest of the riders. He faced her then. "In your eyes Two Wolves is a hero, and I guess I have to say he *is* one in many ways. And marrying you was probably more heroic than riding against the enemy. But he's a man who needs the sun and the stars and fresh air. Do you really think you can pin him to a house with four walls, and to a job among your kind?"

Claire studied the man's blue eyes, seeing genuine concern there. "You're forgetting he's half white, Major. He *has* lived among whites and inside four walls, for several years before his mother died."

"And he came back out here to get away from all that and live the way his heart tells him to live."

"And now his heart tells him he wants *me* as his wife, and he has told me he will do whatever it takes for us to be together."

Ansley removed his hat, a hot wind ruffling the thin hairs left on his head. "I just want you to be sure before there is no turning back."

"There is already no turning back, Major. I belong to Two Wolves in every sense. In his mind, we are already married, and I will not turn around and tell him I don't want this after all. It would break his heart, and being away from him would break *my* heart. We will face whatever we need to face *together*."

Ansley glanced over to see Two Wolves watching them. "Right now, I think your *husband* is thinking about coming over here and knocking my head off. He probably figures I'm trying to talk you out of this."

"He would never harm you. He likes you very much. Right now, he's just really upset about what happened to his cousin, and I don't blame him. They were peacefully camped when those men attacked."

Ansley put his hat back on. "I don't doubt that, Ma'am." He sighed. "And I didn't bring you over here because I think it's sinful that you would choose an Indian for a husband. On the contrary, I see every reason why a woman would be proud to be his wife. I just know how *others* will look at this—not everyone—but *most* people. I just would feel remiss if I didn't point out the problems you'll encounter. Personally, I hope you'll be very happy. I am going to try to find a way to help you out with this thing involving Vince Huebner."

Claire felt like crying. "Thank you, Major, for caring."

"You're one brave woman for your age and your size, I'll say that."

Claire smiled. "It's easy to be brave when Two Wolves is standing with you."

Ansley chuckled. "I agree. He saved my life once, and I saved his, so I guess we're even."

"He would probably say you are *not* even, because you saved both of us back there when you interrupted that attack. Two Wolves was standing them off all by himself. I'm not sure what would have happened if you hadn't come along."

Ansley turned his horse. "I'm not so sure it wasn't the other way around. Knowing Two Wolves and his skills, I might have saved those *ranchers*' lives." He smiled and rode away to catch up with his men.

Claire turned her horse to go back, but she noticed Two Wolves riding toward her. She waited, wishing she could reach out and let him take her onto his horse with him and wrap his arms around her. He halted his horse and just studied her for a moment.

"Did the Major change your mind, *Maeveksea*?"

Claire smiled, thinking how utterly handsome he looked, his long hair blowing in the wind, beaded bands on his biceps, a bone hair-pipe necklace against his chest, an array of weapons around his hips. He wore only a leather vest now, and his powerful arms and muscled chest were beautifully displayed in the sun. She felt a pull low in her belly just looking at him, finding it hard to believe the magnificent man before her had actually mated with her and made her his own.

"*No* one is going to change my mind, Two Wolves," she answered. "Get that through your head. I am your wife and I love you, and that's that. Everything else will work itself out."

He nodded, smiling. "When we reach the fort, I will find a way to be with you in the night, preacher or no preacher."

Claire smiled. "I look forward to it." She watched him ride away, then just sat there a moment watching the whole procession—blue-coated soldiers mixed with Cheyenne Indians, and one man riding with them who was a part of both worlds. "God, please keep us safe," she prayed.

CHAPTER TWENTY-NINE

UPON ARRIVING AT THE FORT, Claire was surrounded by the three soldiers' wives. In a flurry of introductions, she learned their names. Emily Sternaman, the young wife of First Lieutenant Robert Sternaman, held a baby in her arms as Claire dismounted. Sarah Flower, the wife of Captain Stephen Flower, led a three-year-old son down the steps of the veranda in front of Major Ansley's quarters. She greeted Claire with a smile and an exclamation that she would lend her a dress right away so she could "get out of those awful boy's pants" and the man's shirt that was a bit too big for her.

"Oh, my! She's wearing moccasins," Gertrude Becker commented. She was an older, very stout woman who was married to Sergeant First Class Harry Becker. "You poor thing! Major Ansley said he was going out to look for you and that you were wounded in some kind of attack." She glanced at Two Wolves. "Thank goodness you're all right," she told him. "But that looks like a bad cut on your forehead." She looked past him then. "And who are these Indians with you?"

"They are relatives. One little boy is hurt. He is my second cousin. White men attacked their camp, and one of them rode his horse over the boy."

All three women gasped.

Two Wolves dismounted and helped Sits-In-The-Night down from her horse, helping her remove the papoose from her back. He looked at Gertrude again. "I am hoping you will set aside prejudice and help this woman and her children. This is Sits-In-The-Night, and her husband, my cousin *O'Kohm*, was killed in the attack. The wounded boy is hers."

"Oh, well . . . of course," Gertrude told him. "Put them all up in the shed over by the horse corral. It's been recently cleaned out. The other women and I will bring food and the doctor over."

"I am grateful. When the boy is better, I am taking all of them north to join relatives there."

"What about you?" Gertrude asked again. "Do you need the doctor?"

"No. But one should tend to this woman here." He reached out and took Claire's arm. "She was very badly wounded by an arrow when I was taking her to a trading post. It later became infected. I had to reopen the wound myself to drain it. She needs much rest."

"We will take good care of her," Emily told him.

Two Wolves looked down at Claire. "These women will help you bathe and get you clean clothes and some food. I will take Sits-In-The-Night and get her and the children settled."

"Thank you." Claire tried to behave as formally as possible, but she hated the idea of truly being away from Two Wolves. He left with Sits-In-The-Night, and she wanted to run after him. Instead, she was invited into First Lieutenant Sternaman's quarters, where all three women doted on her. Sarah and Emily heated water and prepared a tin tub for her in a small bedroom off the main room. Sarah left with a promise to bring Claire a dress, and clean under-clothes. She promised to send the doctor over to check on her after he tended to the injured Indian boy.

Claire hardly had a chance to think straight. It was a struggle to hide her true feelings for Two Wolves as the women bombarded her with questions about her ordeal. She couldn't help tears as she bathed alone She realized that ever since he first rescued her from the supply train attack, Two Wolves had been by her side constantly. Being away from him now made her feel lonely and vulnerable.

She put on slips and a dress loaned to her, then looked in a mirror. She was actually surprised by her own figure. She couldn't wear a corset because of her still-healing wound, but even without it, her breasts filled the bodice of the dress nicely. She couldn't help the pleasant thought of how Two Wolves had touched them, tasted them. Of how beautiful he'd said she was. What would he think of how she looked in this dress? She had to admit to herself that it felt good to show off the true woman who usually hid behind men's clothes.

She took some combs Emily had given her and pulled back the sides of her thick curls, securing her hair in place. She figured she looked prettier than Two Wolves had ever seen her. She decided that if Two Wolves told her he liked her better in a dress, she would start wearing them.

Someone knocked on the door, announcing he was the doctor. Claire opened the door to a nice-looking man of perhaps thirty who introduced himself as Captain Edward Tower.

"Ma'am, the Major told me to check you over because of a grave wound you suffered."

Claire felt horribly self-conscious. Nor only had she expected a much older man, but she suddenly hated the thought of letting any man but Two Wolves look upon her. "I'm fine. I don't want a stranger checking me."

"Ma'am, I'm a certified, schooled doctor. I'm only here to help."

Claire couldn't help noticing the way he had looked her over when she first opened the door to him. "I don't know you, and I've been through a lot. Two Wolves took the arrow out of me and he saved me from dying from infection. I'm fine now. I don't want a stranger doctoring me."

Tower sighed. "Ma'am, Two Wolves is no doctor. I just want to make sure there is no more sign of infection."

"No. I'll let him look at it. He'll know." She turned away.

"But Two Wolves is an *Indian*. Surely you don't –"

"He's just a man, Captain Tower. And I was in a bad way." Claire watched out the window. "Two Wolves saved my life, more than once. He rescued me from men who intended to kill me. He saved me from a grizzly bear. He almost lost his life defending me against a Comanche man who meant to kill me, and then he took out that arrow himself because he knows about arrow wounds." She turned and faced the captain. "I'm fine now. The infection is gone and my wound is healing very nicely. And if you think it's terrible that I allowed an Indian to tend to my wound, he was all I had. Without him I would have been dead a good two weeks ago. Should I have died, rather than let an Indian man take care of me?"

Tower studied her intently. "You *care* about Two Wolves, don't you, as more than just an Indian scout?"

Claire realized she'd allowed her feelings to show through. She faced the corporal squarely. "That is a personal question, and it's none of your business. Thank you for offering to care for me, but I'm fine. You should go tend to that poor little Indian boy who has broken ribs from a *white* man trampling over him with his horse. He needs your help more than I do. And if you have anything to help the boy's mother sleep, be sure she gets it. Sits-In-The-Night has suffered greatly, losing her husband in that ugly attack, then being displaced from the life she knew and now worrying about her little boy. They are the ones you should tend to."

He nodded. "Fine. I might add that you need to be very careful and give a lot of thought to what you've been through. I can understand why you feel obliged to Two Wolves, but I don't need to put into words what it could mean if you let your feelings overcome common sense. Perhaps as you heal and get back into a normal life you will think more clearly."

Claire wanted to hit him. "Perhaps," she answered.

The doctor left, and Claire sat down on the bed, breaking into tears. She needed her husband. She took a deep breath and wiped away her tears, then walked to the door and into the main room of the small quarters. Emily was tucking her baby into a small bed with high sides. She straightened and looked at Claire.

"Captain Tower said you refused his help. You really should let him –"

"No," Claire interrupted her. "I'm fine. Really. I want to go and see how Sits-In-The-Night's little boy is doing. I saw where they were taken."

"Two Wolves said you should rest."

"I can't right now. I'm too concerned about the little boy."

"They're just Indians, Miss Stewart."

Claire was almost shocked to hear the words coming out of the mouth of the very pretty, seemingly gentle and likely Christian Emily Sternaman. "They are *people*. What if it was your little boy lying wounded and the only ones who could help were Indians? Wouldn't you want them to see you as just a mother needing help?"

"They would most likely be the *reason* my son lay wounded."

Claire shook her head. "Sits-In-The-Night is a woman, like you and me. She's a mother, like you. Are you Christian, Mrs. Sternaman?"

"Of course, I am."

"Then I don't think I need to tell you why I asked if you were."

Emily raised her chin. "Miss Stewart, every time my husband rides out of this fort I'm afraid for him because I've seen what Indians can do to a man. And if Two Wolves rescued you from some kind of attack, the details of which none of us knows, then you surely have a pretty good idea how they fight and how wild and ugly it can be. Surely when you were attacked you saw it with your own eyes."

Claire stepped closer. "I would have–if my attackers had been Indians. But they were *white*, Mrs. Sternaman. *White* men! And believe you me, they, too, can be wild and ugly. They meant to kill me, and the only man who was good and kind to me and risked his life to help me, not just then, but in other events on our way here, was *Two Wolves*!"

"White men? You can't be sure –"

"I'm *damn* sure! White men are out there attacking their own kind just to blame it on the Cheyenne so they will be hated even more and run out of Colorado! Those Indians in the shed are part of a band who saved my life when I was dying from infection. And if we hadn't needed to stop and stay with them because I was so sick, they might have moved on sooner and avoided that attack. Sits-In-The-Night's husband and an old Shaman might still be alive now, and she wouldn't have to uproot herself and her children and flee north. And Two Wolves wouldn't have to *take* them and risk his life yet again protecting them on the way! I feel somewhat responsible for what happened, and I am going over there to help because it's the Christian thing to do."

Claire headed for the door.

"Miss Stewart!"

Claire hesitated.

"You're *sure* it was white men?"

Claire turned to face her. "I told you so. I wouldn't lie about something like that. I *saw* them! I heard them talking about what they were going to do with me. I was hiding under sacks of potatoes. I was scared to death of those white men, but once I got to know Two Wolves I was never once afraid of him, or afraid of those Indians who helped us." The tears wanted to come again, but Claire angrily wiped them away. "Thank you so much for the bath and the clean clothes. I'm very grateful. But I think it's best I go and stay with Sits-In-The-Night and her son tonight. Right now, Two Wolves and I are apparently the only friends she has. Tomorrow the major can decide where I will stay while Two Wolves takes his relatives north. You have a husband, and I'll be in the way if I stay here." Claire opened the door. "I'll be back for the rest of my things."

Claire hurried out and marched toward the shed where Sits-In-The-Night and the others had been taken. A couple of soldiers whistled at her, and one who crossed her path tipped his hat to her.

"Ma'am, you headed for that shed? You ought not to go over there. There's Indians in there."

"A woman and children, and the woman helped save my life. Why should I be afraid of them?"

Claire just kept walking while on the inside she wanted to run. Before she reached the shed the doctor came out, hesitating in the doorway when he saw her coming.

Claire stopped to look up at him proudly. "I'm going to see Sits-In-The-Night."

"You should be resting."

"I can't rest until I see how they are doing. How is the boy?"

"A couple of broken ribs. I gave him some Laudanum. He'll hurt for a few more weeks, but he's in no danger. He's very lucky."

Claire nodded. "Thank you for helping him."

Captain Tower frowned. "Ma'am, you really shouldn't –"

"I wish people would quit telling me what I should and shouldn't do. I'll be fine, Captain. I'm tired of constantly having to tell people that."

Tower shook his head. "At least don't be walking all over the place unescorted, especially at night. There are a lot of men here who haven't seen a pretty, unattached woman in a long time."

"Are you telling me I should be afraid of my own kind? I'm not afraid of those Indians in there. Why should I be afraid of these soldiers?"

Tower closed his eyes in chagrin. "You got me on that one." He smiled a little. "I can see you're a woman who does what she damn well pleases. Just be wise in your choices, Miss Stewart."

The corporal walked off, and Claire hurried inside. She'd barely gotten out of the sunlight and out of sight of the soldiers when Two Wolves grabbed her and pulled her into the shadows.

"Two Wolves!" Claire threw her arms around him and he embraced her fully.

"*Maeveksea!*" He kissed her hair. "How I have longed to hold you."

"Don't let go." Claire broke into tears.

Two Wolves carried her deeper into a corner of the shed. Claire looked up at him and in the next moment his warm, full lips were tasting her mouth as he embraced her so tightly it almost hurt. He raised her up slightly so she could rest her head on his shoulder, her feet off the ground. She breathed deeply of his now-familiar scent, hugging him even tighter around the neck. "I want to be with you tonight, Two Wolves, not with strangers."

They kissed again, a heated, delicious kiss that caused a desperate, erotic need to rip through Claire.

"We will find a way." Two Wolves spoke the words in a voice husky with need.

"Promise me," Claire whispered.

"I promise, *Maeveksea*. For now, you must go back."

"I want so much to stay with you."

"I will come to you tonight." He kissed her again, in a way that seemed like he was making love to her with his mouth. "I saw you coming," he whispered. "You look so beautiful in the white woman's dress."

"I wouldn't let that doctor look at me, Two Wolves. I want only you to take care of me."

"I am glad he did not touch you." He lowered her to her feet, grasping her arms. "You should not stay here too long alone. And we cannot do this here. Someone might come. If I hold you any longer or kiss you one more time I will be tempted to drag you into the hay in the corner and mate with you. It would be very hard for you if we were caught."

"That corporal already suspects I'm in love with you."

"It is better, then, that you leave here quickly."

"But I want to be with Sits-In-The-Night, too."

"She will be fine, and the boy is better. Go, now. I need to wash and change before I see you again. I will see you tonight, and then we will talk tomorrow with the Major. I will take Sits-In-The-Night north, and when I come back we will legally marry. And we will settle things over your attack for once and for all. For now, you must leave here. Go and see the sergeant's wife, Gertrude Becker. Most call her Gertie. I spoke with her when she brought food for Sits-In-The-Night. She is a wise woman and has always been kind to me. Her children are grown, so she has none to keep her busy. She will welcome your company and give you something to eat and will tell you where you will stay tonight. Trust me in this. I will come to you later tonight."

Claire wiped at tears and nodded, feeling better at his reassuring words. She grasped his hand and leaned down to kiss it, then turned away, walking over to Sits-In-The-Night and embracing her. "God be with you and your children. I hope you make it safely to your relatives in the North."

Sits-In-The-Night nodded. "And I hope you and Two Wolves can find your own happiness. You are my sister now, *Maeveksea.* May the Great Spirit bless you and keep you safe."

Claire glanced at Two Wolves once more as she patted the sides of her hair and tightened the combs there. She smoothed her dress and walked out, feeling stronger after just being in his arms. She was never more sure how much she loved him. She couldn't imagine how they could be together tonight, but he'd promised they would be, and she took hope in that promise.

CHAPTER THIRTY

"**Y**OU'RE NOT EATING MUCH, DEAR."

Claire glanced across the table at Gertrude Becker. The hefty, big-bosomed woman looked truly concerned, her blue eyes showing kindness.

"I'm not very hungry," Claire answered. "My life has been turned upside down the last couple of weeks. At least I think that's how long it's been. I've lost all track of time."

Gertrude smoothed back stray gray strands of hair that had fallen from a bun on top of her head. "Can I help?"

After earlier remarks from others, Claire wasn't sure what to tell the woman, but Two Wolves claimed she was kind. Her husband, Sergeant First Class Harry Becker, was outside barking drills, so they were alone.

"I can tell you that I own a freighting business in Denver. I ran it by myself after my father died. Most women don't like me much because I don't even wear dresses most of the time and they consider what I do as something only for men." She picked at some boiled potatoes on her plate. "At any rate, I might not have anything left. I was taking a big load of supplies to Bent's Fort when we were attacked. All my men were killed." She met the woman's gaze. "It wasn't Indians that attacked us, Gertrude. It was white men."

The woman frowned. "Please, call me Gertie. And Emily told me about your claim."

"I *want* others to know it. White men are raiding and blaming it on the Cheyenne. It's not fair. I know the Indians have raided and killed, but it's because of broken treaties and things like what happened to the small camp where Two Wolves took me because I had a bad infection. Those ranchers had no reason to attack the Cheyenne who were there. They were camping peacefully and not harming a thing. I'm sure you and most of the other women and men here probably hate the Cheyenne. But I've seen another side to them. I intend to go to the authorities in Denver City and tell them what I know about these false attacks."

Gertie leaned back in her chair. "That's very risky, Claire. Do you have any proof beyond just your word?"

Claire shrugged. "Why would a white woman make up something like that? I heard them. I saw them. And they talked about the man behind it, who happens to be someone I actually know. He's in Denver City. I can name names."

"Major Ansley told me quite a bit before he left to find you," Gertie told her. "He trusts me, so don't worry that anything you tell me will go any farther. He pulled me aside when you went to Emily's to clean up and told me about you and Two Wolves."

Claire looked at her in surprise. "But Two Wolves doesn't want —"

"Don't worry." Gertie reached over and patted her hand. "I've told no one, although not many miss the way you look at Two Wolves. And, my dear, although most look at him as Indian, he *is* half white, and you have every right to love him. He's a fine man. He does a loyal and thorough job of scouting, and he saved my husband's squad once when he detected a planned Indian attack that would have trapped them in a canyon. In another battle, he saved Major Ansley from a warrior who was headed to land a hatchet into the major's back. I don't doubt you saw his prowess with your own eyes. And I am guessing that since Two Wolves was your only friend and protector the last couple of weeks, it was easy to fall in love with him." She patted Claire's hand.

"He was kind and caring, and he took an arrow out of me and nursed me practically like a mother. He never left my side. And now he's all I have left."

Gertie nodded. "It's easy to see why you would feel that way." She scooted back her chair and rose, walking around behind Claire and resting her hands on her shoulders in a motherly fashion. "Is it true you are in most respects married to Two Wolves?"

Claire hesitated, not sure whether the woman approved or disapproved.

"Yes," she answered. "We intend to be married the Christian way when the traveling preacher comes. We will have to wait until Two Wolves takes his cousin's wife and children north to family there. I'm scared something will happen to him on the way and I won't ever see him again." She fought tears at the thought.

Gertie gently squeezed her shoulders in a reassuring gesture. "You're very brave, Claire. There is nothing wrong with loving a good man, but we both know how some look at such a thing. You come to me any time you need a shoulder to cry on, Claire. How long has it been since you had a mother?"

"Twelve years. All I had was my father after that, but now he's gone, too, along with a couple of good, protective friends who were among the men who worked for me."

Gertie sighed and pressed her shoulders once more before walking back around the table and sat down again, smiling. "Well, now, I am going to tell you something that will cheer you up, my dear."

Claire brightened. "What's that?"

An almost girlish, teasing look came into Gertie's eyes. She leaned back and folded her arms. "Major Ansley's quarters are in the only two-story building here at the fort. His wife is back East, and he saves the upper room for military guests. He said you could stay there tonight. I have a feeling you will get a visitor after dark. I've already taken your supplies over there. The major and I both had a feeling you'd be uncomfortable staying with Emily or Sarah or even me, because we have husbands, and the other women have children to boot. Lord knows these living quarters are small enough that anyone extra is a problem. Ansley has his own room behind his office, so no one will bother you upstairs."

Claire felt her face flush. It was impossible to hide her excitement that she might be able to be with Two Wolves tonight. She smiled and looked down at the plate of food she still had hardly touched. "Thank you for understanding."

"Well, child, I might be an old woman, but I *am* a woman, and I remember being young and in love. And no one will know it if you do have a visitor. Two Wolves is, after all, half Indian, and Indians are very good at not being seen when they don't want to be seen . . . or heard. That's why they are so good at surprise attacks. Two Wolves has learned their ways to the greatest detail. You just remember that his Indian half has a wild, restless heart. It won't be easy for him to settle into a life of order that includes some kind of job to support a family, but he'll do it— for you. I can see the goodness in him, and occasionally I get a glimpse of the young white man who went to school in Chicago and knows how to live that way. Don't give up on that side of him."

"I love *both* sides of him."

"I'm sure you do." Gertie rose, picking up her plate. "And I'm not letting you go over to Major Ansley's until you eat more of that food.

You need rest and nourishment to truly get all your strength back. You will need it for what lies ahead. You and Two Wolves have some big decisions to make, especially this thing about going to Denver City and accusing white men of raids. I hope the major goes with you because it will be very dangerous for Two Wolves to go into that lion's den."

Claire nodded. "I know. If it was just me I might back down, but Two Wolves rescued me because he was out there watching for raids so he could prove they were happening. He's determined to expose the men responsible and show Denver City that not all the attacks are by the Cheyenne."

"Well, God bless the both of you." Gertie carried her dishes to a wash pan. "Now, finish those potatoes and those cooked carrots. I hope I've made you feel better so you can eat."

"Yes, Ma'am."

"Gertie. Just call me Gertie," the woman reminded Claire.

Claire smiled at Gertie's kindness. Suddenly she was very hungry.

CHAPTER THIRTY-ONE

CLAIRE TOOK THE COMBS FROM her hair and changed out of her dress into a night gown Emily had given her. The sun had long set behind the mountains and her hopes began to fade that Two Wolves would really be able to join her. Maybe he'd changed his mind, thinking it was for her own good. She walked to a window that looked out upon the fort's parade ground, where a few men stood sentry. Through a crack in the floor she could tell it was dark downstairs. Major Ansley was likely asleep in the back room of his quarters. The small two-story building was quiet. She turned, then gasped at the sight of a man standing in the room.

It was Two Wolves. He put a finger to his lips. "Close the shutters and dim the lantern," he said softly.

Claire obeyed, feeling light-headed at his almost-frightening entry, for she'd not heard a thing. She hurried to him on bare feet then, and he swept her into his arms.

"I never heard a thing!" she whispered.

"I am an Indian, remember? I can move with no sound." He met her mouth with a hungry kiss, at the same time leaning down a little to pick her up in his arms and carry her to the bed. He laid her on it, moving on top of her at the same time. "The major left one window open a crack," he whispered as he nibbled teasingly at her neck. "I told you we would be together tonight. I keep my promises. And I am hungry for you, *Maeveksea.*"

"I hated that I couldn't be with you these last two days," Claire whispered in reply. "I love you so, Two Wolves. I want to be with you all the time. How will I sleep without you holding me?"

"Tonight I *will* hold you. All night."

Their need was so intense that all talking stopped for the moment.

Two Wolves wore only a vest over his powerful torso. He raised to his knees and removed it, throwing it to the floor. He pushed Claire's gown up and over her breasts, noticing she wore nothing under it. He grinned. "You *were* expecting me."

"You said you would come, and I believed you."

Two Wolves hovered over her, his long hair brushing against her face. "You looked so beautiful today in that dress. I have never seen you that way."

"Then I will start wearing dresses."

"I prefer that you wear nothing at all." He leaned closer, devouring her mouth with tender kisses, searching suggestively with his tongue.

Claire closed her eyes as he moved downward then, tasting her breasts as though they were delicious, ripe fruits, licking his way down over her belly, bringing out a boldness that only a few days before she'd never dreamed she was capable of showing. He gently pushed her legs apart as his mouth found the ripe mound that was swollen with a desire to be touched and tasted and teased.

"Try not to cry out," he said softly.

Claire found the order difficult to obey as his tongue slicked into her folds and inside her, making her squirm with aching needs. He grasped her hips and softly groaned as he worked her into utter ecstasy. She felt herself floating from reality into a realm of erotic satisfaction. She pushed against him, wanting all he could give, until there came the shivering, sweet explosion she'd felt that first night, a dreamy, exotic fulfillment that made her want to scream his name.

Two Wolves kissed his way back over her body, and she felt him fumbling with his Army pants. In the next moment, he shoved his fullness into her, making her gasp with its size. She realized that in desperate need a man could be even bigger than normal, and she took great satisfaction in the fact that it didn't hurt at all this time. It was a feeling she wished she could experience all day long. She could taste herself in his wild kisses, and she found herself arching up to him, moving in perfect rhythm until his life spilled into her. He rose then and completely undressed while Claire did the same.

Completely naked, they joined bodies again. They kissed, tasted, breathed deeply of each other's breath and scent, touched amid whispers of loving and adoring. They made love and made love and made love, hardly able to get enough of each other.

"I will plant my seed deep so that you will remember when I am gone.

Perhaps my son already grows in your belly," he told her.

He raised up and lifted her hips in order to penetrate her as deeply as possible. Claire struggled not to scream out his name. She pulled a pillow over her face to muffle the cries coming rhythmically with his every thrust. Waves of heated pleasure moved through her. He leaned down then, wrapping his arms fully under her back as he finished with her once again.

Claire felt deliciously worn out. Utter exhaustion brought them to fall asleep in each other's arms. Then some time deeper in the night Claire felt her husband moving inside her again. She thought what a pleasant way this was to be awakened from a dead sleep. This time was more gentle and full of soft whispers and no foreplay. None was needed. The pleasure came simply from being united again in the way God meant for a man and woman to join souls, to give and take and share their love. Claire buried her face in her husband's neck as he grasped her bottom in his hands and pushed deep. She felt his life spill into her yet again, and she prayed his child was already forming deep inside her body.

Two Wolves settled beside her then, both of them tired yet wide awake. Claire stared at the ceiling as she settled into the crook of his arm. "I don't even know how old you are."

He pulled the blankets over them and turned on his side, moving one leg over hers. "I am twenty-nine summers. How many are you?"

"Twenty."

He kissed her hair. "Are you all right? I was so hungry for you that perhaps I hurt you."

"I'm fine. It was all wonderful."

Two Wolves grinned, gently caressing one of her breasts. "No pain from your wound?"

"No." Claire rubbed at his powerful forearm. "Tell me about your mother. What was life like in Chicago?"

He didn't answer right away.

"Did I say something wrong?"

"No. Sometimes the memories are hard."

"I'm sorry."

He kissed her hair again. "My mother was beautiful, like you. She had dark hair, but in the sun you could see the red in it. She told me many times how my father rescued her from Pawnee Indians who had killed her whole family in a raid and were going to sell her to Comancheros. They are men–Indian and white alike–who sell women and horses and anything else they can steal, usually to Mexicans. She was afraid of my father at first, but she soon learned he meant her no harm. She was only fourteen. He kept her because he was fascinated by her beauty. He took her to his wives, and she began learning the Indian way and helped them with their duties collecting wood and tanning hides and making clothing and moccasins. When she was sixteen he took her for a wife. She told me she was willing because by then she was in love with the great warrior who'd saved her from hell. After that she became his only wife. The others were older and could no longer bear children."

"And they didn't mind?"

"It is the Indian way–to preserve the clan."

"I hope you know I would never tolerate your taking a younger wife when I'm too old to give you children." Claire could feel his grin.

"That will not happen. I am more white than you think when it comes to certain customs." He kissed her hair. "I was eight when the soldiers came in the night, using their howitzers to blow up *tipis*."

Claire felt him stiffen a little, sensed his anger over the memory.

"Many died, including my father," he continued. "When the soldiers saw that my mother was white, they took her, claiming she was surely an abused, unwilling captive. They were going to leave me behind, but she screamed and begged to keep her son with her. I hated the soldiers then, and I deeply grieved my father, as did my mother. The soldiers took us to a fort. I have no memory of where we were. I only remember being put on a train and going to a white man's city. Everything there was so different. Such filth and bad smells and so much noise. Our lives were completely changed. We were sent to a missionary home, and from there we went to live in Chicago with my mother's brother, who was a preacher. He was kind to us."

Two Wolves stretched out on his back beside her then. "My mother began gradually returning to the life she once knew. They cut my hair and made me wear white boys' clothing. I guess I looked mostly like a white boy tanned from the sun. I already knew English, but I was still shunned by other white children in school. I often got into fights with them, not because of names they called me but because of names they called my mother. She finally took me out of the public schools and hired a tutor. I learned to read and write and learned white man ways ..."

He paused. Claire could tell that the memory was becoming more difficult for him to talk about. He breathed a deep sigh before continuing.

"But in the night, I could see my father lying dead." His hold on her tightened. "And I could hear the drums in my dreams. Feel their rhythm. See the warriors dancing around a campfire, singing songs of war and of Mother Earth and *Maheo*. I always knew part of me could never be white."

He swallowed and didn't speak for several seconds. Claire waited for him to continue, suspecting there was more but that it was hard for him to tell it. "My mother finally re-married. I was seventeen when she died of pneumonia. In the city, she was all I had. I knew I could not stay there after that and keep living like a white man. I longed to re-join my father's people, so I left, and I never went back, but it hurt to know I would never see my mother again. I found my father's family and for almost three years lived only with the Cheyenne. I fasted and had a vision. I saw two wolves, one white and one red, and a voice told me they would always be pulling at me like wolves gnawing at a fresh kill. Thus, I took the name Two Wolves, and I chose to suffer the Sun Dance to prove my Cheyenne blood and to forever be a part of them."

He just lay there then, holding her close. Claire sensed that wild side of him, wondered if she could truly hold this man to her world. She feared she could lose him to the wind and earth and a culture she would never fully understand. She could only pray that God would give her the strength and wisdom to understand his ways and find a happy medium that would help them stay together.

"How did you end up scouting for the Army?" she asked softly.

Leaning over, he kissed her cheek. "I remembered the city, and the fact that there are as many whites as there are stars and that they have industry and knowledge and superior weapons. I am not ignorant of the fact that more will come . . . and more and more . . . and the Indians are in their way. I know that the Cheyenne way of life will someday end. I tried to decide how I could live in both worlds and how I might help the Cheyenne learn to live another way and understand it is useless to fight what is coming. I volunteered to scout for the Army, hoping to be a peace-keeper. I endured the sneers and remarks from soldiers, but I soon earned their respect for my scouting and fighting abilities."

"When you saved them from an attack at a canyon? Gertie told me about that."

"*Aye*. They would have all been killed. I earned their friendship, but there are some here who will always see me as just a half-breed. Some think that is worse than being all Indian. It is usually the new ones who come here and don't know me who treat me with fear and disrespect.

But Major Ansley and most of the others see me as just a friend. While I am gone taking Sits-In-The-Night to her relatives in the North, the major will make sure you are safe. I will not worry."

Claire turned and wrapped her arms around him again. "I don't want you to go. *This* is where I feel safe–right here in your arms. But I feel so sorry for Sits-In-The-Night and I know she surely wants to be with loved ones where she is safest. Please be careful, Two Wolves."

He moved on top of her again. "You know I will be careful, because I will be anxious to get back to you. I must leave you before light so that no one sees me. When I return, we will marry your way. I want to wait until then because if you marry me before I leave, those here who still believe only loose white women lie with Indians will harass and abuse you, married or not. I do not want any of them to know about us until I return and can always be at your side.

"I'll be so lonely when you're gone."

Two Wolves leaned closer and kissed her tenderly as he moved between her legs. "You will stay right here above the major's quarters. You will be safe. And if you want to be with me, just close your eyes and feel my arms around you, as I will feel you with me."

"I'm scared you'll be attacked and won't make it back."

"Is your husband not a warrior? Have you not already seen how I can take care of myself?"

Claire smiled through tears. "I most certainly have."

"Do not fear for me, *Maeveksea*. All I will think about is coming back to you. That will give me strength and speed."

Claire ran her fingers along his hair, pulling it toward her. "I'll dream about you every night."

"And I will feel you beneath me in my own dreams." Two Wolves entered her again as though it was as natural as breathing. With each breath, he pushed in sweet rhythm. Claire felt lost beneath his big frame, loving him for how gentle he was with her in spite of his strength. They enjoyed the heady heights of mating for several long beautiful minutes before they fell into a second sleep.

When Claire awoke, the sun was streaming through the upstairs window. Two Wolves was gone. She never even knew he'd left.

"Two Wolves," she whispered. "God be with you." She pulled the extra pillow against her and wept.

CHAPTER THIRTY-TWO

"ARE YOU STILL SURE ABOUT going after Vince Huebner, Claire? As soon as Two Wolves returns, we need to decide what we will do."

Claire sat next to Major Ansley on the boardwalk in front of his quarters. It had been over two weeks since Two Wolves left to take his family north. The major felt he should be back by now and Claire was worried. Anything could have happened. Knowing it was legal to shoot an Indian on sight made her feel ill.

"I still want to expose Vince for what he is, but I'm afraid it could be bad for Two Wolves," she answered. Since my eyes have been opened to how much hatred there truly is out here for the Indians, and apparently worse for half-breeds, I'm afraid for him to go to Denver City."

"You won't change his mind. He's been trying to prove what's going on ever since he came here wanting to scout for us. Marrying you won't make a difference. And if you don't go with him—and he'll give you that choice—he'll go alone."

"No! He shouldn't!" Claire straightened, looking pleadingly at the major. "Can you go with us, bring some extra men to protect Two Wolves?"

"Of course I will. I wouldn't think of letting either of you go there alone. And with or without Two Wolves, you will be in danger yourself. You're our star witness."

"If anyone will believe me." Claire leaned back in her chair. "I wasn't the most popular woman in Denver, Major. Women are supposed to be teachers and seamstresses and hat makers, not run a freighting business."

Ansley grinned. "You are quite something, Claire. For the spit of a woman you are you sure have spunk, and you're braver than you realize."

Claire stared at the little flowers sewn onto the dress she'd borrowed from Emily. "I'm braver when Two Wolves is with me." Her eyes teared. "I miss him so much. What if he doesn't make it back?"

"Knowing you're waiting for him?" Ansley chuckled. "He'll make it back, all right, and eventually you'll both leave, and I will miss you very much. You're a good cook, and my quarters have never been cleaner or more orderly. I'll also dearly miss your help with my laundry."

"Those are the only reasons?" Claire asked teasingly.

"Of course not. It's been nice having someone to talk to. And I'll miss Two Wolves something awful. He does a great job, and I'm very fond of him. I see that kind of lost little boy look in his eyes sometimes. He hides it well, but he's a very torn young man. I think you've helped him decide which life he's going to follow from now on."

Claire picked up some lemonade she'd made earlier. "I just want him to be happy." She took a sip.

"From what I could tell he's happier than he's been in a long time." Ansley rose. "And you should get your mind off your worries. The men are holding a big pig roast and dance tomorrow night. I hope you'll be there. Let some of them dance with you. I promise I'll make sure they are respectful. Right now, they think you're just resting here to heal and then will be on your way to Denver City. They know you're friends with Two Wolves, but they think it's just because he rescued you. I don't think they know there is more to it, and it's best that way until he gets back. Captain Tower suspects. He talked to me about it. I gave him strict orders to keep his mouth shut. He's single and interested in you, but I told him you've been through enough and aren't open to courting. He's a good man and a good doctor, and part of me wants to advise you to give some thought to letting yourself consider marrying white."

Claire shook her head. "I've given Two Wolves my heart and my soul. I have no interest in considering anyone else. And for all I know . . ." She felt color coming into her cheeks. "I could be carrying Two Wolves child. No white man would ever accept that."

Ansley sighed. "Well, to keep the gossip down until things are legal, I would go to that dance if I were you, and I would accept dances from the men. Have some fun, Claire. I have a feeling you've never gone to a dance or given consideration to any other man even before you met Two Wolves. Even wearing that dress feels foreign to you, doesn't it?"

Claire nodded. "Two Wolves said I looked pretty in a dress, so I don't mind wearing one. They just aren't practical for the kind of business I'm in."

Ansley folded his arms. "Have you thought about what you're going to do about the business? How you and Two Wolves will live a normal life? You certainly can't go running around living in *tipis* with the Cheyenne."

"We'll work it out. If I can bring down Vince Huebner I can have his share of customers and can get on my feet again. I can't think of anyone better than Two Wolves to help me run my business. He's educated, and Lord knows he'd be great riding shotgun for me. And since he speaks both languages and knows the Cheyenne well, he could dicker with them and perhaps make sure I'm never attacked. If people in Denver City don't like us, I couldn't care less. They'd soon find out the kind of man Two Wolves is, and even if not, they'll need my business whether they like me or not. It won't matter."

Ansley's eyebrows shot up. "Well, now, you *have* been thinking about things." He lit a cigar. "I think Two Wolves has found his equal. I think you're strong enough to stand up to him and stand *with* him against whatever comes along."

"I'll certainly try."

"By the way, I need to write to my wife. I'm terrible at writing and wonder if you will help me. I'll tell you what to say."

"I'd like that! Why doesn't she come out here with you, Major?"

He puffed on the cigar. "In case you haven't noticed, I'm not a young man, which means Pearl is not a young woman. Life is hard enough out here on *younger* women. My wife used to follow me around wherever I was stationed, but it just got too hard. Quite a few years ago she lost a baby, and that kind of topped things off. She was never really well after that, so I sent her back to relatives in Ohio. I only have a year left in the army. When I'm retired from this damn job, that's where I'll be going." He puffed the cigar again. "And I want you and Two Wolves to remember that if things get too hard for you out here, you can come to Ohio and we'll help you settle. You'd be accepted, and truth be told, Two Wolves can be very white when he wants to. He has an education, and I've seen him in full dress uniform. It's quite a transformation, except for that long hair. He refuses to cut it."

"I'm glad. I like his long hair." Claire also rose. "Thank you, Major, for the offer about Ohio, and for putting me up here. The other women are more friendly now, but I still feel their silent disapproval of my opinion that white men could be attacking their own kind."

Ansley stretched and got up from his chair. "They'll find out the truth eventually. Let's go inside, dear. It's getting a little chilly out here. I don't want Two Wolves coming back to find you ill."

Claire followed Ansley inside, praying Two Wolves hadn't run into any trouble. He should have been back by now. She couldn't think of a better way to get warm on a chilly night than to lie in her husband's arms.

CHAPTER THIRTY-THREE

AFTER COOKING AND BAKING WITH the other women most of the day before and part of the morning of the pig roast, Claire joined in the annual event. The men themselves roasted the pig and the mess cook provided even more food. After spending half the day eating, everyone felt properly stuffed and ready to work off the big meal through a dance. The men dragged a piano from the mess hall, and two men with fiddles joined the piano player in providing the music. Whoops of joy were mixed with laughter as couples whirled around on a raised wooden dance floor the men had built for the occasion.

Tables made of wooden planks laid over saw horses were still covered with left-over food. Claire had baked two cakes for the occasion and was glad for the distraction of the entire event. It helped divert her worries over Two Wolves still being gone. She had actually enjoyed the company of the other women as they cooked and baked. Most were friendly and accepting now that she was fully rested and recovered. She suspected that, in their minds, she had finally come to her senses about the raids and about Two Wolves. Nearly every woman there mentioned she looked much better and encouraged her to dance with some of the men. Emily even mentioned that she was sure Captain Tower had a romantic eye for her.

Claire refused to reply to the remark. She hated keeping her secret, and she knew Emily and Sarah would likely shun her once Two Wolves was back and their true relationship was revealed. The only genuinely accepting and understanding woman there was Gertie Becker.

The wait was wearing on her. What if Two Wolves didn't make it back? She had to go on somehow, and she remained determined to bring out the truth about Vince Huebner and raids by white men. She owed it to Two Wolves and the Cheyenne. She also owed it to her father and the business Huebner was trying to take from her. Somehow, she would find a way to face Vince Huebner even without Two Wolves. The thought was daunting, but she wouldn't be able to live with herself without telling people what she knew, whether they believed her or not.

She stood beside the major as the little group of musicians began playing a waltz. Lieutenant Sternaman, Captain Flower and Sergeant First Class Becker allowed their wives to dance with some of the other men. Gertie, in spite of being older and much more stout, truly seemed to enjoy herself and didn't miss one dance. Some of the men rousingly cavorted around the dance platform with each other.

Although she hated it, Claire accepted a few requests for a dance just to please the major, who wanted to continue stilling any gossip that might linger about her and Two Wolves. Some of the men there were travelers who'd stopped at the fort. Two in particular worried Claire. They'd arrived the day before claiming to be heading back East after failed efforts at gold mining in the Rockies. They stayed an extra night for the dance and feasting, and though they seemed friendly enough, dancing with them made Claire uncomfortable, knowing Vince Huebner could be searching for her. Did they know him? It seemed to her they asked too many questions. One of them mentioned that one of the soldiers said she'd owned a freighting business in Denver and that her supply train had been attacked. He seemed to press for more information.

"I'd rather not talk about it," she told him, afraid to give details. "It was a terrible experience."

"How on earth did you get away, if I might ask."

"It doesn't matter. It's over now."

"Well, Miss Stewart, I'm sorry about what happened. You seem to be doing well now."

"Yes, I am, thank you." *Do you know Vince Huebner?* She wanted to demand an answer. *Why are you really here?* She decided she would mention her concerns to Major Ansley when the dance was over.

Most of her dances were with Captain Tower, which was a relief from having to dance with the two strangers, even though Tower kept making obvious attempts at wooing her.

"You look well," he told her now. "How much longer will you be staying here at the fort?"

"I'm not sure," she answered. "I have to go back to Denver City and see what's left of my freighting business. I don't know if I can ever recover from the attack."

Tower smiled. He was a handsome man in his own right, shorter than Two Wolves but well-built and well spoken. His dark hair was neatly combed and oiled, and his blue eyes showed kindness. "Then maybe it's time you settled down and took a husband."

I have a husband, she wanted to answer.

"Captain, why do men think a woman is helpless without a husband?" She asked aloud. "I worked alongside my father for years and took over his business when he died. I'm not a woman to sit home knitting and baking."

"I didn't mean to offend," Tower told her.

"I know. I'm just tired of most men's attitude about marriage. My husband will be a strong, respectful man who admires my own strength."

The captain whirled her around the dance floor, watching her closely. "Like Two Wolves?"

His question startled her. She couldn't quite hide her reaction, and she knew he was reading it in her eyes. "Yes," she answered boldly. "He's not like any other man I've ever met. He's good and honest, and respects me completely."

The dance ended. "Well, Ma'am, so am I good and honest. And I most certainly respect you. I hope you understand that my concern is true and has nothing to do with me disliking Two Wolves. I happen to like him very much, and I have abided by the Major's order that I keep what I suspect about you and Two Wolves to myself." He pulled her aside. "It's just that I know how difficult it will be for you if you marry a half-breed. You are beautiful and sweet. I hate to see you suffer."

Claire stepped away. "Thank you for your concern, but I'll be fine."

Tower bowed to her as another dance started. The major asked Claire to dance with him and she gladly obliged.

"Was the captain giving you his sage advice about marriage?" he asked.

She smiled, relieved to be talking to someone who understood. "Yes. I know he meant well, but thank you for rescuing me."

"Well, you can't blame the man for trying. He's single and he's lonely. And as far as I can see, he would be a fine catch."

"Yes, he would, if I was looking. But I'm not." She sighed. "Honestly, Major, do you really think I'd break Two Wolves' heart like that –having him come back to learn I'm interested in some other man? In our hearts, we are already married. And when he gets back everyone will *know* we're married."

Ansley grinned. "You are one brave lady."

"I am also a very tired one. Ever since I got here I've been scrubbing and cooking and sewing, and I've danced practically every dance here tonight. I think I'll go back to my room."

"I'll walk you there."

"I'm sure I'll be fine."

"Nevertheless–" The Major offered his arm and Claire took it, walking with him back to his quarters.

"I hope I get to meet your wife someday, Major. She is married to a fine man."

"I don't deserve her. I'll be glad to get back home, but the whole country is in a mess right now. It's broken–North fighting South back East, fathers against sons, brothers against brothers. And out here so much hatred for the Indians, a lot of it unwarranted, like what happened to Two Wolves' relatives. There is no excuse for that. Sometimes I wonder if we can ever fix it all."

Claire patted his arm. "There are plenty of people who feel the way you do, Major. I'm sure President Lincoln will find a way. I have to believe that, or I wouldn't be marrying Two Wolves. Love can conquer a lot of things. And even just the fact that I'm marrying an Indian shows that people of different races *can* get along, just like someday all the slaves will be freed. I think slavery is barbaric. It's about time this country rids itself of such a black mark against its own shouts of being a free country."

Ansley chuckled. "You and Two Wolves do have one thing in common. You both boldly speak your mind."

Claire smiled and let go of his arm when he led her up the steps. "Thank you for walking with me. You probably need to go back and join the others and keep an eye on the men. I'll be fine."

Ansley nodded. "As you wish." He sobered. "I hope things work out for you and Two Wolves. I'll do what I can to help with the mess over Vince Huebner."

"Thank you. Right now, I prefer to not even think about that man."

The major tipped his hat and Claire walked inside. Before going up the stairs to her room she realized she needed to visit the privy behind the major's quarters. She walked out the back door to take care of things, but when she emerged from the privy, a burlap bag came over her head and someone pulled the drawstring so tight around her throat she couldn't breathe.

"Vince is gonna' be right happy to see you, little lady!" someone growled. "But we're gonna' get a piece of ya' ourselves before we sell you in San Francisco! You might as well get started knowin' what it's like when strange men are havin' at you!"

Claire tried her best to scream, but she began to black out from lack of air inside the dusty bag. Someone grasped her breasts as someone else grabbed her ankles. She struggled wildly as they carried her somewhere and dropped her to the ground. A continued lack of air and the tight cord around her neck left her helpless to fight back as someone pushed up her dress and began groping her. She felt her legs being forced apart.

Suddenly it all stopped. She heard a *thud*, and at the same time a man's grunt. She rolled to her side and struggled to loosen the burlap bag from her neck. Somewhere close by a man let out a blood-curdling scream. Then came the sound of a horse galloping off.

Someone was on top of her then. She felt a knife at her throat and was sure her life was over, but instead the tight cord loosened from around her neck. The bag was yanked from over her head, and fresh air hit her face and nostrils. She gulped it in, gagging and coughing when she tried to scream. She began flailing her arms in an attempt to defend herself. The man grasped her wrists and pushed them to the ground.

"It is all right, *Maeveksea*. It is I–your husband!

The words were like music to her ears. "Two Wolves!" she gasped. She reached around his neck and he grabbed her close and helped her to her feet. Her desperate tears came in deep groans through heavy coughing from the dirt in her mouth and nose.

"Come inside," he told her. "You need water."

"Two Wolves!" she gasped again. "They tried to–"

"I know what they were doing." His voice growled the words. He picked her up in his arms and carried her into the major's quarters as men came running at the sound of the horrible scream from one of Claire's attackers.

"Stay here and drink some water," Two Wolves told her as he set her on her feet inside Major Ansley's quarters. "Do not come out. Go upstairs and wash away the dirt, and I will come soon. I do not want the men to see you this way. We will talk when I get back. Do as I say for now. Go upstairs and clean up. I promise I will come to you soon."

Claire frantically shook dirt from her hair and rubbed some from her eyes. "Two Wolves, where were you? How did you know?"

"Just go upstairs for now. We will talk soon. I must go back outside."

"One of those men who attacked me mentioned Vince! I think they worked for him, and he sent them to look for me." She went into another fit of coughing.

"The one who rode off won't get far in the dark," Two Wolves told her. "In the morning, I will track him. We might get him to talk. The other one is dead." Two Wolves led her to the stairs, then hurried out.

Dead? Claire tried to think straight. If the men who'd attacked her worked for Vince, this could mean huge trouble for Two Wolves if he caught the other man and people in Denver City learned he'd killed one of Vince's men. They might not care that she'd been attacked. Maybe they would think she deserved it if they found out she was in love with an Indian. All sorts of scenarios raced through her mind. She hurried upstairs to listen at a window as men below began shouting and asking questions.

CHAPTER THIRTY-FOUR

"JESUS, HE'S ALMOST CHOPPED IN half!" one of the soldiers commented.

Another turned around and threw up.

"Get the women away from here," Major Ansley ordered.

Several men left, urging Gertie, Emily and Sarah away before they could come close enough to see the man Two Wolves had killed. Two Wolves rejoined them as Ansley told some of those remaining to pick up the body and take it to the fort graveyard. "Go through his things and bring me whatever you can find about his identification," he ordered.

"That's one of them travelers from Denver City, Major," one of the men spoke up. "I think this one called himself Lonnie Best. Where's the other one?"

"He rode off so I would not *kill* him!" Two Wolves seethed. "Someone should go after him."

"It's too dark," Ansley told him. "The man will ride through the settlement outside the fort first to hide his tracks and then high-tail it out of here. We can't track him in the dark."

"Shit, Two Wolves, if I'd seen what you did to this guy, I'd have got my ass out of here, too," one of the soldiers declared. "What the hell did he do?"

"I'll ask the questions," Ansley told the man. "I told you to get this body out of here and bring me his personals."

"Yes, Sir."

Four men picked up the dead man and carried it off, one of them cussing again over the ugly, bloody wound.

"See if you can find the man's horse," Ansley ordered the two remaining soldiers. "It might have run after the man who rode off, but if it's around here somewhere we might find even more evidence of who he is and where he's really from . . . maybe if he has family."

The men left and Ansley turned to Two Wolves, who was pacing. "What the hell happened here?"

"What do you *think*? They were attacking Claire!" Two Wolves walked over and picked up the potato sack, bringing it back to Ansley. "They put this over her head and pulled the string so tight she was choking. I just got back. I left my horse at the horse barn and came here to wait for Claire. Only I found her fighting off two men who meant to rape her and likely intended to ride off with her. I could not shoot because they were on top of her, so I used my hatchet on one of them. The other one ran. I did not go after him because I had to tend to Claire. He got away. That cannot be good. What if they were sent by Vince Huebner? If the other man reaches him, Huebner will know that Claire is alive."

Ansley rubbed at his eyes. "Where is your rifle?"

"On the ground somewhere."

"See if you can find it and then come inside, Two Wolves."

Claire turned away from the upstairs window and hurried over to a pitcher and bowl in her room. She poured water into the bowl and dipped a rag into it, quickly washing her face enough to get the dirt out of her eyes as she heard Ansley come inside. She took a handkerchief from a pocket on her dress and blew more dirt out of her nose, then poured water into a cup and drank some to rinse her mouth as Two Wolves also came in downstairs.

"Did they rape her?" Ansley asked Two Wolves.

Claire felt ill at the ugly word.

"I stopped them, but if I had not come along when I did–"

"Calm down, Two Wolves. My God, did you have to use that hatchet?"

"I could not take the chance of both of them being able to attack me together. I had to get them off Claire and could not use a gun. A bullet could have gone through one of them and into Claire. I could think of nothing else."

Claire hurried down the stairs. The major glanced at her, pain moving through his eyes at the sight of her filthy dress and dirt stains still around her face.

"I thought I left you here safe," Ansley told her.

Two Wolves hurried over and put an arm around her, leading her to a chair near Ansley's desk. She sat down and Two Wolves stood behind her.

"I had to use the privy," Claire said, looking down at her lap. "When

I came out, someone put that potato sack over my head and pulled it so tight around my throat I could barely get my breath. There was so much dirt in it I couldn't even scream because as soon as I took a breath, my throat and lungs were full of dirt." She coughed again. "There is still dirt in my lungs and my eyes," she added, rubbing at her eyes.

"I'm damn sorry, Claire. I should have stayed here once I escorted you back. I trust our soldiers, but I didn't think about those two travelers."

Claire reached up and grasped Two Wolves' hand at her shoulder. "One of them said Vince would be glad to see me," she told the major. "And they said they were going to sell me in San Francisco and said –" She hesitated, shivering at the memory. "He said he'd show me what it was like having strange men–" She didn't finish.

"I *told* you!" Two Wolves seethed. "They were Vince Huebner's men!"

"Well, I'm damn sorry," Ansley told Claire. "The only thing I can say is what they told you will help when we go to Denver City."

"I'm scared for Two Wolves. That man might tell people that it was Two Wolves who attacked me and he and his friend were the ones trying to help. It won't matter to those people what I say. They will be much more ready to believe what that man tells them. Two Wolves used a hatchet to kill a white man and that's all they will care about."

"I am not afraid of what they say," Two Wolves answered. "You will be able to tell them the truth. It is Vince Huebner who will pay for this. I am only worried that the man who rode off will get to Denver City before us now and Huebner will know that you are alive."

"The other man's name was John Hart, if I remember right," Ansley told Two Wolves. "They got here yesterday. Said they wanted to rest up here and stay for the cookout and dance before they left again. They told us they were headed east after giving up on looking for gold in the mountains."

"White men *never* give up looking for gold," Two Wolves grumbled. "Huebner probably has men out in all directions trying to learn what happened to Claire." He stroked her hair. "You did not recognize either of them?"

Claire shook her head. "One of them seemed a little familiar, but Vince has so many men working for him that I couldn't possibly know all of them."

"Then we must find him when we go to Denver."

"Let me handle this, Two Wolves," Ansley told him. "I'll explain this to the men in the morning. And if we find John Hart, you keep your temper in check. We'll need him alive. I know you. You will very much want to kill him, but you can't, understand? You could be in enough trouble killing the other one in spite of what he was doing. You're Indian. He's white. And that's the damn crux of the matter. You go killing the other one in the city and I won't be able to save you from a hanging. I swear, in moments like this I truly wonder if you have an ounce of white blood in you."

"When people learn the truth about Vince Huebner they will know who deserves to hang–for killing his own people."

Ansley nodded. "That's why we need that second man alive. We have to make him tell the truth. That's our only hope because, otherwise, we have nothing to go on as far as pinning anything on Huebner."

Claire suddenly swooned. Two Wolves caught her as she slumped sideways, then hurried around to pick her up out of the chair. "I will take her upstairs and help her wash and get to bed," he told Ansley, turning toward the stairs with Claire in his arms. "I will stay there with her so she is not afraid."

"Two Wolves," Ansley spoke up as he rose from the chair behind his desk.

Two Wolves stopped at the foot of the stairs.

"The traveling preacher gets here the day after tomorrow. You two had better tie the knot and clear things up in that department. People will think what they want to think, but a Christian wedding will help them accept the two of you together."

Two Wolves clung to Claire. "After tonight I will stay at the shed where I usually stay. We will be married the next day." The words were spoken matter-of-factly. He carried Claire upstairs. "Get the papers ready for us," he called down to Ansley. "Show my name as Peter James Matthews." He disappeared into Claire's room then, shutting the door.

Ansley sighed and shook his head. "You're going to have to be Peter James Matthews in more ways than one if you want to get through this without a noose around your neck," he muttered.

CHAPTER THIRTY-FIVE

CLAIRE FELT EVERY NERVE IN her body, both excited and also worried . . . worried she wouldn't look pretty enough. Never had she cared so much about her looks or her hair.

"Are you sure you're all right, dear?" Gertrude Becker finished pinning Claire's hair into a pile of curls on top of her head.

"Yes. I know everybody is aware that those men attacked me, but I'm not going to hang my head. I did nothing wrong, and today I am marrying Two Wolves. I'm proud to call him my husband."

"As well you should be," Gertie chuckled. "Two Wolves is a fine man, brave and able. And Lord knows he is easy on the eyes. But some here will, of course, think this marriage is totally wrong. I know Doctor Tower is upset. He would have liked to court you. Emily Sternaman and Sarah Flower are learning to accept it, but they'll be cool at first. Pay no attention. A woman has to follow her heart, or life isn't worth living."

"Thank you, Gertie. And thank you for helping with my hair and all."

They were together in Gertie's small home, where Claire could have help getting ready for her wedding.

"It's no problem," Gertie told her. "Sarah made you a lovely cake, and Major Ansley ordered all the men to wear their dress uniforms or whatever they have that is cleanest—and to be on their best behavior and not say one word if they don't approve of this marriage. They all like Two Wolves, and most will accept this. You be proud and happy today."

Claire had refused to let Two Wolves help her wash the night of the attack, telling him to leave after he took her to her room. Because they planned to marry so soon, she wanted to wait and sleep with him on their actual wedding night . . . and she didn't want to talk about the attack or what lay ahead of them in Denver City.

Gertie came around to stand in front of her and held up a mirror. Claire studied herself, smiling at the wonderful job Gertie had done with her hair. Springy little curls hung separately around her face. She rose from the chair and walked to better light. "Gertie, you did a wonderful job!"

Gertrude had helped her apply just a little rouge to her cheeks and lips, and for the first time in her life she truly felt pretty and was amazed that her hair could actually be somewhat tamed if it was pinned into place. She wore a pink gingham dress loaned to her by Emily. She thanked Gertie again for all her help and lowered the mirror, sobering. "Gertie, I haven't seen Two Wolves since the night of the attack. Maybe he rode away and decided not to marry me."

Gertrude laughed. "Honey, how can you possibly think such a thing? The man is crazy about you. It's written all over his face. Fact is, some of the men say he rode out of the fort and put up a *tipi* somewhere nearby. That's where he intends to take you after all the celebrating is over. Believe me, he is out there waiting for you. Just remember, dear, that once you tie the knot the Christian way, there's no going back." The woman reached over and fussed with one last pin in her hair. "Is there anything you want to ask me?"

Claire put a hand to her waist. "Just one thing."

"What is it, dear?"

"I think . . ." She swallowed before continuing, not sure how Gertrude would take the news. "Let's just say it's probably a good thing we're having a Christian wedding, because I think I might be carrying."

Gertrude frowned. "Are you asking how you can be sure?"

Claire met her gaze. "Aren't you going to chastise me and tell me what a sinner I am?"

Gertrude smiled and made her sit down again. She pulled up a chair beside Claire, sitting down to face her. "Claire, the Good Lord teaches that he who is without sin can cast the first stone. No one did, and neither can I. The fact is, when Harry first went off into the Army, and I knew he was headed West . . . Well, that was twenty-five years ago, and it was even more wild out here. I was so afraid for him. We were young and in love and scared, but we were just dating then. He wanted to wait and marry after he came back East because he'd only be in the west for one year, and he wanted to be sure he'd make it back. But then desperation and desire got in the way and . . . Let's just say I was lucky not to end up in the situation you are in now."

Claire's eyes widened in surprise. "Before you married?"

Gertrude folded her arms and leaned back, nodding her head. "Yes. I know it's hard to picture now, both of us already gray and me about forty pounds heavier, but yes. You and Two Wolves are not the only man and woman who couldn't wait. And it's even more acceptable for you two because he firmly believes he took you as his true wife the Cheyenne way." She leaned forward then and took Claire's hand. "Now, are you saying you're past the time when you should be having your monthly menstruation?"

Claire could hardly believe Gertie wasn't shaking her finger at her. "Yes," she answered, her cheeks hot with embarrassment. "I haven't said anything to Two Wolves because I'm not sure yet. I think he would be happy, don't you?"

Gertie chuckled. "Men like Two Wolves *always* want children. It's the nature of the Native American man. And most men, especially native men, think it's a sign of their powerful manhood to so easily and quickly get their wife pregnant."

Claire covered her face with gloved hands. "I can't believe we are talking so openly about this."

"What other way is there?" Gertie patted her arm. "Things happen, Claire, and you are young and in love and beautiful and lonely. I can see how you would turn to the man who saved your life and has taken such good care of you. I just hope you understand what you are getting yourself into, dear. You'll have to be very strong in your love for each other because there are some who will scorn you and gossip about you."

Claire straightened. "I've been scorned and laughed at my whole adult life, ever since I was old enough that women thought I should be wearing dresses and fixing my hair and going to quilting bees. I see them whispering behind their fans when I'm working out in front of my supply store with the men." She met Gertrude's gaze. "I grew up around men and thought nothing of it. They were all Father's good friends, and I've never even . . ." She blinked back tears. ". . . had the chance to cry over losing them to that raid. They didn't deserve to die that way. They were like brothers and uncles to me."

Gertie rose. "Well, today is not a day for mourning. Save that for later. Today is a day for happiness. You are marrying the father of your child, who will most certainly be thrilled to know you are carrying his baby. Two Wolves is also half white, so you are getting the best of both worlds. And don't think his handsome looks go unnoticed by the women around here. They just won't admit what a beautiful man he is because he's Indian, and they think that makes it sinful to notice."

Claire felt a rush of desire at the thought of being with Two Wolves that night. "He *is* a most handsome man, isn't he?"

"The other women and I are properly jealous, let me tell you."

Claire smiled. "I didn't know falling in love could be so easy and unexpected."

"It's *always* that way, my dear." Gertie rose. "Now, let's take one more look at you. It's time to go out to the fort grounds and get you two married."

Just then they heard fiddle music playing "Here Comes the Bride and someone pounded on the door. "Mrs. Becker? Major Ansley says they're ready for you. Wait 'til you see Two Wolves!"

Gertrude went to the door and opened it. "We're ready. What did you mean about Two Wolves?"

The soldier removed his hat, looking past her to Claire, his eyes growing wider. "Ma'am, you look–" He swallowed. "You look *beautiful*!"

Claire smoothed the skirt of her dress. "Thank you."

"I asked you a question, Private," Gertie spoke up. "What did you mean about Two Wolves?"

"Oh!" The soldier turned his attention to Gertrude. "I mean he's all done up in his dress blues . . . to the hilt. You don't hardly even know he's an Indian except for that dark skin and his long hair. He's got it pulled back into a tail that he tucked under his uniform jacket. Right now, you'd have to study him real good to figure if he's white or Indian."

"Oh, my!" Claire exclaimed.

"Let's go, dear," Gertie told her. "This I have to see."

"So do I," Claire answered, walking toward the door, not sure what to expect.

Gertrude put an arm around her waist and led her out. They walked together down the steps and toward the center of the fort, where every soldier there and every soldier's wife and their children waited, ready for a reason to dance and eat cake and celebrate, whether or not they approved of the marriage between Claire Louise Stewart and Peter James "Two Wolves" Matthews.

CHAPTER THIRTY-SIX

MAJOR ANSLEY SMILED AS HE took Claire's arm, walking with her through a circle of onlookers at the center of the parade ground. Gertie followed, moving to take her place with the crowd. A very handsome soldier stepped forward to stand near the preacher, and it took Claire a moment to realize it was Two Wolves. She nearly gasped at how different he looked, much more white than Indian except for his dark skin.

Two Wolves broke into a broad smile at the sight of her, looking her over with obvious love and admiration. Ansley walked Claire closer, and the preacher asked, "Who gives this woman to this man?" Ansley answered, "I do." He moved an arm around Claire's waist and gave her a light embrace before leaving her.

Two Wolves walked closer.

"Is it really you?" Claire asked.

He held his chin proudly. "A while ago you married Two Wolves. Today you marry Peter James Matthews."

"You look wonderful," Claire said softly.

"And you have never been more beautiful." Two Wolves' smile faded a little when he noticed bruises on her wrists from her attack two nights before. He took hold of her hand and lightly touched one wrist, lifting it to kiss the bruise. "I am sorry for this."

"It's all right. Don't let it spoil this moment."

Claire could see it was a struggle for him to fight his anger, but he drew a deep breath and looked her over lovingly again. A wave of heat moved through her when he glanced down at the cut of her dress, a square neckline that revealed the crown of her breasts and ample cleavage.

"I am the Reverend Moses Clark," the preacher spoke up, "and today we are joining . . ." He looked down at a piece of paper inside his open

Bible. "Claire Louise Stewart and Peter James Matthews, also known as–" He cleared his throat. "Two Wolves," he finished.

Two Wolves put his arm around Claire and kept hold of her hand as the preacher delivered a short sermon about marriage and unity and devotion and faithfulness before adding the usual marriage vows "for richer, for poorer, in sickness and in health."

Both Claire and Two Wolves had trouble speaking the words "'til death do us part." Each knew how real it was that death could come sooner than later if they went to Denver City and confronted Vince Huebner.

To Claire's surprise, Two Wolves presented her with a ring, a gold band with two small diamonds in it. She was deeply touched to know that when he'd taken Sits-In-The-Night home, he'd thought to stop somewhere and buy a wedding ring. He'd been so "Indian" the entire time she'd known him that she'd given little thought to the fact that he'd spent over ten years growing up and being schooled in Chicago. He was indeed a man who could fit into both worlds, and it struck her that he could more easily help her with the freighting business than she'd even realized.

Their vows were spoken, and the preacher said the magic words. "I now pronounce you Mr. and Mrs. Peter James Matthews. Peter, you may kiss the bride."

Two Wolves grinned and leaned closer, kissing her lightly. "We will do much more than kiss," he whispered in hear ear. "I have missed you."

The crowd around them clapped, and several of the soldiers let out whoops and whistles as they embraced. Claire relished her husband's strong arms around her again, loved this place where she felt so safe. She was never more sure this would work than at this moment in Two Wolves' arms.

"I love you so, Two Wolves," she said close to his ear.

"You can call me Peter."

"No. You will always be Two Wolves to me."

He released her, and the party began. The three-piece band that had played for the dance struck up a waltz, and everyone insisted the bride and groom have the first dance while women began cutting a cake. Claire could hardly get over how full of surprises Two Wolves was. He began whirling her around like any white man would dance at his wedding. She wondered if he'd danced around a campfire with other Cheyenne, painted and heavily armed, and she had trouble picturing him celebrating the Sun Dance, dancing around a lodge pole with skewers in his chest. She began to feel as though she was in love with two different men.

"I am so surprised at how you look, Mr. Matthews," she teased. "And I love you for what you are doing. I know you would rather be in buckskins with your hair long and loose and paint on your cheek bones."

"I want to be what my wife expects me to be–the man who will make our marriage most acceptable."

Claire studied his dark eyes as they turned to the music. "I want you to be the real Two Wolves later tonight," Claire answered. "When we go to Denver City you will have to be Peter James Matthews again, but always at night in your arms, I want you to be the Cheyenne man I fell in love with."

He flashed his moving smile again, his gaze showing deep desire "Then tonight you will give yourself to Two Wolves. We will make love in the *tipi* I built for us, away from the prying eyes and ears of soldiers. There you will become my wife the white man's way, but it will not be Peter James Matthews who makes you his woman. Tonight I will again be Cheyenne, and the man who makes love to you will always and only be Two Wolves."

CHAPTER THIRTY-SEVEN

CLAIRE AND TWO WOLVES RODE together on his painted Appaloosa to the *tipi* he'd put up for their wedding night. A good half-mile from the fort, the dwelling sat alone on the vast plains that spread out from the base of the Rockies. Claire's heart burst with love over the many ways Two Wolves had made sure everything was perfect for her, including complete privacy for this night. They'd left amid whistles and farewells and partying at the fort. Indeed, being well removed from there would be far more relaxing than staying anywhere close.

"So, this is what you were up to yesterday when you stayed away," Claire told her husband. "Two Wolves, this is wonderful! How did you put this up so quickly?"

He dismounted and reached up for her, grasping her about the waist and helping her down. "I brought what I would need from the Northern Cheyenne when I took Sits-In-The-Night to her family there. They said to tell you it is a gift." He put an arm around her and walked her closer. "And I was able to put this up quickly because I learned from my people how to build and tear down a *tipi* on a moment's notice. It is necessary when you are being constantly hunted and attacked."

Claire caught the disgruntled tone to his words. She touched his arm. "I know how you feel about most soldiers and settlers. What about me? Are you sure about this?"

He brushed at one of the springy curls on her forehead. "Why would I have bought you a ring and spoken Christian vows if I was not sure?" He leaned down and kissed her forehead. "It is not the color of one's skin that matters to the Cheyenne. All that matters is who the enemy really is. Vince Huebner is your true enemy, and he is white, and it was white men who attacked you. I am Indian, and I am *not* your enemy. I have many friends among the whites, and those Comanche men I fought were my enemy. For a hundred years, the Crow have been enemy to the Sioux and Cheyenne, yet they, too, are Indian. And now they fight with us against white settlers. It is what is in the heart that matters, *Maeveksea.*" He put a hand to the side of her face. "You are my wife, and therefore you are as much Cheyenne as I." He walked her to the *tipi* entrance and pulled aside the flap. "Go inside, and I will bring in the supplies."

Claire entered, finding it surprisingly cool inside. The floor of fresh grass was soft, and she shivered with desire and anticipation at the sight of a bed made of several blankets over straw. She walked closer and picked up a cup next to the bed that had some kind of liquid in it. It smelled incredibly sweet and invigorating. *Sweet oil,* she thought. He would use it on her again, as he had that first night he took her in the foothills of the Rockies when they'd camped with the Cheyenne. Tonight would be like that first time all over again.

Paintings of horses and wolves and men with spears decorated the inside skins of the dwelling. Another scene seemed to replicate soldiers on horses attacking Indians, the Indians fighting back with hatchets and bows and arrows. Another depicted male figures hanging back from a center pole, rawhide strips tied to something in their chest. Whoever painted the picture even included little droplets of blood dripping from their chest wounds.

The Sun Dance. Claire studied the picture closely, trying to imagine Two Wolves taking part in such a ritual. It hit her, from looking at all the pictures, how little she really knew about his Indian side. What other customs did she still know nothing about? In studying the paintings and an array of his weapons that hung inside the *tipi*, she could almost hear drumming and chanting.

The sun was setting, and a soft breeze whispered under the skins where they were rolled up a few inches from the ground. Claire became anxious when Two Wolves did not come back inside for several long minutes.

She turned toward the entrance, determined to go see what had happened to her husband, when suddenly there came the trilling sound of a flute being played softly. It was a lovely tune, and somewhere in the distance she heard a wolf howl, then another. She felt she was being transported into another world, the world of the Cheyenne. She opened the entrance flap and ducked outside.

There sat Two Wolves, wearing only deerskin leggings and nothing more. His hair was now undone, hanging long and straight over his shoulders and to his waist. White stripes were painted horizontally on his cheek bones. He was a complete transformation from the "white soldier" she'd married and danced with earlier. He seemed to hardly notice her as he played the flute with his eyes closed. Claire sat down across from him and waited for him to finish. Finally, he took the long, wooden flute from his lips and set it aside, studying her lovingly.

"I did not court you as an Indian man usually courts the woman he wants for a wife. For that I am sorry, but circumstances would not permit it."

"That was beautiful, but just being who you are is enough courting for me." Claire smiled. "Our relationship has been anything but conventional, Two Wolves, whether from the White man's point of view or the Cheyenne's. Heaven knows we were thrown together under most unusual circumstances."

He smiled and nodded. "You told me that in the night you wanted only Two Wolves, so now I am he again." He reached out to her, rising and urging her to get up with him. "Come inside. I will relax you again with the sweet oil, as I did that first night I made you mine."

Claire felt a rush of desire as they ducked inside. "This is beautiful," she told him, "so quiet and peaceful. I wish our life together could always be this way."

He put his hands to the sides of her face and leaned close to kiss her lightly. "If only it could be so, but we know it will not. We will have to be strong for what is to come. But tonight is only ours." He pulled the sleeves of her dress down over her shoulders, then ran his fingers across her chest. "So white and velvety you are."

Claire took his other hand and raised it to her lips, kissing his fingers. "I love you."

"As I love you." He began unbuttoning the front of the dress, then pulled it open and on down to her waist, where he took hold of her many slips and pulled everything off together. She stood there in just her ruffled pantaloons and camisole.

Claire stepped out of the dress, and he tossed it aside. Still on his knees, Two Wolves unlaced her strapless camisole and tossed it aside also, leaning up then to softly suckle her breasts, plying them gently. He kissed the scar from her wound, then took hold of the waist of her pantaloons and pulled them down.

Claire breathed deeply with thrilling desire. He had a way of commanding this, yet was so gentle about it. She grasped his head when he began kissing the folds between her legs. He firmly grasped her bottom. She shivered when he ran his tongue into secret places, then kissed his way upward, over her belly, lingering at each breast, her throat, her lips.

"My wife is most beautiful," he told her, groaning then in a deeper, suggestive, invading kiss. He picked her up in his arms and carried her to the bed of straw and blankets.

She was totally at his mercy then, not caring what he did with her, only wanting to enjoy the way he had of bringing her to a place far removed from reality and the present.

He dipped his fingers into the sweet oil.

"Turn face down, and I will massage your back," he told her.

Claire gladly obeyed, closing her eyes and breathing deeply when he moved strong hands gently over her back, from her tense muscles near her neck, down along her spine, over the muscles at her hips and back up.

"You have some bruises on your back, *Maeveksea*, from when those men threw you down. When I removed your underwear, I saw more on your thighs from where they tried to force you. This breaks my heart. I am sorry I did not arrive sooner."

"You couldn't have known."

He massaged over her back again, up to her shoulders and down over the backs of her arms.

"I still feel responsible. I will make sure no one harms you ever again."

Now his fingers plied the base of her neck, making her totally and luxuriously relaxed as a fire burned deep inside to mate with this man who brought out every womanly desire.

"I never fear harm when I'm with you," she told him. "You are the kindest, bravest man I've ever known. I'm so happy right now."

He put more oil on his hands and massaged near her waist again, down over her buttocks, her thighs, her calves, the bottom of her feet.

"Maybe I should do this to you, my husband. It isn't fair that I get all this wonderful enjoyment."

"It is the man's place to make sure his woman is happy and contented. And the more relaxed you are, the more likely my seed will take hold deep inside and become our child."

Claire smiled and turned on her back before he was finished with her feet. "I wasn't sure when to tell you, Two Wolves."

He frowned, moving his oiled hands over her shin bones, her thighs, to her belly. "Tell me what?"

She grasped his wrists. "I think I am already with child. I am far past my time of month. I wasn't sure if I should say anything yet, or how you would feel about it."

A light shone in his eyes unlike anything she'd ever seen there. "This is so?"

She nodded. "Are you glad?"

He moved his hands up over her ribs to her neck, gently rubbing his thumbs along her jaw.

"I knew when I first saw you that you should be mine," he told her. I did not know I could love this much. You honor me like no one has ever honored me. In the Cheyenne culture the women are highly respected as the bearers of life. I had hoped this would happen for us, but to happen this quickly–" He raked her nakedness with a look of intense desire. "You bring out all that is man in me. You have proven my seed is strong, and now you carry my blood inside you. There is nothing that can come between us. If I should die, I will always be alive in the child you carry. I have never loved you more, and you have never looked more beautiful."

Claire sat up and hugged him around the neck. "I'm glad you're happy!"

Two Wolves laid her back and moved on top of her. "How could I not be happy?"

"My father told me once that he knew a man who left his wife because she was carrying and he didn't want any more children."

He stretched out on top of her, nuzzling her neck. "No Cheyenne man would ever do such a thing. Children are vital to survival. I would not care if we had *ten* children." He met her lips in a sweet kiss.

"Well, maybe *I* would care," Claire answered between more kisses. "That's a lot of babies and a lot of work, my husband."

More kisses. "I will never let it be too much for you." He frowned then, raising up on his elbows. His hair fell around her, shrouding her from all but his handsome face. "I will massage you every night if you wish. I will make sure we always have food, and I will even stoop to woman's work and carry the wood for our fires. I will do what is necessary, and you will never be too tired or complain."

"Why would I ever complain when I can lie in these arms every night?"

He kissed her neck. "I did not finish my massage."

Claire's breathing deepened. "There is only one thing I want to feel, and that is my husband inside me," she told him, closing her eyes as he tasted her breasts more fervently.

"And your husband wants nothing more than to *be* inside you, *Maevek-*

sea."

He worked his way downward, and she gladly opened herself to him as he massaged her inner thighs, then the folds of that secret place she'd given to only one man and would never give to another. He tasted her with relish, groaning deeply as he searched with lips and tongue and brought her to the heights of ecstasy until the wonderful explosion of keen desire made her cry out his name. He moved fingers inside her teasingly as he worked his way back up to her mouth.

"The moistness I feel tells me you are ready to mate with your husband again. I am *momata.*"

"What is that?" she whispered.

"Very blessed." He entered her, gently at first. She arched her hips to greet him, and suddenly they could not get enough of each other. His thrusts came in heated, quick rhythm then as he took her over and over for several minutes. Claire cried out with the pleasure he brought in filling her so deeply. He grasped her arms and stretched them over her head, keeping her fully in his control. She was at his mercy, and she didn't mind at all.

Finally, she felt his life pulsing into her again. He kept up the invasion until he was spent, both of them perspiring and relishing the sweet relief of sexual fulfillment

"Do not move," he told her.

"I am very happy right here under you," she teased, smiling.

"I did not hurt you?"

"Most certainly not."

Two Wolves grinned. "Then you won't mind if I feel myself growing inside of you again, and if I take my pleasure in you again."

"I don't mind at all."

He kissed her softly. "*Ne-mehotatse, Maeveksea.*"

She loved the Cheyenne word for *I love you.* "*Ne-mehotatse*" she replied softly.

"Thank you for the child of my seed that you carry."

"Thank you for *giving* me a child. Until now I have never thought about how pleasant it is to be a woman."

"And I do not mind giving you that pleasure, for I take my own in return."

He moved inside her again, and Claire closed her eyes, still in the throes of her earlier climax, still needing more. She suspected not many men could give as much as this man she'd taken for her husband . . . for better or for worse . . . for richer, for poorer . . . in sickness and in health . . . 'til death do they part. She would not think about death. God would never take this beautiful man from her. No god could be that cruel.

CHAPTER THIRTY-EIGHT

IT WAS LATE IN THE afternoon the day after their marriage that Major Ansley rode out to the *tipi* to find Claire and Two Wolves sitting outside. For comfort, and because she planned to wait one more day before getting back to her world as a white woman, Claire wore a simple deerskin tunic Two Wolves had given her to wear, another gift from Sits-In-The-Night. She'd hung a kettle over a campfire outside the *tipi*, where she was cooking potatoes and venison, both from supplies Two Wolves had packed for them.

Claire rose, calling out the major's name in greeting.

Ansley grinned and nodded, dismounting as Two Wolves came out of the *tipi* wearing deerskin leggings and no shirt. His hair hung long and loose, and he wore no weapons.

"You two look very peaceful and happy," Ansley told them as Two Wolves put an arm around Claire.

"We are," he told Ansley. "Today I can offer you only a log to sit on, my friend, but soon we will build our own house. First, we need to see about Claire's business in Denver City and decide where we will live. In the meantime, we would like to stay in your quarters upstairs. It won't be for long. I do not expect my wife to live this way for long."

"Actually, I've enjoyed it," Claire spoke up, smiling. She curled closer into Two Wolves' embrace. "*Tipis* are quite pleasant, Major."

The major removed his hat and sat down on a log near the fire. "Yes, well, you'd change your mind in winter, I'm sure. And for what's coming, you'll both need to behave like whites. You already know that."

Claire hated having to think about what lay ahead. Two Wolves urged her to sit down on a blanket near the fire. He sat down on a nearby stump that remained from a felled pine tree.

"We know what we need to do," he told Ansley, sobering. "I have never told you that the man my mother married in Chicago owned a dry goods store and left her money when he died. She in turn left what she had to me after her own death. I have money in a bank in Chicago, and I have more in my own supplies. The way I live, I have no need of it, but now my wife will need white women's things. I intend to support her as any husband should, in spite of her wanting to keep her own business. We will go to a dress shop in the settlement nearby and buy her more dresses to wear when we go to Denver City. It is time to take care of matters there so we can get on with our lives and be rid of those who threaten Claire."

Ansley nodded. "I'm glad to hear you are wise with your money and intend to let Claire keep her business if she so chooses."

"It is what she is used to. I understand that." He looked at Claire and grinned. "An old Indian told me once that the way for a married man to be completely happy is to make sure his *wives* are completely happy. I have only one, so I am lucky it will not take so much work."

Both men laughed and Claire smiled, loving the fact that her husband cared about her happiness and was allowing her to make her own choices. Someone like Vince Huebner would most certainly clamp down on her freedom and take everything from her if she married him. She'd be left a prisoner in her own home, pretending to enjoy tea parties and quilting bees. "And I intend to give Two Wolves whatever freedom he needs to be Cheyenne," she told Ansley. "There will be times when he has to ride off on his own, maybe even visit some of his relatives. I understand that."

"Our son will also know a free spirit," Two Wolves told the major. "*Maekveksea* is already carrying our child. She told me so last night."

The major smiled. "Gertie told me." He studied Claire with concern. "You're sure?"

Claire pulled a corner of the blanket over her lap. "All the signs are right, Major, and just this morning I felt a little sick. Gertie told me that could happen and that if it did, it was just more proof that I'm carrying a child."

"Well, I know how Indian men feel about children, so I'm happy for both of you." He sobered then, turning to Two Wolves. "But you're right about having to get things settled in Denver City. That's why I came out here. We found some evidence in Lonnie Best's supplies."

Two Wolves came more alert. "Is it something important we can use?"

"I think so."

Claire's heartbeat quickened at the good news. "Thank God," she said aloud.

Ansley stretched out his legs and shifted a little. "Well, let's not jump up and down over it. We have to remember the prejudice we'll run into when we get to Denver City, but it should help that a brand etched into the underside of his saddle, as well as a bill of sale for some tools and a gun in his supplies all read Huebner Supplies. Papers on the horse itself show he got the horse from Huebner Stables."

Two Wolves got up from the stump and walked over to kneel behind Claire, putting his hands on her shoulders. "This will be a big help."

"Best of all, we found a paycheck written out to him," Ansley announced, "from Vince Huebner."

"That's wonderful" Claire exclaimed. "When I tell people what those men said about Vince when they attacked me, Vince *has* to be arrested for what he's done."

Ansley rubbed at the back of his neck and rose from the log where he sat. "It still won't be that simple. The fact remains that it's the word of a woman others in town don't like and who is married to an Indian, against a well-respected businessman. And if we do find the man who got away after attacking you, Claire, he could say that he and his friend saw you being attacked by Two Wolves and they were just trying to help you."

"But he's my *husband*! Why would my own husband attack me?"

"Because he's Indian and he was angry with you for something and was beating you. People believe that kind of thing about Indian men. You need to open your eyes, Claire, to how bad the hatred really is."

Claire's hope dwindled. "What we found *has* to count for something, Major."

"Of course it will. And we did find something else in his gear that had Stewart Supplies etched into it that could help even more."

"What was it?" Claire still clung to Two Wolves' hand.

"A Colt .44. It has initials carved into the butt of the gun. B. D."

Claire jumped up, and Two Wolves rose with her. "Benny Drum! He handed me his gun when he saw the attack coming. He said to use it on myself if I had to." She paced, trying to remember. "When I snuck out of that potato wagon, I took it with me, but then I fell and lost the gun somewhere in the woods. It was dark and I was scared, so I just left it and kept running because I didn't have time to look for it." She turned to Two Wolves. "Lonnie Best must have been one of those who went searching for that Comanche man who chased me. He probably found my gun along the way." She turned to Ansley. "That would explain how he got hold of it. That's good evidence, Major, isn't it?"

The Major sighed. "John Hart, the man who got away the night of your attack, could claim this Lonnie Best bought the gun for himself from your store."

"Why would he buy anything from me if he worked for Vince Huebner?" Claire reasoned. "And why would Benny sell someone his own gun, with his initials carved into it besides? I'll bet that if you surprise John Hart with that gun, you can trip him up. He might blurt something out unwittingly. We just need to find out if Lonnie Best worked for Vince."

The Major nodded. "It might work. It could at least plant some doubt in the minds of Denver's citizens. It would put Vince Huebner on a thin line and would maybe at least stop him from any more raids."

"But he should *pay* for what he's done," Two Wolves insisted. "I do not want to just *stop* him from future raids, I want people to know the *truth*!"

"I'm trying to help you with that, but I still need you to keep your temper in check, Two Wolves. You and Claire have to ride in with me, dressed and behaving as a white married couple who look as though their word might be true. The calmer you are, the more people might listen. But if they see even a hint of an angry Indian in your talk and reactions, their judgmental prejudice will come first, and they won't believe one word out of your mouth. Do you understand?"

Claire felt sorry for her husband, who deserved to be furious and deserved to thirst for the blood of those who'd committed such hideous attacks, not only on Indians, but on their own kind. There was no forgiving such a thing.

"I understand *completely*," Two Wolves growled. "I am half Indian and, therefore, my word means nothing. But my wife is *white*! They should at least listen to *her*. When she tells them about the gun it will all make sense as to how this Lonnie Best got hold of it. We have much evidence. I think we should go to Denver City soon and get this over with. I want Vince Huebner behind bars or dead for what he has done, and because he now surely wants to kill Claire for what she knows. By now John Hart has made it back to Denver and has told Huebner that Claire is still alive. They will come after her."

"After what you did to Lonnie Best?" The major shook his head. "I think they'll be thinking twice about that. But they will surely have something in mind–most likely a good story to refute what Claire might tell people." He closed his eyes and shook his head. "I'm so sorry. I just need both of you to consider all the possibilities and be ready for them."

Claire turned away. "I understand."

The major turned to Two Wolves. "The way you reacted just now is what I was talking about. You can't behave like this in Denver City. Maybe I should take Claire there without you."

"No! Where she goes, *I* go. Someone might try to hurt or kill her. I will not allow it."

"That's what I'm afraid of."

"I am *not* afraid! You will be surprised how *white* I can be when necessary."

Ansley sighed. "That will most certainly help, but the fact remains you obviously have Indian blood."

Claire walked closer to Two Wolves and he wrapped an arm around her.

"Can the two of you be ready to leave in three days?" the Major asked them. "That gives you another day alone together and yet another to go buy some dresses for Claire and pack for Denver City."

"We will be ready," Two Wolves answered, holding Claire close.

"Fine." The Major removed his hat and fidgeted with it as he studied Claire. "I think you and Two Wolves make a beautiful couple," he told her, "and I want nothing more than your happiness. That invitation I extended to come to Ohio still stands. At the least, I think you two should settle here rather than in Denver City. No matter how this turns out, you'll be shunned there. Life will be much easier around here."

"We will decide after we settle with Vince Huebner," Two Wolves answered. "We thank you for telling us what you found and for going with us to Denver City. There is no going back. We must tell people what we know. I will take the chance–for the Cheyenne."

Ansley nodded and turned to mount his horse. "God bless the both of you. Stay here another day and enjoy the peace. God knows there won't be much of that when we get to Denver-City ." He turned his horse and rode off.

Claire moved her arms around Two Wolves' waist. "I'm so afraid for you."

"Do not fear. Those who tell the truth have nothing to fear. It is men like Vince Huebner who should be afraid."

Claire shivered at the thought of Vince. She breathed deeply of her husband's manly scent, feeling so safe right there in his arms. "I wish things could stay just like this forever."

"As do I. But it is not meant to be. We must pray that justice will have its way when we go to Denver City."

Claire clung to him even tighter. "The only good thing that ever happened to me there was the day you came riding down the street and you looked at me." She turned her face up to meet his gaze. "Just like you, somehow, I knew deep inside my whole world would change, and it's been for the better. I can never go back to how my life was before you came along."

Two Wolves leaned down to kiss her gently. "Nor can I, *Maeveksea*. Nor can I."

CHAPTER THIRTY-NINE

MORNING SICKNESS VISITED CLAIRE THE day they left for Denver City. Two Wolves insisted she ride inside a covered wagon for the nearly four-day journey. Claire argued she was perfectly fine, but her husband insisted. Claire feared that in her husband's eyes she would seem weak compared to Cheyenne women.

"If I wanted a Cheyenne woman, I would have married a Cheyenne woman," he assured her with a smile and a kiss. *"You are young, and this is your first child, so you must be careful."*

Two Wolves was dressed fully as an Indian scout, mostly buckskins with only an Army horse and saddle and Army issue for weapons. He intended to change into his uniform when they reached Denver City, but not before.

The trip was difficult for both of them. With Major Ansley along as well as five other men, including Lieutenant Sternaman and Sergeant Becker, they couldn't very well spend time together at night in the back of the wagon. The other three men with them were young privates the Major had brought with them for further protection in case of trouble.

When they stopped to rest the animals on the first day and eat a little lunch, Two Wolves expressed his concern that Claire should lie down in the back of the wagon instead of riding in the seat beside Private Thomas Lake, who'd been assigned to drive the wagon. "You should lie down inside," Two Wolves told her. "That seat is hardly any more comfortable than riding on a horse, the way it bounces and sways."

Claire folded her arms and looked up at him. "I've ridden horses and bounced around in wagons since as early as I can remember. We have already discussed this, Two Wolves."

He pulled her closer. "I watched what you went through when you were wounded. I know your strength, *Maeveksea*, but the child in your belly is not just yours. It is also mine, and it means very much to me, as well as being sure I do not lose my beloved because something went wrong. Stay in the back of the wagon–for me. I do not think you weaker because of it."

Claire sighed. "All right. Besides, I–" Morning sickness hit her again, and she turned away, bending over to vomit. Two Wolves kept hold of her, pulling her hair back from her face and holding it until she was finished being sick.

"Oh, my goodness, I thought this would end by noon!"

"Some Indian women also get sick, so you are no different. And Gertie told me the sickness usually only lasts a few days or weeks and then goes away."

Claire had to appreciate her husband now for insisting she do no work on this trip. She could not do the morning cooking because in the morning all food smelled bad. Besides the wagon for supplies and bedding, they'd brought along a chuck wagon, and Privates Billy Carver and Stan Cooper did the cooking and camp clean-up.

Claire finally turned and rested her head against her husband's chest. "I guess we no longer need to doubt if I'm carrying."

Two Wolves rocked her in his arms. "I am sure you will feel better soon, *Maeveksea*."

"I hope you're right. At the moment, I am very angry that only the woman suffers this. It took both of us to get me this way, so why doesn't the *man* have to suffer something? He gets the fun part."

Two Wolves laughed. "It most certainly *is* the fun part. And the man has to stay strong and still hunt for food and protect his woman," he answered, pretending authority and ruggedness, "so he cannot be allowed to suffer these things. It is very embarrassing for a warrior to be sick."

Claire pushed at him. "I still think it's unfair."

He pulled her close again and rubbed her back as he kissed the top of her head. "I have to agree, but it is the way the Great One made us." He squeezed her tighter. "I miss you in the night, *Maeveksea*."

Claire closed her eyes and breathed in his now-familiar scent. "And I miss you."

"We might not be able to stay together in Denver City," he warned her. "I am Indian. No one will give me a room."

"We'll stay at my store," she told him. "There are living quarters in the back."

He kissed her hair again. "I long to kiss you."

"And I would let you, but right now I don't think you'd enjoy it after I've just been sick."

He let go of her and untied a small leather bag from his weapons belt and pulled it open, reaching inside and taking out a piece of peppermint. "Eat this. Your mouth will taste better, and it will help your stomach."

Claire took the candy. "Where did you get this?"

"Gertie gave it to me. She said if you get sick to give it to you."

"Oh, Gertie!" Claire gladly sucked on the mint. "She's so thoughtful. She's been so good about accepting us together, Two Wolves."

"She is a good white woman, as you are." He grasped either side of her face and leaned down, kissing her gently. "I had better leave you now," he said then, "before I want much more and do something that would embarrass you and the soldiers."

"But not you?"

He shrugged, grinning. "In the *tipi,* a man and woman mate even with the children around. It is a natural thing. Children learn about such things at an early age and they think nothing of it. The man and woman, of course, do it under a robe or blankets, but the children soon understand what is going on and where babies come from. For Whites, it is something to be hidden and whispered about. Some even think it is sinful, even for a man and wife."

Claire smiled. "But not you."

"Of course not. It is an expression of adoration. What is sinful about that?"

She stood on her toes to kiss his neck. "Not a thing."

He picked her up in his arms then and helped her into the wagon, giving her another piece of peppermint. "Promise me you will lie down for a while. I want you and the baby to be strong. I wish we did not have to make this trip, but it is best while the evidence we have is all still fresh. We will find John Hart and we will make him talk."

Claire grasped the wagon gate as he closed it. She longed to have him come into the wagon and hold her. "I hate this."

"It will be over soon." He leaned up and kissed her cheek. "As your husband, I order you to rest."

"I don't take orders easily."

"This I know, but I insist. Promise me."

Claire sighed. "I promise."

Two Wolves squeezed her hands, then left. Claire laid down into a pile of quilts, hating to admit that her husband was right. She needed to lie down. The thought of riding on the bouncing, swaying wagon seat right now made her feel nauseous again. She grabbed a pillow and hugged it, wishing it was Two Wolves. She heard the men talking outside then as they made ready to leave.

"She okay?" Ansley asked.

"She will be fine. It is the sickness women get when they are carrying," she heard Two Wolves answer.

"So, she's certain then?"

"There is no doubt. I wish it had not happened so soon when we have this trip to make. I fear her being upset by things that will happen when we reach Denver City."

"She's a strong young woman. And don't tell me you aren't feeling like the proud warrior right now, with Claire already carrying your child."

Two Wolves laughed. "If I was with the Cheyenne right now, we would be celebrating with dancing around a fire."

"I'm sure you would."

Some of the other men laughed.

"Two Wolves, you said not all that long ago that you had no plans to marry any time soon, and now you not only have a wife, but she's carrying," Captain Flower spoke up. "Sounds to me like it's the woman in that wagon who has the upper hand, warrior or not. You might be strong and brave and skilled outside the *tipi*, but somebody else has you hogtied *inside* the *tipi*."

They all laughed again.

"Say another word, and I will have your scalp," Two Wolves joked.

"Well, after what we saw you do to that traveler the other night, I reckon' I'll keep quiet," Flower told him.

Someone rode off, and then Private Lake climbed into the seat of Claire's wagon and snapped the reins. "You okay back there, Ma'am?"

"I'll be fine," she answered, grateful for the few good friends Two Wolves had made among the soldiers.

Ansley had hand-picked only the men he knew liked and trusted her husband best. She loved him for that. She just hoped they would stick by him all the way if things turned bad when they reached Denver City.

CHAPTER FORTY

VINCE LOOKED UP FROM HIS desk when he heard men's voices and heavy footsteps coming up the stairs.

"You're wrong to do this, Major," someone said. Vince thought he recognized the voice of the town sheriff, Max McKee. *Major?* He thought a moment, wondering if Sheriff McKee could be referring to the Army man he'd met a couple of weeks before.

"What the hell?" he muttered.

He quickly rose when the footsteps approached his office door. Before he could move from behind the desk the door burst open, and in walked Major Ansley with two other soldiers and Sheriff McKee. All defenses came alert as Vince quickly surmised the reason for the visit, reminding himself to be careful what he said. "What on earth are you doing bursting into my office like this?" he demanded of the sheriff, pretending surprise. "And with these soldiers?"

McKee stepped to the side of the room. "Vince, I'm afraid Major Ansley here says he's come to arrest you."

"*Arrest* me?" Vince stayed behind his desk. "What the hell for?"

"For raids on white settlers and supply trains," Ansley spoke up, "raids purported to be by Cheyenne Indians, but by your own men who are out to stir up trouble with the Cheyenne."

Vince couldn't hide his fury. "What in God's name are you talking about?" he growled. He turned to McKee. "You *believe* this?"

The sheriff folded his arms in resignation. "Of course not. But the Army has more power than I do."

"The hell it does!" Vince gripped the edge of his desk. "*Explain* yourself, Major. I am a well-respected business man and land owner in Denver City and in parts of this territory. Why would I have anything to do with raids on ranches and supply trains? What is going on here?"

Ansley rested a hand on his sidearm and stepped closer, wanting very much to shoot Vince Huebner. "I was here talking to you not long ago, Mr. Huebner, and you told me Claire Stewart had not returned from her last trip to Pueblo. I believe you said something about being concerned. Your attempt at sincerity seemed weak, and now I understand why. It was because *you* were the one responsible for the fact that she was missing."

Huebner struggled to appear dumbfounded. "Get to the point," he snapped.

The major ordered the two men with him to move to either side of Vince's desk, then looked boldly into Vince's eyes. "My point, Mr. Huebner, is we have found Claire Stewart," Ansley told him, "and she had an interesting story for us. Things have happened since she was rescued that help substantiate her story."

Vince decided he'd better show come kind of relief and concern. "You found Claire? My God, is she all right?"

"Don't pretend you don't know what happened to her, Mr. Huebner."

"But I *don't*! Where did you find her? What happened?"

"I'll let Claire explain it all. In a *courtroom*. It was your men who attacked her wagon train, Mr. Huebner, and if not for one of our Indian scouts who saw it all and helped her get away, she'd be a prisoner in some whorehouse in Mexico by now, or *dead*! Both by *your* orders! I am locking you up in the Denver City jail for now, until we can have a hearing and get a Federal judge here for a trial. You're under arrest for ordering the murder of five men, for stealing supplies from another freighting company, for the destruction of that company's wagons and remaining supplies, and for planning the attacks and murders of other innocent settlers and other supply trains in an attempt to keep the hatred stirred up among whites toward the Cheyenne Indians–which, in case you don't know, is a Federal offense, and that in turn gives me the right to have you arrested on Federal charges. The government is having enough troubles, what with a Civil War going on, without having to put up with these kinds of troubles with the Indians."

"This is *mad!*" Vince looked at Sheriff McKee. "How can you just stand there? Aren't you going to stop this?"

"I can't, Vince. I'm sorry."

"But there's no *proof* of such absurd charges!" He looked at Ansley again. "You can't possibly be serious!"

"I'm *very* serious, Mr. Huebner, and you need to come along with us now." The other two soldiers moved closer.

"Where is Claire Stewart?" Vince demanded. "That woman *hates* me, you know. She'll make up *anything* to drive me out of business so she can get out of paying back the money she owes me. She's a crazy woman . . . wears men's pants and behaves like a goddamn *man* most of the time. Hell, I've even offered to *marry* her! She'd have everything a woman could want if she married me. Why in God's name is she making up these lies?"

"They are *not* lies. And her name is no longer Claire Stewart. She's already married someone else. Her name is Claire Matthews."

Vince struggled with his rage. "*Matthews!* What in God's name is going on? Whom did she marry?"

"That makes no difference," Ansley told him. "Once you're in jail, you can hire a lawyer and decide how you will defend yourself, but we have plenty of proof against you. John Chivington and his hateful Colorado Volunteers are causing enough headaches for the regular Army here in Colorado. We don't need white men running around attacking their own kind just to give them a trumped-up reason to go after innocent Cheyenne."

"*Innocent* Cheyenne? There's no such thing!"

"I assure you there *is*, Ansley told him. "Now let's get going." One of the soldiers grasped Vince's arm, but Vince jerked it away, glaring at the major.

"Do you really think I'm going to let you march me to jail out there in the streets where citizens will see?"

"That's exactly what we intend to do," Ansley answered.

Vince could tell by the look in the Major's eyes that he meant business. If he put up a fuss, it would only make things more difficult and embarrassing. He walked from behind his desk on his own, stepping closer to Ansley.

"Fine, but let me tell you something, Major. Everyone in this town respects me, and they know damn well I would never do the things you are charging me with. When I am through with you, and with Claire Stewart, or Matthews, or whatever she calls herself now, you will *all* be run out of town! We might even end up with the first *woman* to be hanged! She's not going to get away with this. Not one person in this town will believe one goddamn charge she's bringing. At first I was relieved to know she'd been found, but by the time I'm done with her, she'll wish she'd never invented these lies!"

"And we've already arrested two of your men," Ansley told him. "They haven't talked yet, but they will, Mr. Huebner, especially once we find a Mister John Hart."

"Who the hell is John Hart?"

"You know damn well who he is. I can tell by the sudden alarm in your eyes, Mr. Huebner. Now let's go."

Huebner straightened, buttoning his expensive suit coat. "You've stirred up a bees' nest that's going to sting a lot of people, Major, one that will only make Claire more hated in this town, let alone the Cheyenne. These charges will cause an uprising unlike anything the people here have ever known." He walked past them and out of his office and down the stairs, where he turned to his assistant. "Take care of things here, Jeremy. I have some problems to settle, but it won't take long."

"What?" Jeremy Bates rose from his desk. "What's going on, Vince? I tried to stop these men from going upstairs, but they charged right up without explaining anything."

"I'm being arrested," Vince answered with sarcasm. "Can you believe it?"

"Hell, no!" Jeremy looked at Sheriff McKee with indignation. "What on earth is this about, Sheriff? Mr. Huebner is one of our finest citizens. He's never broken the law in any way."

"There will be a hearing to determine that," McKee told him.

"But this is ridiculous!"

"Just go get my attorney and tell him what's happened," Vince told the young man. "And keep things running smoothly while I'm gone. Business as usual. You know what to do."

"Yes, sir." Jeremy watched in disbelief as soldiers each took one of Vince's arms and walked out with Vince. Major Ansley and Sheriff McKee followed, heading for the jail. Jeremy ran to the front door to step outside and watch Vince being marched down the main street. Crowds began to gather at the sight.

"Mr. Huebner, what's going on?" someone shouted.

"I'm being arrested." Vince yelled the words as though they were a joke. He actually laughed. "Can you believe it?"

"What the hell for?"

"Ask that crazy damn woman Claire Stewart! The woman has finally completely lost her mind!"

"Shut your mouth!" Ansley ordered.

More people gathered, obviously already growing restless. They were too far away now for Jeremy to hear what Vince and the soldiers were saying, but he watched several people gather behind them to follow Vince to jail.

"This is going to be a goddamn circus," he muttered. He hurried toward the newspaper office to tell what was going on. This was big news!

CHAPTER FORTY-ONE

CLAIRE AWOKE TO HER HUSBAND crawling under the quilts with her. "Two Wolves!" she whispered, throwing her arms around him.

He snuggled against her, drawing her close. "I told the two men who stayed behind with us to camp farther away so we can be alone." He met her mouth hungrily, and Claire moved one leg over him and urged him to roll on top of her.

"Are you sure they're far enough away?" she asked.

"*Aye*. They understand, *Maeveksea*." He kissed her again. "Ansley was wise to go into Denver City first," he said softly before caressing her neck with light kisses. "I agree it was best that Vince Huebner be arrested before we come into town. I am sure things are already growing restless there."

"I don't want to talk about it." Claire hugged him tighter around the neck. "I don't care about myself, but once Vince finds out we're married and people realize that you're Indian—"

"The Major will protect us. They will be waiting for us at your place when we go into town. By then people will be doubting Vince Huebner and wondering if our story is true."

"All I know is that you are in my arms right now, and we have tonight. I was so afraid we wouldn't be able to be together this way before we go into town."

Two Wolves ran a hand under her gown and up over her thigh to her pantaloons. He moved a hand into the waist of her underwear and grasped at her bare bottom. "I have missed you so. Tell me you feel all right for this."

"It's only in the morning that I feel ill," she answered. "Make love to me."

He pulled at her pantaloons, and Claire arched up to help him get them off. He pushed up her night gown and she opened herself to him. Each wanted nothing more than to be one again. Two Wolves untied his breech cloth and tossed it to the side of the wagon. In the next moment, he pushed himself inside of her, feeling crazy with the want of her.

Claire arched up to greet his thrusts. He whispered to her in the Cheyenne tongue, keeping his promise that when they were together this way he would be only her Cheyenne warrior. Tomorrow they would go into Denver City dressed as the proper white husband and wife, but in their hearts, he would always be Indian, and she would be his willing captive.

Their kisses were heated and wild. Claire grasped the hard muscle of his forearms as he braced his arms on either side of her and moved even deeper into her love nest. She wrapped her legs around him and raised to meet him eagerly as his life spilled into her with such need that she felt every pulsing surge.

"Do not move," he told her. "We will do this again."

"I could do this all night," Claire told him softly. "I don't mind."

It was dark in the wagon, but Claire could tell her husband was smiling.

"Then we *will* do this all night. I cannot get enough of you, *Maeveksea*." He helped her pull her gown all the way off, then stretched out over her, wrapping his arms around her so their naked bodies could fully touch. He met her mouth again in a searching kiss, running his tongue deep as though there was another way to be inside her. In seconds, she felt his swollen shaft pushing deep again. He began moving in a circular motion, rubbing his penis against that magic spot that built her desire to ecstatic heights and made her whimper his name. She struggled not to cry out, embarrassed that the soldiers camped farther away might hear.

A desperate climax made her meet his thrusts with equal wild rhythm, a sudden fear of what lay ahead making her want to grab him and hang on and never let go. She didn't want tomorrow to come. She loved her husband beyond description, thanking God he'd come into her life and made it so much better.

Again, Two Wolves spilled his life into her with surging desire, leaving both of them warm and damp and filled with aching pleasure and fulfillment. He kissed her over and over before he moved to her side and pulled her into his arms. "We will do this again before morning, unless it is too much for you."

"I can never get enough of you, especially before facing what we will have to face in Denver City." Her tears came then, a release of all her stress and fears. She wept against his shoulder. "What if this is the last time we get to be together this way?"

"Do not cry, *Maeveksea*. It will not be the last time. *Maheo* knows that we are right, and He will see that people learn the truth."

"I've been praying for that on this whole trip."

"As have I. If there was time, I would go away and make a blood sacrifice and seek a vision for more strength and to bring *Maheo* closer. I cannot do that now, and so we have to believe He is with us. His power is with us because of my sacrifice at the Sun Dance. It has made me strong in my beliefs and my convictions."

Claire wiped at her tears. "I want to learn more about that side of you, Two Wolves. You understand the white man's ways, but there is so much I don't understand about the Cheyenne."

"You will learn." He raised up on one elbow, gently wiping at more of her tears with his fingers. "Promise me one thing, *Maeveksea*."

"Anything."

"Promise me that no matter what happens, you will raise our child to be proud of his Cheyenne blood."

"Oh, Two Wolves, you know I want this baby to know where he comes from. Son our daughter, I will always make sure our child is proud. And I believe it's going to be a boy–a son for a Cheyenne warrior."

"We will see. I just want you to promise me one other thing."

"What is that?"

"If something should happen that you are alone with our child, you will go to Ohio and find the Major. Our child will be much more accepted and loved there than here, where there is so much hatred."

Claire threw her arms around his neck again. "Don't talk that way! You said God is with us."

"*Aye*. I believe this will turn out for good, and that people will learn the truth. But there will likely be violence. I only want to be sure that you and my child are always happy and well and cared for."

"I'll do as you ask, but I don't want to think about such a thing, Two Wolves! You said we would be this way forever."

"And we will." He pressed a hand between her breasts. "In here. I will always, always be with you in spirit. Here in your heart."

Claire did not need light in the wagon to know there were tears in her husband's eyes. She felt them. The man well knew how dangerous it would be to go to Denver City and accuse Vince Huebner of heinous crimes.

"I would rather die than be without you, Two Wolves."

"But you are much stronger than that. You will live to raise our child in love and pride, no matter if I am with you or not. I need you to live so that my blood goes on, just as my mother kept me with her and went on without my father. She raised me to be proud of my heritage, just as I know you will do with my seed that grows inside you."

"I refuse to consider having to go on alone, Two Wolves. It's not going to happen. We will be strong in each other and strong in the truth. The truth will free us to be together."

He met her lips again. "This is what I pray for, *Maeveksea.* I only want to be sure you know that I am always with you, in life and in death."

Claire wrapped herself around him again, and Two Wolves pulled the quilts up over them as a chilly breeze suddenly ruffled the wagon canvas and made its way inside through loose openings. He prayed the sudden cold was not a bad sign.

Sometime before dawn they made love again, quietly, gently, in near agonizing need to believe this would never end. By daylight both were properly dressed as Mr. and Mrs. Peter James Matthews, headed for Denver City.

CHAPTER FORTY-TWO

AFTER LEAVING THE COOK WAGON at a ranch outside of town, Claire and the rest of the party headed into Denver City. Private Lake drove the wagon, with Private Cooper and Two Wolves riding beside it and Lake's horse tied to the back of the wagon. Claire felt stares as they made their way along Denver City's main street. Her stomach tightened with anxiety as people gawked, some whispering and mumbling, some pointing.

"It's her!" someone said.

"I thought she was dead," another commented.

"Oh, my gosh, she's wearing a dress!"

Claire didn't turn to see which woman spoke the words.

"Who's the Indian?"

"How dare she accuse Vince Huebner of those awful crimes," a man said, deliberately raising his voice so Claire could hear it. "You're crazy!" he shouted louder. "And what are you doing bringing an Indian to Denver City?"

Two Wolves, dressed in full uniform, glanced her way. They shared a look that warned the other to stay calm. Claire pointed to the building that had Stewart Freighting on the marquee.

"Pull up there," she told Private Lake.

"Yes, Ma'am. You all right?"

"I'm fine. I'm used to being called crazy."

The few sacks of flour left out front over three weeks ago had been hacked open, and flour was scattered over the stoop. Stewart Haggarty was nowhere in sight, and Claire noticed a broken window. The front door opened and to her relief Major Ansley stepped out.

Two Wolves dismounted and walked to the wagon to grasp Claire about the waist and lift her down. More people had gathered, and several women gasped when Two Wolves put an arm around Claire.

"Did you see that?" several mumbled.

"She crazier than I thought," some man said.

"Get inside," Ansley told them. He turned to Privates Lake and Cooper. "Take the wagon around back. There's a barn back there where you can put up the horses."

Claire hurried inside, but Two Wolves walked back to his horse to remove his rifle and other weapons and supplies. He started up the steps, but two men stepped in front of him.

"What the hell are you doing here?" one of them demanded.

He was a big man with a belly that hung over his belt. He smelled so bad that Two Wolves decided he'd be an easy man to track. He wouldn't need to watch the ground. He would just have to sniff.

"I am here to bring justice to the Cheyenne."

The man laughed. "That so?"

"How do you think you'll do that?" the second man asked. He was tall and slim, and his hand rested on a six-gun at his side.

"By proving white men are raiding settlers."

"You're a fucking liar!" the fatter man threatened.

"The Cheyenne do not lie! And if I were you, I would move before I decide to shed my white side and practice my Indian side."

"You a half-breed?" the skinnier one asked.

Two Wolves bristled. "I am just a man."

Ansley opened the door then and stepped out, waving a rifle. "You two get out of the way and let this man come inside."

Looking disgruntled, the fatter man stepped back a little. "We don't like Indians around here, let alone half-breeds," he grumbled. "He got somethin' to do with that crazy woman?"

"Maybe she's not just crazy. Maybe she sleeps with Breeds," the other antagonist added.

Two Wolves dropped his belongings onto the stoop and turned, walking up close to both men. He was taller than both of them and had to lean down to glower right into the more slender man's face. "I warn you not to say one more word about my wife," he said in a low, threatening growl. "I might forget my white blood and turn to my *savage* side, as you would call it! I can easily find where you live, and I guarantee I can get into your house and slit your throat without a *sound*! Do you understand what I am telling you?

Both men stepped back a little.

"*Wife*?" the bigger one snarled. "She's –" He studied Two Wolves' eyes and stepped back even more, deciding not to finish his sentence.

"Two Wolves, come inside!" Ansley shouted to him. "Let it go!"

Two Wolves glanced at the fatter man, dearly wanting to use a hatchet on him and his friend. They both stepped back even more.

"You see that?" the slender man shouted. "He threatened me! That fuckin' Indian threatened me!"

Reluctantly, Two Wolves turned away, stopping to give Ansley a look that told him what he would rather do.

"You can't let their words get to you," Ansley told him under his breath. "You've got to tamp down that Indian pride, Two Wolves, or none of this will work."

Two Wolves leaned down and angrily grabbed up his supplies and took them inside. Major Ansley stepped forward and addressed the crowd.

"This is a Federal matter," he shouted to them. "Anybody who interferes will be put in jail for Federal crimes, so all of you get the hell away from here. And anyone who steps up on this stoop or tries to come inside will be *shot*! That's not a threat. It's a *promise*!" He turned and went inside, slamming the door.

Inside, Two Wolves was fuming.

"Damn it, Two Wolves, I told you to stay *calm*! You'll get yourself hanged before we even have a hearing!"

"They insulted Claire!"

"And you knew that would happen. You just have to put up with it until this is over. If we can bring out the truth, you and Claire will be more accepted. Let's take this a day at a time. And if you are sincere in wanting to help your people, you have to stay calm and do this the right way. Those people out there are just angry about Vince, so they're bound to try to deliberately make you lose your temper, which would prove in their eyes that you *are* a savage and would give them an excuse to shoot you!"

Two Wolves removed his Army hat and threw it across the room, then unbuttoned the top buttons of his uniform shirt as though he needed to do so to breathe. He turned to Claire, seeing the terror in her eyes.

"Don't worry about defending me," she told him. "I can take it, believe me. *Nothing* is as bad as losing you."

"Let's go into the living quarters in back and sit down and talk," Ansley suggested.

Two Wolves noticed then that Claire's store had been ransacked.

"Look at this!" he said, waving his arm at empty shelves where supplies should have been. Broken items and canned goods lay scattered across the floor. "What kind of men do this?"

"This was done before we even got here," Ansley explained. "People thought Claire was dead, so they decided to raid her store."

"They have no honor."

"I agree, but right now let's concentrate on why we are here. Most of the furniture in back is intact, so go sit down. I'll fill you in on what went on before you got here."

"Is Vince Huebner in jail?" Two Wolves asked.

"Yes."

"At least we can be glad for that much." Sighing with frustration, Two Wolves and Claire followed Major Ansley into the rooms at the back of the building. Two Wolves had never seen Claire's living quarters until now. From the small, neat parlor he could see a tiny kitchen and two bedrooms. Claire sat down in a wooden rocker and asked one of the soldiers to get her a glass of water. Two Wolves knelt in front of her. "Are you all right?"

"I'm fine." Her eyes teared as she reached out and touched the side of his face. "You have to think before you act while you're here in town. People will deliberately say things to make you angry. Name calling doesn't bother me at all, but losing you will destroy me. The way you react upsets me, so if you don't want me upset, please stay calm."

He grasped her hand and kissed it. "I will try, *Maeveksea*. It will not be easy, but I will try."

Sergeant Becker walked into the small kitchen and pumped some water into a cup. He brought it back to Claire, who took it while Two Wolves sat down in a stuffed paisley chair beside her, looking far too big and wild, not just for the lovely chair, but for the small parlor itself. Ansley, Captain Flower and Sergeant Becker carried chairs from the kitchen table into the parlor and sat down to join them.

"I arrested Vince Huebner yesterday," Ansley told them. "The news is, of course, all over town now. People are in an uproar, as you saw. The sheriff has agreed to help me keep them at bay while we ride over to the hearing tomorrow morning, where we will present our case and our evidence."

"What about John Hart?" Two Wolves asked. "Have you found him?"

"I have a feeling he's long gone. If he came back here, Vince probably told him to get the hell out of town. The man claims he doesn't know anything about a John Hart, and it is possible Hart never came back at all. He might have been too scared to tell Vince what happened, or scared of being caught for that attack, after what he saw you do to his partner. We'll have to rely on what Claire saw and heard when her wagon train was attacked and again when Hart and Lonnie Best attacked her. And we have the items from Best's belongings that are the property of Huebner Freighting, plus that paycheck. I think that's enough to at least make people wonder. That's our best bet. Plant the idea, make them think twice. And maybe we can somehow trip up Vince himself in our questioning. He's professing complete innocence, of course. I'm anxious to ask him in front of everyone why, if he doesn't even know John Hart or Lonnie Best, did most of Best's gear come from Huebner Freighting? And why did the man have a paycheck on him signed by Huebner himself?"

"Vince is very clever, and he has the town behind him," Claire told Ansley, despair in her voice. "People will find it hard to believe he could possibly commit these crimes." She rubbed at her eyes. "I know him. He's planning his answers right now, with the help of his lawyer, I'm sure."

"Then we have to do some planning of our own," Ansley answered. "And do a lot of praying. There is supposed to be a judge here who will rule whether this should go to a full trial, but you can bet Vince probably has him in his pocket. The men and I will surround both of you when we ride to the hearing tomorrow. The flood wiped out the courthouse a few months ago, and the new building isn't finished yet. We have to meet someplace else."

"It's finished enough to use for this hearing," Claire argued.

Ansley rubbed at his forehead. "Sheriff McKee and the town council say it's not safe to meet in an unfinished building."

"Then where?" Claire asked, feeling alarm.

Ansley sighed. "I'm afraid we're meeting at the Silver Horse."

Her eyes widened in indignation. "*What?* The Silver Horse is a *saloon*! Half the people in there will already be drunk when we get there."

"I know that." Ansley rose and paced. "I argued about it, but the judge said he can keep the crowd smaller at the saloon, and they've had other trials there since the flood. He's picking six men to help decide if this should go to a full trial and agreed that, if so, it can be held in a different venue because Vince is so well known here in Denver City."

Claire grasped her stomach, feeling ill. "This isn't good. I don't like the sound of any of it. Holding the hearing at the Silver Horse could create a mob atmosphere. It's dangerous."

"I promise to keep you and Two Wolves well-guarded, and the judge promised to keep order. The sheriff will help."

Claire shook her head. "Sheriff McKee is friends with Vince Huebner and John Chivington both. He has no more use for the Cheyenne than Chivington does, let alone being in Vince's pocket. He'll help because it's his job, but he most certainly will not risk his life for Two Wolves."

Ansley leaned against a stone fireplace. "I'll make sure he does his job, and I'll do mine. We can at least say we tried—and we can plant the seed of doubt."

"It is as Claire said." Dark anger showed in Two Wolves' eyes. "It could turn into a mob. No one in this town will believe us, but I do not care. We have the truth behind us, and when we are through, people will at least wonder about Vince Huebner, especially when they learn the man who attacked Claire carried a paycheck signed by Huebner."

"And no matter how much Denver's citizens might hate Indians, they will hate even more the idea of whites attacking their own kind just to turn people against the Cheyenne," Ansley added. "That will taste pretty sour in their mouths, so planting that doubt is really important."

"What we need is a miracle," Claire said quietly.

They could hear shouting outside in the street—name-calling and threats. Lieutenant Sternaman came inside and walked into the back room.

"They're already getting ugly out there," Sternaman told the others.

"You take first watch," Ansley responded. He stood and turned to Captain Flower. "Keep an eye out back. Sergeant Becker and Private Lake can relieve you and the Lieutenant in a few hours." He scanned the room. "And I want all of you to get some sleep tonight, if that's possible."

"Claire must get some rest, but I will not sleep," Two Wolves told Ansley. He rose and walked over to peek out of a side window. "I am too angry, and I do not trust the people outside not to try to break in here in the night. You need an extra man to keep watch."

"That's your choice, but be careful," Ansley warned. "We don't need even the smallest excuse for the people out there to shoot you, so keep you temper. Try to stay calm, and close your eyes for a little while. It's going to be a long night, and tomorrow will be an even longer day."

Claire stood up and walked over to Two Wolves, moving her arms around his middle and resting her head against his chest. "God help us all," she said softly.

CHAPTER FORTY-THREE

IT WAS INDEED A LONG night. Shouts and name-calling continued into the wee hours, and someone threw a rock through one of the windows. The behavior of Denver City's citizens made Claire ashamed of her own race. If she could brave this out and help bring some kind of justice to the Southern Cheyenne, fruitless as that effort might be, it would be worth the horrors of what was happening right then.

She slept fitfully, afraid someone might try to set fire to her store. It was the same for Two Wolves, who stayed awake all night with the soldiers who took turns keeping guard.

Morning brought relative peace, with only the sounds of chirping birds and an occasional passing of horses and wagons. Two Wolves walked into the small bedroom where Claire had slept to find her already dressed but bent over a bucket with morning sickness. He rushed to her side.

"This is not good for you. Let me go to the hearing alone. You should stay here and rest."

"No!" Claire straightened, wiping perspiration from her brow with a towel. "I'll not let you go alone. I'm the one who was attacked, and I know what I heard. I need to testify."

She poured some water from a pitcher beside the bed into a glass and rinsed her mouth, spitting into the bucket. Two Wolves noticed her hand shaking a little as she wiped her lips with the towel. She put a piece of the peppermint he'd given her into her mouth, then took a deep breath and turned to rest her head on his chest. "I'm so sorry for the awful things those people out there are saying."

Two Wolves kissed her hair. He loved her more than he ever thought possible. "Do not worry about me, *Maeveksea*. I only worry about the child in your belly, *our* child."

Claire straightened and wiped at her eyes. "Maybe one of Ansley's men can make us something to eat. I'll be all right now. I think I should get something into my stomach. Then we all have to get ready for the hearing."

Two Wolves brushed her cheek gently. "Stay close to me today, and do not listen to their ugly words."

"I'm not afraid of it. I'm only afraid for you. I love you more than anything on this earth."

"As I love you." He kissed her forehead. "We will get through this and at least have our say. And we will go to the hearing as Mr. and Mrs. Peter James Matthews, and hold our heads high."

Claire stood on her tip-toes to kiss his cheek. "I have to try doing something to this hair," she told him. "Maybe I can tame it down with some combs."

Two Wolves smiled. "I love it the way it is, but I suppose to impress the arrogant women of Denver, you should try to tame it a little." He put a hand to the side of her face. "When this is over, the only woman I want is the one with the wild hair and the free spirit. The woman who is independent and who talks right back to me and gives me orders."

Claire smiled. "No one gives you orders. You do what you will do, and there is no changing that. I don't *want* to change that."

Two Wolves kissed her lightly. "I will go and see about getting you something to eat." He left her and walked to the kitchen to see Major Ansley was making coffee. The major lifted the plate to one of the burners on the wood-fired cook stove and added some fresh wood to hot coals left over from the night before. "She all right?"

"She was sick again. I am worried because she is carrying."

"I am, too, but she's a strong, healthy young lady, as well as brave and determined. She'll make it through this." Ansley set a kettle of water on the stove, then glanced at Two Wolves, who stood there in buckskin pants and no shirt, looking fierce even without any weapons. "I take it you'll wear your uniform today."

"Of course."

"That uniform shows you are on our side, so to speak. Might make you more believable and less apt to be shot. For now, I don't want you stepping one foot outside until you *are* in uniform and we're ready to leave. You go out looking like you do now, and someone will use you for target practice."

"I will never understand such unwarranted hatred."

"It is what it is. Fear and ignorance make people do some pretty stupid things."

Two Wolves folded his arms. "I thank you for what you are doing . You have gone out of your way to help us."

Ansley shrugged. "I'm rooting for both of you. I firmly believe Vince Huebner has done the things Claire says he's done. I don't know if we can prove it to others, but we'll damn well try."

Two Wolves nodded. "You are one of the rare white men who see me as just another man. And what is even more rare is that I trust you. There are not many Blue Eyes that I trust, especially when they wear a soldier's uniform."

Ansley grinned. "Well, I could say the same. I don't exactly trust all Indians when I'm *wearing* this uniform."

Two Wolves smiled sadly. "Do you think the day will ever come when Whites and Indians live peacefully together?"

"I wish I could say yes, but sadly I can't. Maybe it will happen, but it's not likely to happen in my lifetime. Maybe not even in yours." He put out his hand. "Good luck today, Two Wolves. Or, I guess for today I should call you Peter."

Nodding, Two Wolves firmly shook Ansley's hand, then squeezed it before letting go. "Peter it is. For today." He stepped back. "You are a good man, Major. I always describe you to the Cheyenne I come across and tell them to please never try to take your scalp."

Ansley laughed lightly. "Thanks for your thoughtfulness."

"Of course, when I describe your scalp, they scoff and say they would not want it, anyway."

Both men laughed, and Two Wolves relished the moment they'd been given to enjoy the morning and put away thoughts of what this day could bring.

CHAPTER FORTY-FOUR

CLAIRE RODE HER HORSE CLOSE beside Two Wolves, both of them flanked by Private Lake and Captain Flower. Ansley and Lieutenant Sternaman rode in front of them and Sergeant Becker rode behind with Sheriff Max McKee and a couple of his deputies. Claire still didn't trust McKee, but they had no choice. She had to hope he would put duty before personal hatreds.

Two Wolves wore his uniform–boots, pants, buttoned shirt with crossed-arrow patches to indicate he was an Army scout. He continued to surprise Claire with how White he could look when necessary.

As they approached the Silver Horse, the crowd grew, some shouting out "slut" and "liars" and "Redskin" and "Breed" and "troublemakers" and a host of other names. Some raised their fists. Claire just stared straight ahead, noticing a few prostitutes standing on a balcony over the saloon, most of them clad in embarrassingly revealing dresses, a couple wearing only ruffled pantaloons and corsets, with only thin, silky-looking housecoats over them–housecoats that were deliberately left open. One of them smiled and nodded at Claire.

"He's damn handsome," she called out. "If you get tired of him, honey, he can come see us!"

"Go get 'em!" another prostitute yelled down.

"Yeah, honey, Vince needs his tail shaved," a third shouted.

All of them shrieked with laughter.

They reached the saloon entrance, and the soldiers continued to surround them as they dismounted and made their way inside. The courtroom, if anyone could call it that, was packed. Vince Huebner and a man Claire recognized as Attorney Ezekial Howard stood near the bar, behind which stood a rather austere-looking, bearded man Claire guessed to be the judge. He pounded a gavel on top of the bar to try to quiet the excited crowd as Major Ansley and his whole party, along with Sheriff McKee, gathered opposite from where Vince and his lawyer stood. They all faced the judge.

Claire glanced at Vince, and if looks could kill, she knew she would be dead. If not for Two Wolves standing beside her, she would be terrified of Heubner's dark, piercing gaze.

He actually had the gall to nod to her then. "Glad to know you're all right, Miss Stewart … or I guess I should say Mrs. Matthews," he said, loudly enough for others to hear. "I heard you married an Indian." He smiled then.

Claire made no reply. She took hold of her husband's arm and could feel his muscles, rock hard and tight with a desire to attack Vince Huebner then and there.

"You stay calm," Major Ansley again told Two Wolves, keeping his eyes on Vince as he spoke. "I can feel your anger without even looking at you."

"The man should *die*," Two Wolves said quietly.

As more people poured into the saloon, the judge finally ordered men at the back of the room to close the doors and let no one else inside. Some of those left outside stood at the windows, piled up against each other in an effort to see and hear the proceedings.

Again, the judge pounded his gavel until finally the crowd quieted.

"This is a legal hearing regarding charges brought against Mister Vincent Huebner by Miss Claire Stewart," he announced.

"*Mrs.* Peter Matthews," Major Ansley spoke up.

Whispers moved among the crowd.

"I stand corrected," the judge said, glancing at Claire. "I apologize, Mrs. Matthews. Mister Huebner did just say you had married. Is your husband with you?"

"Yes." She took Two Wolves' arm. "He is standing right here beside me."

"Oh, my God, she really did marry that Indian," a woman behind her said softly.

"You two are legally married by a Christian ceremony and a Christian minister?" the judge asked Claire.

"Yes," Two Wolves answered. "I am Peter James Matthews. My mother was white, and I was raised and schooled in Chicago. I have served as a scout for the United States Army for the past three years."

More mumbles among the onlookers.

"Private First-Class Matthews is one of the Army's best scouts," Ansley told the judge. "He is a peace-maker, and in one incident he rescued me and my entire unit from a planned ambush by Sioux Indians farther north. He is not a liar and not a troublemaker, as some here seem to think. As a Major in the United States Army, I will gladly vouch for every word this man and his wife speak here today."

"And you are?" the judge asked.

"Major John Ansley out of Fort Collins. Peter Matthews, also known as Two Wolves, is under my command."

The judge appeared a bit surprised. Claire suspected he'd been told that the person accusing Vince was nothing more than a wild Indian out for vengeance. The man straightened and pounded his gavel again when more rumblings moved through the crowd.

"We will have quiet here," he shouted. "I am Judge Harvey Kieler, This hearing was arranged to discuss Claire Stewart . . . uh . . . Claire Matthews and her husband's claim against Vincent Huebner that he has been behind raids against white settlers and freighters, hiring white men to paint themselves up as Indians in order to stir up more hatred for the Southern Cheyenne."

The crowd broke into shouting and fist-raising, swearing such charges against a well-respected Denver City business man were an outrage. The judge had trouble quieting them again.

"I want to remind all of you that this is simply a hearing, not a trial. People here in Denver City need to know the truth, if indeed these charges are proven. I find the thought of whites raiding against their own kind more reprehensible than the Cheyenne attacking Whites. The Indians may think they have good reason, but for white men to kill their own as well as women and even children, there is no forgiveness."

"She's a liar, judge," someone yelled. "That woman slept with an Indian, and now she's on their side!"

The gavel fell again, and Judge Kieler ordered that anyone who shouted out their opinion without him asking for it would be immediately expelled from the saloon. He pointed to two of Sheriff McKee's deputies.

"Make sure you act on that order," he told them.

Both men nodded. As soon as things quieted down, Kieler asked Claire to step forward and give her evidence against Vince Huebner. Two Wolves squeezed her hand for support before she left his side and walked up to the bar, turning then to face the crowd.

The judge glanced at a man sitting at a table nearby scribbling notes. "Take down as much of her statement as you can, Cal." He turned to Claire then. "Speak slowly, Mrs. Matthews, so that the court reporter over there can write down what you have to say."

"Yes, sir." Claire reiterated what happened to her and her men in the raid on her supply wagons, how she had managed to hide and get away. Her heart pounded wildly through her entire statement, and the hatred and disbelief in the room were palpable. "Before I escaped, I saw and heard our attackers through a crack in the side of the wagon." She looked straight at Vince. "A couple of them really were Indians, and I have learned since then that they were Comanche, not Cheyenne. The rest were White men, and they all worked for Vince Huebner."

"Liar!" someone shouted.

Again the judge had to demand order.

"Mrs. Matthews, are you sure about all of this?" he asked Claire. "You were under great distress."

"The fact that they were white only made me *more* distressed!" Claire answered. "One of the Comanche men said Vince had promised him he could take me as part of his prize for helping." She looked down at her gloved hands. "I don't even want to mention what his intentions were. One of them even said something about . . . about selling me in Mexico."

The room erupted with objections. Vince pointed directly at Claire, calling her a liar. Once things quieted, the judge asked Vince to step forward and state his name and give his side of the story.

"Your Honor, that woman just wants me out of business," Vince argued. "Her own freighting business is failing. I've offered several times to help her out and I . . . I once even cared enough for her that I asked her to marry me." He feigned disappointment. "She refused, determined to prove she could handle the business herself. Her father was a gambler who owed a lot of money to several people, including me. This is just her way of getting me out of the picture and taking over the freighting business for Denver City. She is lying, Your Honor. And how can you trust the word of a white woman who would lay with an Indian?"

More rumblings and gasps moved through the crowd. Ansley grabbed Two Wolves' arm in a firm grip that told him not to react to the crude remark. "Show them your civilized side," he warned quietly.

Two Wolves jerked away and stood before the judge. "Let me tell you what I saw and have seen *before*," he begged.

Kieler pounded his gavel again. "I'll have order in this courtroom," he shouted, "and Mister Matthews here should be allowed to testify."

"He's an *Indian!*" someone shouted. "He's got no rights!"

Again the gavel came down. "He is half white and an honorable scout for the United States Army," the judge announced. "These are serious charges and I intend to hear all sides. Mister Matthews will be allowed to testify." He nodded to Two Wolves in a gesture to say what he had to say.

"I have lived among the Cheyenne half my life," Two Wolves told the judge. "I have come upon families who were the victims of raids conducted by whites. I know the signs of Indian raids. The horse tracks I found were from shod horses. The Cheyenne do not use horse shoes. Many times the arrows I found were not Cheyenne arrows. They were not even the arrows the Sioux or Crow or Shoshoni any other Indian Nation anywhere near here would use. They were poorly-made arrows made by someone who knows nothing about Cheyenne weaponry or markings. I even often found boot prints instead of moccasin prints. There are many ways to tell what Indian tribe committed an attack, and I assure you that what I found indicated no Indians at all. In many cases the dead were shot, and most of the Cheyenne can't even get hold of guns. Not only that, but the arrows I found in bodies were deeply embedded, yet the victims were also shot. That means they were shot first, and then some-one stood over them and shot arrows directly into them to make it look like an Indian attack. This tells me whoever shot the arrows into them were not adept at actually killing someone with bow and arrow from a distance, like the Cheyenne would be. And often no horses were taken. They Cheyenne would not leave good horses behind. And the Cheyenne do not –" He hesitated. "In some cases the women were violated."

The few women in the crowd gasped.

"I am sorry to be so blunt in my accusations, Judge," Two Wolves told the man. "But it is all evidence. The Cheyenne might kill white women, but they would not violate them. And they would steal a child before they would kill a child. The attacks I came upon were not committed by Cheyenne! They were by men who know nothing about Cheyenne ways."

"He'll say anything to protect his People," one of Vince's attorneys argued.

"Perhaps," Judge Kieler answered. He looked at Claire. "Do you have anything more to add, Mrs. Matthews?"

"Only that I haven't lied about one thing," Claire announced. "The night my freight wagons were attacked, my husband had followed them because he'd already seen the results of such attacks before. He knows the comings and goings of the Southern Cheyenne. He knows practically every move they make, and he knows when they are the ones who do the raiding, and when it's not them. If not for Two Wolves … I mean, Peter … I would be dead now, or suffering something *worse* than death, all at the orders of Vince Huebner. Every one of my men was killed and dragged off to rot in the sun. They said they would burn my wagons because then it would look more like an Indian raid. They shot arrows into the wagons and into my men's bodies to make it look more real, just like my husband said they had done to other victims. And I saw one of them pull off a wig of long, dark hair!"

"How *dare* you?" Vince practically screamed. "You've wanted to put me out of business ever since your father died. I offered you the world, and you wouldn't take it. No woman should be running a freighting business *alone*! Do you know how that makes you look?" He turned to the judge. "Your Honor, she's not a woman to be honored and respected. The day that Indian over there came riding through Denver City with soldiers when there was a meeting with Governor Evans, I saw how she watched him–brazenly. She lusted after that half-breed and somehow–I don't know how–they ended up together. And for some reason they have plotted against me. She's a Cheyenne lover now and thinks this is a way of helping them. I'm a respected business man in Denver City. I would *never* do the things she's accusing me of."

Vince's words created more commotion. The judge kept pounding his gavel until finally some kind of order again prevailed.

"Ask him why two of his men attacked my wife at Fort Collins recently when they visited there and learned she was alive," Two Wolves pleaded. "They said that Vince would be pleased they had finally found her and that once they let him know, she'd be sold in Mexico. I fought them off, killing one of them. The other one rode away. We kept the gear of the first man, and he was carrying a *paycheck* signed by Vince Huebner!"

The crowd quieted a little more.

"Do you have the check with you?" Judge Kieler asked.

"I have it," Ansley spoke up. He walked up to the bar and handed the check to the judge. Judge Kieler studied it, then took a flask of whiskey from under the bar and opened it to take a swallow. He looked at Vince. "This is a check from Huebner Freighting," he told Vince. "And it has your signature on it."

"A lot of men work for me, Judge," Vince argued. "Once they are paid, I'm not responsible for what they do when they leave. I have no knowledge of any of my men going after Claire Stewart, or I should say Matthews. If that man abused her, it was his own decision. He just used me as an excuse. Maybe he had no respect for her because he knew she'd lain with an Indian. And I'd like to point out that Peter Matthews just admitted that he killed one of those men … a *white* man! Mister Matthews is standing here today pretending to be white, but he takes the Indian name of Two Wolves, and it's obvious that in his heart he's Cheyenne. He had no business killing a white man!"

"And I would do it again!" Two Wolves answered. "He was attacking my wife!"

No, Two Wolves, don't say that! Claire thought, heart pounding.

The room quieted.

"And how do we know those men weren't trying to stop *you* from beating on your wife?" Vince suggested. "Everyone knows what Indian men are like. They're wild and vicious and they abuse their women! How did you end up half white, Mister Matthews? You say Cheyenne men don't rape white women. I beg to differ, and I'm betting that's how *you* came to be!"

Two Wolves started to charge toward Vince, but Major Ansley and two other soldiers held him back. "You see?" Vince glowered. "His first reaction was to come after me, probably to kill me, like *all* Indians react!"

"Judge, Vince Huebner is deliberately insulting and baiting Mister Matthews here to take the attention away from all the proof we have brought against him!" Ansley shouted above a growing crowd commotion. "He is guilty as hell and we've brought you plenty of proof!"

"The Cheyenne are raiders and rapists and murderers!" Vince shouted, easily working up the crowd.

The judge pounded his gavel fruitlessly as shouts both in favor and against Two Wolves began to build.

"And settlers and travelers out there beyond the city are defenseless, thanks to the Army being short-handed out here!" Vince continued. "The Major over there told me so a couple of weeks ago, when he was in Denver pretending to need supplies! He was setting me up for this! If people want to believe these lies, or that I could be responsible for such atrocities, then so be it. But I'm telling you here and now that Mister Matthews is an *Indian*, trying to take the attention away from the

Cheyenne by blaming their own atrocities on an innocent man like me!" He pointed to Two Wolves. "He's the guilty one! He murdered a White man for attacking a White woman. I contend it wasn't that way at all! I contend he was the one attacking her, and that it was my man who tried to stop it and got killed in the process. That man should be hanged for *murder*! Who knows how many other white men he's murdered while out scouting alone!"

The crowd erupted in furious arguments. Claire tried to shout above them. "That's a lie! Why would I marry a man who would attack me?"

Her words were lost in all the shouting. The crowd, mostly all men, surged, grabbing hold of Two Wolves. One man landed the butt of his gun against Major Ansley's head, knocking him out. Lieutenant Sternaman and Sergeant Becker rushed to Claire's side to drag her out of harm's way, and Private Lake and Captain Flower stayed with their commander as the crowd dragged a struggling, unarmed Two Wolves out the door, amid chants of "Hang him! Hang the lying Indian!"

CHAPTER FORTY-FIVE

THERE WERE SIMPLY TOO MANY for the soldiers to be able to help Two Wolves. Claire struggled against Sternaman's and Becker's grip.

"Help him!" she screamed.

"Ma'am, we can't shoot into a crowd like that!" Sergeant Becker told her. "We'd kill innocent people, and Major Ansley and all of us would be court-martialed!"

"They're going to hang Two Wolves!" Claire felt as though someone was ripping her heart from her chest. Her husband was going to die! She kept jerking at the hold the soldiers had on her.

"Let go! Let go! We have to stop them!" Everyone was already out the door, including Vince Huebner, Sheriff McKee and his two deputies. Claire knew instinctively they would do nothing to help Two Wolves. Lieutenant Sternaman finally let go of her and she turned to the judge in wide-eyed terror. "Stop them!"

Judge Kieler swallowed more whiskey. "I tried, Ma'am. A crowd like this can't be controlled. You shouldn't have tried accusing a man like Vince Huebner of such a hideous crime."

He smiled a little, and Claire realized he'd never been on her side to begin with. In a panic, she turned and fled the saloon. Becker and Sternaman charged after her, but she'd already reached their horses outside and had pulled a rifle from Ansley's horse. She chambered a round and aimed the weapon at them.

"Ma'am, you can't do anything to stop this!"

Claire waved the rifle. "If either of you tries to stop me, I'll *shoot*!" She turned and ran toward the crowd, who'd already made it down the street to the livery. The livery's barn had a beam protruding from the roof's peak with a pulley for lifting heavy items to the loft.

Claire realized they were going to use the pulley and rope to hang Two Wolves. She headed into the crowd, where men pushed and shoved her, one knocking her down and calling her a whore. He tried to take the rifle from her but Claire hung on. The rifle fired into the air by accident. The shot caused everyone to stop for a moment as Claire got to her feet and aimed the rifle at the men nearest Two Wolves. She wanted to scream at the sight of her husband, his face bloody from a beating, his shirt half ripped off.

"Do not do this," he told her. "Go away from here!"

"I'll kill the first man who tries to put a noose around my husband's neck!" Claire declared. She cocked the rifle again. She held the gun steady then, aiming it straight at the man closest to her husband. "I am carrying that man's child, and we are going to raise it together. We've told you the truth! You have no right hanging this man! It's Vince Huebner you should be hanging!"

"Please go, *Maeveksea,* before they hurt you, too!" Two Wolves pleaded, blood pouring from a cut on his head. "They are fools and full of hate. They will not listen!"

Claire kept the rifle in a firm grip, turning then to aim it directly at Vince Huebner, who stood just a few feet away from Two Wolves, grinning. "Vince Huebner is the man who deserves to die here today," she shouted, loud enough for all to hear. "If anybody tries to grab this gun away, it will go off and he *will* die. Now, let my husband go!"

"Wait!" A man stepped out of the crowd. His skin was wrinkled from a lifetime in the sun, in a way that made it difficult to tell if he was really as old as he looked. Tall and lanky, he wore a blue cotton shirt with brown cotton pants covered with dirt stains, signs of a hard-working farmer. His pants were held up by suspenders. He seemed nervous as he stepped farther away from the crowd. It was obvious he was normally a quiet, shy man who didn't like to draw attention. He walked closer to Claire.

"This lady and that Indian man over there are telling the truth!" he announced.

Claire froze in place, hardly able to believe her ears. The whole crowd quieted, and by then Lieutenant Sternaman and Sergeant Becker reached her. They halted close by, as if not sure what their next move should be. She was still holding the rifle on Vince.

"What the hell are you talking about?" Vince asked the farmer. "Who are you?"

"My name is Hubert Huff." The farmer turned to address the crowd. "I raise potatoes south of here to sell to the miners. I ain't never once had trouble with Indians. But a while back, maybe three or four months ago, I had trouble all right, with *white* men!"

Mumbling moved through the crowd.

"What are you talking about?" Vince growled. The look on his face began to give away the fact that he knew exactly what Huff meant.

Claire hoped the whole crowd noticed.

Huff looked back at Vince. "I'm talking about losing my wife to an Indian attack. At least that's what I thought it was at the time. Our farm got raided, horses trampling over the potato sprouts, which hurts their undergrowth. They trampled a smaller garden and set fire to my barn. I was way out in the fields and couldn't get there in time, but my wife had run out of the house, and they shot her down. A *woman*! They shot down a woman. I started runnin', and one of them shot at me, grazed me–right here." He pointed to a deep scar across the left side of his head, where the hair would no longer grow. He turned so that everyone could see it.

Claire lowered her rife, and Lieutenant Sternaman carefully took it from her. He and Becker moved closer to her, Becker gently taking her arm.

"You said it was Indians!" someone shouted.

"I said I *thought* it was Indians. The shot knocked me down and knocked me out for a few minutes. One of 'em rode up to make sure I was dead, and I pretended I was. I hoped they figured it was so. One of 'em yelled to the others I was a goner. And there was no doubt by his voice and how good he talked that he was a white man!" He pointed a finger at a man Claire recognized as Bill Powers, one of Vince's wagon drivers. "That man there. He was the one who came to check on me. He bent over and picked up a rock, and he didn't know I'd opened one eye and saw his face. He threw the rock at my plow horses to chase them off."

Powers looked around, suddenly appearing desperate and very guilty. He backed away and looked as though he might run. A couple of men from the crowd grasped his arms.

"Let's hear Mr. Huff out," one of them yelled at the crowd.

Huff rubbed at the back of his neck. "I ain't no Indian lover, but I don't believe in a man dyin' for somethin' he didn't do." he stated. "If the Indians attack soldiers or whites, then we have to do something about it. But there ain't no forgiveness for white men who attack their own kind.

I laid there and I listened to them talk about how they could make the attack look like Indians did it. My head was sideways and I opened my eyes to see them shoot down my cows and put arrows into them. They shot arrows into the front of the house and they even–" He stopped, his voice choking. "They even shot arrows into my wife." He swallowed, wiping at his eyes. "I can only pray she was already dead." He turned to Claire. "Ma'am, you said you was carryin'. I can't let these people hang your child's father when I know he's innocent."

Claire blinked in disbelief. The night before she'd said they would need a miracle today, and that miracle was standing in front of her. "Thank you, Mr. Huff."

The crowd had turned amazingly quiet, most of them also listening in disbelief.

Huff nodded to Claire. "It's only right, Ma'am." He turned to the crowd again. "While I was lyin' on the ground, I heard one of the men say 'Mr. Huebner will owe us extra for this one.' Them was his exact words. He said they weren't even supposed to make this attack, but they figured one extra would bring them more money."

Vince stepped even farther forward. "You're a liar!"

Huff shook his head. "I ain't got no reason to lie. It's like I said. I'm no Indian lover, but what's fair and right is fair and right, Mr. Huebner. I just happened to be in town today and found out what was goin' on. I've been watchin' and listenin', and I couldn't abide keepin' my mouth shut any longer."

"Why didn't you come into town and report the attack in the first place?" Sheriff McKee asked.

Huff glanced at Claire. "For the exact reason Mrs. Matthews here was probably afraid to speak up. Nobody would have believed me." He closed his eyes and shook his head. "I'm ashamed now that I didn't say nothin'. But I'm just one man. Vince Huebner is rich and well liked in this town, and those men were vicious. I was scared." He looked at Vince. "I was afraid I'd be run out of town on a rail if I accused Mr. Huebner of such a heinous crime, or that those men would come back to my place and finish me off."

He stepped closer to Vince. "I ain't got one reason to hold something against you, Mr. Huebner. You said this lady here just wanted to run you out of business because you're her competition. But it's not that way for me. People ought to understand I've got no personal reason to expose you. I'm not tryin' to protect the Cheyenne, and I've got no business dealings with you. I don't even know you, but I know your name, and I know what I heard and what I saw. If the lady here says it was men hired by you who attacked her freight wagons, then I believe her, because I know what you've been up to. A human being is a human being, and the Southern Cheyenne–and that man you're wanting to hang–don't deserve this. If I don't stop you, who will?"

The men holding Two Wolves let go of him. Two Wolves shoved them away and walked up to Hubert Huff, a bruise forming on his left cheek, his clothes torn and filthy.

"You are an honorable man," he told Huff. "And a brave man. The Cheyenne would honor you with a ceremony if they knew this."

"Like I said, this ain't for the Indians, but you seem like a good man, and these soldiers seem to respect you." He turned and pointed at Vince. "That man deserves to go to jail, and some of the men who work for him, too. I can attest that him and his men planned and carried out attacks on white farmers and settlers–and I believe this lady here when she says they attacked her freight wagons and killed all her men."

Vince Huebner and Bill Powers both suddenly took off running. Two Wolves grabbed Claire close to his side and whisked her off the street, ducking into a nearby hardware store with Becker and Sternaman as the crowd chased after the fleeing men. Before long the throng dragged Vince Huebner and Bill Powers back to the blacksmith's barn.

Claire and Two Wolves could only stand and watch from inside. Claire gasped and turned away when both Vince and Powers were strung up with the barn pulley. She rested her face against Two Wolves' chest, and his arms came around her. He watched both men struggle and kick until finally the life went out of them. "Finally, some justice," he said sadly.

"I didn't want it to end this way," Claire wept.

"This is not your fault." Two Wolves watched Hubert Huff turn away, shaking his head. He walked away from the ugly events while the crowd cheered over the hanging.

Two Wolves pulled Claire even closer. "You did a brave thing holding that rifle on Vince, but you shouldn't have. Those people could have hurt you. You could have lost our child."

"I had to stop them," Claire answered. "I thought I was going to see *you* hanging up there!"

He petted her hair, glancing at Sternaman and Becker. "One of you go and see about Major Ansley. I hope he has not been killed. He is like a father to me. Take him to Claire's place. And try to find that farmer and take him there, also. I wish to speak with him.'"

"I'll go see about the Major," Becker told him. "You and Claire had better take a back way to her place while Lieutenant Sternaman looks for Mr. Huff." He looked around the store. "This place seems to be empty right now. Stay here for a few minutes until that crowd settles a little." He put a hand on Two Wolves' shoulder. "I'm damn glad this didn't end the way it looked like it might. I'm damn sorry we couldn't do more. I never dreamed they would get that crazy or things would get that out of hand."

Two Wolves nodded. "I understand."

"I'll be back soon."

Both men left, and Two Wolves kissed the top of Claire's head. "It is over, *Maeveksea*. It is over. I have proven what I wanted to prove, and you made it happen. You will be greatly honored by my people when they learn of this."

"I'm just glad you're alive," Claire answered, relishing the feel of his arms around her. If only the hatred of the Cheyenne could also be over. "I love you so."

"*Aye. Ne-mehotatse, Maeveksea.*"

"When they dragged you off–" Claire clung to him even tighter.

"All I could think of was you being left alone to raise our child," he told her. "We need to go back to your place now. You need to rest."

Claire looked up at his bloodied face. "And we need to take care of those cuts." She reached up and touched at blood that was beginning to scab. "We need to clean this off." Her eyes brimmed with tears. "I'm so sorry for all the ugly hatred. It made me sick to hear some of the things they said."

"I have heard it for years. I can bear it because I know it is their own ignorance that makes them say such things." He wiped at her tears with his thumbs. "We will wait here a while longer."

Claire smiled through tears. "God was surely with us! I prayed last night for a miracle, and there he stood in the form of that farmer."

He pulled her close again. "It is good to know there are some white men who are good and honest, like Major Ansley and Mister Huff." He rocked her in his strong arms. "And good white women, like my mother. And you."

"I'll be so glad to settle into a normal life together, if that's even possible."

"We will *make* it possible." Two Wolves watched the crowd in the street, many of them disbursing, some looking as though they sorely regretted what they'd just done, others still shouting that Vince Huebner deserved to die.

"He's no better than the damn Indians," one man swore.

Two Wolves closed his eyes, realizing that in the end, life as the Cheyenne once knew it would have to change forever. This was just the beginning of more war and heartache for both the Whites and the Cheyenne. Part of him regretted dragging Claire into all of it, yet now she there was no changing it. He would spend the rest of their married life protecting her from the kind of ugliness that milled about outside in the street.

"Come," he told her. "We will go out the back way. Your building is not that far from here. I am anxious to find out about Major Ansley." He kept an arm around Claire as he led her out the back door.

CHAPTER FORTY-SIX

CLAIRE RUSHED OVER TO MAJOR Ansley where he sat in a large stuffed chair holding a towel to the back of his head. She knelt in front him, worried at how pale he looked.

"What can we do?" she asked him.

"I think ice might help," he answered weakly.

Claire turned to Private Lake. "Two streets over is an ice house–blocks of ice packed in straw. They bring it down from the mountains. Go and see if they have any."

"Yes, Ma'am." The private quickly left.

"Don't go out of your way," Ansley argued.

"Nonsense," Claire told him, touching his arm.

Ansley looked up at Two Wolves, pain moving through his eyes at the sight of his battered face. "I'm damn sorry, Two Wolves. Thank God for that farmer. Lieutenant Sternaman told me what happened. Otherwise, you'd be strung up by now, and I never would have forgiven myself. I thought we had enough men to protect you."

"It could not be helped." Two Wolves moved behind Ansley. "Let me look at your wound. I am the one who is relieved, that you were not killed today." He grimaced a little at ugly cut on the back of Ansley's head, easy to see because of his thinning hair. "The swelling is showing," he told the major. "That is good. It is when things swell on the inside that there could be worse damage. I agree that ice will help."

"You need to take care of your own wounds," Ansley told him. "Looks like you were beat up pretty good."

"I have suffered far worse. Cheyenne warriors are trained for this."

Ansley smiled weakly and shook his head. "Of course they are."

"Let me wrap this so you do not have to hold your hand to it. And you should remain sitting up. It is best to stay awake for a while after a head wound. Sitting up will keep too much blood from rushing to the wound."

Claire found some gauze Becker had left lying on a table beside the chair. She handed it to Two Wolves and remained kneeling in front of Ansley.

"You all right?" the major asked.

"Pretty shaken, but I'm fine."

Ansley reached out and squeezed her hand. "You two did it. You proved what you wanted to prove. Things didn't work out exactly like we thought they might, but at least people know it's the truth. I'm happy for both of you."

Someone knocked on the store's front door. Becker walked through to open it and greet Hubert Huff and Lieutenant Sternaman. "Come in," he told Mr. Huff. "Two Wolves wants to speak with you. He's very grateful that you saved him from a hanging."

Huff entered hesitantly. "I didn't save him. The *truth* saved him."

Becker nodded. "Agreed." He led Huff back to Claire's living quarters. Huff glanced at Major Ansley.

"I'm sorry, Sir, about your injuries." His gaze fell on Two Wolves then. "Yours too, Mr. Matthews. If I'd spoken up sooner . . . but I–I just didn't know it would get so out of hand."

"No one did." Two Wolves stepped closer. "I am the one who sent for you. I wanted to tell you again how grateful my wife and I are for what you did. I wish to know where your farm is. I will tell the Cheyenne never to touch it. And I would like your permission to bring some of the braves to your farm so that they can give you a gift. You will be greatly honored."

Huff shook his head and smiled humbly. "Heck, that's not necessary."

"It *is* necessary. It is the way of the Cheyenne. You will never need to fear an attack by *real* Indians, and after this there will never be another attack by outlaws posing as Indians. I am sorry about your wife. I would be deeply grieved if I lost mine. Speaking up was a brave thing. Some might see it as defending the Cheyenne."

Huff slowly nodded. "In a way, I suppose I was. And after meeting you I can tell some of them are fine people."

"They are just that, Mr. Huff–people. They are as human as all of us in this room–little children who have to be taught the right way–mothers and grandmothers, and fathers who love their sons. They are not so different from white families. Men like Chivington keep the hatred going. I had to stop letting white men make things worse."

"Two Wolves is my best scout," Ansley spoke up from where he sat. "He's as good or better than any white man I've known. We have to work on keeping the peace, Mr. Huff, and men like you can help."

Huff studied Two Wolves. "Don't take offense if I tell you I'll still keep my rifle handy when I'm working out in the fields. It will still be hard for me to trust Indians who come riding to my place."

"I understand, but you must trust me that no Cheyenne will come there and bring you harm. The Cheyenne are men of their word, and they honor bravery and truth. You have earned their trust." He touched his own forehead. "When they touch their foreheads this way, you will know they mean no harm. Tell me where to find your farm and I will tell the Cheyenne."

Huff frowned. "I can't believe I'm standing here talking to an Indian. I mean, I know you're half white, but you pretty much look all Indian. I never thought I'd be talkin' straight on to a Cheyenne man."

Their gazes held in mutual understanding. "And you see that I am just a man, the same as you."

Huff laughed lightly. "Well, not exactly the same as me. I expect I can't hold a candle to you in fighting skills and such. I wouldn't want to have to go one on one with the likes of you, but yes, I reckon' we're both just men who want the same thing–to be left alone to live the way we want." He put out his hand. "I guess I'll never get the chance to actually shake the hand of an Indian, so maybe we should. If I ever remarry and have children, I'll have somethin' to tell them."

They shook hands. Claire blinked back tears at the sight. If only all white men would just shake hands with the Indians and come to some kind of peaceful agreement, but she knew it would never happen and that more treaties would be broken.

Huff glanced at Claire. "Today must have been a terrible ordeal for you, Ma'am. I'm awful sorry, and I'm glad you're all right."

"Thank you."

Huff glanced at Sternaman. "I'd best leave now and let all of you get some rest and make ready to leave tomorrow." He asked for a piece of paper and an ink pen. He used them to draw out the boundaries of his farm and describe to Two Wolves the lay of the land and a couple of physical markers to look for when trying to find his home.

"I will bring some of my Cheyenne friends there. They will bring gifts, and you will no longer need to fear an attack by my people."

They grasped hands, and the farmer nodded. "I believe you." He gave his well wishes to Major Ansley, then turned then and walked out.

Two Wolves turned to Claire. "Go and lie down. I will help Major Ansley when Private Lake gets back here with the ice."

Claire felt suddenly a bit lost. "Where do we go from here, Two Wolves? What about my business? And what about you? I want you to be happy."

Two Wolves walked over to her and put a hand to her waist, leading her into her bedroom. He closed the door and made her sit down on the bed. He knelt in front of her. "I *am* happy. I have proven what I wanted to prove, and the woman I love is carrying my child. Do not worry about what comes next. We will go back to Fort Collins and take some time alone before we make any decisions." He took her hands and leaned up to kiss her lightly, his lips too bruised and cut for a full kiss. "We can reopen your business in Denver City if that is what you wish, or we can move your business to the settlement near Fort Collins. I will let it be your decision because I know it is important to you. If we live at Fort Collins, I can continue to scout and work as an interpreter for the Army, which will allow me to visit the Cheyenne and continue to help keep the peace. And I can go with you to protect you when you make your delivery runs."

Claire threw her arms around him. "I thought I'd watch you die today!"

He rose, pulling her up with him and keeping her tight against him and nuzzled her thick curls. "You did a brave thing today. My people would be proud of you. We will be all right, *Maeveksea*. It is over now. And our love is strong. *Maheo* brought you to me, and I will never let you go. You are the wife of Two Wolves, and I will protect and love you forever."

"As I will love you forever," Claire answered, breathing deeply of his familiar scent. She felt a flutter in her belly. Life. His life. Life that would continue the blood of the Cheyenne. Their future together would be good and sweet and right. God had brought them together, and no man, white or red, was going to tear them apart.

FROM THE AUTHOR...

O N NOVEMBER 29, 1864, AT Sand Creek in southern Colorado, Colonel John Chivington and his troops of Colorado Volunteers attacked a peaceful camp of Cheyenne and Arapaho Indians led by the very peaceful chief, Black Kettle, who waved both a white flag of surrender and an American flag as he was shot down. The camp consisted of mostly women, children and the elderly. The atrocities committed there by Chivington and his men would today compare to what terrorists are doing to their victims. They were so disgusting that I can't even write them here.

You can look up the Sand Creek Massacre of 1864 on the internet. I will tell you, though, that Chivington and his men called it a "victorious battle" and rode through the streets of Denver City to celebrate, sporting tobacco pouches made from Indian women's breasts, Indian scalps (including those of children and a newborn baby), and men and women's genitals dangling from poles. Eventually, the truth was discovered, mainly from men who refused to take part, some of whom broke down on the witness stand when testifying as to what they saw that day in a massacre that lasted for eight hours.

This heinous act became a mark of shame for Colorado, and today the place where it all happened is a National Historic Site in southern Colorado. To this day, the Federal Government continues to keep a strong hold on our Native Americans, a people seemingly forgotten amid all the other issues of today's time. Little is taught in our schools about our Native Americans, who still struggle to hang on to what land is left to them.

To learn more of the historical truth about the gradual demise of America's Natives, I recommend reading *Bury My Heart at Wounded Knee*, by Dee Brown. And be sure to visit my web site at *www.rosannebittner.*

com to learn about the over 60 other books I have written, many of them about Native Americans and the real history surrounding them as the United States was settled.

ABOUT THE AUTHOR

ROSANNE BITTNER HAS PENNED OVER sixty books since her first book was published in 1983 and has won numerous writing awards, including the prestigious WILLA award from Women Writing the West, a RITA nomination from Romance Writers of America, and a nomination for Best Western Romance for 2015 from Romantic Times for DO NOT FORSAKE ME. Her stories involve real American history, events and locations, from the Revolutionary War through the discovery of gold, the Civil War, the building of the Union Pacific, the Indian wars, the founding of today's great western cities and the late 1800's Yukon gold rush. Through her memorable fictitious characters, America's phenomenal growth takes place in exciting action, adventure and romance. She has been dubbed the "Queen of Western Romance" by the well-known romance magazine Romantic Times Reviews, and 92% of Rosanne's books on Amazon have garnered five-star reviews.

Rosanne belongs to several historical societies throughout the country, is an active officer in a local charity organization, and is a member of Romance Writers of America and Women Writing the West. She and her husband of over 50 years live in southwest Michigan.

To learn about all of Rosanne's books, visit her web site at *www.rosannebittner.com*. Check out her blogs at *www.rosannebittner.blogspot.com*. You can also find Rosanne on Facebook, Goodreads, Twitter and many other internet venues.

Made in the USA
San Bernardino, CA
20 March 2018